THE SWEET SWING

THE SWEET SWING OF JINGLES PLUMLEE

LEE STONE

Copyright © 2013 by Lee Stone.

Library of Congress Control Number:		2013915378
ISBN:	Hardcover	978-1-4836-9024-7
	Softcover	978-1-4836-9023-0
	Ebook	978-1-4836-9025-4

All rights reserved. No part of this book may be reproduced or transmitted in any form or by any means, electronic or mechanical, including photocopying, recording, or by any information storage and retrieval system, without permission in writing from the copyright owner.

This is a work of fiction. Names, characters, places and incidents either are the product of the author's imagination or are used fictitiously, and any resemblance to any actual persons, living or dead, events, or locales is entirely coincidental.

This book was printed in the United States of America.

Rev. date: 10/09/2013

To order additional copies of this book, contact:
Xlibris LLC
1-888-795-4274
www.Xlibris.com
Orders@Xlibris.com
120405

Foreword

The game of golf, as we know it today, evolved on Scottish pastures in the Middle Ages. Today, in America alone, over twenty thousand golf courses dot the landscape and nearly thirty million golfers drive, chip, and putt across them.

The simplest description of the sport is that a golfer attempts to move a ball from point A (the tee) to point B (the hole) in the fewest number of swings, or strokes, possible. That process is repeated eighteen times to complete a round.

While there is varying leeway as to how accurate strokes must be to efficiently reach the proximity of the hole, such forgiveness disappears once the golfer reaches the final destination, the green. The cup is a mere 4.25 inches in diameter, precisely the size of the random piece of drainpipe used to punch holes in the ground that were officially adopted as regulation by the Royal and Ancient Golf Club of St. Andrews in 1891.

While the game is allegedly steeped in tradition, few sports have seen such changing technology. Clubs first fashioned with hickory shafts and persimmon heads gave way to metal shafts and heads that in turn were replaced by graphite and titanium. Each nuance served to simplify the game by adding more distance and control to shots leading to the greens. The ball itself evolved from a piece of wood to a leather bag of feathers, to a high-tech package of energy encased in surlyn resin with over three hundred dimples on the surface. The resulting 1.68" sphere is as aerodynamically perfect as rocket scientists can make it.

Regulation par for a typical golf course is seventy-two, based on the principle that an average distance of four hundred yards to each green should be covered with two stokes, and the hole should be completed with two additional strokes or putts. Given that putting is so crucial in determining a golfer's score, technological efforts have focused on trying to improve that part of performance as well. The variety of putting clubs (putters) available to modern golfers is now infinite. Putter heads are shaped and weighted in ways to promote proper alignment and impart efficient spin. The lengths of shafts vary from thirty-two inches to fifty-two inches, allowing putting techniques to vary dramatically to fit individual preference. Videos and devices purported to improve putting are advertised everywhere.

However, despite it all, today's golfers are no more proficient at putting than their predecessors. The reason is simple. Rolling a ball into a four-and-a-quarter-inch hole is a function of hand *and eye* coordination. Regardless of how much we try to train and assist the hand, the eye remains the limiting factor. Encumbered by mere 20/20 vision for the most part, a golfer's putting potential is capped by how well he or she sees the cup and the terrain leading to it. Advancement of visual acuity beyond that norm has never been achieved . . . *until now* . . . *and the game of golf will never be the same.*

Prologue

Monday, September 1, 2014

The five department heads of Eagle Optics, one of a dwindling number of companies specializing in the manufacture of rigid, prescription contact lenses, were gathered in the conference room for their weekly morning meeting with Herman Winston, the owner. While awaiting his arrival, they speculated about the unusual centerpiece on the table, a silver ice bucket sporting two bottles of champagne. Why a celebration? In the morning no less?

Standing away from the well-dressed executives and lost in his own thoughts, Karl Zimmer wore his three-quarter length white lab coat. Technically speaking, Karl was a sixth director. His office door at the Eagle Optics facility read: Research and Development Department. Beyond that door, however, was just a single unused desk. By cooperative arrangement, all of Karl's work took place thirty miles away at the manufacturing plant of the company that supplied Eagle Optics and many other prescription lens providers with the buttons they converted to lenses. This was only the second meeting he had been asked to attend during his tenure with Herman's company. The first had been for his formal introduction to the group five years ago, when he first arrived in Arizona from Germany.

Through a tinted window, Karl squinted at the barren desert beyond the parking lot, looking through just his right eye. The only sign of life was a solitary coyote, moving at a slow trot, tongue and tail flopping in rhythm. He could point out the animal to the others, but what was the point? They would see nothing. *The animal was over six hundred yards away.* That was the miracle of the contact lens he invented and now wore on that right eye.

He turned his attention to the parking lot, specifically to the shining white Mercedes sedan he purchased over the weekend. It was a gift to himself, a tribute to the success he chronicled in his latest report on the lens. There was simply no substitute for German engineering.

The concept of the telescopic contact lens had taken root at his family's dining table in Dusseldorf thirty-seven years earlier, when Karl was twelve. His father, an optical engineer for Focus, Europe's leading producer of binoculars and telescopic rifle sights, often discussed the future of eye prosthetics over boiled potatoes and gravy. *What if,* he would say, people could walk through life wearing binoculars in the form of advanced contact lenses? *Think what could be accomplished!* His reference point was always the same: a marksman with a traditional open sight on his rifle could hit a six-inch circle at a hundred-yard distance perhaps once in ten tries. With a four-power scope on the same rifle, the shooter could hit the target every single time! *Visual acuity was the only variable!* His father was convinced that improving technology would one day allow the science of the scope to be incorporated into contact lenses that would dramatically raise the bar for human performance at a whole host of activities.

Although cancer took his father ten years later, Karl kept the vision alive. He became an optical engineer and took a job with Focus as well, which had branched into the rapidly growing contact lens manufacturing business. By 2004, he was convinced that advancements in materials and microfabrication made development of new magnifying lenses possible.

The concept was relatively simple: by imbedding a concave crystal lens within a conventional, acrylic convex lens, images could be enlarged by a factor of three or even four. Unlike a telescope, which had to be adjusted to produce clarity at a specific distance, the entire field of vision figured to be clear because the lens rested directly on the eye.

However, despite his own confidence in the *lens within a lens* theory, conservative Focus executives proved reluctant to turn him loose on the project. He had remained shackled to the mundane chore of developing material for more durable conventional lenses.

Ironically, a severe economic downturn in another country provided the lift he needed. When the U. S. Congress approved an Economic Stimulus Package in February of 2009, the government committed itself to virtually handing out money to spur business growth. Karl put together a sample proposal for research funding and sent it to a dozen optical companies in the U.S. to gauge interest. Eagle Optics had been the first to respond. When a five-year grant for a total of $9,000,000 was approved within six months, he was on a jet to Phoenix.

Karl's two-hundred-page report, "The Status and Future of Eaglevision," detailed the design of the lens and reviewed both the advantages and limitations. It also outlined the methodology and required budget for the FDA approval process, which he estimated would take only a year. By frequently wearing the lens himself for the last month, he had eliminated doubt of its viability.

In hindsight, his invention should have been approved and on the market two years ago. Producing a functional lens had taken just a year. The grand opening of an aided eye for the first time had been a revelation, a rare instance of actuality matching anticipation. 20/5 vision. The roadblock had appeared when he opened two aided eyes at once; binocular vision produced nothing but a staggering blur of shapes and colors through both eyes. Fascinated and challenged by this phenomenon, he spent the next three years toying with the invention, changing the size and angle of the interior lens, hoping to find a solution. With time winding down on his contract, he had made no progress. Open one eye, either eye, and the lens worked like a charm. Open both and all was lost.

Inspiration . . . salvation . . . had arrived two months ago from a most unlikely source: a play-by-play commentator on an Arizona Diamondback baseball broadcast. His simple comment that a batter had "a good eye at the plate" changed everything. Although it was just an expression, like keep an eye on the ball, it signaled to Karl that his preconceived notion that eaglevision had to be binocular was only a distraction. One miraculous eye was far more valuable than two good eyes. In fact, why not wear the magnifying lens on one eye and a normal lens on the other? Open one and see the world as we've always known it; open the other and benefit from an incredible close-up view!

Unchained from his previous notion, Karl realized the benefit of his lens was not just a game-changer but a world-changer. Current norms for eye/hand coordination went out the window. How did he know? Even the neighborhood tavern provided ample proof. With a new lens on his right eye, the balls on a pool table took on the size of cantaloupes. Each pocket seemed cavernous . . . large enough to crawl into himself. The calculation of angles and aiming points was beyond simple: *he didn't even seem to have to think about it, he just knew!* Though basically a novice at eight-ball, he felt equipped to become a champion if he didn't have more important things to do. Fellow bar patrons that had routinely taken his dollar wagers in the past would no longer play with him. The dartboards on the wall provided even less challenge. When he stood at the eight-foot tossing distance, it seemed as if he could reach out and stick the darts into the target without even letting them go. The only challenge was in seeing how many he could fit into the fifty-point circle in the center. While these were merely games, enhanced performance would have implications in a myriad of human activities that really mattered.

Eaglevision was about to change the entire world view of eye prosthetics. Instead of being a corrective measure for sub-normal sight, his contacts would enhance all eyesight. The market for the product would basically be everyone . . . at least everyone that could afford the exorbitant price that Herman Winston would likely demand.

Given the benefits of his invention, Karl didn't see its limitations as unreasonable at all. Due to the added light the lens captured, eye protection was required for outdoor use in particular. Sunglasses seemed to suffice. Secondly, the lens seemed to have a drying effect on the eye that required the remedy of frequent lubrication. Finally, the lens could be worn for only short durations, even with lubrication, before causing irritation and potential damage to the eye. That aspect needed advanced study.

Karl's thoughts were interrupted by a loud thump behind him. The finance director had rapped the table with a fist.

"So," the director said loudly, "enough of this idle speculation about why we're looking at champagne. Someone has to know what this is all about." He pulled one of the bottles from the ice, held it up, and looked directly at Karl. Perhaps it was a farewell party for the R&D man; his five-year grant was expiring. Why else would he be at the meeting?

Karl smirked but said nothing. The answer was as clear as the tiny words, Contains Sulfates, at the bottom of the label of the bottle the speaker held. Through his right eye, he could read the words from eight feet away.

The manufacturing director pointed to the bottle. "Oh, look at the label! It's sparkling cider!" The others moaned.

"Just kidding," he added. "It's Chateau Montenegro. That's not even the cheapest stuff."

"It's not far from it," the personnel director added. "I think that goes for eleven dollars a bottle."

The manufacturing director snickered. "You'd know, wouldn't you?" He paused while the others chuckled. "Actually, I think the crabby old duffer made a hole-in-one or something like that. We all know he spends more time at his country club than he does here."

"Well, I've seen him play," said the head of Marketing. "I'd bet a year's salary against that." The others laughed with him.

"Herman just pulled in," the personnel director announced as she watched a cream-colored Bentley drive into the lot. "We'll soon have our answer!"

Karl took an empty seat and pulled a vial of ophthalmic solution from one of his many pockets. Tilting his head back, he shook a few drops onto his right eye.

Slipping his left hand into another pocket, Karl grasped the two acrylic buttons with embedded second lenses that he brought to the meeting. The buttons, blanks from which contact lens are lasered to individual prescription, were identical in size and appearance to conventional buttons and could be prescription cut with the same technology. He planned to pass them around so the others could appreciate their overt similarity to the regular product. Giving them a shake like a pair of dice, he tossed them on the mahogany veneer table in front of him. If they had dots like actual dice, Karl knew they would have totaled seven. When the marketing director looked at him curiously, Karl swept them up and hid them in his hand. He would show them off soon enough.

Hearing the door open, Karl looked through his left eye as the kindly Martha Porter, Mr. Winston's personal secretary, entered the room. She was followed by Herman and another man Karl met five years ago and hadn't seen since, the company attorney.

The owner followed his arrowhead nose to the head of the table and stood behind his chair, squeezing the backrest with both hands. He looked solemnly around the room before speaking, like a statesman preparing to make a significant pronouncement.

"Remember the date. August 31, 2014. It happened to me yesterday on the fourteenth hole at Desert Springs."

Eyes shifted to the manufacturing chief, who seemed to have guessed correctly. "So you finally made an ace," he said, standing up to applaud. The other directors stood as well. "That's the par three with the pond in front of it, right?"

Herman glared back and shook his head. "If you must know, I put my drive in the water, hit the green in three, and took three putts for a triple bogey. That's not the point.

"I had a revelation as I walked off that green. I turn sixty-seven this year and I'm not getting younger. If I'm ever going to break ninety, I'm going to have to turn my full attention to golf. I've decided to put the company up for sale."

The news buckled knees, dropping everyone back into their chairs. How might a sale affect their jobs? How were they supposed to enjoy champagne now?

"We're going into full cutback mode immediately. I want to show strong numbers for the final quarter. That's what a buyer will want to see. I'm going to begin by eliminating R and D."

Karl's body went limp. He dropped the buttons from his left hand, and they fell to the carpet. "That can't be, Mr. Winston! Didn't you read my report? We're about to make optical history. We *have* made history! I've given Eagle Optics a real eagle's eye!"

That awful accent, Herman thought, shaking his head. *How have I put up with it for five years?*

Actually, Herman knew exactly why he put up with it. R&D had paid for itself with government money and had given his company 27 percent of $9 million as administrative overhead. He had been able to charge other unrelated costs to the grant that added even more to his bottom line. His total profit from Karl's venture was about $3 million. Not bad. *God bless America.*

"I've read your outstanding report in detail," Herman lied. In truth, he looked mostly at the potential risks. He didn't believe it was negative thinking to consider problems more than benefits. It was good business. Liability was everything. "However, FDA approval could take some time and there is inherent risk. I'm not willing to take that step, especially not now."

The finance director looked at the confusion on Karl's squinting face and wished he could give him a translation. Didn't he get it? The grant funds were exhausted. Herman wasn't about to spend any of *his* money on anything short of a sure thing. He never believed in the concept in the first place. The party is over.

In a panic, Karl fumbled through his pockets until he found a spool of thread with a needle stuck in it. "Watch this, everyone! You have to see this!"

His audience watched as he pulled thread from the spool and wet the end in his mouth. Holding the thread and needle at full arm's length and staring through a single open eye, he slipped the thread through the eye of the needle and stood up, smiling and nodding.

All but one of the people in the room looked at Karl in bewilderment. Was he crazy? Why would he thread a needle at the conference table? Was he going to mend a hole in his pants next?

Martha Porter, the secretary, was the only seamstress in the room and nearly fell out of her chair. She sewed every day, and it often took three or more tries to thread a needle w*hile wearing reading glasses and holding the needle inches in front of her nose!* What Karl had done was impossible! She vowed to express her admiration after the meeting.

Herman audibly cleared his throat. "Sit down, Karl. You need to hear me out."

Karl was amazed at the seeming indifference to his demonstration. He had calculated the odds of such an accomplishment at roughly one in a hundred for a person with normal vision. He could do it every time. "I think I've seen and heard enough," Karl said, refusing to sit and turning to leave, "I'll have to take my lens to another company."

"Sit!" Herman commanded, motioning with his right hand. "You should know perfectly well that everything related to the lens is now the property of Eagle Optics. That includes all the research you brought with you. It was all part of the contract you signed when you came to work here."

The attorney sat at the other end of the table, watching the drama unfold. Karl was very naïve, he thought, or maybe business was conducted differently in Germany. Yet again, Karl may have been distracted by the sizeable $270,000 annual salary in his contract. Nevertheless, he shouldn't have signed it before review by his own attorney. Under its terms, he didn't have a dime of compensation coming from Herman after the grant expired at the end of September. His income would disappear right along with the rights to his own invention.

Karl returned to his chair and slumped in it. What would he tell his wife? Moments ago, their future was beyond bright. He was ready to collect a Nobel Prize. How could he even face her now?

"I'm a reasonable man," Herman continued. "I'm going to give you a three-month option to purchase all the rights to the product for fifteen million dollars. If it has one tenth the potential you say it does, you should have no problem finding a buyer. Go out and make yourself a very wealthy man!" Fifteen million seemed like a good number to Herman. After all, he came up with it on the fifteenth hole.

At the far end of the table, the attorney shook his head, wondering why Herman was discussing this matter in front of others. Perhaps he thought he was showing off his business acumen. More likely, he was finding pleasure in ridiculing Mr. Zimmer.

Karl sat up straight. "You want me to pay fifteen million dollars for my own research?"

Herman shook his head. "Of course not. I want you to find someone else who will pay thirty or forty million. Everything over fifteen is yours! Sell it to the Department of Defense. You said they needed it in your report. Or maybe try some of the major players, like Bausch and Lomb or CooperVision."

Karl reflected for a moment. He was suddenly embarrassed by his initial reaction. The destiny of *eaglevision* was now in his hands alone, at least for three months. The potential financial benefit was enormous. There was no time to waste.

"I gladly accept your offer, Mr. Winston," Karl answered confidently. "I'll make us both a lot of money."

Herman nodded to the attorney and looked back to Karl. "The exclusive right to buy is yours until the end of the workday on December first. I'll excuse you and my attorney from the meeting. He can review the option for you in my office. Come back for champagne at the end of our meeting if you like."

Herman watched them leave. He was banking on having the most highly motivated salesman in the world working on his behalf for the next three months. Karl *did* have a gift. He h*ad* convinced the government to give his company millions.

Would someone out there pay $15 million for the rights to a contact lens that had to be watered more often than an Arizona lawn to avoid damaging or even destroying a dang eye? Improbable. Would a company go fifteen large for a lens that could only be used by people walking around looking goofy with just one eye open? Highly doubtful. Would they pay big money for the right to spend even more to get the lens tested and approved? Maybe one chance in a hundred. *Or a thousand*. Still, he would be getting valuable free advertising from Karl for the next three months. Maybe it would lead to at least some kind of offer after the option expired. It was all gravy.

Hours later, Martha Porter was alone in the conference room, putting everything back in order. She found an inch of champagne in one of the bottles and poured herself a toast. There was no point in wasting good bubbly.

In the process of realigning the chairs, she saw a contact lens button on the carpet and then another. She knew they had not been cut yet, or she wouldn't have seen them at all. A finished lens was almost clear, except for a hint of blue hue. In precut form, they had a slightly gray, frosty appearance.

She was tempted to toss them in the wastebasket because manufacturing already had thousands. However, she remembered Mr. Winston had stressed the importance of keeping costs to a minimum. Upon leaving the conference room, she carried the buttons all the way down the long hall and stopped beside the last door on the left. She took a pair of safety glasses from the box on the wall and put them on before she entered. As it turned out, the precaution was unnecessary. The Money Factory, as Mr. Winston called it, where hundreds of buttons were cut to prescription daily, was deserted. Glancing at the clock, she realized it was already lunchtime. She walked to the closest of the twelve work stations and tossed the buttons into a hopper that held countless others. They would all be cut to prescription and sent to customers throughout Arizona and other Western States.

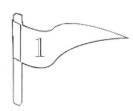

1

The retirement community of Leisureville, Arizona, is a thirty-minute drive from downtown Phoenix, but a world away from the bustle and buzz of working America. Like thousands of similar developments in warm weather locations throughout the southern states, it is a haven where senior citizens from all parts of the country congregate to pursue their hobbies, reduce the discomfort of arthritis and allergies, share stories of glorious younger days, and find compassion from others who are beginning the inescapable process of withering away.

Meticulous Spanish-style stucco homes, painted in the owner's choice of three different shades of beige and roofed with deep red tile, line streets that are shaded only by a few palm trees. The rock gardens surrounding each home feature a variety of bushes, flowers, and cacti that residents are free to choose from a list published by the homeowners' association. Matching mailboxes are perched beside each driveway, with the house numbers relief-carved into each stained wood post, a feature most residents agree is an elegant touch.

There is no need for speed bumps on streets that carve the development into neat square blocks. Drivers are respectful of the 15 mph limit that applies to both cars and golf carts, and more than a few of the residents spend the better part of each day watching the trickle of traffic from their porches or windows, ready to report any violation immediately.

The streets and grounds show no trace of litter. All garbage is sealed in plastic bags and placed in trash barrels with tight-fitting lids. These, in turn, are left next to the mailboxes every Monday morning for pickup before 10:00 a.m. An eight-foot chain link fence covered with dark green fabric surrounds the entire gated community and prevents the invasion of refuse from the outside world. In the unlikely event that a gum wrapper somehow gets loose within the compound, volunteers on patrol in carts are ready to pounce on the problem.

A twelve thousand square foot entertainment facility stands in the center of Leisureville. It features a ballroom that houses biweekly association meetings, movies, concerts, dances, and other organized activities. The building also has a library, exercise room, billiards room, and space for sewing groups and other crafters. A large swimming pool and tennis and shuffleboard courts adjoin the building.

Two golf courses comprise the emerald core of the development. The many ponds that serve as hazards for the golfers provide domain for fish and waterfowl. Hundreds of migrating Canadian geese and mallard ducks, referred to as *snowbirds* like many of the human residents, make Leisureville their home in the winter. However, an increasing number of the birds and people alike, all with tiring wings perhaps, make the peaceful setting a permanent home.

Beneath a predawn sky and the roof of one of Leisureville's 960 homes, seventy-two-year-old Ray Plumlee stirred between sheets patterned with the layout of the famous Pebble Beach Golf Course. The bedding had been a Christmas gift from one his four children, though which child or which Christmas might be hard to recall. In fact, the gift may have even been a birthday surprise. Admittedly, it was getting a little harder to remember such things.

The alarm clock on his nightstand was set for 6:30 a.m., but he rarely needed its hum to wake him, especially not on a golf day. He reached over, flicked off the alarm switch, and fumbled to find his eyeglasses on the nightstand, where he routinely placed them before drifting off.

"Here they are," his wife Pat whispered from the adjacent pillow. "You fell asleep watching TV last night." She lifted the glasses from her own nightstand and handed them over, then pulled the covers back to her chin and instantly dropped back to sleep.

He climbed out of bed cautiously, testing the left knee that was often stiff in the morning. It felt okay, but he favored it with a slight limp out of habit. After shaving and dressing as quietly as possible, he collected the Arizona Republic from the front doorstep and extracted the sports page. He glanced through it at the kitchen table while eating the bland fiber cereal and small dish of prunes that Pat prescribed as his regular breakfast. When the

The Sweet Swing

clock showed six-fifty, he washed and dried his dishes, returned them to the cupboard and stood by the window to admire the sunrise.

The kitchen window faced east, just like that in his former home in Wasilla, Alaska. It had been the only feature he insisted upon when his wife and he shopped for a retirement home in Leisureville, although a fairway location would have been wonderful too. While the sun now rose over tile rooftops instead of snow covered mountain peaks, the effect was still spectacular. He loved his old Alaska home but didn't long for it. He was living in the right place at the right time in his life.

As departure time approached, he refolded the Monday paper exactly the way it arrived and delivered it to Pat's nightstand along with an insulated carafe of coffee and her personal cup. He knew she would wake soon after he left.

When Ray entered the double garage in stocking feet, he caught a faint whiff of gasoline, which prompted him to tap the door opener and allow fresh morning air to enter. He never noticed the odor with his old Explorer, but since replacing it with a slightly used Lincoln a couple weeks back, it had become the norm. It was a minor inconvenience to endure after getting such a bargain on a luxury car with low mileage.

He immediately sat down on a four-by-eight-feet piece of carpet that he kept on the concrete floor. Five minutes of exercise was all he needed to get loose before a round: a handful of pushups and leg raises, a few standing jumping jacks, and a dozen swings with a weighted club. His golf buddies marveled at his perceived ability to walk right to the first tee and hit the ball without preparation, so he never disclosed his home workout routine. Why not let them marvel?

A dozen hats hung in a row on the wall, from darkest on the left to white on the far right. He went with red and the local Phoenix Cardinals logo. He wore white on Saturday and his round hadn't gone well. His putting game was deteriorating by the day.

After pulling the power cord from Birdie Chaser, the golf cart parked next to the Lincoln, he hopped aboard and backed out of the garage before suddenly stopping at the end of driveway. Something didn't feel right. He looked down at his foot on the break. No shoe. He had forgotten to put on his golf spikes! After a deep breath and quiet curse, he pulled back into the garage. Getting older had its downside. Like one of his friends often said, aging was an increasingly slippery slope.

With that in mind, he hurried back to the kitchen to take some fish oil capsules. He tried to swallow two each morning because they reportedly enhanced memory, but often forgot to take them. Ironically, he always remembered his golf scores, information he would rather forget these days.

Returning to the garage, he studied a neat line of six pairs of golf shoes before slipping into brown and white saddles. Now he was running late.

Stepping back in the cart, he noted the empty space in front of his seat. He forgot the two brown paper bags on the kitchen counter. He kicked off his golf shoes, reentered the house, and came back with the bags. He had to untie his shoes before he could slide them back on and left before retying them, leaving that chore for the first tee.

As he whirred down the palm-lined street, he reminded himself that there was nowhere in the world he'd rather be and nothing he would rather be doing. At the same time, he wondered why he had to remind himself of it. During his first years at Leisureville, he had plunged into each day like a kid on summer vacation. Now his days were becoming . . . robotic?

To what could he attribute this malaise? Was it the erosion of his golf game? Was he so shallow that his happiness was linked directly to his handicap? Would sagging play simply become intolerable at some point? Was there life after golf?

He tried to purge his mind of dark thoughts as he braked to greet Mrs. Flannery, who was walking her tiny poodle. He reached into one of the bags below his seat and grabbed a Milk Bone, broke it in half, and tossed a piece to the dog, which stood on hind legs in anticipation.

The poodle made the catch, just like always. Ray said, "Nice grab, Shadow!"

Mrs. Flannery scrunched her face into a raisin. "Her name is Michelle, Mr. Plumlee!"

"Oh, I'm so sorry. Michelle!" He waved, stepped on the accelerator and forgave himself for the error. There were as many dogs as people in the development and he knew that at least a couple of them had the Shadow handle.

A block later, he saw Harvey Green, tall and slender as a lamppost, standing at the end of his driveway, watching him approach. For the past two years, Ray picked up his playing partner five mornings a week. Never, not once, had Harvey not been ready and waiting.

Lucy, Harvey's wife, walked out of the house in a long, white bathrobe. She carried a tall travel cup of her five star coffee and handed it to Ray along with her regular greeting. "Good morning, Mr. Bailey!" She alone called him by that name because he reminded her of Jimmy Stewart, who played George Bailey in one of his signature roles in *It's a Wonderful Life*. She claimed the similarity was as much in his voice as his appearance.

"Did you remember to tell Pat that our bridge game has moved to my house today?"

Now that Lucy mentioned it, Ray remembered her request from yesterday. He lifted the cup near his nose to savor the aroma and the heat of it fogged his glasses. "You better call and remind her," he said, grinning. "I could be losing it a bit. I drove away from the house without shoes on today!"

Lucy stared at him and shook her head. "And you forgot something else. Your tooth is missing."

Ray immediately dropped his smile. It wasn't just the tooth to the right of his upper two front ones that was missing, but two upper molars that were normally out of view anyway.

When the visible tooth fell victim to a popcorn seed a year ago, he remedied the problem with a partial denture that included all three missing teeth. Given that the prosthetic was half the cost of a single implant and killed three birds with one stone, it seemed like a fine idea at the time. No one told him how uncomfortable the thing was to wear or how easy to misplace. He should have sprung for an implant.

"The dang thing is right where it belongs, in a glass by the bathroom sink," Ray said.

"I'll go for comfort over good looks today!"

Harvey slid onto the seat beside him. "We can go back to your house for it," he said, patting Ray on the shoulder. "You don't want to hear the guys joking about it for eighteen holes, do you?"

Ray headed straight for the course. "We're already late. I'll just have to keep my mouth shut today."

Before the men covered a single block, Harvey whispered, "Speed bump!"

Ray eased off the throttle. There were no actual speed inhibitors on the streets, but most Leisureville men understood the code. It meant that Ingrid Samuels was out and about. *Slow down and savor the view.*

Ingrid was a widow child in her late forties, fifty at the most. Her long legs, however, looked no more than eighteen and were always showcased by sundresses that revealed all but an inch of them. The men speculated that she had the only naturally unwrinkled face in the whole development. Adding to her mystique, she was from one of the Northern European countries where they assumed all women were born drop dead gorgeous and spoke English in a way that made the language exotic. Because her deceased husband had been thirty years older than she, most Leisureville women called her a gold-digger. The men figured if that were true she would be living in a castle, not a ranch home.

Ingrid disappeared through her front door as they drew closer and Ray sped toward the main golf course. Although resident golfers had unlimited access to both the regulation and executive courses for an annual fee of $3,000, they preferred the challenge of full-length golf.

As they drove past empty fairways on their way toward the first tee, they inspected their playground. A small maintenance crew was mowing the greens and raking sand. A scattering of rabbits grazed on grass sparkling with dew. Ducks rippled the large pond between 17 and 18 and a large bass splashed after his breakfast.

They had the earliest tee time because they loved the freshness of the morning, the sight of steam rising from the greens as the sun rose, and the tracks of balls on the grass for the first few holes, until the moisture evaporated. Beyond the aesthetics of early play, they also preferred to avoid the hottest sun and inconvenience of waiting for foursomes ahead of them.

When they pulled up to the first tee, Mulligan Wettman and Knickers Collins, the balance of the regular group, were warming up in their own unique styles. Knickers, or Mickey as he was named on his birth certificate and known to people outside Leisureville, knelt on one damp knee, like a batter awaiting his turn at the plate. He flexed broad shoulders and twirled his Big Bertha driver in a variety of exercises. Mulligan, whose given name was Irvin, sat in the passenger side of Knickers's cart, swilling coffee and puffing on his front-nine cigar.

With an exaggerated wave of his smoke, Mulligan greeted his competition, "I was worried after the whipping we gave you Saturday that you might not be showing up."

Knickers added, "I was worried that after drinkin' *Old Arizona* after three straight rounds, you might be throwin' up!"

The standard wager between the competing pairs was twofold. The losing team not only paid for the beer at the clubhouse tavern after the round, but they had to drink Old Arizona, the blandest brew on earth, while watching the winners enjoy frosty mugs of draft Sam Adams. The tradition was set in stone.

The same group had been grinding out rounds and gulping beer, both good and bad, for two years. Prior to the inclusion of Harvey, the others played together four additional years.

Ray's former partner, Tom Klein, succumbed to a stroke while standing over a twelve-footer on the seventeenth green. While his death was a shock at age seventy-one, he had gone out in style. He was even par at the fatal moment, with an excellent chance for a birdie.

As Mulligan pulled out his driver, Harvey called to him, "I hope you brought your wallet, there's a scent of lemons in the air."

The lemon reference was tied to Mulligan's working career as a Ford dealer in Chicago. He always referred to his own errant shots as lemons, like the occasional troublesome cars that passed through his lot. However, his lemons were rare.

In fact, Mulligan was a former Leisureville club champion, just as Knickers and Ray and the late Tom Klein had been. Between 2007 and 2011, the succession of champs had been Tom, Ray, Knickers, Mulligan and Ray again. As a result of their collective accomplishments, local residents referred to the quartet as not *a* foursome but *the* Foursome. Much to Harvey's delight, the group still enjoyed that recognition despite his own failure to win a title thus far.

"I won't be making any lemonade today, Harv," Mulligan returned through teeth that clenched his stogie. "Although you'd probably prefer it to the beer you'll be drinking."

Always first to drive at the start, Mulligan teed his ball. At seventy-three, he was the elder statesman, at least by a few months. Like the rest of what *he* referred to as the Four-Eyed Foursome, he wore bifocal glasses. Barely 5'4" in golf spikes, he described himself as a short glass of water. Knickers often joked that his playing partner was more like a shot glass because the closest thing to water he ever drank was Old Arizona. In truth, however, Mulligan's persona was larger than life. As the president of the Leisureville Homeowners Association for the last five years, he was the development's best known figure. Although he had a heavy hand in all business related to the community and occasionally was loose with the application of the rules, there were surprisingly few complaints from any of the residents. He had a knack for explaining things.

As both a talented and perpetual talker, Mulligan regarded the golfers' code of whispery silence with disdain. He was even known to talk during his own swing. "Good morning, America!" Mulligan hollered as he began to backswing a driver that seemed as tall as he.

He lurched into his swing with a ferocity that lifted both feet from the ground. The resulting drive ripped a trail through the grass and eventually stopped rolling about one hundred yards out.

"Good morning, worms!" Knickers responded. "That'll teach those night crawlers to get back in the ground before your tee time!"

Mulligan already had a second ball on the tee and launched it 240 yards down the left side of the fairway; therein explaining his nickname. A mulligan, in golf terminology, is the playing of a second ball after hitting a poor initial shot. It was a practice normally reserved for beginners, but the Foursome permitted a single mulligan a day, on the first tee only, if the golfer chose to use it. It was a rule that only Mulligan utilized, and he did so routinely. It was his way of warming up. No practice swings. No stretching. Just rock and fire and then fire again.

"Way to give them the old one-two, slugger," Knickers said, taking over the tee.

Knickers Collins enjoyed honored status among the men because he spent his whole working life in professional baseball. As a catcher in the St. Louis organization, he played ten years in the farm system before a call-up to the major league team for just fifteen days. Some might say he had his cup of coffee in the big leagues, but Knickers called it an espresso . . . short but stimulating. In any case, he had two hits in the official record book, both singles. He played another four years in AAA before working as a minor league bullpen coach for another thirty-eight years.

Perhaps in tribute to a lifetime of wearing a baseball uniform, maybe in deference to golf tradition, or probably just to be different, he wore knickers on the course each round. Because no one else in Leisureville wore them, and maybe no one else in all of Arizona, he, like Mulligan, was especially well-known.

Knickers was also the official founder of the Foursome. After retiring to Leisureville, his first order of business had been to recruit the most elite golfers as his playing partners. Competition was in his blood.

The old ball player with the oversized nose and belly teed his ball and deliberately assumed his stance, just as he had in the batter's box for so many years. He held one of the long shafted huge-headed drivers that everyone was using these days, but did so begrudgingly. To him, the new equipment was an insult to the true essence of the game, just as the aluminum bat was to baseball. Still, he saw what the big drivers had done for the rest of the Foursome and wouldn't concede an advantage. He uncorked a nice draw that settled into the light rough.

Rough wasn't really an apt description of the area off the fairways at Leisureville. The grass there was barely longer than the fairways themselves, which was the way most senior golfers liked it. Because of that and other characteristics of the layout, the men referred to themselves as *Leisureville scratch* golfers, meaning they could play this particular course or others similar to it in close to regulation par. The distances from tee to green were appreciably shorter than championship level country clubs and the short cut fairways added length to their drives. The sand traps were shallow and relatively easy to escape. Greens they had played a thousand times were predictable. Mulligan, Knickers and Ray had all shared the resident record of sixty-seven, a score each achieved in his youthful sixties, until that record recently fell to a punk early retiree in his midfifties.

Harvey was smiling as he took the tee, delighted with life in general. As a career teacher and then principal at an Indiana high school, golf had always been his escape from the commotion of noisy halls, stress of parent conferences, politics of advisory school board meetings, and mediation of teacher power struggles. Now he played with three former champions and was dedicated to becoming one himself.

His drive made him shiver with pleasure. The low liner landed a couple hundred yards out and rolled another sixty down the sparse right side of the fairway; ideal position for an approach to the green.

"Nothing but perfect," Ray said, as he passed Harvey and slapped his shoulder. They were Ray's first words of the morning; he was conscious of the missing tooth and trying to keep the gap hidden from merciless opponents.

"You must have landed on a sprinkler head, Ichabod," Mulligan complained. "No way that ball should have rolled so far."

Ichabod was Lucy Green's special nickname for her husband that she used only in rare moments of anger. At 6'4" and around 175 pounds, Harvey could be described as gangly. He also had a long neck and pronounced Adam's apple. Toss in the fact that he was a teacher and there you have it: *Ichabod Crane*. Harvey hated the reference. Therefore, the other men loved it and figured Lucy was a true genius.

And Knickers was a true menace. Not long after the nickname slipped into his playful hands, he arranged a surprise for Harvey when he and Lucy returned from a weekend trip. The Greens drove up to their house and were greeted by a blaze orange sign installed in their front yard. Measuring four feet long and three feet high and supported by beams anchored in cement, it christened the home *Sleepy Hollow* in black, Old English-style letters. While the mini billboard was well outside the boundaries of Leisureville's bylaws, Mulligan was a dangerous sidekick for a prankster of Knickers's ingenuity and approved the waiver. The professionally made sign and installation set Knickers back $1,500.

Harvey had been ready to rent a chainsaw and remedy the situation, but Lucy layed down the law. She told Ichabod he should feel honored to have a name for his estate and that it was a compliment that Knickers made such a large investment in the name of friendship. She even had a spotlight installed to showcase the monument at night.

Ray limped to a spot midway between the white markers for his tee shot. Unlike the others, who wore light jackets in the chill of an October morning, he was in short sleeves. A lifetime in Alaska had thickened his skin.

While the others played golf most of their lives, Ray never picked up a club until after his fiftieth birthday. Most folks in his home state grew up with a fishing rod or shotgun in their hands. Outside of hunting and fishing, his only outdoor sporting pursuit had been decades of slo-pitch softball. However, when the growing tourism industry near his Wasilla home led to development of a golf course, he was one of the first to give it a go. He felt comfortable with his first swing and the game became a passion. Within just three years, he played a round in par.

Knickers always paid special attention when Ray addressed a ball. While most golfers had *something* to worry about during each swipe . . . the position of the head or an elbow, the pressure of their fingers on the grip, the turn of their hips and shoulders . . . Knickers was convinced his friend thought of nothing at all. He swung as easily, as freely, as confidently as a major leaguer taking batting practice. Mulligan called him a machine. Harvey described him as a natural. In any case, Knickers had never seen Ray have to fish a ball from the water or look for his shot in the bushes. He could just walk down the middle of the fairway until he tripped over his Titleist. It hardly seemed fair.

Before Ray hit his drive, he stood back and took in the vista of the distant green for a moment. He visualized a perfect drive, a stiff approach, and a single putt for a birdie. It would be the first of eighteen birdies and the beginning of a perfect day. Wasn't that the right way to think?

Ray's drive was routinely center cut, and he slid behind the wheel of Birdie Chaser with dreams of a great round and turnaround. His game had been slipping, as evidenced by a gut-wrenching seventy-seven on Saturday that added a new frown line to his forehead. Would he ever make a putt outside of three feet again?

And so they went. Four kids in their seventies, dressed in flamingo pink, lemon yellow, kelly green and powder blue, lost to the world for another four hours.

On the sixteenth green, Harvey reclined on elbows and knees with his right cheek on the grass and his rear end high in the air. With his left eye closed, he squinted at the eight feet of landscape between his ball marker and the cup. It was the first time any of the men took on grass strains in pursuit of excellence.

"I think it will break two or three inches to the right," Harvey said to Ray, who stood behind him, surveying the situation as well.

Mulligan and Knickers stood silently, just off the green. Normally, Mulligan would be commenting about the label on Harvey's underwear that was peeking above his belt, perhaps asking why he wore his boxers inside out. Knickers might also be messing with Harvey's fragile psyche but not today. Harvey was two under par. The best score he had ever recorded was a one-under seventy-one. It was just one of those amazing things; Harvey was feeling it.

His round had been improbable in so many ways. He knocked in putts from all over the greens, a few from twenty feet or more. He chipped in for an unlikely bird on twelve when his wedge shot from the bunker crashed into the flagstick a foot above the ground and dropped straight into the hole. Most unlikely of all, he had recorded no bogeys.

Generally, Harvey's overall game could be described as erratic. While the other three men made the occasional bogey, they carded a nearly equal number of birdies. Their double bogeys were rarer than rain. That was why, even with their games trailing off over the last couple of years, they maintained handicaps of just a few shots. Harvey could hit his driver a mile and launch iron shots so high they seemed to disappear in the sky, but there was no place on a scorecard for style points. Accuracy was his issue. That and dealing with adversity. He wanted to excel so badly that his excitement often got in his way.

The addition of a six handicapper to the Foursome after Tom Klein's passing had been the result of divine intervention; Ray's wife dictated it. Harvey's Lucy was her best friend and bridge partner and the future of the Foursome had been determined across a card table.

It had been a stretch to add Harvey to the group because of the delicate balance of competition. Tom Klein had the same tiny handicap as the others. With his new partner, Ray was living on bad beer that he to pay for himself. Nonetheless, he didn't seem to care. Therefore, Mulligan and Knickers didn't mind either.

As it turned out, Harvey's participation did have benefits. He loved keeping score, a task the others happily delegated. Beyond that, he spent countless hours on his computer tallying statistics from the Foursome's results. On any given hole, off the top of his head, he could tell each player their average score, how many birdies he made, and his success rate for hitting the green in regulation. The others surmised that the former principal had grown accustomed to compiling numbers like student test scores, graduation rates and so forth. It was kind of weird, but really cool. Harvey's enthusiasm was contagious.

When Harvey finally rose to his feet, Ray whispered that it was a straight putt. "Just knock it in, Harv. This will be your best score ever!"

Lightheaded, Harvey stood over his ball, focusing on stiff wrists, pendulum shoulder action and a smooth follow through. He hadn't felt this way since standing in the delivery room, watching the birth of his first child. The memory got him thinking of the importance of proper breathing. He tried to remember. *Take a deep breath and push.* He pushed the putter and closed his eyes. The sound of his Titleist striking the bottom of the cup hit him like Harvey Jr.'s first cry. He raised his arms and hollered.

"Three under par," Ray exclaimed. "None of us has shot a score like that in years."

"You had that sixty-eight almost two years ago," Harvey said, recovering his ball.

"That's the best round any of us played since I joined the group."

"Just par out for your personal best," Mulligan said. "I'll have a victory cigar ready for you!"

"We'll all be watchin' you on the Champions Tour if you keep this up," Knickers added.

Back in Birdie Chaser, Harvey reached into one of the bags his partner brought, the one with *his* biscuits, not the Milk Bones. His biscuits were Oreos that Ray brought each day exclusively for Harvey, who could consume any amount of anything and never gain a pound.

He popped the last of what had been a dozen into his mouth. "This is the last bit of energy I need to push past these last two holes! I can honestly say this is the best day of my life!"

The best day of his life, Ray thought. Which was the best day of my life? The day I got married? The day my first child was born? The day I bought my first and only business license? The day the Little League team I coached won a state championship? Or possibly the day I won my first Leisureville club championship? There had been lots of best days. The glow of thinking about them made him feel all the more excited for his friend.

As Harvey stood over his ball on the seventeenth tee, he was thinking big. No, he was thinking huge. *If he made two more birdies he could match his friends' best scores.* Today, anything was possible.

He turned and said, "I have you guys to thank for all this. You inspired me from the first day I played with you. I've learned so much."

With five iron in hand, Harvey looked at the flag just 178 yards away. Yesterday he hit his best shot from this very spot and stuck his drive ten feet from the hole. Barely missed the birdie putt. He wanted to duplicate that swing and tried to recall exactly how he did it.

As Harvey continued to stand over the ball, twitching his shoulders and shuffling his feet, Ray got an uneasy feeling. A golf swing was all about rhythm and repetition. Harvey should have swung by now. He glanced at Mulligan and Knickers and both raised their eyebrows.

Suddenly and inexplicably, Harvey gave the grip a white-knuckled squeeze and unleashed a too wicked cut. His ball soared far to the right of his target, toward a pond that was normally out of play, even for him.

At first Harvey was convinced the ball would wind up in the water. However, as his *Titleist* sliced even further right, there was hope it might carry beyond the hazard into the adjoining fairway. In that case, there would be no penalty. He could hit a wedge to the green and still conceivably make par!

The ball cleared the water and bounced on the far side and the men collectively sighed relief. On the second bounce, the ball caught the edge of a concrete cart path and ricocheted right back into the lake. Harvey was still frozen in his follow-through, a veritable statue. No one spoke until the last ripple from the splash disappeared.

Ray cleared his throat first. "You can take a drop over there and still make a bogey! Heck, you can birdie the last hole and still shoot sixty-nine!"

The other two men said nothing. They knew the writing was on the wall and the message wasn't pretty.

Five minutes later, Harvey stood zombie-like in the bunker in front of the green, where his third shot landed after he took a penalty stroke. The others stood on the far side of the green, their heads bowed as if they were at a funeral.

Harvey took an anxious swing, lifted his head too soon, and saw his three friends dive and duck as his ball rocketed straight at them. It flew over their heads, glanced off the roof of Birdie Chaser, cleared shrubs that normally protected a fairway home, and came to rest on a chair on the Olson's rear patio.

Harvey immediately dropped his wedge, picked up the rake, and calmly tried to clean up his mess. After finishing, he recovered his club and suddenly went Jekyll to Hyde. Spitting profanity, he took three running strides toward the lake, whipping the club around his head like a helicopter propeller. When he let go, it spun in a high arc before splashdown a good hundred feet out. Then, without looking back, he started walking across the fairway in the direction of Sleepy Hollow.

"That was hard to watch," Mulligan said, glancing back at the seventeenth tee. "I'm glad no one was following close behind to witness it. You think he'll be okay?"

"Of course he will," Ray said. "He'll be right back in the saddle tomorrow. He loves the game. Last time something like that happened he invited us all out to dinner. Remember?"

"Hell," Mulligan grunted. "He doesn't have to act as if his house burned down though."

Knickers stared after Harvey, who seemed to pick up speed with each long stride. "Give the guy a break, Mulligan. If his house burned down, he could build another one. He'll never have that round back. They don't sell insurance for that kinda thing."

"That's an excellent point," Ray added, thinking of the scorecard in Harvey's rear pocket. "What are the chances that he'll ever have that chance again?" He knew that Harvey would be looking at that incomplete scorecard at least once a day for the rest of his life.

"All right," Mulligan conceded. "I guess there's nothing wrong with feeling a little passion at our age. I was just a little worried his heart was going to blow up like a grenade there for a second. I'd hate to lose two friends on the same damn hole."

"Which reminds me," Knickers said. "There's somethin' I want to talk about with you guys. Now's a perfect time. Let's just pick up our balls and go over to Tom's bench for a bit."

Tom's bench referred to the fancy redwood bench under the large mesquite tree behind the seventeenth green, where their previous partner Tom Klein prematurely met his maker. Tom's widow had disclosed that it was her husband's wish to be buried somewhere on the golf course he loved. However, even Mulligan was unable to get board approval for a burial that was contrary to township zoning ordinances. Instead, the widow purchased the commemorative bench with a brass plaque on the backrest that read:

In Loving Memory of Thomas Klein
2007 Leisureville Club Champion

Mulligan, Knickers, and Ray had subsequently filled a Sam Adams bottle with some of Tom's ashes and buried it beneath the bench. They scattered the rest of his remains in the very sand trap that Harvey just raked, so their friend would always be in play.

Knickers motioned for the other two men to take a seat while he paced silently in front of them for a full minute. Finally, he said, "I have somethin' serious to talk about, and this seems like the right time and place."

Ray and Mulligan sat at attention. They often joked that an x-ray of Knickers's entire body wouldn't reveal a single serious bone. He was the class clown.

"We never talk about money much," he began. "I think we all assume that each of us is well enough off that we don't worry about money. Is that a fair assumption? Do we all think our lives are about as perfect as we'd like them to be?

The men were caught off guard by the subject matter, but nodded tentative agreement. Each wondered if Knickers was setting them up for a joke.

"Last night Bess and I were watching Wizard of Oz on TV. You know, they show it every year around this time and we never miss it. Bess was saying how the Foursome reminded her so much of the characters."

Mulligan narrowed his eyes. "So this is the serious stuff you wanted to talk about? I swear, if you say I'm the mayor of Munchkinland, I'll deck you. Enough with the short jokes! I was beating you by two strokes today."

Knickers still held his putter and lifted it as if he were about to club Mulligan. "I know it's hard for you to listen for more than a few seconds, but shut up for a little while, will you?

"Anyway, you Mulligan, are the lion, the king of the Leisureville jungle."

Mulligan smiled at the comparison for a moment, then blurted, "But not cowardly, right?"

Knickers raised his club again. "Are you going to listen or not? As the lion, you always talk a good game and generally lead the community in the right direction, but you seem terrified of those old witches on your board of directors."

"Hey," Mulligan said. "That's politics. You wouldn't understand. Sometimes you make concessions so that you'll have their votes when it really matters."

"Well," Knickers continued, "I thought honoring Tom's wish for a proper burial on the golf course really mattered."

Mulligan stood up. "I'm telling you for the hundredth time, it was against the friggin' law!"

Ray said, "Besides, you figured out a way around the problem, Knickers. We did bury Tom on the course, at least in our own way."

Knickers continued to stare at Mulligan until he sat back down. "And Harvey is the tin man. He's a true blue friend and would go to war for you in a second. At the same time, he can be a little high maintenance.

"Ray is the scarecrow. His golf swing is so loose and easy it's like he's made of straw. He's so good natured that he's gone through his whole life with a smile painted on his face."

Knickers grinned. "I came up with the straw thing. The painted smile was Bess's idea."

Ray laughed and nudged Mulligan. "If I only had a brain, right?"

"If only you weren't missing your tooth today," Mulligan returned. "You'd at least look a little smarter!"

Mulligan turned to Knickers. "So who does that make you, Dorothy or Toto?"

Ray couldn't help laughing again, especially when Knickers rolled his eyes and shook his head.

Knickers coughed and said, "Well, I'm the wizard, of course. I'm here to coach you all into being heroes . . . the best you can be!"

Mulligan and Ray stared. How had Knickers delivered that line with a straight face?

"So this is the serious stuff you wanted to talk about?" Mulligan asked again, shaking his head. "One minute you're talking about money and the next you are skipping down the yellow brick road."

"No," Knickers said. "It's what you call an introduction. Up until now, our golden years have been all about golf. We spend half our time playin' and the other half-talkin' or thinkin' about it. Well, I can't speak for you, but the game is losing a little of its glow for me. How long will it be before we are takin' half a swing and chasin' our balls a hundred yards at a time like some of the old farts around here? I'm not sure I want to go out that way. In fact, I'm damn sure of it."

Ray was looking past Knickers, watching the following foursome hit their drives toward the green, but listened closely. The words of his friend could well have been his own.

"So you think we're getting old?" Mulligan said.

Knickers nodded. "I think it's a proper time to build what my wife calls a legacy. What if we can do more than just amuse ourselves? What if we can actually help change the world in some great way?"

Mulligan and Ray suddenly felt a little uncomfortable and started to twitch on the seat. Their legacy? Change the world? It was all so out of left field. There had always been an unspoken rule on the golf course: No talk of politics, religion, philosophy, economics or anything else of substance.

"Now, back to money," Knickers continued. "Bess and I have been talkin' about what we are gonna do with our money when we die. We've been talkin' for two years now, ever since Tom passed away all the sudden like he did.

"Mulligan, you have a couple kids. I have no doubt that you will just leave your estate to them. Harvey has two children, so same goes for him. Ray, you have so many kids and grandkids that you probably can't even remember all their names. Bess and I have nobody to leave our money to. She has one rotten brother she'd rather forget."

Mulligan and Ray knew this was a difficult subject for Knickers. His only son, Mickey Jr., died in a car accident the night of his high school graduation.

"So what do we do with the money? Leave it to charity, right?" He looked at the others for a show of agreement, but they stared blankly.

Ray realized he had never even given this subject a thought. His children would get his estate, just as Knickers suggested.

Mulligan, out of habit, was about to joke that Knickers could leave the money to him, but bit his tongue. His friend was in serious mode, just as advertised.

"Our problem is that after two years of talkin', we still have no idea what charity would be the right choice. Therefore, I'm going to make the Foursome into a board of directors of this charitable trust or whatever you want to call it. Together we are going to decide where the money goes."

Ray glanced at Mulligan to see his reaction, but he was uncharacteristically stoic.

"What about your wife?" Ray asked. "Doesn't she have an equal say in all this?"

Knickers shook his head vigorously. "She's tired of the whole discussion. She says the money is my doin' and my problem. As long as I'm happy, she's happy."

Mulligan asked, "How much are we talking about here? How much do you plan on leaving behind?"

"I'll tell you what," Knickers whispered, aware that the next group of golfers was nearing the green behind him. "We'll get together tonight and I'll explain more. Just don't say nothin' to the wives." Knickers winked at Ray, who understood the subtle message. It wasn't Pat who posed a problem, it was Mulligan's wife, Mary. She was a wonderful lady but a world class networker. Very little happened in Leisureville that she didn't know about or freely discuss.

"Let me go over and see Harvey now," Knickers added. "I think this news will cheer him up."

After his friends drove off, Ray headed to the driving range, where he had business to transact before going home. Not surprisingly, he found only four people on the range under the noontime sun. Tommy, the young man who maintained the facility, was filling divots with sand. An elderly fellow in bermuda shorts and a broad-brimmed straw hat lounged on a chair in the shade. The new club pro, whose name Ray couldn't recall, was giving a lesson to Gladys Beckerman.

"How you doing, Tommy?" Ray whispered when he drew close. He didn't want to distract the Beckerman widow, who was taking some wild hacks just a few yards away. She was a small woman, but could beat the pattern off a rug with those swings.

"Hey, Mr. Plumlee," Tommy returned. "How they hangin'?" He greeted all the men that way.

"Lower all the time," Ray said and grinned. He pulled out his wallet and withdrew a ten dollar bill. "I have a favor to ask."

Tommy smiled at the sawbuck. "Let me guess. Mr. Green lost a club in the water again."

"You make it sound like a regular occurrence," Ray said. "It only happened once before."

Tommy grunted. "It's at least the third time, but who's counting, right? Where do I swim today?"

Ray described the location of the wet wedge as closely as he could. Tommy was familiar with the entire layout of the course, especially the hazards. He spent lots of time recovering lost balls from the ponds and hedges, which he sold for half a buck each. It was an excellent supplement to low wages in a locale where errant shots were common, energy for finding them was limited, and most folks appreciated a fifty-cent bargain. Tommy agreed to drop the wedge off at Sleepy Hollow on the way home. Everyone knew where Harvey lived.

Behind him, Ray heard the pro telling Gladys to slow down her swing and relax her grip, which was always good advice. Suddenly the widow shrieked. If Ray hadn't turned his head to the sound, the flying three iron may have harmlessly brushed past his ear. However, it was the warning that doomed him; the blade caught him flush between the eyes.

Seconds or hours later, Ray found himself on his back, staring into the blurred face of the club pro. It must have been seconds. "Can you hear me?" the pro asked. "Can you see me? Are you okay?"

Ray heard a woman's hysterical crying, and her wailing too. "I killed Ray Plumlee! Oh, I've killed Ray Plumlee!"

The pro looked at Tommy and asked him to console the lady, or at least shut her up. Tommy and the man in shorts walked her to a nearby chair.

"I'm going to call an ambulance," the pro said to Ray. "You took a hard blow and were unconscious for at least a few seconds. You're bleeding from a cut on your forehead and it looks like you lost a tooth."

Ray's head was clearing quickly. He wasn't going to any hospital; he wasn't going to scare his wife that way. And his mouth felt fine. The pro only assumed he lost a tooth.

"I'll be fine," he said, hoping it was true. He certainly couldn't see very well, but then he never could without his glasses. "Do you have my glasses?"

The pro shook his head. "I'm afraid they didn't make it."

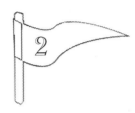

The waiting room at Sturrock Optometry was nearly empty in the midafternoon, with only the Plumlees filling any of the dozen chairs. It had taken Pat just two calls to find a doctor with an opening in his afternoon schedule.

"This is so romantic," she said, patting Ray on the knee.

"Romantic?" He asked, not certain he heard correctly. He wasn't sure what kind of pain medication was administered at the emergency room, but he felt pleasantly groggy.

"Because I think you look like Jimmy Stewart without your glasses. You're going to be so handsome! You'll have contacts just like mine!"

"You got that from Lucy," he responded, shaking his head.

Pat giggled and jammed an elbow into his side. "I happen to agree with her."

"Well, I only said I would try contacts for you. I'm getting glasses too. It's hard to teach an old frog new kicks."

Ray glanced at the assortment of magazines in front of him and picked up *Time*, not one of the many golf publications that seemed as much a part of Arizona doctor offices as the waiting room itself. He didn't think about it until Pat registered surprise.

"You really are struggling with your vision," she said. "You didn't pick up *Golf Digest* or *Golf World*."

He could barely read the names on the magazine covers, but the subconscious choice was significant. Golf had meant everything until recently. Now the game served to convey the clear message of Father Time: Life was winding down. Perhaps he glimpsed his own Grim Reaper in the form of Mrs. Beckerman. Ironically, her scythe had been a golf club. Maybe it was time to think about more productive uses for the remaining years of his life.

Ray thumbed through the magazine, unable to read a word on the hazy pages and barely able to see the pictures. It didn't matter. His thoughts were on Knickers and his unusual request. What would he and Pat do with their estate in a similar situation?

"Pat, if you had a bunch of money to donate to a charity, which one would you choose?"

Pat dropped *House Beautiful* and wondered what triggered such an unusual question. "What are you reading about?" she asked.

"I'm not reading anything. I just want to know what charity you think is most important."

"I guess they are all important in their own way. I'm probably partial to charities for children, maybe ones that help prevent birth defects or assist the babies that are born with them."

Ray nodded. "Who could argue with that?"

"What's to argue about?" she asked. "People support all kinds of causes for all kinds of reasons. Some believe education is most important. For others it's environmental protection. I heard from Mary Wettman that one of our neighbors gave her entire estate to the *Humane Society* because she loved her pets so much. But I'm dying to know why you brought this up."

Ray knew she would ask. Always curious. "I'm just thinking that I ought to be a more charitable person. I should be doing more for other people."

Pat stared at her husband for a moment, perplexed. She had taken him to the emergency room for x-rays and stitches and the doctor said Ray had a mild concussion. Could that explain unusual behavior?

She leaned close and kissed his cheek. "You are the most charitable person I've ever known. It's one of the reasons I love you so much. For over forty-five years we ran our business and you never said no to any group that came looking for a donation. You sponsored teams in every youth sport. I know. I kept the books. I'd say we donated an average of over five thousand a year to different things.

"And goodness sakes, what about the coaching? You coached a Little League team for almost thirty years! And you were the only coach in the league that wasn't there because your own child was on the team. You've paid your dues. You deserve to spend your retirement years enjoying life."

With Knickers prepared to give up his entire life savings in the name of charity, Ray remained unconvinced. He turned toward Pat, returned a kiss to her cheek, and said, "You know what? I think I'm going to cut back on golf to just a couple days a week."

Pat stiffened. "Excuse me?" On the two days Ray didn't play, he paced around the house like a newly caged tiger. All the other days, he golfed all morning, came home with beer breath, and took a long nap after lunch. His schedule for those days was comfortably set, just the way she liked it.

"I'm thinking about doing some community service stuff," he said in a sober tone. "I know where there's a homeless shelter not far from our place. Maybe I can get up early and go cook breakfast there or something."

Pat's laugh came out like a snort. "Don't you think the homeless have it rough enough already?"

Fair point, he thought. He wasn't known for his artistry in the kitchen.

However, he was an expert in the world of cleaning and building maintenance. He had built a life around it. After graduating from high school, he worked for a janitorial service at night as a means of saving money for college. He had vacuumed, scrubbed, mopped, buffed, and polished his way through half of that summer before his employer suddenly left town, leaving his employees and clients in a lurch. One of the major clients, a bank, asked Ray if he would be interested in assuming the janitorial contract himself. He applied for a business license the next day. In filling out the paperwork, he had to think of a name for his undertaking. He was already dating Pat back then and her parents owned a plant and flower business called the Greenery. She came up with the Cleanery.

Most of his former employer's other clients contracted with him soon after. He hired all his high school friends that weren't commercial fishing or doing something else that paid better. Before long, Ray wasn't even doing much cleaning himself. He drove around town, visited with customers, and acquired additional contracts. In the meantime, Pat arranged work schedules, did the banking and payroll, and ordered supplies. When September arrived, bringing the first day of college classes, Ray and Pat were not on campus. They were making better money than most of the people employed in the buildings they serviced! The Cleanery grew and flourished. By the time Ray and Pat would have been graduating from college, they were married, had their own home, and had three white panel trucks parked in the driveway, all with the business name scripted in black and gold letters. That was four children, thirteen grandchildren, and four great-grandchildren ago.

"Maybe I can volunteer to clean the shelter every day," Ray said, nodding his head, prodding her to agree.

She shook him off again. "I think they let the people who sleep and eat there do most of those kinds of things. It helps them feel like they are giving something back.

"Let's just think of you right now. I've been trying to get you to have your eyes examined forever it seems like. You can't read road signs until you are right on top of them! And aren't you tired of having other cars honk at you to move when the stoplight changes? How long have you been wearing those same glasses?"

Ray shrugged.

"I'll bet you've been wearing them for twenty years or more. Think back to when you lost that other pair. We got two pairs and you lost one of them a week later. I remember that clearly. And the second pair has made it through all these years."

Ray warmed to the memory of losing the first pair. He was landing a huge king salmon on the Kenai River. His son tried to capture the fish with a long-handled net and accidentally poked him in the face with the end of the handle. In hindsight, he was struck on the bridge of his nose, just like today! The glasses dropped into the river and were swept away in the current. That was twenty-three years ago.

"Maybe your golf game will get back to normal if you can see better," Pat offered. *And maybe you'll stop complaining about it*, she thought. Ray never complained about anything his entire life, until recently. Higher golf scores were weighing him down.

"And if you want to think of others," she added. "How about the rest of the foursome? How would the other guys ever get by without you?" She had just been reminded of the strength of their bond when Mulligan, Harvey and Knickers stormed the emergency room shortly after Ray arrived there. They wouldn't leave until the doctor met with them personally and conveyed a favorable diagnosis.

Dr. Sturrock's receptionist called Ray's name and he rose from his chair. Patting his wife's shoulder, he said, "I can do more with my life than spend the rest of it chasing golf balls."

A jovial Stanley Sturrock greeted him in the examination room. "I heard you had a little accident on the golf course," he said, grinning at his new patient. "It can be a dangerous game!" He laughed loudly at his own humor.

Hmm, Ray thought to himself. *This Dr. Sturrock must be a comediologist or something. Maybe an opticometrician.* He decided he liked him.

"Take a look at that eye chart across the room," the doctor said. "Let's start by having you read it to me with your left eye. Cover the right with your hand."

Ray squinted at the letters. "Without my glasses I can't see much, just the three letters on top and, I guess, the four letters after that. Can I use my glasses?"

"Hey, that would be cheating," the doctor said sternly. "You don't kick your ball out from behind a tree, do you?"

Ray wasn't sure what to say and just stood there until Dr. Sturrock started laughing again.

"I'm just messing with you. Of course you can wear your glasses. That'll tell us where you've been so we'll know how much better we can get!"

Ray fished his broken glasses from his shirt pocket. Pat and the hospital receptionist had attempted a repair job while the doctor was sewing up the divot on his forehead. The frames had snapped in the center and were both super glued and taped. The left lens was cracked diagonally. He lifted them gingerly to his eyes. The next two lines of letters on the chart appeared with enough clarity to identify. He could have tossed guesses at the next line, but saw little point.

"All garbledygook," Ray said, shaking his head.

"I should be able to help you quite a bit," the doctor responded. "Even with your glasses, your vision isn't close to normal. When is the last time you had an exam?"

"It's been a while," Ray admitted. "It never occurred to me that I needed one."

"And you've been driving your car all this time?"

"Sure."

"That's plain scary."

Opticomediologist, Ray thought once again.

The doctor lifted the glasses from his patient's nose and looked at them. "Everyone needs an exam every year or two. Your eyes are forever changing. It's especially important as you get older. Now, let's get busy! Take a seat."

As Ray looked at images through the doctor's diagnostic equipment, first with the left eye and then with the right, he was amazed at how easily a gray blob turned into the razor sharp image of a letter. He suddenly felt better about returning to the golf course.

There was a tap on the door and Pat looked into the room. "I just wanted to see how everything is going, doctor."

"Just fine," he answered. "I'm going to dilate his pupils and make sure everything is okay structurally, but I think he'll be fine."

"We'll want two pairs of hard contacts and two pairs of glasses," Pat said. "I want lots of spares."

Dr. Sturrock was used to having seniors ask for the outdated hard contacts. They were easier for them to put on and remove. Many had worn them for a long time and just didn't want to change.

"How soon can I pick them up?" Ray asked.

Dr. Sturrock heard that often as well. Everybody wanted everything right now. It was the way of the world. "We should get the lenses for your glasses back here in a week. You can pick out frames in our showroom before you go. The contacts will come straight to your house by priority mail. No more than a week. They come from a company just thirty miles from here. Eagle Optics."

In the car outside the optometrist's office, Ray sat uncomfortably in the passenger seat. Normally, he did the driving. He cupped his right hand above his crooked glasses, shielding his pupils from the light.

"We need to stop at a florist and get Mrs. Beckerman some flowers," he said. "Seriously, I thought I was going to give her a heart attack with all my falling and bleeding and everything."

"Yes," Pat said, chuckling. "You can be very difficult. Actually, I already ordered her yellow roses while you were getting stitches. It's all you talked about when you got home from the golf course, so I took care of it. She probably has them by now."

"You sent a card with the flowers, right?"

"Of course there was a card. It said: 'Dear Gladys, I am sorry to have given you such a scare. I have been meaning to get contact lenses for some time now, so you have done me a favor. Please don't worry about me, I am just fine. Best wishes, Ray Plumlee.'"

"Perfect," he said, leaning back on the headrest and closing his eyes.

A moment later, he sat upright. "Since when did you start going to the gas station to fill the car?" Getting gas had always been his job and he'd been meaning to ask her about it for several days.

Pat shook her head. "You know I don't get gas. You always keep the tank full."

She looked at the gas gauge. "And it's full now."

"Well, there's something wrong with the gauge," Ray said. "I haven't put a drop of gas in this car and we've had it for two weeks. Didn't the Tanner widow say everything worked fine?"

"As far as I know," Pat said. "I didn't pay much attention."

The attendant at the front gate of Leisureville left his security station and walked toward the Plumlee's car as they drove up to the barrier at the entrance. Pat lowered the driver's side window.

The man said, "I just wanted to thank you for the birthday card and gift certificate. The wife and I used it at the steakhouse last night."

Ray leaned toward the window, and squeezed Pat's knee. The lady remembered everything. "Glad to hear it, Charlie. Happy Birthday!"

Charlie studied Ray's face for a moment. "Sorry to hear about your accident today. Are you going to be all right?" News traveled quickly.

"I'll be fine, just not as pretty for a while."

Charlie laughed and returned to his office to open the gate. Moments later the Plumlees were in their driveway.

As soon as Pat was out of the car, Ray slipped into the driver seat. "I'm going to go get gas," he said. "We have to be running on fumes. I'll get the gas gauge checked out too." He was gone before Pat could even object to his driving with sensitive eyes and a concussion. His only thoughts were how much a repair might cost and how long it might keep the car out of commission.

Fortunately, the closest gas station was only a half mile away. While driving he considered how embarrassing it would have been for his wife to run out of gas. How could he have a car for two weeks and never think about refueling? Sure, the gauge said the tank was full, but two weeks? They routinely used three quarters of a tank every two weeks in their last car. The Lincoln figured to burn nearly as much fuel. Was he getting so old he would have to start carrying a list of basic chores? Would he forget to check the list?

After pulling up to a vacant pump, Ray struggled to find the switch to open the tank cover. He looked at the dashboard to the left of the steering wheel, where the button was located in his old car. Nothing. He found it on the floor to his left.

He swiped his credit card at the pump, lifted the fuel nozzle, placed it in the intake, and leaned on the car for the long wait. However, before the meter read even two gallons, the pump kicked off. Knowing the tank had to be close to empty, he squeezed the handle and held it. Gas flew out of the intake like a geyser and soaked his pants.

The manager watched Ray from inside a station window. He shook his head at the old guy with the bandaged forehead looking for something in the puddle around his feet. Reluctantly, he got out of his chair and walked outside.

"What seems to be the problem?" he asked.

"I dropped my glasses," Ray said, looking around.

That's not all you dropped, the manager thought. *You dropped about a quart of gas on your clothes and another on my lot. I'm glad my shift is over in fifteen minutes. It's been a long day.*

The manager picked up part of Ray's glasses. "Here's half of them."

Ray held the half with the cracked left lens up to his left eye and read the name on the manager's shirt. "Hello, Bob. I'm Ray. Sorry to have made a mess here, but something is wrong with my car."

Bob located the other half of the glasses and handed it to him. Ray held both halves in place with his hands at each temple.

"You see, we've been driving this car for a couple weeks, probably a hundred miles or more, and the gas gauge is broken. It says full all the time."

Bob looked at the gas meter and back to Ray. "They'll generally read full when you're only down a couple gallons," he said, shaking his head. "That means your gauge is working just fine." *Certainly a lot better than your brain is working*, he thought. Man, he was ready to go home and enjoy a cold beer.

"Have you noticed me here fueling this car before?" Ray asked. "Like sometime in the last week?" Despite asking the question, he was pretty sure he had not gassed up. He couldn't even find the switch at first. At the same time, he *must* have gotten gas.

Bob looked at his watch. Thirteen more minutes. "I don't really notice the customers. I only pay attention when they spill gas because I have to clean it up. I don't remember seeing you." *Most old people looked alike to him*, he thought, *but Ray seemed wackier than most. Probably Alzheimer's.*

Ray didn't know what else to do. He'd have to go home and try to figure things out. He lowered his glasses, held them out toward Bob, and asked if he could borrow some tape.

Upon returning to his garage, Ray removed his shirt, slacks and underwear, put them in a plastic bag, and tossed it in the trash can. He didn't want to stink up the house or have to explain their condition to Pat.

At least he didn't stink up the house. Pat was waiting for him when he entered the kitchen wearing nothing but a pair of navy blue socks. She just stared.

"I took off my clothes in the garage," he said. "I had an accident."

Her eyes widened as her jaw dropped. "Oh no! In the new car?"

He shook his head and wondered how the day could get any worse. She was actually thinking he peed his pants. "I spilled gas on them at the service station!" He placed a receipt from the station in a wicker basket on a small table near the door.

"Accidents happen," Pat said with obvious relief. "Is the gas gauge fixed?"

"Well," Ray said, walking toward the bedroom to gather some fresh clothes, "there doesn't seem to be anything wrong with it. The car took less than two gallons."

Pat followed him as he spoke. "That can't be. I checked my records while you were gone. There were no receipts for gas for the last two weeks."

After a lifetime of managing the finances of The Cleanery, Pat was well organized. Every receipt for every expenditure went in the basket into which Ray had just dropped his credit card receipt. The action was automatic. Pat emptied the basket every Sunday and updated their finances on *Quickbooks*.

"How much did you drive since we got the car?" Ray said. "It seems like you've been out fairly often."

"Just shopping," she answered. "Same old thing."

Ray understood the complex meaning of *same old thing*. Groceries were the least of it. There were gifts and cards for every occasion for a cast of recipients that was continually growing. There were all their children and their spouses, thirteen grandchildren and seven more spouses attached to them, parents of spouses, and the great-grandchildren. There were Pat's two sisters and their related family trees, which kept growing like her own. There were lifelong friends in Alaska that had to be remembered right along with new friends in Arizona, like Charlie at the gate. Every event was recorded on a calendar in her computer and she tried to stay a month ahead of things.

Pat tried to retrace her steps. "It just seemed like an average couple of weeks, except I really like the way the Lincoln drives. I also like that it's lower and I don't have to climb so high to get into the driver's seat. The Explorer was getting too tall for me."

Ray had looked at the odometer on his way home from the gas station. Unfortunately, he couldn't recall exactly what the reading was when he bought the car. He only knew that it was eleven thousand and something. "I think I'll go next door and see Mrs. Tanner. Maybe the Lincoln just gets incredible mileage, especially compared to the Explorer."

"She's out of town," Pat said. "Visiting family in Montana."

Not knowing what else to do, Ray went to the garage and wrote down the present mileage on the odometer. He folded the paper and put it behind the visor.

At 6:30 p.m., Ray and Pat were watching the end of the local news over dessert when there was a tap on the front door. Mulligan had dropped by with a twelve pack of Sam Adams.

"Knickers called a meeting for tonight," he announced. "We knew you wouldn't be doing anything." Ray eyed the beer and the sweat on it shouted *ice cold*.

"Hi, Irvin," Pat said from behind Ray, then nudged her husband. "He can't even think about drinking while he's taking medication, but we're glad to see you."

Ray rolled his eyes and shrugged as Knickers parked in the driveway beside Mulligan's car and Harvey arrived by foot. The four men settled in the den and Pat disappeared into her office to give the guys their space.

"So," Knickers said, cracking a beer, "why aren't you wearin' new glasses? You went to the optician, right?" He raised his bottle in a toast, and the other two guests followed suit. They all took a swallow, smacked their lips in exaggerated fashion, and winked at Ray.

He shook his head at their cold humor. "I won't get them for a week. I ordered contact lenses too."

"Hmmm," Knickers followed. "Are you going to be able to play wearing those?" He pointed at Ray's crooked, taped glasses. "They look a little shaky."

Ray was reluctant to even turn his head quickly out of fear that the glasses would come apart. "No golf for me for the next week, not until I get my new ones. I'm going to be able to see a lot better then. You guys better watch out."

"No golf for a week?" Mulligan said. "Why not just put those lenses in new frames? You could get by."

Pat's voice came from the other room. "Forget it, you guys. He has a concussion. No golf for at least a week." Advancing years had not diminished her sharp sense of hearing.

Knickers whispered, "You've got to take one for the team, Ray. We're not talkin' about tackle football here."

Pat entered the room to talk this time. "You think I can't hear you, Knickers Collins? It's time that you grow up and have a little compassion!" She gave him a long stare, then looked at Harvey, who understood he was expected to support her.

"I googled concussions this afternoon," he said. "Ray needs to wait until the doctor clears him to play. You have to be cautious."

Pat nodded her satisfaction. "There you have it, words from an educated man." She spun and left the room.

Harvey looked apologetically at Knickers and cleared his throat. "I've done some thinking. We could use Ray's average score for the last year, which is seventy-five. I'll fill in the scorecard with all pars except for bogeys on two, nine, and twelve, which are statistically his worst holes. That way we can still compete."

Knickers scratched his chin. "But Ray still comes with us right? He drives you around in Birdie Chaser. We have business to discuss on the course." It was agreed.

Knickers got up, walked over to the pocket door that could close the den off from the rest of the house and slid it shut. After sitting down, he announced that the meeting would now begin.

"Like I told you earlier," he started, "we're gonna figure out what to do with my money. I plan on givin' most of it away soon, so I can enjoy feelin' good about it for the rest of my life . . . and you fellas can too."

Mulligan was confident that they weren't talking about much cash. Knickers just didn't behave like he had a thick wallet. The only real exception was the money he blew on the sign at Harvey's house. "Don't you think you should hold on to your money 'til both you and Bess are gone?

You never know what's going to come up." He had certainly learned that lesson himself.

"I'm not as stupid as I look," Knickers said, before draining the rest of his beer. "I'm going to hold back a couple million, just in case."

Ray stared in disbelief, then grabbed a bottle from the case on the floor. *Hold back a couple million?*

"You need to stop your bullshitting, Knickers," Mulligan said, shaking his head. "We know you too well. You're yanking our chains."

Knickers just glared back.

Mulligan started to sputter. "Stop it! You drive a car that's older than me!"

Knickers laughed at the predictable response. "If you change the oil every year, a Chevy will run forever. Mine has a hundred forty thousand miles on it. You wouldn't know. You sold Fords."

Harvey pulled a piece of paper from his pocket. "Knickers knew we wouldn't believe him, so he had me make a copy of his stock account off my computer when he came by."

He handed the paper to Mulligan, whose eyes widened then narrowed. "Twenty-four million dollars and change? I have to hand it to you, Harvey and Knickers, this looks real. How did you fake this?" He passed the paper to Ray.

Knickers sighed. "Here you go, my simple story. Back in 1989 I was in Louisville, coachin' the pen for the triple A team. I got to know this guy that sat along the bullpen railin' almost every game. He wasn't just your average fan. He could watch a pitcher throw for a few seconds and tell you exactly what he was doin' wrong. He was a helluva lot smarter than me. Anyway, he was on the board of a company called Dell Computer. He said I should buy the stock, they were the coming thing.

"My father had just passed away and left me sixty grand. I never owned a share of stock, but I really respected this fan big time. I bought forty-eight thousand worth of Dell stock and got my car with the rest.

"After that season, I never saw the guy for like ten years. One day he pops up again in Memphis, where the team had moved. I didn't even know what to say to him. My stock had gone crazy, and I still had every bit of it. I mean, what were Bess and I gonna do with millions of dollars? We lived the way we lived and we liked it. Anyway, he's really impressed that I held the shares all that time but says he moved to the board of a company called Apple. He said to sell my stock and buy Apple's, so I did. We had to pay so much in taxes that I wouldn't even write the check. I made Bess do it. I think the taxes alone were more money than I made my entire life! As you can see on that paper, though, everything seems to have worked out even though it used to be worth a lot more."

Mulligan decided the story was strangely believable. Why would Knickers joke about something like this? He'd know full well that he'd be expected to pay for all the beer after the disclosure.

"Just think for a second," Mulligan said. "What if you had invested the whole sixty thousand instead of buying that crappy car!" All the men laughed and looked at Knickers a little differently than before.

At five the next morning, a shadowy figure approached the side door of the Plumlee garage. He carried a Jerry Jug of gasoline, a flashlight, and a roll of paper towels.

Like Mulligan, Knickers had been entrusted with a key to Ray's home long ago. Unlike Mulligan, he finally found a good use for it.

Ray had raved about his car purchase during an entire round of golf a couple weeks back. He paid low *Blue Book* for a Lincoln that was four years old but had less than twelve thousand miles on it. It even came with a full tank of gas!

During almost half a century in baseball clubhouses, Knickers had earned a reputation as a dedicated prankster. A recap of his stunts could fill a book. Still, he was confident that this could be one of his career highlights.

Inside the garage, he took the set of keys from the hook on the wall beside the door into the house, where he knew they were stowed. He gained access to the fuel tank with the pull of a lever. He barely started to pour and the tank was full.

"Crap!" Knickers said under his breath. They didn't drive much yesterday. He quickly replaced the cap and went to work with the paper towels, drying the side of the car and absorbing the drops that hit the floor.

He had poured over twenty gallons of fuel into the Lincoln over twelve consecutive nights and still not a word from Ray. What could his friend be thinking? What did he think about a car that didn't burn gas? What would anyone think?

However, Ray should have started talking about his car by now. What if Ray somehow knew what he was up to? What if the joke turned out to be on him? That would be completely unacceptable.

Knickers decided that a satisfying conclusion to this time-consuming gag had to be on the immediate horizon. He wasn't sure exactly what the outcome would be, but the thought of toying with Ray's mind, and Pat's too, excited him to no end.

He opened the side door to the garage and held it open for a full five minutes, allowing the gas vapor to escape. Satisfied, he closed the door, picked up the heavy gas jug, and waddled off down the street.

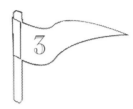

A week later, Ray sat at the kitchen window, staring at the mailbox in front of his home. Mike, the postman, generally pulled up to the box in his white van around 2:00 p.m. It was now 1:52. Ray had been on vigil for twenty minutes. He learned a lot about himself since his injury, not the least of which was how much he valued being part of the Foursome. He was ready to start hitting the ball again.

Although the game now seemed secondary to the discussion of where to donate Knickers's money, Ray had been drinking lots of the good stuff at the Nineteenth Hole the past week. Harvey was shrewd in negotiating use of a full year's average of his scores because the mean over the last month alone was a couple strokes higher. While their opponents pulled out their wallets each day without complaint, they never failed to mention that they looked forward to having the *real* Ray back.

As a spectator, he enjoyed watching the others more closely than usual. He even made a few suggestions for improving their games, mostly based on stuff he watched on the Golf Channel. He noted that Harvey, with his feet close together in his stance, tended to stab down at the ball too much. While that approach resulted in some towering shots, accuracy suffered. By spreading his feet a few more inches, he could sweep the ball with a more consistent blade angle. As for Knickers, the only detectable flaw was in his putting stroke. Despite being a student of the game, he ignored the cardinal rule of following through with his putter after contact. He jabbed at the ball as if he were bunting a baseball. Mulligan's main problem was psychological;

he rarely used enough club. If Knickers could hit his seven iron 160 yards, Mulligan figured he should too, despite the fact that he was a much slighter man. As a result, he swung too hard and lost control too often. When Mulligan ignored his advice, Knickers intervened, explaining that it was the number on the scorecard that mattered, not the one on the bottom of the club.

The most interesting aspect of the week, however, was the new direction of their conversation. Instead of behaving as joking, wisecracking caricatures of themselves, as they had for years, they actually turned more reflective. No one took Knickers' unique request for help lightly, especially not with so much money on the table.

Not surprisingly, Harvey had done his homework. He informed the others that over $300 billion had been donated to charities by Americans in the last year alone. Churches were the top beneficiary of that generosity with almost a third of the total. Nearly $50 billion was donated in the name of education, with colleges leading the way. In total, there were over a million registered and active charitable entities serving every imaginable cause. Fortunately, there were also rating services available that detailed how efficiently those entities operated.

Ray assumed Mulligan would be a dominant force in the discussion because he was a natural leader. He also guessed his friend would make a compelling case for cancer research. Although Mulligan never discussed the subject himself, most everyone in Leisureville knew his wife Mary was a cancer survivor. A decade earlier, her name was nearly chiseled on a gravestone before she was miraculously saved by a new, experimental treatment. However, Mulligan instead championed the Veterans Administration, citing the incredible care his brother received over a decade of battling a variety of health problems before ultimately succumbing to pancreatic cancer at the age of fifty-nine. Until now, the others were unaware Mulligan even had a brother!

That disclosure led to others. Harvey, while an advocate for education for the most part, believed Hospice deserved special consideration. Lucy's mother and father received loving attention and support through that organization in their final months, while she and Harvey were busy with their jobs most of the time. This led the others to talk about their own parents, about both their lives and their passing.

Ray himself shared thoughts about the importance of environmental protection, a regular topic of discussion in Alaska over the years. He shared stories about mining projects that destroyed salmon spawning grounds and the infamous oil spill near Valdez back in 1989. Subsequent questions from the others about Alaska spurred hours of conversation, during which he told much of his life story for the first time.

Through all the discussions, Knickers mostly smiled and nodded, causing Ray to think that maybe the old baseball man *was* coaching them to be better people, just the way he suggested he would.

Inspired by it all, Ray had risen early on Sunday morning and drove to Friends, the homeless shelter not far from Leisureville's southern gated entrance. He didn't have the deep pockets that Knickers did . . . hell, his were empty in comparison . . . but he wanted to do something to help people. Upon entering, he was greeted by a smiling young man who appeared to be the host. Ray asked if he could talk to whoever was in charge and the man responded by directing him to the breakfast line.

"You don't have to ask for help here," the man said, patting Ray on the back. "Have a healthy meal, and we'll be over to get a case file started."

"You don't understand," Ray returned. "I want to volunteer to help. I can clean and even cook. I can do whatever you need."

"That's a great attitude," the host responded. "I'll bet we can find you a paying job somewhere and get you back on your feet in no time."

And then it was clear. The host assumed he was homeless or destitute! It wasn't that much of a reach, he realized. He had a bandage above his nose and poorly mended glasses drooping across his eyes. Although his clothing was fashionable . . . yellow slacks, a navy blue and green-striped polo shirt, and a green ball cap with the Leisureville insignia . . . he looked no different than the twenty or so people eating breakfast at the tables. Apparently, the senior population of the area was dying off rapidly enough to keep the shelter well supplied with donated clothing. The group looked like customers at the Nineteenth Hole.

Impressed with the immaculate and friendly facility but dispirited that he didn't seem to be needed, Ray dropped fifty dollars in the donation box before heading back home. He would have to find a different way to help mankind.

Tired of looking up the street for the mail truck, Ray walked to the living room and picked up a Ping putter that leaned in its customary spot in a corner. The club was a twin to the one he called *Pinger*, which rested in his golf bag. There were three balls on the floor beside it, and he pushed them to the center of the room. His target, a corner leg of the dining room table, was nineteen feet away and four inches wide, almost the size of a regulation cup. He knew, from attempting the putt a good thousand times previously, that the ball would break two inches to the left if struck with the right touch. He missed first to the right, then the left, and again to the right. It didn't seem long ago that he could hit the leg fairly often. Discouraged, he put the club back in the corner.

His next glance out the window was rewarded; the mail had arrived. He went to the refrigerator, pulled out a can of the green tea Mike liked, and went out to meet him. In addition to the normal collection of envelopes and advertising, Mike held a small white cardboard box. The men quickly exchanged gifts.

Mike popped the can and took a swallow. "You're the best, Ray. Thanks!"

"No, you're the best," Ray returned, looking at the Eagle Optics label on the box. "I've been waiting for these babies."

"Glad they arrived then," Mike said, sliding back into his truck. "Give my best to Pat."

"As soon as she gets home."

At the kitchen counter, Ray grabbed a steak knife and cut the seal around the box. Two white plastic lens containers and a small bottle of ophthalmic solution were nestled inside.

Grabbing one of the cases, he rushed to the bathroom to install his new eyes. After opening the compartment labeled *L*, he put the lens on the tip of his left index finger and removed his glasses. Tilting his head back slightly and holding his eye ajar with his right thumb and index finger, just the way Pat showed him, he dropped the lens into place and blinked rapidly. Bull's eye!

He studied himself in the mirror through the single eye. Where he had removed a bandage earlier, the bruise looked more ominous than it had a moment before. *So much for clearer vision*, he thought. In spite of the damage and stitches, though, he loved the sight of his more vivid image. He looked all around the bathroom and nodded his head excitedly. The words h*igh definition* came to mind. If only he knew this possibility existed years ago!

"Watch out Mulligan and Knickers," he announced. "There's a new man on the tee."

Now the right lens. He placed it on his eye, blinked, and was stunned by an explosion of light as if someone had taken his photo with a flash. He closed the eye and reopened it cautiously. The brightness returned, but he tried to stare through it. He seemed to be on the other side of a camera now, looking through the viewfinder, a circular viewfinder. Had he put the lens on upside down? Was that even possible? Something was very wrong.

He opened his other eye to see through both. All of his sight instantly disintegrated into a mass of indistinct images and pain shot through his forehead. He squeezed his right eye shut and exhaled when normal sight immediately returned. He stumbled to the toilet and sat down to collect himself.

The Sweet Swing

After removing the problematic right lens, he returned it to the case and went to the kitchen to retrieve the second set of lenses. The other right lens proved to be perfectly fine, as did the left. Obviously, the one bad lens was a mistake, a lemon. He would send it back to Eagle Optics for replacement, or at least Pat would take care of the chore after he told her about it.

Feeling energized, Ray hurried to the garage and backed Birdie Chaser into the driveway. After removing Harvey's and his clubs from the back, he unwound the garden hose and started scrubbing down the cart. She would look her best for his return to the course in the morning.

While working, he constantly looked up at the new grandeur of the neighborhood. The bushes and trees were no longer just shapes but clusters of individual leaves. The flowers in the garden were brilliant, inviting his nose to sniff them.

Knickers's recent reference to the Land of Oz whirled into his mind. Nope, he wasn't in Kansas anymore. This world was pure technicolor. Had it even looked so glorious when he was a boy? He couldn't imagine it. Thank you, Gladys Beckerman!

Out of nowhere, a huge head popped into his imagination. He was still exploring Oz, apparently, because it was the giant face of the mighty wizard that appeared before him, the same one that frightened the quartet of Dorothy and her friends when they first visited the Emerald City. The image metamorphosed into an oversized version of his own face, one that he now realized was looking back at him through the viewfinder in that odd right lens. The mere presence of the peephole had shocked him so much that he barely realized what he saw within it. He dropped the hose and rushed back into the house.

In the bathroom, he returned the odd lens to his right eye and studied his image, which became increasingly clear as the eye adjusted to the light. The view triggered a surprising flashback. He was young again, a boy of maybe ten. He was visiting an amusement park in California while on vacation with his family, enjoying an attraction called the Funhouse. A hallway had a series of full-length mirrors that distorted his image in a variety of weird ways. One mirror made his legs appear to go all the way to his chin. Another made him look like he weighed three hundred pounds. Still another, like the one he was looking into right now, made his head look far too large for his body. In overall effect, he was looking at himself through a magnifying glass. A circle of clarity was surrounded by light gray fog at its perimeter that darkened as it extended outward. Vision was limited to what was directly in front of him.

His nose was grotesque. Each gaping pore seemed big enough to hold a flagstick. The depressions on the sides of his upper nose, the result of forty years of wearing glasses, looked like bunkers. Hideous gray and black hairs jutted from all over his cheeks and chin like willows on Alaska's winter tundra. He reached out to touch the mirror, perhaps to confirm the reality of it all. However, his fingers touched nothing but air. He was lost in space.

Shutting his right eye, he opened the other. There was his hand, just inches in front of his right cheek, nearly two feet from touching the mirror that appeared to be so close. It was all an illusion.

Was it some kind of trick gadget? Could Knickers be playing one of his elaborate practical jokes on him? Was he sitting somewhere laughing, wondering what his friend's reaction would be? Knickers' pranks had surprised him more than once over the years.

No. It couldn't be. He knew Knickers well enough by now that he could see through his darned tricks. There was simply no way he could pull off something this difficult.

He took a couple steps back and looked around through the new toy on his eye. The bathroom mirror looked ten feet tall! The washcloth folded beside the sink looked like a bath towel. The sink itself was big as a bathtub.

Concerned with the length of his whiskers, he decided to shave again. He gathered a can of shaving cream and his razor from the medicine cabinet, and chuckled at the sight of them. They looked like more like a barrel and a rake through the lens! The mundane chore was suddenly a challenge because he had to adjust his movement to compensate for the lie his eye was telling him; nothing was anywhere near as close as it seemed. It was like learning to use his hands all over again. After a shave that did little good, he decided he would have to get a new razor.

He decided to tour the rest of the house, his Funhouse, with the odd lens. The bedroom, which appeared tidy a few minutes before, was now a mess. The royal blue carpet looked as if Mulligan had dropped cigar ashes all over it. Actually, it was covered with lint, hair, and other clinging debris that were invisible through his left eye. He hauled out the vacuum and went over the entire surface twice but couldn't get it cleaner. Now he would have to buy a more powerful vacuum!

In the living room, his right eye was drawn to Pat's substantial library, which was shelved on the far wall, about twenty feet away. He could read every title and the name of every author. He felt as if he could reach out and grab one from where he stood.

He glanced toward the dining room. The leg of the oak table at which he putted earlier was now a telephone pole! How could anyone miss that?

He looked over at his jumbo putter and three baseball-sized Titleists. Grabbing the club, he pushed the balls into a line and stroked one toward the giant target. It rolled barely halfway to the table.

"Remember," he whispered to himself, "you have to compensate." His second putt was a foot short. The third took a chip from the oak.

He proceeded to putt all over the house for the next several minutes. Every chair, coffee table, and end table leg became a flagstick; and he was missing none of them. Pure magic. A supersized putter was simple to align. The larger ball was easier to steer. The pin was the proverbial side of a barn.

But there was more. The living room carpet was slightly worn, particularly in regular traffic lanes. As a result, most of his putts veered somewhat between his putter and the targets. Nonetheless, his aim was always true. The question that suddenly flooded his light head was why. He wasn't consciously making allowances for the breaks in the rug surface, was he? He didn't seem to be thinking at all. His putter seemed to be on autopilot. *Autoputtit*, he thought and laughed out loud.

Dashing to the telephone, he tried to decide which of the guys to call first. He picked it up, but set it back down before pushing a button. *Why would he tell them about it?* That would only ruin his fun. What would they say when he started making putts for a change? He could hardly wait to see their reactions.

Moments later he was in Birdie Chaser, heading for the practice putting green near the clubhouse and pushing the speed limit. His newfound jewel was secure beneath his right eyelid so he could steer with his ordinary left eye.

During his first year or two at Leisureville, he spent an hour on the practice green almost every day, trying to find a way to knock a few strokes from his scorecard. All the rest of the clubs in his bag seemed to know how to perform; his darn putter *Pinger* was the problem.

Although Harvey suggested that he experiment with a different model or style of putter, he stayed loyal to his old mallet. A divorce from Pinger seemed outrageous after all their close years together, not to mention those two club championships.

However, the mechanics of putting were another story altogether. He tried every kind of grip he could imagine. He spread his hands, overlapped them fully and partially, and even tried his left hand below the right. He interlocked four fingers, just a couple, and none at all. The same went for his stance. He stood with his feet close together and far apart, toes pointed in and pointed out, knees flexed and straight, bending over and standing tall. He even copied the exact form of his favorite pro only to find that the pro himself changed styles the very next week!

Over the last year, he hadn't been to the practice green even once. Now he felt as if he was heading there for the very first time. As he drove, he smiled and waved at the drivers of cars and carts and the dog walkers too.

A few of the pet owners frowned in return, perhaps at his excessive speed or possibly because he didn't stop to deliver a treat to their pup, as he normally did. Most of the folks grinned back at him and seemed to wink, as if they already knew his secret.

But how could they know? Was this all just a dream? Of course not, he realized. They winked at him because it looked like he was winking at them! One of his eyes was pinched shut.

He stopped behind the tee at the par three ninth and admired the view through the new contact lens on his left eye. There had been so many spectacular sights in Alaska . . . majestic Mt. Denali, calving glaciers, streams teeming with salmon, and herds of caribou that dotted the tundra as far as you could see. Still, nothing touched his heart like the sight of a golf course.

Remembering that his right eye would give him an altogether different perspective, he opened it. The sun blinded him and the eye snapped shut, sending his mind reeling. *So* he wondered, *that's it? I'm going to be a great putter in my living room and can't take it outside where it matters?*

A familiar short-legged fuzzball of a dog at the end of a long leash appeared beside his cart and started barking. Ray looked apologetically to the owner, a cotton-topped lady who apparently had both her hair and the dog's styled by the same beautician.

He held up his hands, and shrugged. "I'm so sorry, I don't have any Milk Bones today. I left the house in a hurry."

The lady wore sunglasses and a sympathetic smile. "That's what happens when you spoil her all the time, Mr. Plumlee. Little Wendy is always on the lookout for you!"

"Sunglasses!" Ray yelled out. "I need sunglasses, that's all."

"My sunglasses?" she asked. "You want my sunglasses?"

He had to laugh. "No, no, no. I need sunglasses . . . like . . . yours. They look so great on you."

She nodded her agreement. "You aren't the first man to tell me that."

Ray wondered where he could get a pair of sunglasses. He never wore them in his life. The bill of a baseball cap had always provided sufficient shade.

"In fact," the woman continued, taking off her glasses, "a lot of men think I still look very young for my age, although I'm really not that old." She batted her eyelashes and beamed.

Ray nodded. "And you'll stay looking young if you keep up with your regular walking. Have a great day!"

He touched the accelerator, then the brake. Harvey kept sunglasses in his golf bag! And the bag was right behind him! Seconds later, he was wearing wraparound shades and they felt great. After all these years, glasses seemed as much a part of him as his nose or ears.

The scene changed dramatically when he opened his right eye this time. The woman's departing dog looked like a polar bear! The ninth green, which he knew to be a couple hundred yards distant, stood just a chip shot away. He instantly recognized the three golfers on it. Heck, he could see their mouths moving as they talked! Ray felt a tingling sensation on his eye, which reminded him of his mission. It was time to putt.

A lone person stood on the practice green when he arrived, the same man he saw on the driving range a week ago. The broad brimmed hat and long shorts were a dead giveaway. Ray pulled Pinger from his bag, along with five balls, and joined him.

Even through his left eye, the green looked newly inviting. Nine holes were scattered around it, each with a short flagstick. He dropped his balls about twenty feet from one of them, kneeled behind them to gauge the break, and turned to his right eye. The condition of the grass carpet changed even more dramatically than the rug in his home. Scattered clumps of grass stood taller than the rest and clods of dirt were everywhere. Granules of fertilizer reminded him of the rock salt he used to scatter on his sidewalk and steps in the winter. But most incredibly, the cup itself appeared to be as large as a bucket and only a few feet away. He stepped back from his Titleists and switched to his left eye. The distance to the hole jumped to seven yards again and the putting surface was smooth as a table top.

He stood over a ball, opened his stance to allow a better one-eyed view, and focused on the center of the flagpole. To his surprise, he noticed his hands were quivering. His knees started to tremble. The toes of both feet started bouncing around in his shoes. Was he nervous or afraid? Or just plain excited?

He stepped back from the ball and drew a couple deep breaths, releasing them slowly. He remembered the leg of the dining table. This was no different. Why was he making it different? Why was he suddenly worried about a soft grip, locked wrists, and coordinated shoulders? In the house he just looked and stroked without thinking.

He stepped back to the ball and gave it a whack. It tracked right at the pole before stopping a few inches short. He shook his head and groaned. While there were many ways to miss a putt, coming up short was the most inexcusable.

Moving to another ball, he realized that he blocked the cup with his first. He aimed at the final *T* in Titleist, at what appeared to be the center of the roadblock, and hit the second ball. It struck the target perfectly and knocked the first ball right into the bucket.

He proceeded to knock the next two putts into the hole as well. The final ball would have joined them had there been more room in the cup around the flag.

To confirm the reality of his accomplishment, he checked the scene with the left eye. There were his balls, seven long strides away, gathered around the flag, overflowing the cup.

How often did he make putts of that length on the course? In his heyday, a few years back, maybe once in five tries. Nowadays he rarely made any. Overwhelmed by a wave of emotion, he felt an explosive need to urinate. He dropped his club and ran toward the clubhouse restroom, already peeing down his left leg. He couldn't remember ever doing such a thing, but didn't care a lick.

After cleaning himself with paper towels, he returned to the green. The man in the straw hat was holding Pinger, examining the club closely.

When Ray drew near, he handed back the putter. "That's some putting stick you have there, Mr. Plumtree. I never saw anybody make so many long ones like that."

Ray figured Plumtree was close enough. "And what's your name?" he asked, offering a handshake.

"It's Harold Perkins. I saw you get clobbered on the driving range last week. Whew! That was a bad one."

Not as bad as you think, Ray thought and grinned. "It's good to meet you. Let's see if I can keep it up."

He turned and looked toward another hole, this one thirty feet off. His previous putts only foreshadowed his true capability. After removing the flag from the cup this time, he made four of the five putts while Harold whooped and hollered. Even at an amazing forty feet, he drained three more! There was slope to the green, and a fair amount of accompanying break, but it didn't matter. Somehow he simply saw the right path to the hole. All he had to do was keep Pinger moving in a straight line and hit the ball hard enough.

As he continued, the tingling sensation on his right eye became an irritating sting, and then an aggravating burn. Maybe eyedrops would help, but the little bottle was still in the kitchen. He closed his right eye and rubbed the lid, triggering even more pain. It was time to head home.

While driving, he tried to think through the growing discomfort on and behind his eye. How could he putt like that? How could anybody? While the holes seemed huge, they weren't disproportionate to the size of his golf balls, right? Why was it all so easy? It made no sense.

Or did it? Was it a matter of focus? When he looked at his target through the strange window, it was all he seemed to see. It reminded him of the 4X scope on his old Remington hunting rifle. As long as he remained still when he squeezed the trigger, there could be no miss. That was especially true if the caribou or moose was motionless . . . like the hole in the green.

On the other hand, how did that account for the way he could read the terrain? A bullet is fired in a straight line, with just occasional allowance for wind or distance. Putts on a golf course are rarely straight, not even at Leisureville. Somehow he was able to see the breaks better. He could glance at the tilt of the green, the slant of the grass and simply *know* what to do.

Forget about *how* he was able to do it. Why was he, of all people, doing it? What kind of contact lens was this? Why did *he* have it? If there was some kind of miracle lens on the market, wouldn't he have heard about it? Certainly Harvey would have read about it and told him. Wouldn't all golfers be wearing them?

He waved to three elderly women, all lined up and power walking, striding and pumping their arms in perfect unison. Amanda, Dorothy, and Linda . . . no, Lois. Very impressive. Maybe he would start exercising more vigorously when he reached octogenarian status.

A thought hit just after he passed them. He U-turned and caught up.

Matching their speed with the cart, he called out, "Hey, Amanda."

She glanced over at him from under the bill of a white ball cap, a ponytail of her natural gray hair bouncing behind it, but didn't miss a stride. "Hi, Alaska. I thought that was you, but the sunglasses kind of threw me. I haven't even had a chance to write and thank you and Pat for the anniversary card."

He could only wonder when the anniversary may have been; Pat was clutch. "Save a stamp, I'll let her know. How's your Sid doing?" She and her husband always called each other *my* Sid and *my* Amanda. Real lovebirds. Pat and he used to socialize with the couple when they first arrived in Leisureville.

"He's home packing the car. We're off to Minnesota tomorrow." Ray remembered that they owned a cabin on a lake there. In fact, it was a remote place where they stayed all winter without electricity or anything. He spent days on the lake ice fishing and she mostly sewed and baked. Everyone joked that they were reverse snowbirds, but *tough old birds* was a more apt description.

"I was thinking," Ray said. "Wasn't your Sid an eye doctor?"

"He was an optometrist."

"Do you think he'd mind if I dropped by to say hello?"

"Of course not. He'll be delighted."

The Wexlers lived only a block from Ray's house. The men had met at the golf course and played a few rounds together, which led to a few dinner invitations back and forth. However, that was seven years ago. Ray felt guilty that he hadn't worked at maintaining the friendship, but his new friends in the Foursome absorbed all his time. The garage door was open and Sid was packing the trunk.

"Are you off to the far north?" Ray asked, after Sid noticed him standing in the driveway.

Sid's face broke into a broad smile. "Alaska! It's been too long." In the shade of the garage, Ray removed his sunglasses and gave Sid a hug.

When the older man stepped back, he noticed the ding on Ray's forehead. "What in the world happened to you?"

"You're probably the only person in Leisureville that hasn't heard. I got hit by a golf club that got away from Mrs. Beckerman."

"Gladys? I didn't know she was a golfer."

"She's not. She was taking a lesson."

"How serious was the injury? You've got an eye shut. Did she hurt your eye?"

"Naw, she just broke my glasses. Now I have contacts. I know you're busy getting ready to leave, but I wondered if you could look at one of my lenses. I think it's unusual." He removed the right contact and felt immediate relief.

Sid took the lens on his fingertip and stared at it for a moment. "Let me go get my Loupes," he said, referring to a magnification device. He went into the house and returned a minute later. "I want to look at this outside, in better light, but it appears you got a defective lens."

Holding the lens up to the sky with his left thumb and forefinger, he looked at it through his magnifier and nodded. "I'm not that familiar with the manufacturing side of things, but I've seen countless lenses and I know how they should look. This looks like maybe some air got trapped in the acrylic when they molded it. Come here and I'll show you."

Ray looked at the magnified lens through his left eye. Sure enough, there was something inside it, something round. Maybe it was a thin crack?

Sid said, "Yep, only an air bubble would turn out perfectly round like that. See the clear circle within the lens? It has to be a defect. Can I see your other lens?"

Ray removed the left one, handed it over, and the former eye doctor checked it out. "This is a healthy lens! Send the other one back and they'll give you a new one."

He turned and looked at Ray. "Now open that right eye and let me look at it. I thought I saw some inflammation."

Sid looked through his Loupes at the eye and shook his head. "Ooohh, your eye is very irritated. Now why would you wear that lens for more than a second? It has to distort your vision."

"It's definitely not like the other one," Ray acknowledged.

58

"A contact lens directs light to the center of your eye, where it needs to be for normal sight. That flaw in your lens would interfere with that."

"It makes things look bigger than they really are. Much bigger."

"See? That's distortion. Take this magnifying glass for example. It has a convex lens, meaning thicker in the center. It bends light rays in a way that changes how we see an object.

Your lens could be thicker in the middle than it should be because of that bubble, or at least the bubble has that effect. I would send it back immediately. And by all means, don't ever put it on again. It really rubs your eye the wrong way."

"Don't worry," Ray said, taking the lens back. "Have a safe trip. That's a long way to be driving." He turned to leave, then glanced back. "And don't catch all the trout in that lake! Leave a few for the fair weather fishermen."

What an incredible stroke of luck, Ray thought. *His newfound putting ability was all due to a manufacturing error. What were the odds of that? Was it heaven sent?*

Back at home, he found the Lincoln in the garage, meaning Pat was home. Before entering the house, he put the right lens back on his sore eye so he could demonstrate his vision.

"Where have you been?" she shouted at the sound of the door closing. "It's four o'clock and we have to be at Lucy's for dinner at five."

Ray found her in the bedroom, modeling a red dress in front of the mirror. A couple others were on the bed.

"You aren't going to believe this," he said, beaming.

"Why are you squinting?" she asked.

"Never mind that. Let me take you to the practice green so you can see what I can do!"

"You're kidding, right? I have to get ready."

"My contacts arrived today. It's unbelievable."

She stepped closer to her husband and looked at him. "Why is one eye closed?"

He opened his right eye and automatically closed the left. He stared at his wife in disbelief. She had a full-blown mustache! He immediately shut the wicked eye.

"Your one eye is bloodshot," she said. "And what was that shocked look on your face?"

"Don't worry about the eye," he countered, "I think maybe a bug flew into it." He had fibbed on the fly, but after fifty-three years of marriage, he knew sometimes dishonesty was the best policy. If she knew what Sid Wexler said, the lens would be gone in a second. For his part, he would learn to live with some discomfort. What was the old expression? No pain, no gain?

She shook her head and twitched her nose. "What's that smell?" She lowered her eyes to the stain that ran from his crotch all the way down a leg of his tan slacks. "Oh, my! How did that happen?"

He hurried from the room to put his pants and underwear in the washing machine. On returning, he said, "I got excited is all. The most excited I've ever been in my life."

"I knew you'd be happy with contacts," she said, picking up a blue dress from the bed.

"Happy? I'm not happy. I'm exhilarated. Reborn! I can putt like a pro. How can you be taking this news so lightly?"

She held the dress in front of her and posed. "You've always been a good golfer. I'm reminded of it every day!" She pointed to the two Leisureville Championship trophies on the dresser, 2008 and 2011.

He was getting nowhere. "See the painting on the wall over there?" he said, reopening his right eye. "What's the name of the artist in the right hand corner?"

"I already know, Dear. It's Francis or something. I picked out the painting."

"It's Frankson. F-R-A-N-K-S-O-N."

Pat turned and looked across the room at the painting of a fishing boat anchored in a picturesque cove. She couldn't even see a name.

"So," he said, "what do you think about that?"

"Well, I think it's probably time for me to get an eye exam too."

The pain in Ray's eye was spreading to his entire forehead. He went to the bathroom, removed the right lens, returned it to the storage case, and replaced it with the normal one.

His wife called to him from the bedroom. "Put some drops in your eye. You know where I keep them. And take a shower!"

He followed her instructions and added a couple aspirin to the list. Under the shower, he took stock of the situation. As much as he wanted to tell everyone about the lens, he sensed it would be better to say nothing, at least for now. Pinger could do his talking. He tried to imagine how Knickers and Mulligan's would react.

Still, as he slipped on clean trousers, he couldn't help himself. "It's amazing that I could read that name on the painting, don't you think?"

"It's the eighth wonder of the world," Pat deadpanned.

It was exactly that, as far as he was concerned. "Why do we have to be at the Greens so early?"

"You know they don't believe in eating after six. It's a health thing. Cocktails are at five and dinner's at five-thirty. They want to show off their

The Sweet Swing

grandsons, who are staying there for a few days while their parents are on a second honeymoon."

Ray put on a sports jacket and was set to go. He took the contact case with the special lens and slipped it under his pillow for safekeeping.

"If you need something to do for the next fifteen minutes," Pat said, as she slipped into a flowered white dress, "you can get some gas in the car. I drove all over the place today."

The Lincoln! He hadn't given the car a thought since he wrote down the mileage a week ago. "Does the gauge still say the tank is full?"

"Yep," she answered. "But I know better."

He grabbed the keys off the hook in the garage and got in the driver's seat. From behind the visor, he took the paper with the mileage number. He wrote the number from the odometer above that mileage and did the subtraction. The car had been driven 149 miles in the last week. That's a lot of shopping!

"Okay," he said to himself. "Let's get this mystery solved right now."

He drove to the gas station and slid his credit card into the pump. The flow into the tank stopped in just seconds—2.1 gallons! He squeezed another couple tenths into the tank, and it was completely full. Seventy miles to the gallon? In traffic? Suddenly, he sensed there was an explanation.

Back at home, Pat still wasn't ready. She was applying makeup in the bathroom. He looked at her in the mirror, over her shoulder. "What did Mr. Tanner do for a living?" Ray remembered he had been a scientist or something in his working days and that he always tinkered around in his garage until he passed away six months ago.

"He was chemical engineer, wasn't he?" Pat said. "Remember the box of heat packets he gave us at Christmas one year? He helped develop those."

Everything was getting clear. You could take a packet and scrunch it up with your fingers. The chemicals inside reacted in a way that gave off warmth for hours. They were perfect for stuffing in your boots or gloves in cold weather. Quite phenomenal really. And there were the gel packs in his freezer too. Mr. Tanner also helped design those. You could put them in your cooler and keep beer cold all day. Mr. Tanner was an inventor! Obviously, he came up with a way to make his engine more efficient. That was the answer! A person that could a turn a packet of granules into an all-day furnace could do anything.

Ray hurried to examine the car. He had the hood up, looking for something unusual, when Pat came into the garage.

"Time to go," she said, settling into the passenger side of Birdie Chaser.

He noticed nothing abnormal about the engine, but why would he? Automotive mechanics were generally a mystery to him. He slammed the hood shut.

"Do you realize we've been getting seventy miles to the gallon in this car?" he exclaimed.

"That's good, right?"

"Good? No. It's fantastic! It's the best mileage I've ever heard of. Motorcycles get mileage like that!"

Pat smiled and nodded. "What do you suppose we're having for dinner?"

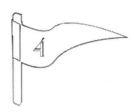

The three guest couples arrived at Sleepy Hollow at the same time, exactly five o'clock. Knickers and Bess pulled up in their golf cart and parked in the driveway right behind Birdie Chaser. Mulligan and his wife Mary filled the other side of the driveway with their Ford Fusion.

Harvey, two young grandsons, and Lucy, who held a silver tray with six flutes of champagne, met them at the front door. The visiting grandsons wore new St. Louis Cardinals jerseys in Knickers' honor.

Shawn, the younger of the two boys at eight, nudged his brother Sam, who was ten. "Which one is the famous baseball player?" Harvey smiled at Knickers and shrugged his shoulders.

"Well, it's not the little guy," Sam offered. "He's too small to be a major leaguer."

Ray playfully elbowed Mulligan. "And it's not me," he laughed. "I'm a golfer." He surprised himself with the impulsive response. Was he already bragging?

Mulligan reached into his breast pocket and pulled out a pair of baseball cards, official Topps rookie cards for Mickey Collins. He handed each boy an autographed card.

Knickers had bought hundreds, maybe thousands, of the cards when they were printed. He had autographed them all and been prepared to hand them out to fans at every request. Unfortunately, supply proved greater than demand and he still had most of them. Mulligan had swiped a supply and forced them on people whenever he traveled with Knickers.

Both boys looked back and forth between the photo of the player and Knickers, the seventy-two-year-old. "Your pants look really funny in the picture," Sam said.

"Really baggy and short," his brother added. "I heard about these old baseball cards. They came with gum, right?"

"Yeah, where's the gum?" Sam asked.

"Here it is," Ray said, producing a pack of Juicy Fruit from his pocket. He gave each boy a stick and they bounded back into the house.

Inside, Ray quickly drained two glasses of champagne while listening to the chitchat, much of it about his new appearance without glasses. The women called him dashing and the men thought he looked weird, all par for the course. In response to Pat's joking about how much his vision had improved, Ray assured them the change was unbelievable; each and every one of them looked more beautiful than ever.

The drinks went straight to his bladder, so he went off to the guest bathroom to relieve himself. Lucy was a world class entertainer and her bathroom reflected it. Fresh flowers graced the top of the toilet tank, elegant floral towels hung everywhere, and a dish of little colored soaps shaped like rosebuds sat by the sink. The toilet seat cover was fitted with a plush pink minirug that matched the larger one on the floor.

Ray stood over the toilet with his head back and eyes closed, enjoying the sensation. Champagne always passed through his system so quickly! Suddenly the toilet seat fell down on him, destroying the moment altogether. He dribbled all over the right leg of his black slacks and the tile floor beside the toilet.

"Shit!" he exclaimed loudly, then heard audible laughter from the other side of the wall. Little boy laughter. Hysterical little boy laughter.

After spending a minute to clean up his mess with a damp washcloth, he walked into the adjoining guest bedroom. Shawn and Sam were still rolling on the floor, all yucks and guffaws.

Before Ray could say a word, the smaller boy pointed at him. "The toilet seat got you, didn't it?"

"It got me too!" Shawn said. "Grandma put that rug on the toilet cover this afternoon and it makes the seat fall down every time!"

"We've been waiting for someone to use the bathroom," Sam said proudly. "You can hear pretty good if you put your ear against the wall."

"It takes about three seconds," Shawn said. "We timed it. It's the same every time."

Ray cleared his throat. He wanted to handle the situation properly. "You have to realize that what you did was impolite, boys. You should have told

The Sweet Swing

your grandma about the cover so she could remove it." The boys looked at him like he was speaking a foreign language.

"Think of your grandma," he continued. "She would be very unhappy if she knew her guests were having a problem."

Sam interrupted. "Listen! Somebody else just went in the bathroom!" They both put their ears to the wall and looked at each other, wide-eyed and grinning.

They could all hear Mulligan singing lyrics to his favorite song. *He was bad, bad Leroy Brown, baddest man in the whole damn town . . .*

Ray raised his eyebrows and leaned closer to the wall too.

Badder than old King Kong, meaner than a junkyard . . . damn!

When Ray returned to the festivities, everyone was gathering at the dining room table. All Lucy's best china and silverware were on display.

Mulligan was last to join the group, and walked into the dining room pointing to a large wet spot on the leg of his olive green pants. "When will I ever learn to drink champagne from a flute without spilling half of it on my lap?"

Ray laughed along with the others, exchanged glances with the boys, and continued to smile as they all sat down for dinner. Halfway through the meal, and after the boys were excused to run off and play video games, Mulligan's wife Mary started the conversation, as she often did.

"So, ladies," she said, looking down the table to Lucy and Pat, "did you know that our husbands remind Knickers and Bess of the lion, the tin man and the scarecrow from the *Wizard of Oz* movie? Isn't that positively hilarious?"

Bess immediately kicked Knickers' ankle under the table, punishment for sharing a private conversation. At the same time, Knickers wanted to kick Mulligan for the same reason, who in turn was thinking about kicking Mary.

Harvey recognized a hint of tension and came to the rescue. "I'd much rather be the tin man than Ichabod Crane!"

Mulligan wanted to redirect the conversation. "Hey, Lucy, we already know that Harvey is your Ichabod and Ray's your George Bailey, but how about the rest of us? Who do we remind you of?" Everyone looked at their hostess, hoping she would entertain them.

She took a sip of water and studied the ceiling for a few seconds. "Well, I actually think quite a bit about all of you, and I do have my ideas. You know I watch a lot of television."

"Tell us then," Mary insisted. "I can hardly wait!"

"Well, Mary, your husband is *My Cousin Vinny*. Did you see the movie?"

Harvey belly-laughed, delighted that someone would have to share his pain. "Joe Pesci! He *is* Mulligan Wettman!"

"*My Cousin Vinny* with a dash of his role in *Good Fellows* thrown in," Bess added.

Ray laughed with everyone. It was a great comparison. Mulligan had an air about him that suggested he could do anything, or at least thought he could. And he certainly had the gift of gab.

"I think Joe Pesci is a little taller," Knickers said. "Joe must be at least five-four."

Mulligan sat and smiled contentedly. Clearly, he was on board with the Vinny thing. After all, Joe Pesci was a popular star.

"How about my husband?" Bess asked. "That ought to be good!"

Knickers sat more upright in his chair, folded his hands in front of him on the table, and shot Lucy his sweetest smile. He was a portrait of a perfect angel.

"For me," she said, "Knickers is the easiest of all."

Harvey interrupted. "Tell me it's Fred Flintstone. Please, let it be Fred. Knickers and Mulligan should be Fred and Barney Rubble."

"Actually," Lucy said. "It's Lieutenant Commander Quinton McHale, U.S. Navy."

"Ernest Borgnine," Mary exclaimed. "There's a very strong resemblance."

"*McHale's Navy*," Knickers said. "Who didn't love that show? He was a great American! Good-looking too."

"He was a wise guy who was forever messing around," Mary pointed out.

"Yes," Pat agreed. "Always up to something . . . mostly mischief."

Lucy nodded enthusiastically. "My thinking exactly!"

Lucy's eyes settled on Bess. "You are June Cleaver, always having to deal with little Beaver Cleaver."

Harvey interrupted. "Now wait, Lucy. Is Knickers McHale or Beaver Cleaver? You're confusing me."

"He's both," she said. "Beaver is what McHale must have been like as a boy!" Everyone agreed, even Knickers.

Lucy turned her attention to Mary, who slumped in her chair as if she wanted to slip under the table and hide. "You are the Sugarbaker sisters from *Designing Women*, a combination of both. You have all the finest qualities of each of them!"

Mulligan clapped his hands and grinned at his wife. "Can I just call you Sugar?"

"It's very true, Mary," Bess said. "You know everything going on in Leisureville. I get all the latest news from you."

"You are also so smart and sophisticated," Pat added. "And the best-dressed woman I've ever known."

"And then there's Pat," Lucy said. "The perfect mother who is always putting her family first. She is my Donna Reed. You all remember her show."

"Hey, Pat," Mary said. "You even got to marry George Bailey in *It's a Wonderful Life*! What a coincidence that is!"

Only half-listening, Ray thought Lucy's reflections were pretty much on target. He knew Pat would be delighted with the Donna Reed comparison. At the same time, half his mind was back on the practice green, making one long putt after another. *How could he not think about that?*

"Actually," Lucy said, quietly, "Ray reminded me of someone else last week. The similarity almost floored me."

This disclosure got Ray's full attention. What happened to George Bailey? He was fine with that.

"Do you all remember the show *Wild Bill Hickock*?" Lucy asked.

Ray flashed to the heroic Wild Bill, played by Guy Madison. This wasn't going to be so bad after all!

"No way," Harvey objected. "There's no way that Ray is Wild Bill!"

"Maybe more like his sidekick Jingles," Mulligan suggested.

Everyone stopped talking and chewing and stared at Mulligan, then Lucy. Ray smelled trouble.

"That's it!" Lucy said, lifting her champagne. "Here's to Andy Devine as Jingles!"

Laughter erupted around the table. Everyone reached for their champagne to toast Lucy's brilliance. Pat, in particular, seemed amused.

Ray tapped his glass with a fork, but not to propose another toast. "You'll have to explain this one to me," he said. "I don't think I look like the Jingles character at all. Besides, all I really remember about Jingles is that he was always whining about something in that funny voice of his."

There was silence. Everyone stared at Ray with a knowing grin. *Oh no,* he thought.

"I'm getting so old," Mulligan mocked, trying to sound like Jingles. "I can barely get around the golf course anymore!"

"I can't make a putt to save my life," Knickers said, in a similar voice. "Last year I was makin' putts all the time."

"I swear I've lost twenty yards off my driver in the last month alone," Harvey said, and then started choking on his laughter. "They keep raising the membership fees every year, but the course never gets any better,"

Mulligan said, nearly crying. "And that was just last week you said that! You never complained when you were shooting par."

Even Pat got in the act. "I'm just wasting my time playing golf," she said, in her own attempt at a whiny voice.

"It hit me last week," Lucy said. "He was picking up Harvey and said he couldn't even remember to put on his shoes or put in his teeth anymore. When they started to drive off, I said to myself, 'There goes Jingles.'"

Ray hung his head. Their quotes were indisputably accurate. *He had started to complain.* In doing so, he violated an unspoken code within the Foursome: no complaining about anything. Not ever. Living in a community of seniors, they all knew that whining was a habit for many and an outright preoccupation for many more. The Foursome's refusal to take the low road was one of the important bonds between the men.

Ray looked up at Knickers and Mulligan and saw the sparkle in their eyes. He knew that he had just been sentenced to Jingles for life, or at least until he changed his tune. Nonetheless, Lucy had actually done him a favor. It was time to refocus and be positive. *Refocus.* That shouldn't be difficult with his new lens!

Lucy served dessert and Ray got a welcome reprieve from the teasing. Everyone tore into the chocolate mousse cake and the room got quiet.

Knickers was thinking about the Christmas decorations in boxes in his garage. Surely there were some jingle bells in there. Yes, they were affixed to red ribbons that he hung on the tree. He would have to hang some on Birdie Chaser's rearview mirror!

Another thought on Knickers's mind wasn't quite so pleasant. Still another week passed and Ray hadn't said a single word about the car that burned no fuel. The joke *would* be on him if he poured any more unleaded into that gas hog of a Lincoln.

He decided to give the subject a little push. "Mulligan, Bess and I are thinking about gettin' a new car," he said casually.

"We are?" Bess asked.

"I'm sorry," Knickers said, looking at his wife with a hint of annoyance. "I was gonna surprise you with a new car and I ruined it."

Bess felt Knickers' foot kick hers this time. As his confidant in everything . . . the yard sign in front of the Green's house was her design . . . she knew exactly what her husband was up to. She had tossed a playful curve to see how he would handle it.

"You have anything special in mind?" Mulligan asked.

"Not really, just something reliable."

Harvey entered the conversation. "Well, with gas at these prices, I'd get something that would be affordable to run." He winked at Knickers, expressing his secret knowledge that his friend could buy an airplane if he wanted one. Knickers' wealth had grown by another two hundred thousand dollars that very day. Still, he enjoyed keeping the secret from the wives, particularly Mary, who would spread the news worldwide if she got wind of it.

Ray struck his glass with his fork a second time. "Well, if you're really lucky, Knickers, you can find a car like ours. We're getting about seventy miles to the gallon."

Knickers thought he was going to fill his pants! It had been three long weeks of hard labor, much, much longer than anticipated. All those trips to the gas station, all those early walks to Ray's house, all the worrying about getting caught . . . over! Now it was payday! He and Bess kicked each other at the same time.

Mulligan blurted, "Could you repeat that, Jingles? I couldn't have heard you right."

Jingles, Ray thought. He knew he wasn't going to like the sound of it. To make matters worse, everyone else laughed. "I said our Lincoln Continental is getting seventy miles to the gallon. It's a fact."

Mulligan looked at Harvey. "I'm afraid our friend has had a little too much of your champagne."

"Or maybe played hooky from too many math classes." Harvey added.

Did Harvey really just say that, Ray wondered. Mulligan or Knickers might make that crack, or even Pat, but Harvey? He would have to pay him back for that one.

Harvey must have read his mind, or at least his facial expression. "I'm sorry, Ray, but that sounds kind of impossible. I don't know much about cars, but I'd say our Toyota gets better mileage than a heavy car like a Lincoln. We get about twenty-eight on the highway and less driving stop and go."

"Well, I know *everything* about cars, especially Fords," Mulligan said. "If you are getting more than twenty driving around here, *my* name is Jingles!"

Knickers sat back and enjoyed the scene. Commander McHale would have put his stamp of approval on this night. Beaver too.

Pat joined the fray. "You may not know as much about cars as you think. I pay all the bills at our house and we hardly buy any gas since we got this car."

Knickers glanced at Pat and nodded his sympathy for her argument. Getting Pat in the mix was even better!

Mulligan coughed and stared at Ray. He didn't like to argue with women. There was no winning. "Listen, Mr. Devine Jingles, I'm just telling you that what you are saying is preposterous."

Ray didn't like the way Mulligan was using the ugly nickname at all. They were friends, great friends, but there had to be respect. Instead of explaining that his deceased neighbor had obviously made some unique improvement to the car, Ray decided to get even. "So, Mulligan, do you want to bet?"

"Bet?" Mulligan said. "Bet about what? Bet whether Gladys Beckerman knocked you silly when she hit you with her club?"

Lucy quickly rose at the end of the table. "Now, now, be nice. Why are you arguing over a silly old car?"

"Because my silly old car gets seventy miles to the gallon and Mulligan and Harvey won't believe it," Ray said.

"Tell you what, *Ray*," Mulligan said, trying to be civil. "The Cardinals are playing the Giants at the stadium next Monday night. The four of us will drive to the game and back in your super car. We'll get great seats on the fifty yard line. If your car gets better than say, *forty* miles a gallon for the trip, I'll pay for the seats. How's that for a deal?"

Such a wager was a joke in Ray's mind. His car got almost double that mileage. "And if it doesn't, I'll pay for the tickets."

"Wait," Pat said. "Wouldn't you girls like to go to the game too? Let's make it eight tickets!"

Pat didn't get feisty very often, Ray knew, but she could be a real trooper when she got fired up. Mulligan must have upset her. He squeezed her knee beneath the table.

"How much are tickets?" Mary asked, looking at her husband.

Harvey answered instead. "Must be about two hundred dollars each." Then he turned to Ray. "Maybe you should go for end zone seats."

"Fifty yard line it is," Ray announced.

"It's about fifty miles each way," Mulligan said. "We'll fill the tank before we go and fill it again when we get back."

"I'll take my car too, if the ladies are coming," Harvey said. They all nodded approval.

"Wait, wait, wait," Ray said. "We're going to have to pay for the tickets in advance. Why don't we settle the bet tomorrow afternoon after golf? We'll drive to Apache Wells for the matinee at the dog track. That's about a hundred miles round trip too. My tank is already full. I just went to the station before I came over here."

That sounded perfect to Knickers. No more trips to the Plumlee garage! "You can count me in," he said.

"Me too," said Harvey.

Mulligan nodded. "It's a date then. And a bet!"

On the drive home in Birdie Chaser, Pat's face was still flushed. "Can you believe that Irv Wettman? He's usually such a gentleman!"

Around women he is, Ray thought and smiled. He recounted the story of the toilet seat to Pat. Naturally, she had sympathy for Mulligan's misfortune. No sense of humor. He knew she would be on the phone to Lucy the moment they walked in their door, warning her of the dangers of her bathroom.

He said, "Realistically, you have to understand Mulligan's point of view. I know I would think exactly the same thing if someone said their car got that mileage. If it's okay with you, we'll share the cost of all the tickets with Mulligan after I win the bet tomorrow. I wouldn't feel right about winning so much when I already know the outcome."

Pat knew the expense would put some strain on the budget for the month, but she agreed. At least Irvin and the others would learn that she and her husband should not be underestimated.

"And we can't forget about Mrs. Tanner," Ray said, pulling into the garage. "She deserves some flowers for selling us her wonderful car."

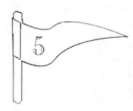

The alarm woke Ray with a start in the morning. He actually overslept on the biggest day of his golfing life.

"Are you okay, dear?" Pat mumbled.

"I'm fine. I couldn't fall asleep last night. All I could think about was getting to the course today." He had gazed at the ceiling long into the night, as if it were a huge projection screen, watching himself putt from all over every one of the Leisureville greens. He never missed. The defective lens was the cure for the defect in his game. The lens with the bubble. The ultimate gift. He took the contact case from under his pillow and fumbled his way to the bathroom.

Both Harvey and his wife stood at the curb when Ray pulled up, but Lucy didn't hold the customary stainless steel cup. This one was white. She turned it so he could read the word printed on it with a dark marker: Jingles.

Ray's jaw dropped. "Perfect, Lucy, just perfect. How will I ever be able to thank you?"

She just grinned and blew him a kiss.

"You're wearing sunglasses now?" Harvey asked, with a curious tilt of his head.

"Actually, they're yours. I remembered you kept them in your bag. I'll buy some at the pro shop after our round."

"Those are old ones, not even prescription," Harvey replied. "I don't even know where I got them. They've just been in the bag as long as I remember."

The Sweet Swing

"Well, they've sure come in handy. With my contacts, it's too bright outside."

The men headed off and Ray sampled the coffee, which tasted as good as always, even in the embarrassing cup. Harvey reached into the Oreo bag to enjoy his first cookie of the day. He nearly bit into a dog biscuit before he realized the bags had switched places. The change could be no accident, not after two years. Ray was chuckling.

"Oh, so now *you're* a wise guy too?" Harvey said. "You've been hanging around Knickers too long."

"Didn't I tell you? I took a wise guy class as a high school senior. Never played hooky!"

Ray looked at Harvey for a response, but his friend just touched his glasses with his index fingers and then pointed ahead. Ingrid Samuels, *Speed Bump*, was walking her toy collie, an animal almost as elegant as she.

Because she was on the right side of the street, it was Harvey who had the privilege of pulling a Milk Bone from the bag. When Ray pulled up beside the walkers, his partner put the bone between his teeth and delivered it to the dog mouth to mouth. Only Ingrid's dog rated Harvey's special delivery and it always made her giggle and jiggle.

"Eeenjoy your gawf, boys," she said through perfect pearly whites and waited a moment for them to respond. When they only nodded, she moved on.

"Can't you even be sociable and say hello?" Ray asked.

"I tried, but nothing came out," Harvey admitted.

"Ditto," Ray said, and slapped Harvey on the knee.

Mulligan waved his cigar at the new arrivals. "Morning, Harvey. What's up, *Jingles*?"

Ray's back stiffened but he decided to ignore the tease. *Ignore it and it will go away*, he told himself. Better yet, maybe he should pretend to like it.

Knickers looked at Ray and cocked his head, exactly the way Harvey had. "What's with the shades? You look like one of the Blues Brothers. No, one of the *Bruise* Brothers."

Ray reached up and touched the spot where the stitches had been. Got it. Very funny.

"It's the new Jingles look," he said. "A new look for my new name."

Harvey pulled the driver from his bag. "By the way, Jingles and I hit a speed bump on the way."

Both Knickers and Mulligan stiffened, shifting their scrutiny to Harvey. While each member of the Foursome was joyfully married to the love of his youth, they also had a common appreciation of art, at least as represented in

73

the sculptured perfection of the Leisureville goddess. Mulligan asked what she was wearing. Knickers wondered if they talked to her.

Ray gave the report. "She told us to 'eenjoy our gawf' and called us boys."

"Now I know your bullshittin'," Knickers said. "She didn't really call you *boys*, did she?"

"It's a fact," Harvey said.

"And Harvey kissed her dog," Ray added. "Right on the lips!"

After the others teed off, Ray stood over his ball, oddly flustered. He planned on using his left eye for his swings and the right eye to putt. However, his one-eyed practice swings felt awkward; he should have spent some time on the driving range. He caught the ball too low with a tentative cut and sent up a rainmaker that dropped barely a hundred yards down the fairway.

Mulligan dropped his stogie. Harvey gasped. Knickers wondered about the concussion.

"Okay, okay," Ray said, walking back to Birdie Chaser. "I hit a moonball."

"Ray Plumlee doesn't hit moonballs," Knickers said. "I've played with you for six years. I can walk two hundred and twenty-five yards down the middle of this fairway, draw a ten yard circle, and every single drive you ever hit would be inside that circle. That's the miracle of Ray Plumlee!"

Ray forced a laugh. "Just call me Jingles then."

With the green still 280 yards away, Ray took the three wood from his bag and overcompensated for the previous mishit by topping the shot and mostly rolling the ball just another 120 yards. When he returned to the cart, Harvey stared at him in disbelief.

"When's the last time I didn't get up in two?" Ray asked.

"I can't tell you," his partner said. "We're on new ground here. The top pros on tour only hit greens in regulation 70 percent of the time. Your stats are closer to eighty. Heck, if you just added a couple yards around the perimeter of the greens to the equation, you'd be near 100 percent."

Ray knew that was true. It was something he took for granted. He hit the ball low and straight and always square, until a few minutes ago.

"Well," he said. "The Leisureville links hardly measure up to Pebble Beach. On this course, the pros would probably hit a 125 percent of the greens."

Harvey scratched his ear. "That's interesting math, Jingles. How do you figure?"

"They'd hit all our par fives in just two shots, right? That's better than regulation.

And almost a quarter of the holes are par five . . . four out of eighteen anyway. That's where the hundred and a quarter comes from. Just do the math."

"I'll have to think about that," Harvey said, figuring it probably made more sense than seventy miles to a gallon. "Anyway, in one of your rounds last week, you hit every green but two and still shot seventy-seven. That means you had almost forty putts. Over half your score was putts!"

"I'm going to turn that around," Ray said. "My new contact is going to help."

"You mean contacts, right?" Harvey asked.

His partner just smiled.

Ray stopped on the cart path when they reached the distance of Harvey's drive. Since Mulligan had taken over as association president, carts were no longer allowed off the paths in order to optimize the condition of the course. Although the rule slowed down play, few of the golfers at Leisureville were in much of a hurry. While Harvey walked out to his ball, Ray opened his right eye to check out the surroundings more closely.

When Harvey returned to Birdie Chaser, there were five golf balls on his seat. "Check 'em out," Ray said. "I found them all right here, stuck in the bushes. There's even a blue smile there!" The blue smile was actually a *C*, identifying it as one of Knickers Collins' balls. He marked all his balls that way with a Sharpie.

"That's amazing," Harvey responded, as he examined Knickers' ball. He hooked one over here a couple months ago. That's the only time I remember."

Ray drove only a few yards before stopping once again to extract a couple more abandoned balls from the bushes. "They're everywhere!" His right lens held nothing but surprises.

"How did you see those?" Harvey asked. "Seven found balls on the first hole? We haven't found that many total in the last two years!" Without a doubt, he was going to get his own eyes checked out as soon as he could.

Ray was a little more comfortable hitting his third shot, but still left himself a few feet short of the putting surface. Only lots of time on the driving range would cure the one-eyed swing dilemma.

At the green, Ray grabbed Pinger and headed for his ball. Through his left eye, he saw about forty feet to the hole, three or four of which were through the fringe. To his right eye, the shot didn't look difficult at all. He stroked the Titleist and knew at once that he yanked it left; maybe he was too amped up. It slid past the left edge of the gaping hole and went three feet by.

He walked after the miss, stopped at the hole, and just reached out and backhanded the ball back into the cup for a bogey.

Now Harvey was worried about the concussion. "Careful there, Jingles! That was no gimme. You could have very easily missed that."

Knickers and Mulligan looked at each other in surprise. The Ray they knew would have walked around surveying the short putt and then taken his time with it. He was a deliberate player. Why would he slap at a putt like it meant nothing?

Ray neither heard Harvey nor noticed the quizzical looks from the others. He just wanted to get to the next green.

With better swings, he managed to do that in style. Even with just one eye, he put a seven-iron approach within six feet of the hole.

"You can make that," Harvey told him, although he doubted it. Statistically, the pros on tour made putts of that distance 62 percent of the time on average. On the easier Leisureville greens, Mulligan could make six-footers three-fourths of the time because he was brilliant with his belly putter. Knickers and he both made them over half the time. Ray was another story.

He had been averaging a miserable thirty-five putts a round for the last few months and showed no sign of improvement. Mulligan averaged only twenty-nine putts. Knickers and he averaged about thirty-one. In effect, Ray had been spotting them all five or six strokes a round on the greens. If one could combine Ray's overall game with Mulligan's putting, the hybrid would average sixty-eight!

Nonetheless, Ray stroked his birdie putt straight into the hole, and did the same on three of the next four holes as well. His only miss came on a thirty-five-footer with a double break.

"I don't know about you, Mulligan, but I'm gonna get myself some contact lenses," Knickers said on the sixth tee.

Mulligan, though disappointed that he and his partner were already down by three holes, tried to stay lighthearted. "I'll bet Mary already made an appointment for me. She wants me to look more like Joe Pesci!

"And what's with Jingles? Did we piss him off or something? I sure haven't heard any whining today."

When Ray walked to the seventh tee, Knickers watched him even more closely than usual. While Mulligan figured he was having a lucky day like Harvey had the previous week, Knickers wasn't quite so sure. From the very start, there had been extra bounce in Ray's step. His limp had nearly disappeared. His approach to putting was different, and it wasn't just the new open stance. Instead of standing over the ball with a frown of resignation, he looked confident. There was no celebration when he jarred a thirty-footer on the last hole, which made no sense! Ray rarely made a long putt and always danced when he did. Heck, he didn't normally make all that many short putts! Ray was suddenly all business. Maybe he had been half blind before and didn't even know it.

Continuing his run, Ray hit another accurate approach to the green, leaving no more than ten feet for still another birdie. However, the joy of the day was rapidly fading. His right eye was killing him.

The assumption that eye drops would cure the problem had proven wrong. His shirt collar, already wet from all the drops that leaked down his cheek, now absorbed tears triggered both by pain and frustration. The amazing bubble lens was nothing but a cruel joke. It showed him its magic and then punished him for its use. He was done. He couldn't go on. His head was throbbing worse than in the aftermath of his clubbing by Mrs. Beckerman.

At the seventh green, he delivered the news. "I'm sorry, guys. I have to go home now and lie down."

The objections came as expected. What about your round? How can you possibly leave when you are playing like this?

Instead of saying anything, he took off the sunglasses and showed the men his right eye. They leaned close to look, then frowned as one.

"What's happened?" Harvey asked. "Did you scratch it or something?"

"Maybe it's an allergy," Knickers offered.

"Right, Knickers," Mulligan said, shaking his head. "He has an allergy in just one eye!"

Ray put the shades back on. "I'm afraid I wasn't meant to wear contacts, or at least that one. I need to lie down is all."

"We can go to the track some other day," Mulligan said. "Don't worry about it."

Remembering his car and the wager lifted Ray's spirits slightly. Removal of the contact eased his pain, at least the physical part of it. "No, we'll still go this afternoon. Just meet at my house at twelve thirty or so. I'll be fine. Maybe Harvey can run me home and come back to finish your round."

Back at home, Ray lounged on his bed with one of Mr. Tanner's ice packs sitting on a washcloth over his right eye. The pain had subsided, but now his ears were on fire. Pat had her volume turned up a few notches for effect. "If one of your lenses gave you all that trouble yesterday, why on earth would you just put it on again today? What kind of person does that?

"And why didn't you just tell me the truth about it yesterday instead of making up some story?"

He lifted his hands and showed his palms in surrender. "I told you already. I can see better out of that lens. It helped me with my golf game, but it's over now. We'll take it back to the doctor tomorrow."

"No, I'll take it back now," she said, softening her tone. "Your glasses are ready to be picked up too. Dr. Sturrock's office called just before you got home."

"It's in the container by the bathroom sink," he mumbled. He lifted the ice bag and watched her through normal lenses as she scooped up the case and dropped it in her purse.

She was almost out the door when he remembered the wager and jumped up to stop her. "Wait, Pat! The tank is full and I have the bet to settle with Mulligan, remember?"

With an exaggerated sigh, she turned and dropped the purse on the kitchen counter. "I guess your glasses will still be there tomorrow."

He returned to the bed, sprawled out, and stared at the two trophies on the dresser. He couldn't help but wonder what score he might have shot today. Already three under par through six holes and another birdie awaited him on seven. Four under through seven and he would never know the outcome!

The lens had been fine for over an hour, just like yesterday, before things started going south. If only he could play a round in an hour instead of close to four, his world would be perfect.

Closing his eyes, he pondered the situation. He *used* the lens only to putt. Why not *wear* the lens only to putt? It was awkward trying to swing off the tees and fairways with just his left eye anyway. Couldn't he wear his regular lenses from tee to green, then just switch right lenses in the cart. Why not?

How long did he spend on each green anyway? Five minutes? What was eighteen times five? Less than an hour, right? No, wrong. It was more like an hour and a half. Still, his eye would be resting under a regular right lens most of the time. It could work!

He bounced off the bed and headed for the kitchen, passing Pat's office on the way. The door was slightly ajar, and he saw her at the computer. After snatching the contact case from her purse, he returned it to safety beneath his pillow. There was no point in trying to sell her on the idea; he would have to show her. He would show everyone!

As 12:30 approached, Ray filled an ice chest with beer for his friends to enjoy on the drive, Sam Adams for everyone. He placed the cooler in the center of the backseat, between where Harvey and Mulligan would sit. Shotgun was reserved for Knickers, the only one who hadn't challenged his claim about his car's mileage.

The men showed up on time and were delighted to see that their friend had recovered. They immediately set off on the fifty-four-mile drive to Apache Wells. Along the way, the passengers opened multiple brews and talked mostly about Jingles' mastery of the course that morning.

"Do you realize that we saw history made?" Harvey said. "Jingles' three under par for the first six holes was the best start any of us ever had, at least since I've been playing with you guys."

Mulligan leaned forward to talk in Ray's ear. "What I want to know is when did a cup become a bucket? You kept saying the hole looked like a big ole' bucket."

"It's my contacts," Ray answered. "That's the way the hole looks to me now."

Contacts? He meant *contact*, of course, and was bursting with desire to tell them all about it. However, he wanted to show them its magic first, over a full eighteen holes. He wanted to see that much for himself!

Mulligan passed Knickers another beer and said, "Well, the cup must look more like a thimble to my partner. He three-putted his way around the whole course today."

When they arrived at the dog track, Ray checked the gas gauge and the needle still pointed toward full. In three or four hours, he would pull into the gas station back home, fill his tank with less than two gallons, and get his satisfaction. The look on Mulligan's face would be priceless!

Once inside, the men took their customary position near the finish line, where they huddled along the rail, studied their race programs and sipped more beer from plastic cups. Their standard practice permitted each man a wagering limit of $40, which he had to gamble in its entirety. Whoever had the most money at the end of the day got the balance of everyone else's money too. On the previous trip, a couple months ago, the competition ended in a four-way tie. Each of them lost his entire forty bucks.

In the past, Ray struggled to read much of the program other than the names of the greyhounds in each race. With his new contacts, he could read and analyze all the details of past races that appeared in much smaller print beneath each name.

Each of the men had his own preferred method for losing his money. Mulligan was purely a numbers man and didn't really need a program. He always bet on Two to win, Five to place, and Seven to show. His address, coincidentally, was 257 Leisure Way. Knickers liked to ignore the odds and statistics. He focused on the *athletes* themselves. He placed his bet on the entrant that looked fittest and fastest, with just a single exception. If a dog stopped to defecate before the race, it earned Knickers' wager. Harvey was a true handicapper. He studied past performance so thoroughly that he predicted, in handwritten numbers, the entire finish of each race, first through last. Although he only bet on his top dog to win, he loved comparing all his guesses to the actual results. Ray was strictly a *name* bettor, possibly because the names were the largest print on the program. Even with all the new data at his disposal, he decided to stick with following his heart. Old habits were hard to break.

The men were late for the first race, so Ray studied the field for the second. The lineup was rich in quality names: *Wedding Bell Blues, Willy's Blue Moon Rocket Racer, Just Call Me Angel in the Morning, PJ's Black Alco, the Exterminator, Nash Bridges, Laughing Game,* and *Patsy's Special Birthday Wish.* Tough choices.

"Just look at these wild names!" Mulligan exclaimed.

Knickers laughed. "Yeah, whatever happened to Fido and Spot?"

"What do you do if your dog gets off his leash and you have to walk around the neighborhood calling him?" Harvey asked. "Do you walk around hollering names like these?"

Mulligan started doing just that. "Just Call Me Angel in the Mooorrrning! Come hoooome! Just Call Me Angel in the Mooorrrning! Heeeere, girl!"

Knickers cupped his hands in front of his mouth. "Willy's Blue Moon Rocket Racer!" he shouted. "Where aaaaare you? Willy's Blue Moon Roooooocket Racer! Come home to Daaaddy!"

With no inhibitions whatever, the two of them started walking around, calling their dogs at the top of their lungs. All the spectators within earshot, a substantial distance in this case, looked at the yellers like they were nuts.

Though they wouldn't dream of emulating the odd behavior, Harvey and Ray were amused. Both envied the natural wit and bravado of their buddies, but were satisfied to play straight men to the comedy team of Knickers and Mulligan.

Ray's decision boiled down to two dogs. "Wedding Bell Blues" was a Fifth Dimension song. The lead vocalist, Marilyn McCoo, was maybe his very favorite female singer of all time. However, *Patsy's Special Birthday Wish* was right there too. Patsy wasn't Pat, but it was close.

He splurged right off the bat, betting five bucks on Pat to win and another five on Marilyn McCoo to place. A quarter of his allotted funds might be gone after a single race, but he felt right about this one. He felt right with everything.

The stuffed rabbit circled the track, the doors on the cages opened, and the lean muzzled dogs were off in flying pursuit. Ray's two picks ran side by side throughout the race, joined at the hip. They finished just a nose apart in sixth and seventh place.

When the track announcer called out the names of the winner and second place finisher, Ray knew the day belonged to Knickers and Mulligan. *Just Call Me Angel in the Morning* and *Willy's Blue Moon Rocket Racer* finished first and second. The stars were aligned.

"Oh boy," Ray whispered to Harvey. "This is going to be good!"

Hundreds of eyes focused on their two friends, who had dramatically identified the top dogs. Mulligan raised his arms and stared right back at them. "What?" he yelled, looking around. "You didn't bet on my dog?"

The third race featured a sister to *Just Call Me Angel in the Morning*, a brindle called *Top of the Morning to You*. According to the fine print on the program, the mother of both had the shorter handle of *Morning Glory*.

Ray and Harvey watched their friends go to work, wondering what they might be doing for an encore. Mulligan walked among the crowd, shaking hands like a politician, and greeting them all with, "Top of the morning to you!" He also handed each stranger a Mickey Collins rookie card and pointed out his friend.

With the card in hand, many of the people approached Knickers so they could meet a real major leaguer. He responded to each with the words: "Some kind of wonderful to meet you." *Some Kind of Wonderful* was the number 4 dog in the race.

Dozens of patrons scrambled to the ticket windows to invest their retirement or Social Security income on those two dogs. Ray and Harvey were part of the stampede. The odds on both dropped quickly as they attracted a flood of wagers.

When neither dog ran in the money, Knickers and Mulligan shrugged their shoulders and lit cigars. Neither of them had placed a bet on the race, or even the previous one when they foretold the top finishers. They were having too much fun screwing around.

One of the bolder patrons shouted at them. "Look at you two, just blowing smoke up our asses!"

Mulligan deliberately blew out a huge cloud of smog. "What? You expect us to be right every single time?"

That's right, Ray thought. *Nobody could be right every time. And nobody could make every putt. Or could they?* He was going to try to do that very thing in the morning. The world had changed in a matter of days. Putting with his new vision was like betting on the stuffed bunny that the dogs chased around the track. A winner every time!

On the drive back to Leisureville, Harvey gloated over his winnings for the day. By shrinking his $40 to $8.60, he performed the best. When he counted the handful of dimes that Knickers and Mulligan had left, he came away with nearly $10. Ray hadn't cashed a single winner.

Knickers continued to rave about Ray's golf that morning and about how new eyewear had benefited many baseball players as well. He talked of pitchers that saved careers with improved control, outfielders that got a better jump on fly balls, and hitters that raised batting averages by fifty points, all with the help of glasses or contacts. He also analyzed Ray's new putting stance and said there was no single, right way to hit a baseball or a golf ball. Each player had to find their own special formula for success.

Mulligan said nothing. He slumped against the left rear door, snoring loudly.

Ray just drove without speaking. His good spirits had fallen right along with the needle of the fuel gauge. The moment he left the track, the dang needle had started to dip. It was now well below full and moving downward with every turn of the tires. How was that even possible?

After glancing around to be sure nobody was watching, he thumped the gauge with a finger. Something was horribly wrong! With his shirt starting to stick to his skin, he turned up the air conditioning.

Meanwhile, Knickers watched Ray's every move out of the corner of his eye. The timing of the drop on the fuel gauge was predictable. You always had to burn a few gallons off the top of a tank before the needle moved. He barely contained a grin when his friend tapped the gauge. He could see sweat beaded up on the poor guy's forehead. It was beautiful.

When Ray finally pulled up to a pump near Leisureville, he was sick to his stomach. Almost a quarter of his tank appeared to be gone!

Harvey elbowed Mulligan to wake him and all four men climbed out. Ray's knees were so weak he leaned against the car.

Mulligan walked to the pump, swiped his credit card, and took hold of the nozzle. "It's my treat, Jingles. Just open the tank cover!"

Ray looked down at the switch on the floor by his seat. He swore it had a skull and crossbones on it, but sucked in a big breath and pulled it.

"Let's bet on how much it takes," Mulligan said. "Five bucks."

Knickers had drifted away from the car, but Harvey answered. "I'll take that action. How about you, Jingles?"

"I think the wager is big enough already," he said, barely recognizing his own voice. What was he going to tell Pat?

Harvey seemed to understand. "All right, Mulligan. You guess first."

"Five point two."

Harvey smiled at his trick of getting Mulligan to go first. "I'll take five point three."

Knickers stood admiring the scene, perhaps like Da Vinci may have stood to study one of his paintings. Mulligan and Harvey stared at the numbers flying by on the meter, fists on their hips, nodding their heads. Ray's face had lost color and his expression was a reverse Mona Lisa.

When the meter stopped at 5.1, Harvey passed Mulligan an Abe Lincoln and turned to look at Ray, who had collapsed into the driver seat. "What in the world were you thinking?"

Mulligan returned the nozzle to the pump and started singing. *Take me out to ball game, take me out to the crowd, buy me some peanuts and . . .* He stopped abruptly when he saw Ray slouched in the seat with his forehead resting on the wheel. Was he crying?

"Are you all right, Jingles?" Mulligan and Harvey asked in unison.

In response, Ray mumbled something about the twilight zone.

"Ooh," Harvey said. "Twilight zone is how he refers to Alzheimer's. Remember? I've heard him say that."

Ray felt himself slipping out of control. Life as he always enjoyed it was officially over. His greatest fear had come to pass. He was losing it! What would Pat think? How would she deal with him? Would he have to enter a nursing home? He started to groan, oblivious to the others.

Mulligan circled the car to check on him and gently patted his shoulder. "Don't worry about the money, Jingles. We can all buy our own tickets. We all knew that you miscalculated or something. It's no big deal."

Harvey said, "That's right. We love you even if math isn't your best subject!" He forced a laugh, hoping it would cheer his friend.

"Good gosh, Jingles!" Knickers said, returning to the car. "Don't be such a crybaby! It could have been Mulligan or Harvey just as easy."

Mulligan stared at Knickers for a second and then fell into the back seat, laughing so hard it hurt. "Holy crap! You did this to him . . . you did this to all of us, didn't you? Holy double crap!"

"Knickers did what?" Harvey asked. "What does Knickers have to do with this?"

Knickers sat down in the Lincoln, smiled and continued to savor Ray's misery. Without a doubt, it had been a perfect execution.

Mulligan started to cough from all his laughing. Recovering, he started to speculate. "Have you been putting gas in his tank, Knickers? Oh, my aching gut! You have, haven't you? Holy triple crap!"

Ray grabbed the steering wheel with both hands, squeezing so hard his knuckles whitened. In his mind, the wheel was Knickers' neck.

Knickers nodded. "I can't even remember how many gallons I put in that car! Almost twenty trips to his garage worth."

"But how could you get to his car without him knowing?" Mulligan asked.

"I went over at five in the morning, every day. Jingles gave us keys, remember?"

Slowly Ray released the tension in his grip. *He should be thankful*, he thought. *At least he wasn't losing his mind.* Suddenly the relief was as overwhelming as the pain had been just a minute earlier! He was fine. It had all been a joke! With a burst of energy, he leaned across the center console and wrapped his arms around Knickers' shoulders. He kissed his cheek with a loud smack.

Knickers shoved him away. "If I had known you were going to kiss me, I wouldn't have gone to all the bother!"

Harvey was speechless . . . dumbfounded. All he could think was how fortunate he was to be part of the Foursome!

As the men drove home, Ray described every detail of his thinking about the car and even the explanation that he had manufactured for himself. The words played like a symphony to Knickers, who basked in the praise of all his friends. Finally, the trickster announced they were indeed going to the Monday Night football extravaganza; Bess already bought the tickets. He had decided to sell a few shares and have some extra fun.

Inside his house, Ray started telling Pat about Knickers' prank. He got no further than the part about his friend sneaking into the garage each night. She gave him an icy stare, turned, and walked away, saying, "Get our house keys back."

Wonderful woman, he thought, *but no sense of humor.* "Pat, we got almost thirty gallons of free gas!"

When she didn't respond to that, he added, "I'll get even on the golf course, where it really counts!"

"Good luck with that!" she said, without turning.

He scratched his head. *Now what was that supposed to mean?*

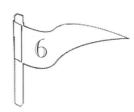

Ray blinked awake five minutes before the scheduled alarm and reached to the nightstand for his glasses. Fortunately, he realized, he didn't find them. They were part of the old Ray, a fellow he wouldn't miss one bit on the golf course.

In anticipation of an extraordinary day, he had selected his attire last night: yellow shirt, matching socks, and white slacks, all bright and celebratory. After dressing, he glanced in the mirror and gave himself a high five.

Tiptoeing back to the bed, he reached under his pillow to gather up his special lens case. He felt nothing! He lifted the pillow to confirm it. Nothing. He dropped to his knees and felt around on the floor. The case was gone.

Catching a movement from the corner of his eye, he stood and looked at his supposedly sleeping wife. Had he just seen her eyes open? After studying her for a few seconds, he was convinced she was wide awake beneath closed eyelids. They were twitching.

Her words from last evening came back to haunt him: *Good luck with that!* When she barely spoke a word to him the rest of the night, he assumed she was angry at him for having a friend like Knickers. That wasn't it at all. She had both discovered the case was missing from her purse and found his hiding place. Impressive. His wife was a worthy adversary.

He quietly walked out of the bedroom, closed the door, and took his panic to a chair at the kitchen table. This was it . . . crunch time. He had to think clearly.

Could she have disposed of the lens? Would she flush it down the toilet or something?

His gut said no, she would want to return it to the doctor for a replacement or a refund. She definitely had the lens.

Could he discuss the matter with her? Could he convince her that his new plan for its use would eliminate any hazard? Could he just demand that she return it? No to all three. He burned that bridge when he lifted the lens from her purse. *Wait, who was he kidding?* There had never been a bridge to burn; that's why he sneaked the lens from her purse in the first place. When she made up her mind about something, that was it. The only way he could win an argument was to avoid it.

He thought back to when he was only twenty-one and married for less than a year. He returned from a week-long fishing trip with an ice chest full of trout and a brand new habit of smoking. When Pat saw the Marlboros in his breast pocket, there was fire in her eyes. She told him she didn't marry a smoker and had no intention of being married to one. When he reminded her that many of their friends and even her mother smoked, she just looked down at her watch and told him he had ten seconds to decide. The smokes went into a waste basket at the seven second mark.

Confrontation was out. His only hope was to find the case and do it fast. Where would she put it? If it was under her pillow or elsewhere in the bedroom, the game was over. She would know he was looking for it and he'd never see it again. He could only hope it was stashed somewhere else, a place he'd never think to look.

He stood and walked straight to the War Room, which was actually just the smaller of two guest bedrooms that served as her office. Pat named it the War Room because it was the operation center from which she waged the battle of tracking and servicing the countless birthdays, graduations, anniversaries, and holidays for a vast and growing list of family and friends. Finding, buying and mailing gifts and cards had become a full-time job for his wife. At least half of their annual budget was consumed by it.

He eased the door shut behind him and turned on the overhead light. The bed served as a large work table. It held wrapping paper for all occasions, tape, markers, and stacks of priority mailboxes in various sizes. Along one wall, dozens of gifts were assembled. There were toys of all kinds, computer games, CDs, boxes of candy, fruit cakes, and clothing boxes from different department stores. Every box or package had a yellow Post It stuck to it, with the name of the future recipient.

As he gawked at the sheer volume of stuff, he recalled Lucy Green once telling him he should feel guilty about not helping his wife with the task.

Actually, he didn't feel any guilt at all. Pat didn't play golf; what else did she have to do? Besides, he did all the housecleaning.

Her desk with the computer, printer and other accessories sat under the single large window. He didn't even know how to turn on a computer and had no interest in learning. Quietly, he began sliding the drawers open. When he opened the third drawer, the contact case was sitting front and center, seemingly smiling up at him. Unbelievable! That lens and his right eye were meant to be together.

After stealing the case back, he took a pen and drew a smiley face on one of her yellow sheets. Beneath the face he wrote: *Don't worry. Everything will be just fine! Thank you for hiding it in the first place I looked. Love, . . .* He started to write Ray but decided on Jingles. He placed the note where the case had been and closed the drawer.

The sight of Harvey and Lucy, standing at the end of their driveway to welcome him, made Ray reflect on Pat again. It was she who brought this wonderful couple into their lives. He hoped she wouldn't be too angry when she opened that third drawer.

Harvey yelled the first greeting. "Hey there, Jingles, top of the morning to you!"

Ray remembered the dog and laughed. "So it's going to be Jingles all the time?"

Lucy said, "It has a nice *ringle* to it, don't you think?"

Ray took the coffee from her and set it in a holder in the cart, then walked over and gave her a big hug that surprised all three of them. "That's for being such a great friend to Pat and me, and for being so tolerant of Ichabod. You're the best and so is your coffee."

"I'm just glad you survived Knickers' prank," Lucy said, when he released her. "Harvey actually thought you were going to have a stroke or something."

Ray shook his head. "Knickers is a hard man to love."

While they drove, Harvey was chatty. "We went to the movies last night with Mulligan and Mary. All he talked about was your golf yesterday. Well, that and the car. He thought you could have put up a special score if your eye hadn't acted up. You think you'll be okay today?"

"I think so, especially if you'll drive the cart. I'm going to be cleaning and rotating my lenses pretty often. That should help me."

Knickers was in the midst of telling Mulligan something when they arrived at the first tee. He nodded hello, but kept on talking. "Anyway, the dentist tells me I need to brush my teeth religiously! What kind of talk is that? What does brushin' your teeth have to do with religion?"

Harvey chuckled. "I think the dentist meant that you should brush your teeth every Sunday, whether they need it or not."

"Or maybe you should use holy water to brush," Mulligan said.

"And do it on your knees in front of the sink, like you're kneeling at the altar," Harvey added, chuckling at his own wit.

Ray's only interest today was golf. "Religiously means regularly, Knickers. Regularly."

Knickers tossed up his hands. "Since when?" The others could only laugh.

On the tee, Ray went through his regular ritual of envisioning the drive, the approach, and the single putt, just like always. The fairway looked special through two good eyes, emerald green and sparkling after a light rain shower during the night. His swing was relaxed and rhythmic and the contact was pure.

"What a surprise," Mulligan shouted. "Right down the middle."

"Way to let the big dog bark," Knickers added.

When Ray returned to his cart, there was a string of jingle bells hanging from the rearview mirror. "It feels like Christmas over here, Knickers," he called out. And it actually did.

Ray already had his five iron on his lap when Birdie Chaser drew even with his ball. His approach on the first hole was always a five, except for yesterday when he muffed his drive.

Instead of walking out to his ball in the fairway, he jogged. The view of the pin was better than ever with two matching lenses and he took careful aim. His target was ten feet in front of the green, from where he could expect a couple bounces and some roll to carry his ball an additional thirty feet. The shot was true and rolled as expected. He had no more than ten feet left for birdie.

"Great shot, Jingles," Harvey said. "That was some kind of wonderful."

Ray removed his sunglasses and reached for the contact case so he could make the lens transfer. He was off to the races.

After the ninth hole, three of the men walked off to the restroom and soda machine while Ray sat in the cart, holding his head in his hands. His eye felt fine, perfect even. He was three under par and should be walking-on-a-cloud ecstatic. It matched his best score ever on the front side, and the other came a full six years ago, when he was still a young buck. So why wasn't he jubilant? Worse yet, why was he acting so glum in front of his friends, who were cheering him on like his biggest fans? He kept telling himself to lift his spirits, to be as gleeful as the day warranted, but his mind just wouldn't listen. As he considered his unexpected problem, the answer became clear. Despite his score, he wasn't living up to the potential of his miraculous right lens. He wasn't holding up his end of the deal.

With the exception of a single hole, he had birdie opportunities. After leaving a straight-in fifteen-footer short on the fifth, he had missed totally makeable putts on the next three holes: a push; a pull; and one that hit the back of the cup and popped right out. His right eye always said *yes*, but his faulty mechanics answered with *no* too often.

The only bogey on his card was simply bad luck; nothing to fret about. His approach from the fairway was barely off-line, but took a horrible bounce to the right and landed under the lip of a trap that took two shots to escape.

Knickers returned from the vending machine at the tenth tee and handed Ray a Diet Coke. "Hey, Mr. Ed, why the long face?" he asked. "You're takin' us behind the barn and givin'' us a whippin'!" In truth, Knickers couldn't decide if he wanted to punch Jingles or kneel at his feet. The guy was unconscious.

"Mr. Ed, the talking horse from the television show!" Harvey said. "That's hysterical, Jingles. Get it? Why the long face?"

"Are you getting a headache again?" Mulligan asked. "I hope so, because you're giving me a headache and a pain in the ass too, the part of my ass where my wallet sits."

Ray decided to choose his words carefully. What would they think if he said they hadn't seen anything yet? He was still making mistakes, making adjustments. What good was knowing exactly where to putt if he couldn't execute the stroke properly? He had to relax.

"I'm worried about the back nine," he responded. "How long can luck like this last?"

As the foursome moved through the final nine holes, conversation slowed and then stopped altogether. Ray's luck didn't continue, it got a whole lot better. The putts that looked like they should drop, did drop.

When he retrieved his ball from the cup on the final hole, Harvey asked if he could have it. After all, he just watched his best friend birdie seven of the last nine holes and post a score of 62. *Sixty-two!* He had the scorecard to prove it!

Knickers had been silent since the twelfth hole, when Ray dipped to six under and put the Leisureville resident scoring record in real jeopardy. Over decades in baseball, he had seen many improbable things. There were the batters that couldn't hit a loud foul, that didn't have a homerun in their last four hundred at bats, that walked on the field one day and inexplicably blasted two of them. There were pitchers near the end of their careers, barely hanging onto their jobs, that found magic or luck on the mound for one spectacular day and tossed a no-hitter. Ray was pitching a perfect game at the age of seventy-two. Improved eyesight alone couldn't be responsible for that. He was just *in the zone*. Knickers would have bet any amount against the possibility of Jingles ever breaking seventy again, and he just carded a sixty-two!

Mulligan dashed off to the clubhouse, eager to tell the club pro about the score, and anyone else that happened to be around. "Sixty-two!" he shouted as he ran. "Jingles Plumlee just shot a sixty-two!"

"Today a story has been written," Harvey said, hugging Ray. "The Legend of Jingles Plumlee! I didn't even think it was possible to shoot a score like that."

The now-legendary Jingles looked up into the cloudless sky. The round had begun with religion for Knickers in a dentist's office and ended with what he considered to be his own religious experience. Everyone had their own view of what heaven might be like, he supposed, but this worked just fine for him. He found himself giving thanks for the wonder of life itself, with all its twists and turns, disappointments and joys. Today was pure joy.

Knickers grabbed Ray's shoulder, ending his reverie. "Let's go have the coldest beer of our lives, Jingles. I'm buying!"

"And today we are all drinking the good stuff!" Ray exclaimed.

In the Nineteenth Hole, Harvey, Knickers and Ray just sat down at their regular table when Mulligan rolled in, his face red with excitement or exhaustion. He went straight to the bar.

"Nick, you better send us a round on the house! Jingles smashed the course record with a sixty-two! Six, two, sixty-two!"

"Who is Jingles?" the bartender asked. He was always polite to Mulligan regardless of what he said or did. Mulligan was the main man in Leisureville.

"It's Ray Plumlee, of course. Leisureville Golf Course record holder Ray Plumlee!"

Nick eyed the three regulars at the nearby table suspiciously, and Knickers in particular. As the regular barkeep, he picked up on just about everybody and everything. He knew about the reputation of Knickers Collins and suspected some serious bullshit. Hell, he had seen plenty of it firsthand!

Maybe four years ago, Knickers had Ray get him some fresh, whole salmon shipped down from Alaska, guts still in them and everything. He hired old Sam Isaac to sit beside the pond on seventeen all morning with a fishing pole and a stringer full of the twenty-pound salmon in the water in front of him. Old Sam couldn't talk or hear, so nobody could ask him anything. With all the golfers passing by and seeing the old guy and huge fish, it wasn't long before a hundred people surrounded the pond, some even in wheelchairs. They cast every kind of lure imaginable and snagged nothing but each other. It all topped off when a guy wearing an Arizona Fish and Wildlife uniform showed up and started issuing tickets for fishing without a license. He said it was a $100 fine. The officer was a fake, of course, but the people didn't know that. All the old fishermen started running like hell. Nick had seen funny things in his life, but watching old folks try to run for the first time in twenty or thirty years was real entertainment.

Yes, Nick had watched *that* drama unfold right in front of him. Knickers, Ray and Mulligan had been sitting right there, at the same table by the window, watching the whole thing and laughing it up like high school kids. Ray Plumlee shot sixty-two? That story smelled worse than those fish must have smelled after a day of soaking in the warm pond.

Nick yelled over to Knickers. "Would you like some fresh caught salmon with those free beers?"

"So you remember, Nick? That was a truly great day," Knickers said, smiling fondly at the memory. Today would be even better if he could have some fun with the bartender.

"Tell you what," Knickers said, getting up from the table. "You're a young guy, what, forty? And I hear you're a damn good golfer too. How about you let me watch the bar for you while you go play Jingles a round for a hundred bucks a hole right now?"

Nick was aware that Ray, or Jingles, or whatever he called himself, had been the club champion a few years back. He looked toward the wall with the Big Board, as everyone called it, and saw Plumlee's name twice. Still, he thought about calling the bluff and accepting the offer. He carded a seventy-three the last time he played and Plumlee was no spring chicken.

"What are you waiting for?" Knickers said. "He's old enough to be your father!"

"I would, but you'd give away all the booze," Nick said. Knickers had to have some kind of gimmick in mind.

"Then bring us a round of Sam," Ray said. "I'll be picking up the tab."

"And a bottle of Old Grand-dad," Knickers added. "It's a day to remember!"

The foursome finishing behind Ray's group rushed up to him when they entered the bar.

"What did you shoot today, Ray?"

"We saw you knocking down putts from everywhere!"

"Never saw anything like it!"

"I can't even remember you missing a putt!"

Ray had played more slowly on the back nine and the following golfers watched the drama unfold as they stood in the fairways, waiting for each green to clear.

"He shot a sixty-two," Harvey announced.

The other foursome collectively sucked in their breath. One asked, "Is that even possible?"

The next hour passed like a minute for Ray as he drank one beer after another to cool the sting of the shots of whiskey. He listened as Mulligan tried to convince everyone that came through the door that the course record had been shattered. A few golfers rushed to congratulate Ray and some only nodded politely. Most looked at Mulligan with understandable skepticism. A majority assumed their association president was drunk before midday and were a little disgusted.

Annoyed, Mulligan returned to the table and sat down. "What's with these people? They look at me as if I'm telling them I'm having an affair with Speed Bump or something!"

Harvey said, "If you were home sick today or something and I just called you and said Jingles shot a sixty-two, would you believe me?"

"And Harvey is very honest compared to you, Mulligan," Knickers added.

"What do you mean?" Mulligan said. "I just watched and I don't believe it. That doesn't mean it didn't happen though."

Ray drained four beers and an equal number of shots, giving birth to a complete stranger. The stranger stood and said to the entire room, "It's not right that you don't believe my friend Mulligan. He would never lie about golf. I'll prove that to all of you tomorrow."

"We don't play tomorrow," Harvey said, stunned by Jingles' bravado. "Tomorrow is Thursday."

Knickers looked at Jingles and chuckled. Through all the drinking and talking, he had been thinking more and more about the round he just watched. With the new contact lenses, his old friend was like a completely new person. He hadn't witnessed only good luck; it was more like a transformation. Much improved vision had uncaged a beast of a golfer.

Knickers stood up beside Jingles. "I'll bet every one of you and every other resident of Leisureville that Jingles here can shoot sixty-five or better on Friday. Nick over there at the bar is going to take a list of names that want to take me up on the bet. Let's say the wager is five dollars in bar credit."

Nick nodded enthusiastically. The bar was a winner either way!

One of the patrons said, "Hey, you guys said he shot a sixty-two! Why is the bet for a sixty-five?"

Knickers said, "Would you have believed he shot a sixty-five?"

"No way!" a dozen voices hollered out.

"There you have it," Knickers said. "I'll cover every name that's on the list by the end of the day tomorrow. Just sign up and give Nick your five bucks. And be sure to tell your friends!"

"Leave it to Knickers to put a little extra shine on a day," Mulligan said. "Friday is going to be our most fun round ever."

Harvey stared at Knickers, then Mulligan, in disbelief. "How can you do that to Jingles? That puts ridiculous pressure on him!"

Knickers smiled as a line formed at the bar, where the other golfers were signing their names and handing over their money. Mulligan was right. Friday's round would be the best ever.

"Do what to Jingles?" Mulligan asked. "What pressure? It's Knickers' money to lose and no doubt our free beer to drink if he breaks sixty-five!"

Harvey said, "You're missing the point! Jingles doesn't want to cost Knickers all that money!"

Jingles filled a shot glass and pushed it toward Harvey. "Sissty-five is no problem. Don't worry, Icha . . . Ichabod! Ichabod Crane!"

Clancy Schmidt, an early retiree of fifty-seven and the reigning club champion, had watched the commotion from a corner table. A former hedge fund manager from New York, he had taken Leisureville by storm two years earlier when he and his young wife arrived in a yellow Corvette. As a former collegiate golfer at Duke, he also dominated the golf course, setting the acknowledged resident record of sixty-five. Knickers Collins was no friend of his. For two years running, he had knocked the goofy old guy in the funny pants out of the club championship match play tournament. On both occasions, Knickers had refused to shake his hand at the end of the round.

Clancy stood and yelled across the now full tavern. "Hey, Collins! How about we spruce up the bet a little between you and me. Let's make it a thousand cash." The room was suddenly so quiet that the birds outside could be heard.

Knickers grinned at the one local resident he despised. Clancy Schmidt was one of those guys that just didn't respect the game. During their matches, Knickers had often seen him nudge his ball into a better lie on the fairway or rough when he thought his opponent wasn't watching; strictly against the rules. Every time Clancy marked his ball on the green, it would wind up several inches closer to the hole when he replaced it. It had been no surprise to learn that Clancy had been forced into early retirement due to some "irregularities" in his business practices, a tidbit Harvey discovered on Google.

"I'll tell you what, Clancy," Knickers said across the room. "Let's you and I do better than that. If Jingles shoots sixty-five or better Friday, you strip naked and jog the whole course from the first tee to the eighteenth green right after the round. If Jingles doesn't do it, I'll do the same."

Everyone started to hoot and holler while watching Clancy for a response.

"Let me get this right," Clancy said. "You're going to strip to your skivvies and run the whole course?"

Knickers said, "Who said anythin' about skivvies? I'm talkin' bare to the bone, baby naked."

One old fellow immediately started to pound his table and shout. "Streaker! Streaker!"

Others immediately picked up the chant. The chaos in the Nineteenth Hole was unprecedented.

Clancy held up his hands in effort to quiet the place, but had to shout over the din. "I think that's illegal. I don't want you to have to break the law. Besides, I don't think you should be hurting everyone's eyes!"

Mulligan jumped to his feet in support of his playing partner. "Legal, shmegal! If the police show up, I'll tell them it's a sponsored Leisureville event!"

"And if there's a fine, I'll pay it for you," Knickers added.

"Everyone will just assume the streaker is senile," a man from the crowd yelled. Many shouted agreement.

Clancy stared at all the nodding heads in disbelief. They actually wanted to see Knickers streak the golf course? So be it. "I hope you won't mind if I decide not to take in the view."

"And I want you there for the whole round," Knickers added. "Watch Jingles closely to make sure he doesn't break the rules." He glared at Clancy in search of a reaction, but got none.

"I wonder what Jingles would have to say about all this," Harvey said, pointing to his friend, who was snoring softly and using the table for a pillow. "Looks like he had a little too much fun."

"How much did he drink?" Mulligan asked. "It's hard to tell because Nick took most of the empties."

"Maybe four or five beers," Knickers offered. "That many shots too. He was real thirsty today."

"He was entitled!" Mulligan said. "Now, let's get to you, oh knickered wonder that you are. Do you actually think Jingles can putt like that again on Friday? Nobody putts like that more than once in his life. Do you have an angle or do you just want to dangle?"

"Dangle," Harvey chuckled. "Are you an exhibitionist, Knickers?"

"Hell, no. My bare body wouldn't even get an R rating. I just have a feelin' we haven't seen the last of Jingles. He's a completely different man out there with his contacts. He musta have been playin' blind before."

"I honestly don't know what to think," Harvey said. "Betting all that bar money will put a lot of pressure on him."

Knickers took another long swallow of beer. "I don't think it matters. He barely knew we were on the course with him today. He was in another world."

"Look at it this way, Harv," Mulligan added. "You and I can't lose. Jingles either puts this place on its ear or bares Knickers' rear. That's a good day either way in my book!"

Harvey nodded happily, then dropped the smile. "We've got a problem! If Pat sees him like this . . . well, she can't see him like this, that's all there is to it." He scratched his head, considering the problem. "Let's take him to my house to sleep it off. Maybe Lucy will call Pat and say we all went out to lunch somewhere and we can take him home later."

"You can lie, Harvey, but Lucy can't," Mulligan said.

"Actually, lunch sounds good to me," Knickers said. "We'll take him to my house to sleep it off. My wife knows how to keep a secret."

"There you go," Harvey said. "I'll call Lucy and have her let Pat know! No tall tales."

By dinnertime, Ray realized that he was indeed alive. After a long shower, he took a couple Advil and chased them down with two aspirin before gargling mouthwash until his gums went numb.

When his friends, who had spent the entire afternoon playing Pinochle, assured him that he actually shot a sixty-two, his headache subsided.

"Thanks for everything, guys," he said. "It was the best day I can barely remember!"

When Ray dropped Harvey off at Sleepy Hollow, his friend grinned and quipped, "Want to come in for a cold beer?"

Ray forced a smile. "That's a kind offer. Oh, wait. Why not just whack me on the head with your driver and save a perfectly good beer?"

They both laughed, and Ray drove home to face the music. Before entering the house, he looked around the garage for a suitable hiding place for a contact lens case. There could be no risk of having her find it again. His life, as he wanted to know it, depended on that. He lifted the cover from his putter, sat the case atop its large metal head, and replaced the cover. Never in a million years!

Pat sat at the kitchen table, glaring at him, when he walked in the door. She looked as though she'd been there for hours.

"It's the most amazing thing," he said, walking over to the refrigerator, opening the door, and looking for nothing in particular. "My eyes have never been better!"

She said nothing.

He took out a bottle of cranberry juice and grabbed a glass from the cabinet, feeling her eyes on him all the while. "Would you like a glass?" he offered.

Still she was silent.

Ray walked over to her, removed his sunglasses, and knelt on the floor in front of her, which made him dizzy. "There, look at my right eye. It's just fine."

A tear appeared on his wife's left cheek. Another started to form under her right eye. "You scared me to death, Ray Plumlee! I get a call from Lucy and she tells me you'd gone off to lunch. I was sure they actually took you to the hospital or something . . . that something serious happened to your eye! You never just go off like that without calling me yourself! Never! I could only assume the worst, especially when the whole afternoon passed and I never heard a word."

If only she knew, he thought. "We were celebrating my round of golf. I shot a sixty-two. Can you believe it?" Pat was looking into his right eye, indifferent to the news.

"Listen, Pat, I shouldn't have taken the contact from your drawer, but I knew that I could use it without causing any problems. I put it in only when I putt and then . . . pfft, right back out. I know that you didn't want me to hurt myself and I love you for that. I just knew I could manage it and that I couldn't make you understand."

"Both your eyes are a little bloodshot," she said, concern wrinkling her forehead. "But your right eye does look much better than yesterday."

Ray kissed the tear on her right cheek. "Let's do something fun tomorrow. Tell me whatever you'd like to do and we'll do it!" She smiled in a way that told him he was off the hook.

The phone rang and Pat got up to answer. He never answered when she was home.

"Hello, the Plumlees," she said. "Yes, Emily."

Pat's smile did a complete flip flop. "Your husband saw Ray being what? *Carried out of the Nineteenth Hole?*"

Ray hustled straight to the garage. It was a perfect time to head for the practice green and put his lens to work. And maybe pick up a hamburger at the clubhouse too.

After putting, he hit three buckets of range balls before it got too dark to see where they landed. As many as a dozen people at a time gathered behind him to watch; that was a first. Word of his round was leaking out.

On the drive back to his house, he began reentry to the real planet Earth. Why couldn't Pat simply be happy for him? He played the round of his life and he celebrated too much. Big deal. All he did was doze off. What harm in that?

As soon as he walked into the kitchen, Pat rushed up and gave him a bear hug, squeezing the breath right out of him. He looked at her in disbelief

The Sweet Swing

while she led him to the table. A hot plate of spaghetti and meatballs sat beside a big tossed salad. It was his favorite meal.

"You'll excuse me if I don't offer you any wine," she said and actually giggled. He was speechless.

"Irv Wettman called right after you left." Among the women, only Bess Collins called Mulligan by his nickname. "When I told him you were gone, he said he called to check in on the world's greatest golfer.

"When I asked about what happened at the Nineteenth Hole, he told me everything."

Ray drew a deep breath. "Everything?"

"Yes. He said you were caught up in the moment, that you did something no one thought possible. He said you were Superman and your only kryptonite was drinking beer on an empty stomach!"

Leave it to Mulligan, he thought. All the women loved him. It wasn't just because he was an incredible ballroom dancer, which he certainly was. It wasn't about his natural charm, which he had in spades. It was all about what he did for his wife Mary. A dozen years ago, she had been diagnosed with breast cancer. Doctors in Chicago gave the bleak news that the disease had been discovered too late and there was no way to save her. Unconvinced, Mulligan sold his car dealership and took his wife on a worldwide odyssey in search of a cure. The search ended in Zurich, Switzerland, where doctors reported success with a new form of treatment. Two and a half years later, her cancer was in full remission. With most of a substantial fortune gone to medical expenses, they chose Leisureville as an affordable place to spend the rest of their lives together. In the eyes of the local women, Irv Wettman walked on water. The men were more than a little impressed too.

"He asked if we were going to the big dance on Saturday night," Pat said, begging with her eyebrows. "You know it's Leisureville's biggest dance of the year, right?"

"I'll tell you what," Ray said, eager to jump into the meal under his nose. "I'd absolutely love to be your escort to the dance. More than that, I am actually going to dance with you!"

On the few occasions Ray attended dances in the past, he spent the night rubbing elbows with Knickers, Harvey and other men while the women took turns doing the waltz, cha-cha or samba with Mulligan and other happy-footed men. Now, out of the blue, he felt like dancing himself!

Ray was playing one of the holes pictured on his sheets, the Island Par Three at Pebble Beach, when the ring of the phone woke him on Thursday morning. He picked up the clock and held it close to his face. 9:15.

Pat called him from the kitchen. "Are you awake in there? Tim Scott is on the phone for you."

Tim Scott? Didn't ring a bell. "Who is that?" he asked, rolling across the bed to where a phone stood on Pat's nightstand.

"He's the club pro, the new club pro," she called back.

Ray picked up. "Morning."

"Do I call you Ray or Jingles?" Scott said. "Irv Wettman says its Jingles now."

"You can call me anything you want after you helped me last week. Lying on my back at the practice range wasn't my best moment."

"Well, according to Mr. Wettman, yesterday was your best. He says you played the course in sixty-two." The pro knew Ray to be one of the top resident players and admired his smooth, uncomplicated swing, but the sixty-two had to be total bullshit. There was no shortage of bullshit in *Seizureville*.

"Maybe for the front nine," Ray joked.

"Right, right. Anyway, the reason I called is that I saw you guys didn't have a tee time today. I'm off too and wondered if you wanted to play Flowering Cactus with me. I've got free privileges if we start after one." He wanted to give the kind of lesson *he* enjoyed!

"Flowering Cactus! I've always wanted to play there!" *But never felt like I could afford it*, Ray thought.

"Well, let's do it then. I'll pick you up at twelve-thirty. What's your address?"

Tim Scott hung up, rolled over in his bed, and nuzzled the neck of his sleeping girlfriend. It was just good business. If Jingles Plumlee had suddenly become even half as good as Wettman said, he would get mileage out of word that he spent a full day giving him pointers.

Ray knew he had to accept the invitation. He had to! Flowering Cactus Country Club! The only problem was getting Pat's okay. Her heart was set on doing something together. There had to be a reasonable solution.

He got up and found her sweeping the sidewalk out front. Still in his underwear, he stuck his head outside. "Pat, there's a card on the bulletin board at the clubhouse that advertises ballroom dance lessons."

"I know," she said, looking up. "The lady that teaches lives a few blocks from here."

"Maybe she could come over the next couple of evenings and teach me a thing or two for Saturday night."

Pat dropped the broom. "That's the best idea ever! I'd like to learn more too. I'll come in and call her right now."

Within minutes, lessons were arranged for seven to nine the next two nights. The instructor would bring the music.

Ray waited what seemed like an appropriate amount of time, a half an hour or so, and hit his wife with the news of the offer to play Flowering Cactus with Tim Scott that afternoon. She readily okayed the plans! It was like taking candy from a baby!

Pat was proud of her husband's attempt at manipulation, amateurish as it was. After all, she taught him everything he knew on the subject over the past fifty years. Still, she had to chuckle. She knew so much more and was so much better at it. She had already planned to spend the afternoon shopping for a dress for the dance.

On the drive home from Flowering Cactus, Jingles was aglow. Tim Scott continued to question him about his unusual open putting stance. He had been asking about it through most of the round and even started to mimic it on the back nine.

Ray had been overwhelmed by the beauty and condition of the ritzy country club course. It was hard to imagine teeing off at Leisureville tomorrow after such an experience!

The men hadn't kept a scorecard, but Ray knew that he played the course in five under par. He beat the teaching pro by about seven strokes, but knew he could shave another few shots from his score if he had a second try at the layout. Naturally, he did most of the damage on the greens, where he rolled in lengthy putts all afternoon. The greens were a different grass than those at Leisureville and cut much closer. As a result, they were quick, especially in the late afternoon. The lumpy contour and speed of the greens had not made them more difficult, however, just more interesting.

His right eye seemed to have a mind of its own now. When he looked over a putt, the eye did the talking and his body just listened. Now it was even telling him exactly how hard to hit the ball. The message was conveyed directly to his shoulders without ever passing through his head! Pinger seemed to line up each putt without even checking with him.

His tee to green game was a revelation as well. The bump and run style that served so well on Leisureville's sparse fairways was less effective on a plush course, where the grass stopped a ball more quickly. He had adjusted by adding one more club for each approach shot; what had been a seven iron at Leisureville was a six at Flowering Cactus.

The only thing holding him back was distance, or, more accurately, his lack of it. There had been two par fours that Ray couldn't even reach with two solid shots! However, there was no remedy for no length at his age. Even Viagra couldn't help that.

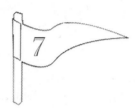

7

On this late October Friday, a few dozen of the senior residents gathered around the first tee of Leisureville's regulation course not long after dawn. A similar number sat in carts lined up on the path to the left of the first fairway. All had bundled up in sweaters and jackets to bear witness to the headline story in Leisureville, the sudden alleged golfing prowess of Jingles Plumlee.

News that a resident oldster carded a sixty-two on their treasured course had spread like wildfire. Most of the local golfers attributed their sizable handicaps to a view that the Leisureville layout was an uncompromising test of skill. The thought that the course could be conquered in so few shots was hard to fathom. That it could be done by a seventy-two-year-old seemed out of the question.

Most of the residents, sensing that Knickers Collins was pulling another prank, slept soundly. Even though it had been four years since salmon appeared in a local pond, the story was Leisureville lore. Someone had photographed the huge silver fish on the stringer, the large group of people fishing, and finally the crowd scattering wildly to avoid apprehension. Those photographs, blown up to twenty-by-twenty-four inches and framed, hung among others on the wall of the ballroom. The sleepers had no desire to be among those photographed at the first tee today. The picture was sure to be posted on the ballroom wall with a caption: Hundreds turn out to watch Jingles Plumlee break eighty. However, many thought it might be fun to turn out for the end of the round to watch Knickers Collins get naked.

The Sweet Swing

When someone in the group recognized Jingles approaching the tee in a cart driven by Harvey Green, the buzz began. While half of those present knew Plumlee, or at least that he was a two-time past champion, they all whispered the name *Jingles*. The nickname had spread right along with news of his "reported" accomplishment on Wednesday.

Harvey hit the brake when he saw the crowd. "What the heck is this?"

"Ouch!" Jingles yelped, as hot coffee spilled over his lap. He twitched in his seat as the brew penetrated his underwear. It was the wrong day to wear light green slacks.

Jingles took in the sight ahead and shook his head. "I think we can assume that Knickers' wager attracted a lot of takers. You know he's just trying to mess with me." *The people should be here,* he thought. *They are going to see something they never saw before! I left some strokes on that front nine Wednesday and I can do better than 62!*

"He's messing with me too!" Harvey said. "If you think I'm going to play in front of an audience like that, you can forget it."

"Let's just go along with it," Jingles said. "Let's wave at all the people and pretend that everything is perfectly normal. Knickers won't expect that."

Harvey stepped on the accelerator and drove to the tee. Mulligan burst out of the cluster to meet them.

"Can you believe this?" he said. "The Rip Van Wrinkled have risen from their slumber to come see you play, Jingles! And that means they'll be watching the rest of us too!"

The Rip Van Wrinkled, Jingles thought and grinned. He wished he came up with that. Mulligan should be doing stand-up comedy or something.

"They won't be watching me," Harvey announced. "I'll chauffer Jingles around the course like he did for me last week."

Jingles noticed a giant plywood scoreboard secured to the back of one of the golf carts. Someone went to a lot of trouble to paint a four-foot square replica of a Leisureville scorecard. A single golfer's name was written in neat block letters: Jingles.

Jingles stepped out of the cart and approached Knickers, who knelt beside the tee, flexing with his driver. He lifted his sunglasses, which were now as much a part of his wardrobe as his pants and shirt, and looked at Knickers eye to eye.

Knickers winked at him. "I know what you're thinkin', Jinglehopper. You're thinkin' I want to put some pressure on you. All I did was make a little wager. I have total faith in you and your new contact lenses."

"You really don't know what I'm thinking," Jingles returned. "I'm thinking how great it would be to see you prancing around naked. I might have to miss a putt on the last green and shoot sixty-six."

Knickers studied Jingles for a moment, weighing the significance of the inference that he could score sixty-five or better if he felt like it. Jingles had never been a braggart about anything . . . far from it. The Alaskan was a slice of humble pie. This was going to be interesting.

Knickers then noticed his friend's stained pants. "You aren't nervous are you? It sure looks like you are."

"It's coffee," Jingles said. "The best coffee I never drank."

Knickers walked to the tee and held the head of his driver in front of his mouth like a microphone. "Welcome, welcome, welcome," he bellowed.

The small crowd clapped enthusiastically and one of the men hollered, "It's supposed to be warm this afternoon! At least you won't catch cold running around naked!"

Knickers laughed and yelled back. "If you're going to see me naked, you'll have to follow me into the shower!"

Everyone laughed and the man yelled, "No, thank you."

The old ball player continued his introduction. "Leading off, our shortstop, Mayor Mulligan Wettman!"

Mulligan threw back his shoulders and walked to the tee, where he shook hands with Knickers and made an exaggerated bow to the congregation. After teeing his ball, he stepped back and took a practice swing.

"That's a first," Harvey whispered to Jingles.

Mulligan addressed his ball and let loose with a cut even more vicious than usual. He topped the drive and sent it bouncing down the fairway just thirty yards before it struck one of the red wooden blocks marking the ladies' tee and bounced right back toward him. It came to rest a mere six feet in front of him.

"Holy cow," Harvey whispered again. "That must be why he's called shortstop!"

Jingles looked in amazement. He never figured Mulligan to choke in front of a crowd, especially not *his* crowd. Then again, his first drive of the day was often a foul ball anyway.

Mulligan quickly put his hand in his pocket and touched the spare Titleist he always carried to the first tee. Just as quickly, he removed the hand and waved to everyone and laughed.

"Clearly," he yelled. "I am no Jingles Plumlee!" To Knickers alone, he whispered, "No mulligan today. You can just call me Irvin."

Knickers stepped between the markers, smacked a solid drive down the center of the fairway, and raised a hand to acknowledge the clapping. He wondered if this might be *his* day. Sixty-four more shots as great as that one and he could shoot sixty-five!

"And now," he hollered into the head of Big Bertha, "the man you have all come to see, and a man that can now see you! After getting contact lenses this week, he fired a sixty-two on this course on Wednesday. I was there. I saw it. I swear it on a stack of salmon!"

Most laughed and a few asked others what Knickers meant. Many wondered if this was an admission that it was all just another joke.

"The artist formerly known as Ray . . . Jingles Plumlee!"

As each person looks back upon his life, a mere handful of days or events can later be viewed as defining moments. They could be related to getting a job or a promotion, meeting the girl or boy of one's dreams, the birth of a child, the passing of a parent or other loved one; so many things, both euphoric and tragic. One thing they all have in common, however, is you rarely knew in advance how those events may ultimately impact your life. As Jingles stood above his ball, he sensed his round today would be one of those events. Somehow his life was never going to be quite the same. It was a sensational feeling.

He crushed his drive 235 yards down the center of the fairway and felt like *The Hulk*. He tipped his hat and went about his business with an ease only he understood.

On the tenth tee, Jingles looked at his huge scorecard on what turned out to be Harold Perkins' cart. The man in the straw hat had meticulously painted the score for each hole on the board. It was the five posted for the fourth hole that grabbed Ray's attention and caused his discontent. There had been a straightforward 140-yard approach to a pin directly in the center of the green and he caught a perfectly good lie, as he normally did. Unlike the carpet on a stairwell that is worn in the center, the middle of the Leisureworld fairways got the least amount of use. But out of the blue, he hit his seven iron more like 150, and buried his ball in a bunker behind the green. He never practiced sand shots because he rarely encountered them. After taking two shots to get free of the trap, he made bogey.

Jingles looked at the rest of his scores and scolded himself. He *was* a whiner! Through nine holes, he putted almost perfectly; just a single two-putt green and only two greens missed. Six birdies, two pars, and the one bogey added up to thirty-one on the front side.

Still, he could have scored lower. For whatever reason, he was hitting the ball further than in years. He nearly reached the 510-yard, par-five seventh green in two shots. From eight feet in front of the putting surface, he had a straight twenty-four-footer he may have drained with his putter if not for a dang divot! A golfer from the previous day chopped a chunk of turf and left a mess behind. He was forced to chip over the gouge and nearly made an eagle anyway.

An eagle! How could a person golf for twenty years, most every day for the past seven, without ever making a single eagle? Just ask Jingles! His three partners had probably made a couple dozen eagles between them. He knew that Knickers alone made five holes-in-one! Jingles witnessed three of them. Mulligan and Harvey each recorded a couple aces too. And then there was him; an eagle virgin at age seventy-two! Over the years, he had hit quite a few flagsticks from distance, but never had the pleasure of seeing his shot disappear into the cup. At least today had yielded a great opportunity.

Knickers was displaying his *A game* for the spectators, like a true professional. In front of a crowd that now numbered around three hundred, he carded a one under thirty-five, which was his best front nine in over a year, according to Harvey. He tipped his cap after every shot and smiled when Mulligan magically produced a supply of his rookie cards and disbursed them.

Mulligan's game was a wreck. He got into a running banter with a vocal spectator, actually his next door neighbor. The man kept chastising Mulligan for moving his feet in the middle of his swing. Mulligan, in turn, came up with dozens of places toward which the neighbor could start moving *his* feet if he didn't shut up. Still, Mulligan subconsciously tried to quiet his feet and his game went even further off track.

A true showman, however, Mulligan didn't let his score affect his performance. When it was clear that Jingles was on his game again, Mulligan made a show of looking at each of Jingles' putts and motioning how they would break. When Mulligan holed out from a bunker on the ninth, his only highlight, he feigned a heart attack and dramatically collapsed in the sand. Everyone laughed except the few that ran to assist him or called 911 on their cell phones. Even with that birdie, Mulligan totaled forty-one.

Harvey watched the entire spectacle, wondering how his own game would benefit when his contact lenses arrived next week. He had purchased new prescription glasses only two years ago, but hoped his eyesight had deteriorated badly since then. Unfortunately, the optometrist said the change in his vision was only slight. But at least there was hope.

As Jingles got set to take on the back nine, Harvey whispered, "If you can hold it together the rest of the way, you will win the bet no problem! I can't believe any of this. I feel like I should be asking for your autograph."

Jingles turned his attention to his friend, whose words triggered a wave of compassion. What must Harvey be thinking? How could the world change so dramatically almost overnight?

"I've been given the gift of amazing vision," Jingles said. "I'll tell you all about it after the round."

As the round progressed, more and more Leisurevillians found their way to the course, which became a fairground. Carts with signs advertising fresh baked goods, coffee or cold drinks for sale weaved their way along the crowded cart paths. The widow Thompson, owner of a fairway home along the dogleg thirteenth, set up a table in her yard to sell golf balls picked from her garden over the years. She had hundreds for $.25 each. Beside the fifteenth green, a couple set up a grill and sold sausages and hamburgers. The aroma was overwhelming and even the golfers stopped for an early lunch. The chefs insisted that Jingles eat for free.

Many decided the long trip around the golf course was a perfect occasion to take their dog or dogs for a walk. Over the years, the number of canines in the development had seemingly surpassed the number of residents. In the original bylaws, one dog or cat was permitted per household. Eventually, that limit was extended to two for "humanitarian" reasons; no pet should be forced to live alone. However, when Mary Wettman decided to bring a third Scottish Terrier under her roof, her husband engineered still another change to the rules.

Jingles and Pat had a preference for Labrador retrievers after living with a series of them throughout their years in Alaska. However, the bylaws limited the size of dogs to what amounted to tiny so that none would serve as lunch for another. There was also fear that larger dogs might create unwanted speed bumps with their excrement. Therefore, the Plumlees went without a pet.

With so many dogs towing people, the yapping was predictable. The little dogs pulled on their leashes and barked at one another. Owners of the dogs barked at other people's dogs to behave, which triggered barks of reprimand from their owners, who told them to yell at their own dogs, which in turn many were accustomed to doing anyway.

One cockapoo broke free and snatched Mulligan's *Titleist* from the fairway and took off with it. Mulligan chased the dog in vain while the owner scolded him for getting the dog too excited.

By the time the parade reached the final green, all agreed it was Leisureville's finest hour. Seemingly the entire community surrounded the round stage to watch what would surely be Jingles' last putt of the day, a twelve-footer for still another birdie.

"The dance floor belongs to you," Knickers said to him. "You are the primo ballerino!"

Jingles looked at the crowd around him through his right eye, which allowed him to take in every detail of every expression. They all loved him, or at least his golf. He could feel it in their eyes, the upturned curl of their lips. Those who didn't particularly care about his golf score simply appreciated that he brought the whole community together on an otherwise routine morning.

However, there was one person in particular he didn't see. "Knickers, where's Clancy Schmidt? Isn't he supposed to be performing in a few minutes?"

"He disappeared on about the fourteenth hole," Knickers said with a wry smile. "Hopefully, he went to put his house on the market. Everybody knows about the bet."

Jingles wasn't surprised, just a little disappointed. "That's too bad. I figure most of these people are here to see somebody get naked."

Jingles noticed that Bess, Mary and Lucy stood together, holding hands. He wondered where Pat could be. She had to know what was going on at the golf course.

He got his answer when the crowd separated to allow his wife to come forward. She was pushing their neighbor from across the street, Kat Kelso, in her wheelchair. Pat looked at her husband, the throng of people around the green, and back to him. She raised her eyebrows and hands in disbelief.

Jingles took an extra practice stroke without knowing why. He found he did best when he didn't think too much. Tuning out the talking, the barking, and all the motion and commotion around him, he saw only the few feet of grass and a cup that looked big enough to swallow him. After waiting for a ladybug to pass out of his line, he put shot number sixty of the morning in the hole.

Jingles walked to his wife to catch the ceremonial first kiss and got the second from Mrs. Kelso. He then hurried through the cluster of well-wishers to Birdie Chaser to remove his right contact, which had started to bother him.

Harvey took his now customary seat behind the wheel and hugged his friend. "Unbelievable doesn't begin to describe it, Jingles! Twenty putts! That's it." Jingles noticed that Harvey's hands were shaking; his friend was more excited than he!

A roar erupted from the crowd as Harold Perkins dashed onto the green wearing nothing but his straw hat. He waved at all his neighbors, encouraging them to join him, then took off down the fairway.

The throng's reaction seemed more of delight than shock, which prompted Jingles to ask Mulligan why he wasn't following Harold's lead.

Mulligan always had a ready response. "If everybody saw how much my junk has shrunk, I'd never get elected again."

"Well," Harvey said with a straight face, "there's always the sympathy vote."

A half dozen of the other men did accept the odd invitation, at least to the extent of stripping to their underwear, and took off after Harold. Even a white-haired lady decided to join the exhibition in her bra, underwear and

The Sweet Swing

support hose. Her jog lasted only ten yards before she lost her breath and broke into a walk.

Mulligan busied himself forming a reception line to Birdie Chaser. Everybody wanted to greet Jingles and nobody wanted the party to end.

A boom box on the front seat of Knickers's cart, just a few yards away, started to blare the song *Zippity Doo Dah*. *My oh my, what a wonderful day, plenty of sunshine headed my way, zippity doo dah, zippity aye.*

Jingles watched as Bess Collins, the culprit, cranked up the volume even more. People all around him started singing along with the lyrics.

"*Mr. bluebird's on my shoulder,*"

"More like bluebirdies, right Jingles?" Harvey said, leaning close.

It's true, it's actual, everything is satisfactual.

It certainly is, Jingles thought, and started shaking hands and absorbing flattery.

The next song on the playlist was "When You Wish Upon a Star." Obviously, Bess was a Walt Disney buff. "*When you wish upon a star, makes no difference who you are, anything your heart desires, will come to you.*"

Jingles got teary listening to the words. Had he wished upon a star? Was it stardust in his right eye? How in the world could this be happening?

If your heart is in your dreams, no request is too extreme.

Knickers was in the Nineteenth Hole with a free beer in his left hand and a phone book in his right. He fired a seventy-one, his best round in recent memory, and lost by eleven strokes! He wanted to call Jingles' optometrist and make an appointment right now.

Pat informed her husband she was heading home with Kat and would see him at the house for lunch. Before departing, she took in the scene around her one last time. Hundreds of people were dancing on the grass, singing and laughing. *Wasn't the big dance supposed to be on Saturday night?* She shook her head the entire six-block walk back home, trying to understand the overwhelming reaction.

Jingles turned down a dozen offers of cold beer and settled for sweet iced tea. When he realized that some of the residents were congratulating him for the second or third time, he decided the party should end, at least for him.

Harvey stepped out of Birdie Chaser at Sleepy Hollow and watched his very popular friend start to drive away. He stopped him with a holler. "Maybe you should consider changing Birdie Chaser's name!"

"To what?" Jingles asked. "Birdie Catcher?"

"Close," Harvey said, dazzled at how close Jingles came to guessing his answer. "I was thinking of Dream Catcher. Golfers half our age only dream of doing something like that and you just showed a bunch of old folks that anything is possible. Age doesn't have to be a deterrent. I think that's a big part of what has everyone so excited."

Jingles thought about his friend's observation and suddenly felt conflicted. It was a defective right contact lens doing the lion's share of the work for him. He was just lucky to have it.

Or was it not simply luck but destiny instead? Should fate be questioned? Perhaps there was a reason that the mysterious lens found its way to his eye. That thought soothed him, even satisfied him. You don't have to apologize for winning the lottery, do you?

Jingles studied Harvey's face for a moment and said, "I just want you to know that it was the last round I'm going to play without you. I'll do anything to get you back on the tee, even change my name back to Ray!"

Harvey shook his head and chuckled. "I think it's too late. Jingles isn't going away any time soon. Everybody loves the name." *And you*, he thought.

Jingles went down for a nap after lunch and slept three full hours. When he rose and walked into the kitchen, he wondered if he might be sleeping still! The table was covered with bottles of liquor and wine, each with a card attached or sitting beneath it. Fifteen bottles? Maybe more. The long kitchen counter was full of great-looking baked goods including frosted cakes, some with the name Jingles, some with the big number 60, others with both, and cupcakes and cookies galore, enough to keep a bakery in business for a day. The pies, with aromas that permeated the house and the surrounding block, included apple, peach, blueberry, chocolate, and coconut cream. The booty extended into the dining room, where a half dozen flower arrangements graced the table. Most appeared to be handpicked from some of the many lovely gardens that residents faithfully attended.

Pat stood amidst it all, talking on the phone. "Yes, Mrs. McCory, we love the flowers your husband brought over." Pat looked at her husband, shrugged her shoulders, and listened.

"Yes, we'd love to come over for dinner some evening. I'll call you next week and we'll set a date. Thank you so much for calling." She put down the phone and started to write herself a reminder. Before she finished, the phone rang.

Jingles looked at the bottles on the table and opened one of three Crown Royal boxes. He didn't drink much hard stuff, but liked the distinctive blue velvet bags that covered the fancy bottles.

Walking over to the counter, he picked up a chocolate chip cookie and sampled it. Nice. Real nice. He grabbed another but Pat cleared her throat and shook her head.

He started looking at the cards that accompanied the celebratory gifts. There were names that he recognized and far more that he didn't.

Pat concluded her conversation, jotted another note, and pulled the phone plug from the wall. "People have been parading to our front door for the last two hours and the phone has been ringing all afternoon, Mister Popularity. I disconnected the one in the bedroom so you could sleep. I planned on calling the kids this afternoon to tell them about your big day but haven't had time to make even one call. People from all over Leisureville are now anxious to socialize with us. We're at the top of the A list!"

Jingles hugged her. "Don't worry. I'm sure I'm just the flavor of the day. People will forget about it before you know it." *He hoped that wasn't true!*

"I don't know," Pat said, kissing his cheek. "It's like you are President of the United States or something."

He kissed her back. "Oh, I don't know about that. What president ever came close to shooting a sixty?"

She laughed and shoved him away. "How in the world are you playing golf like that? It's ridiculous!"

"I've tried to tell you how many times now?"

"I know, I know. The difference now is that you have my attention."

He thought for a moment about how to best describe what he saw through the odd lens, but hesitated. Wouldn't her knowledge of how easy the game had become somehow diminish his accomplishment in her eyes . . . in everyone's eyes? That didn't seem right, or even fair. It was him swinging the club and making the most of good fortune.

The doorbell chimed and Pat went off to the door. A moment later she summoned Jingles to the entry. "These are the Conwells. Samantha and Herb."

He recognized them from the reception line beside the final green. Herb held out still another bottle of Crown Royal. "Please come in."

When they stepped inside, Samantha looked into the kitchen and all the goods on display. "I see we're not the first to thank you for all the happiness you brought to Leisureville today."

"People are very gracious here," Pat said. "I plan on taking all the sweets to the dance tomorrow night. Will you two be attending?" They said that they would be there.

"Heck," Jingles added. "I should be the one saying thank you for all the support I had out there this morning. It was the best round of my life."

Herb walked into the kitchen and put his gift with the other bottles. "That was the best round of anybody's life. I've never seen anything like that, Jingles. I watch the golf channel all the time and I've never seen anybody come close to making every putt like that."

"I missed that thirty-five footer on twelve," Jingles said, recalling the slight push with a twinge of regret.

"You were amazing," Samantha said. "Even out of this world amazing. Our grandson is coming to visit over Thanksgiving. He's a freshman in high school and wants to try out for the golf team. We were wondering if you could give him some pointers when he's here."

"Wow, that would be an honor! I can hardly wait. Just give me a call when he's ready. We're having company ourselves over the holiday but I'm sure there will be an hour or two that works for everybody."

There was another knock on the front door and the Conwells excused themselves. They were replaced by Tim Scott, the pro.

Tim shook his hand and kissed Pat's. "Well, I caught a few holes of your round with everyone else this morning, Jingles. That's what I call kickin' ass."

He quickly looked at Pat. "Please excuse my language."

She smiled at his concern and laughed inside. She grew up in a town full of commercial fishermen. At least half their nouns and all of their adjectives were *real* profanity. "Ass" without a profane adjective preceding it would be considered wimpy.

He handed Jingles a bag with a box of new Titleists and some fancy head covers. "These are a gift from the club. By the way, I understand that the bar and restaurant did record business today."

"Can't thank you enough," Jingles said.

"I was wondering," Scott added. "Do you think you'd be interested in working for me giving lessons?" He had a dozen requests for lessons from Jingles already and knew he could put him to work at least twenty hours a week if he was willing.

Pat was suddenly alert. "What does that pay? Would he get paid by the hour?"

"Of course. Lesson fees get split with the club, but I think your husband could clear thirty an hour, no problem."

Pat did the math on twenty hours a week. *Very interesting.*

She squeezed her husband's arm and he got the message. "That sounds promising," he said.

"You could probably even give Mrs. Beckerman some lessons," Scott said with a laugh.

"Her lessons would be free," Jingles said. "I have her to thank for the turnaround in my game. My friends think that knock on the head jarred my brain and changed everything."

"Well, think about it over the weekend and let me know on Monday. I'll start scheduling you some afternoon hours on Tuesday if you like."

"I'll find you on Monday and let you know," Jingles said, and bid farewell.

Pat guided her husband to a chair by the kitchen table and sat next to him. "Even a few hundred a month would make a huge difference for us. I

The Sweet Swing

think you should do it. Besides, you've been talking about wanting to help people."

"Teaching is an art in itself, Pat. I'm going to have to sleep on the idea for a couple nights."

"Oh," she said, remembering a call from Knickers. "The Collinses invited us to a barbecue at their house tonight with the Wettmans and Greens. I told him about our dance lessons and that we were sorry."

Sorry wasn't the word for it, he thought. "Taking dance lessons was a good idea. Telling Knickers about it was another story. I'm going to pay for that."

"Oh, stop it," Pat scolded. "Knickers needs to grow up. I'm going to tell him so."

Good luck with that, Jingles mumbled to himself, remembering the very words she had directed at him a few days ago. "Let's either eat pie for dinner or go out to a restaurant."

"Why don't you go pick us up some Chinese or something," Pat said. "I have forty or fifty *Thank You* notes to work on, thanks to you."

The foxtrot and cha-cha lessons with their neighbor Sheila proved tolerable for Jingles. It was a cool, comfortable night and the back terrace served as a suitable dance floor. Not a single neighbor complained about the music. Looking into his wife's sparkling brown eyes as they moved under Sheila's supervision, Jingles felt guilty. She loved to dance so much and he had always been too stubborn or self-conscious to give it an honest effort. Now anything seemed possible. It was a matter of confidence. Almost overnight, he was turning into a different man altogether. Pat seemed to like the new guy and he did too.

In the kitchen, Pat pulled the checkbook from her purse and asked the teacher how much she was due. Sheila explained that her normal rate was $20 an hour for a total of four hours, but, seeing all the liquor on the kitchen table, she offered to take payment in-kind. The deal was consummated with the four bottles of Crown and a tip in the form of a medium-size chocolate cake.

Pat reconnected the phone for the first time in several hours and it rang immediately. She sighed and answered. A moment later she called out, "You aren't going to believe this! Jane Friend from *Newswatch* wants to talk to you!"

Jingles walked quickly to the kitchen and made Pat repeat what she said.

"Hel . . . lo," he said into the phone, his voice cracking.

"Am I calling too late, Jingles? Were you sleeping?" she asked.

It was indeed *the* Jane Friend. He'd know that voice anywhere. He wasn't sure how she could actually smile with her voice, but Jane did it six nights a week from six to six-thirty.

As far as he knew, the entire Phoenix area population regularly watched her anchor the news. At the ripe old age of twenty-eight, she was an institution.

"No, it's not too late at all," he said. "We watched your show tonight while we had dinner. It was great."

Pat whispered into his spare ear. "Tell her I loved her hair tonight."

Jane said, "Well, I want you to know that I've been calling for a couple of hours and just now got through to you. Your phone has been busy."

Or disconnected, he thought. "My wife wants you to know that your hair looked great tonight." Actually, Jingles remembered it himself. It was swept into a bun on the side. Jane was a regular fashion model for sure.

"Well, tell her thanks! I try not to be boring. Anyway, I got an e-mail late this afternoon with a photo album attached. Apparently you are quite the sensation over in Leisureville!"

"Who sent you an e-mail?" he asked, and immediately worried he may have been impolite.

"It was a Mary Wettman. Evidently her husband has been your golf partner for a number of years."

"Yes, her husband Mulligan is one of my best friends."

She cracked up on the other end of the line. "Mulligan, you say? His name is Mulligan?"

"His name is Irvin. Mulligan is just a nickname."

"Is Jingles your real name or a nickname too?"

"Everyone is calling me Jingles, even though I don't like it. My name is Ray."

"Would you mind if I call you Jingles? I have to tell you, I *love* that nickname."

"Well, if you like it, Jane, that would be fine with me." He decided that if she liked Jingles, that's exactly who he would be from now on. He didn't feel like the old Ray Plumlee anyway.

"So tell me, Jingles. How does a young man like you go from being a four or five handicapper to shooting scores like sixty in the blink of an eye?"

Jingles laughed at her choice of the words, *in the blink of an eye*. "If you saw pictures, you probably know I'm not young. I'll be seventy-three in February."

"Okay, you caught me. I knew you were seventy-two, but I don't think you are feeling that age right now."

"Between you and me, I've never felt better in my life. After wearing glasses for over forty years, I got contacts this week and they changed everything. No one can fully appreciate how well I can see."

"That may be, Jingles. At the same time, everyone in Leisureville appreciates how well you can golf. After tomorrow night, I'd like everyone in Arizona to appreciate it too."

"What do you mean?"

"I'd like to come over to Leisureville tomorrow morning with a camera crew. We'll tape some of the action, talk to a few of the locals, and put together a little feature for the end of *Newswatch* tomorrow night. Are you game?"

"Are you sure you don't have more important stories to cover?"

She laughed. "That's a good one. Tomorrow night's special feature was going to be the Phoenix Dog Show. I think it can wait until Monday. Your story is an original."

"Today was a dog show here. There must have been a couple hundred of them following us around the course."

"No way! I wish I could have seen that."

"I have a feeling that you will. Drive safely!"

"I promise. We'll find you on the course at about ten. Good night, Jingles." Jane closed her cell phone and smiled. He told her to drive safely. Totally cute.

From the moment she read Mary Wettman's e-mail, the Jingles story had been on her mind. The last photo was a close-up of the big scorecard totaling sixty. Over half her show's demographic, 56 percent, was sixty-five and older. When was the last time they had their own sports hero? Tomorrow was sure to be fun.

Pat had listened to the entire conversation on the bedroom phone. Because Alaska Standard Time made it an hour earlier there, she had time to call each of her children with the day's surprising news. Ray was going to be on television!

Over two thousand miles away, in New York City, *eaglevision* inventor Karl Zimmer reclined on the king-sized bed in his twentieth floor hotel room, watching a very late night movie. This was an exciting time for the German, and sleep didn't come easily. The Big Apple was a fabulous city for people of means, and he planned on being wealthy very soon. Within days, over a month before the expiration date of his option, he would notify Herman Winston that the $15,000,000 payment for his option would be forthcoming on December first.

The seven weeks that had passed since Karl walked out of Eagle Optics for the last time had been a blur of activity. While he was supremely confident that the major corporations in the optics field would be blown away by his new lens and would line up for the chance to buy the technology,

113

he wanted to avoid yielding control to others if at all possible. And of course there was the financial aspect. Why should he be shortchanged on the potential payoff by selling out? He had hired a financial consultant to review his options.

Karl had decided that finding an investment banker was his best choice and worth a quick try. The payoff would be the start of his own company, Zimmer Optics. Despite cautionary words from the consultant, Karl decided that he would give that search a month before taking his research, The Status and Future of Eaglevision, to other well established companies.

The idea that tilted the process in Karl's favor came in asking his consultant to find a prominent investment banker with a passion for pool or billiards. If he could *show* the lens in action to appreciative eyes, perhaps ears, and hopefully a giant wallet, would open.

Mark Sherman of Sherman Macpherson in New York City met the criteria. He couldn't resist an offer to witness what was promised to be a mind-boggling pool exhibition. Karl flew all the way across the country for a lunch date with Sherman at a private club on Madison Avenue.

Once Karl chalked his cue, his lens took over. In nearly six weeks since that day, Karl had not left New York. His project was at the top of Sherman's priority list and the financier didn't want the inventor out of his sight. Over the last month, Karl's aided vision was tested by an entire battery of optometrists. His research was forwarded to top research scientists for confidential review, after which he fielded their questions in teleconference after teleconference at the investment firm offices.

The plan for *eaglevision* now entailed organizing and incorporating Zimmer Optics over the next ninety days. Sherman MacPherson would provide $30 million in funding, half of that to satisfy the option obligation and the rest for operating funds deemed sufficient to get the lens through the FDA approval process. Other experts concurred with Karl's suggestion that approval should take no more than a year.

Zimmer Optics would initially be owned equally by Karl and the investment banker. Upon government approval of its product, Sherman MacPherson would take the company public in an IPO to capitalize the cost of commercial development and hopefully make a fortune for both the banker and the client.

With his eyes finally heavy, Karl turned off the television and crawled under the covers next to his wife, who was having no difficulty sleeping. America was all he hoped it would be after all.

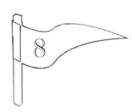

On TV Saturday, Jingles gazed up wistfully at a cloud-heavy sky that threatened to ruin everything. On the way to the course, Harvey reported a 40 percent chance of rain by midday. Would Jane Friend even be making the trip?

Only a handful of residents milled around the first tee, and a few more lingered along the fairway. Harold Perkins, now fully clothed, had crafted a second identical scoreboard overnight and attached it to the rear of his cart. Actually, it was not quite identical. All four of the golfers' names were listed now. Jingles had called him and suggested the addition after Jane Friend announced her intentions last night. He could only imagine how disappointed the others may have been with yesterday's slight; after all, they were the Foursome.

The arrival of Birdie Chaser was greeted with a smattering of applause and Knickers and Mulligan walked over to greet them. Mulligan wore a blaze orange shirt and trousers that almost matched and his partner had on a yellow shirt and a loud pair of plaid knickers with stockings the same color as the shirt. Knickers even sported a fresh haircut.

"I'm going to try playing today," Harvey announced. "Jingles bribed me with homemade cookies."

"Glad to hear it," Mulligan said. "But I'll warn you right now, the back nine is going to be a circus. Jane Friend has even more admirers than Jingles."

Jingles had dressed in all black, a tribute to his all-time favorite pro, Gary Player. "And let me guess," Jingles said. "Everyone in Leisureville knows Jane is coming."

"Leisureville and beyond," Mulligan answered. "It's in everyone's interest to put our fine community on the map. You know, property values and so forth. And hell, everyone wants to be on television!"

Knickers looked at Jingles' attire. "You look like you're goin' to a funeral, Fred Astaire."

"Yeah, our funerals," Mulligan said, glancing at Knickers. "You'll be dancing on our graves, Jingles! We aren't even worthy of playing with you anymore. When it comes to the ballroom, though, you can't take enough lessons to keep up with me!"

Jingles knew that was true. The women lined up to waltz and tango with Mulligan. The dance ran from 8:00 p.m. until midnight, and Mulligan only sat when the little orchestra took a break.

Harvey shook Knickers' hand. "Your stock is headed for twenty-six million. They're forecasting good Christmas sales."

"Well, I have a little announcement to make about that," Knickers said. "I would have told you guys last night, but Jingles wasn't there." He shot Jingles a quick glance, a reprimand for missing the barbecue. "I filed paperwork yesterday to transfer a little over a million in stock to Hidden Valley Community College. That's where my son was enrolled to play baseball and maybe go to some classes too."

Knickers and Bess had given birth to a single child, Mickey Jr. As the men knew and never talked about, the eighteen-year-old was a promising baseball player, a catcher like his dad. His life ended on senior prom night when the car in which he was a passenger left the highway and struck a power pole.

"I've been talking to them for some time about upgrading their baseball facilities. They are going to put in shaded bleachers, a new scoreboard, a clubhouse so that players have access to lockers and showers on site, and new fencing around the whole facility. Oh yeah, and one more thing: A big sign over the scoreboard that says Mickey Collins Jr. Memorial Field."

The other men were quiet for a moment and lowered their heads in respect.

"That is just wonderful," Jingles finally said. "I am so happy for you and Bess." The idea of Knickers giving back to the game he loved seemed touchingly appropriate.

"It was the smart move financially too," Harvey pointed out. "By donating the stock itself, you pay no taxes on the appreciated value, which is huge. The whole thing is a charitable donation." Harvey quickly calculated the donation to be roughly 4 percent of Knickers' wealth.

"That's what the school's attorney said," Knickers added. "Anyway, all the improvements will be finished in less than four months."

Mulligan said, "Let's make plans to attend the first game on the new field!"

Knickers yanked the driver from his bag. "Hey, let's just play golf . . . if Jingles can take a break from his dance lessons!"

By the time the men finished the front nine, the crowd had grown to double the size of the previous day. Residents had invited friends from the surrounding area and the parking lot overflowed. Cars now lined the streets for several blocks around the course.

The pending television coverage had energized the spectators too. Many created homemade signs that were mounted on carts or held like mini-billboards. Most were a tribute to senior citizens and Jingles was the poster boy.

"Which is your favorite sign?" Mulligan asked the others, proud of how well his wife had publicized the day.

"Jingles' Bell Rocks is my choice," Knickers said, pointing to a lady near the tee. "A few minutes ago there was one sign like that, now there are three or four."

"Getting Old Is No Handicap, Just Ask Jingles. That has to be the best," Harvey offered.

Jingles thought the funniest was the Lucy Green creation. As he stood on the tee, surveying the crowd, he saw her holding a sign that said: Jingles is like fine wine.

When she knew he was looking, she flipped it over. The opposite side said: Jingles is like fine whine. An inside joke.

However, new creations were popping up so frequently it was hard to judge the best. Who's your granddaddy? Age seventy-two, score sixty. Jingles all the way. He's Plumlee, not Prunelee. Old time rock and roll. Welcome to Jinglesville.

Mulligan had risen to the occasion today and played consistently. In fact, he played so well at near even par that he didn't feel a need to fool around like yesterday. However, he did take advantage of the opportunity to sign his autograph for a few of the seniors that didn't know one golfer from the other.

Knickers was in his element. Discipline and focus were no problem for a man who played the most challenging position on a baseball diamond for so many years. The noisy fans weren't a distraction; they were motivation. He carded a one-over thirty-seven at the turn.

Harvey had decided to withdraw from the play after six holes, again choosing to join the spectators. His partner golfed like a pro and he didn't want to miss a thing.

Jingles' game seemed to be settling into a pattern in Harvey's eyes. If he put an approach shot within thirty or maybe even thirty-five feet of the cup, it was an automatic birdie. He had done that four times on the front nine. He had come amazingly close to holing a couple longer putts too.

Harvey had never been around many people that wore old-style rigid contact lenses, at least that he really noticed. Watching Jingles struggle with his, always taking them in and out, constantly squirting them, he was glad to have ordered the more comfortable soft and disposable kind.

Jingles tightened up his iron play on the back nine, sticking four straight approaches within *his* "automatic" range, resulting in four birds. Harvey wondered if even the record score of sixty would stand.

However, a five iron on number 14 took a wicked bounce in front of the green and kicked to the right fringe, leaving Jingles all of forty-five feet for a birdie.

Harvey pointed toward the green as he drove. "There they are! The WAZA news crew!"

Jingles watched as a cameraman set up a tripod a couple yards behind his ball. Another climbed atop a golf cart with his camera.

As Birdie Chaser drew closer, Jingles popped his putting lens onto his right eye and looked at the lovely and famous face of Jane Friend. She wore her hair in old-fashioned pigtails, perhaps for the old-fashioned crowd gathered closely around her. Her eyes settled on the scorecard on the far side of the green and she nodded approvingly.

"I hope she likes my score so far," Jingles said to Harvey.

"You hope she likes it?" his partner said in disbelief. "Have you lost your mind? Every golfer in the world would love to have your score! Personally, I'd give practically everything I own to play like you for even one day! I'd sell my soul if anyone would buy it."

Jingles wasn't sure what to say. Again, he failed to consider the others. None of his partners showed any signs of jealousy, at least not outwardly. They seemed to take his transformation as merely a result of getting contacts; that somehow a supreme talent had been unleashed. He favored that assessment himself and tried his best to accept it. Still, in the back of his mind, there was that nagging knowledge that without the bubble lens he was basically . . . them. He tried to tune out the back of his mind.

Harvey continued, "One week ago, Jingles didn't even exist. I mean the man did, but not the name and not the legend. After the news show tonight, your name will be on the lips of millions! Smell the roses, friend. You'll

The Sweet Swing

probably even make this impossible putt and nobody will be surprised . . . especially not you!"

Jingles stepped from Birdie Chaser to the loudest applause of the day, and pulled Pinger from the bag with the flourish of a black knight pulling his mighty sword from its scabbard.

Passing Harvey, he whispered, "I'd give myself no better than a fifty-fifty chance of making this putt." He lifted his sunglasses, seemed to wink and walked off.

Harvey shook his head. The best golfers in the world make forty-five-footers about what, 2 percent of the time? *He figures he's got an even chance.*

For Harvey, there was now no earthly explanation for Jingles' performance. He had been thinking about that and nothing else for the past few days. Corrected vision could explain a few strokes of improvement for sure. But shooting close to sixty for what looked to be three straight rounds? No way. Pro golfers make only one of five putts from twenty feet. Jingles made every single one! It was one thing to be hot for a single round. *He was doing it day after day*!

Jingles walked to his ball, ignoring everything else. He stepped off the distance to the pin and came up with forty-four feet. Returning to his ball, he saw a line that amounted to a three-foot break from right to left. He looked from the ball to a single blade of grass at the center of the cup and back, took two practice strokes, and focused on a long follow-through. For the most part, Pinger seemed to align itself.

His Titleist was just halfway to the target when he knew. He raised his putter triumphantly in the air and started walking after the ball, which found the hole during his fifth step. *Just another drop in the bucket.*

The massive gathering roared approval, shook signs in the air, and pumped withered fists. Dozens of women blew kisses toward the hero.

The cameraman behind Jingles looked anxiously toward the second cameraman, hoping he got a better view of the entire shot. The old golfer had stepped right in front of his lens and obscured the sight of the ball dropping into the hole. He got a thumbs up from his co-worker.

Standing next to Knickers, Mulligan slapped himself on the side of face. "It's official! I have now seen everything!"

Knickers stroked his chin and said, "He's got a set of balls like watermelons."

The next two holes were proof of golf's challenge, even to Jingles. He missed a nearly straight twenty-seven-footer on 15 that curled around the cup and refused to drop. On 16, he shot straight for a pin concealed behind a bunker instead of playing safely to the open side of the green. He failed to clear the trap by a foot and settled for par there also.

On 17, the par three, he dropped a lofted four iron within inches of the cup and it rolled just three feet from the flag for a tap-in bird. The timing couldn't have been better for his best shot ever on the hole.

It all ended on 18 with a no-brainer from twenty-five feet. His score was sixty-one. Jingles had no complaints.

Bess fired up her boom box again, this time with Jingle Bell Rock. Boisterous, rejuvenated residents danced and put on a show for the cameras and each other. Seniors that had been neighbors for years and never met, hugged each other. Countless dogs howled and yapped.

A man from the crowd ran up to the foursome with a Leisureville scorecard on which he recorded Jingles' sixty-one. He asked all of the group to sign it.

Recognizing a good idea, others ran to the clubhouse to get scorecards of their own to fill in and present for signatures. Some of the cards had the day's score of sixty-one, others were reproductions of yesterday's record sixty. They copied those from the original Perkins' scoreboard that still rested against the side of the pro shop.

Jane and her crew recorded comments from Jingles and his playing partners after leading each to an area away from the commotion. Less than half an hour after the round ended, Jane waved good-bye and told everyone to tune into the night's show. She left carrying all kinds of gifts from her fans and wearing a Leisureville jacket.

Pat invited Jingles' golf group and their wives for dinner and the *Newswatch* program before the dance. Mary brought her famous sausage lasagna, Bess baked fresh bread, and Lucy tossed a salad. Wine and desserts were Pat's contributions. Her kitchen overflowed with both.

"Holy smokes," Mulligan said, checking out the alcohol covering the kitchen table. "You're set for years!"

"Most of it came yesterday," Jingles said. "Still more rolled in this afternoon. I was answering the door and phone calls from the moment I got home. We have the phone off now so we can enjoy dinner and the news. It's been a madhouse!"

Knickers picked up a bottle of his favorite scotch. "Can we open this one?"

Jingles said, "I've got one open in the liquor cabinet. You can take that one home with you. You can all take whatever you want."

Harvey grabbed a bottle of Old Grand-dad and pulled a pen from his shirt pocket. "This is the one that bit you on Wednesday. Could you autograph the label for me?"

Jingles scribbled "with love from Jingles." He was getting used to signing that name. He must have written it five hundred times after the morning round.

At six o'clock, everyone assembled in the den in front of the giant flat screen television, a group gift from the children for their last anniversary. Jingles sensed everyone shared his excitement.

They didn't have to wait long for some coverage. *Newswatch* opened with a side view of Jingles stroking the long birdie putt from just off the fourteenth green. It showed him celebrating the birdie while the ball was still twenty feet from the cup! He didn't realize he'd done that. The scene switched to the crowd and the signs, settling on Plumlee, Not Prunelee.

"Where did your limp go?" Knickers wondered. "You hardly limped when you chased after that putt."

"It's a medical miracle," Jingles laughed.

Jane's voice said there was a very special sports story tonight that viewers would have to see to believe. The screen showed a close up of the huge scorecard with the sixty.

"His name is Jingles Plumlee. His age is seventy-two. And his story is coming up at the end of the show! Welcome everyone, to the Saturday edition of *Newswatch*!"

Jingles listened jubilantly as everyone else talked at the same time.

"I think I saw Lucy with her Fine Wine sign," Bess said excitedly.

"Me too," Lucy said. "I think I saw me too!"

"That was me holding the pin," Mulligan said.

Knickers laughed. "Yeah, you made the pin look ten feet tall!"

"I recognized so many of the people," Mary added. "This is so exciting!"

"Just think of it," Harvey observed. "It was a monumental event. When have you ever seen so many senior citizens look so excited and happy."

"I'm surprised Harold Perkins kept his pants on today," Mulligan snickered.

"I can't wait to get to the dance," Pat said. "Everyone is going to be in high spirits tonight."

They all waited patiently as Jane waded through the day's local news and the weatherman did his thing. It didn't look like any rain would materialize after all.

Finally, before *Newswatch* broke for a final commercial ahead of the big story, Jane said, "When we get back, you'll hear the story of Jingles Plumlee, the senior golf sensation of Leisureville, who will share the secret of his record-breaking success."

Once again Jingles filled the screen, knocking down that long putt still again. He quickly disappeared in favor of a Phoenix City Bank commercial.

Jane returned with more of the characteristic laughter in her voice than usual. "Tonight's special story is dedicated to the golfers out there and those who'd like to hear about a real life miracle in our local sports world. Ray "Jingles" Plumlee played a darn good game of golf prior to last week. He had a four handicap that most of us would envy.

"However, when he teed off Wednesday with his regular foursome, he shot a course record sixty-two. On Friday, he beat that with an incredible sixty. In case you're wondering, this is on a regulation seventy-two par course." The scorecard appeared on screen. "And then this morning, in front of *Newswatch* cameras, he followed that up with a sixty-one!

"Were there witnesses? Were there ever! Here are scenes from Leisureville, where folks are high on their senior sensation!" Fifteen seconds of footage showed the crowd lining the fairways and surrounding the greens, the barbecue behind the fifteenth green, the plethora of dogs, and close ups of the handwritten signs.

Suddenly Jingles stood there, right next to Jane. "Wow," Jingles said. "You can still see where I had the stitches!" Seven voices simultaneously told him to shut up.

Then Pat whispered, "No more whining."

"So, Jingles," Jane said. "How do you shave about sixteen shots off your score in the blink of an eye?"

"The only difference is that I got contact lenses." Jingles removed his sunglasses, as if that would allow everyone to see the contacts, and pointed to his right eye. "All along I thought I could see, but I really couldn't. You could say that contacts have made all the difference."

Jingles disappeared and there was Jane with none other than Dr. Sturrock. He appeared to be sitting by a small swimming pool. Jane said, "So, Dr. Sturrock, what did you discover when Mr. Plumlee came to see you recently?"

"I found a man who had just been in an accident and broke the eyeglasses he wore for over twenty years. His eyes had changed over time, you could say deteriorated, and he needed a different prescription."

"Is it unusual," Jane asked, "for new eyewear to have such a dramatic effect?"

"Well, I'm not a golfer, but I do know that excellent vision is an asset to people in everything they do."

It was Tim Scott's turn to be interviewed. *Jane certainly got around.* "Tim, you're the pro here at Leisureville. What's your take on Jinglesmania?"

"The guy has some serious skill, Jane, especially for his age. I was able to spend a few hours with him recently and we talked about the mechanics of putting."

The Sweet Swing

"Do you think you helped him?"

Tim shrugged. "I'd like to think so."

Harvey had a serious expression when he spoke next. "It has to be the contact lenses. Pro golfers average twenty-nine point three putts per round. Jingles averaged only twenty-one point four over his last three rounds. Most golfers will never do that once in a lifetime, whether they wear contacts or not. He's done it over and over. It's supernatural. Last week he couldn't make a putt and now he can't miss."

Knickers came on the screen, smoking one of Mulligan's cigars and winking at Jane.

"You've played with Jingles for six years, what's changed?" she asked.

"Well, maybe it's my vision that's improved. I'm seein' stuff on a golf course I've never seen before. Seriously, Jingles is in the zone. If you gave him ten horse shoes right now, he'd toss you nine or ten ringers."

Mulligan's face appeared and he looked directly into the camera, just as he had in car commercials over the years in Chicago.

Jane said, "And this is Mulligan Wettman. You heard right, Mulligan! He's also been golfing with Jingles for a long time."

Mulligan said, "He had a serious accident about two weeks ago. He got hit in the head with a golf club. A lot of us think that it did something to his brain, maybe rearranged it or something. I can't explain his golf any other way, but one thing is for sure, it's the greatest sports story ever and it happened right here in Leisureville."

Dr. Norman Swartzmann, the general practitioner that gave Jingles his stitches, was next to speak with Jane. "So doctor," she said. "Could a head trauma have caused the improvement in Mr. Plumlee's golf game?"

"The human brain is very complex," he said. "I took x-rays and examined them and there was evidence of only a minor concussion. No one can know with absolute certainty, but based on what you've told me, I'd say it's his improved vision that's making the difference."

They all gasped in surprise at the sight of Gladys Beckerman, as Jane explained she was the lady who accidentally injured Jingles. Gladys stared at Jane and reached out to touch one of the pigtails. "I think he was hurt more than people think. Before I hit him with my club his name was Ray. Now he's Jingles. He's forgotten his own name! The reason he is playing so well is because he is so nice. I almost killed him and he sent *me* flowers! How many people would do that? I've been praying for him."

Then Knickers was back for an encore. "If it's Jingles' contacts makin' him play this way, I want the same prescription. If it's a knock on the head, I'll take two. If it's eatin' lima beans, I'll eat those too. And, man, I hate lima beans."

Laughing, Jane wrapped it up. "Well, whether you like lima beans or not, you have to love Jingles Plumlee. We here at WAZA salute you, Jingles, and all the friendly people at Leisureville. This has been Jane Friend, see you Monday night."

The camera cut to scenes from Leisureville as the *Newswatch* credits rolled down the screen. They played the audio of Jingle Bell Rock and showed the elderly dancers around the giant scorecard.

Mulligan stood up to address the others. "That was a great show. It was great for the community. But I have to get rid of that Tim Scott! Imagine him taking credit for Jingles' putting!"

"I thought the same damn thing," Knickers said. "He had nothin' to do with anythin'."

"Wait," Pat said. "He's very nice. He even offered Jingles a job giving lessons." The men looked at Jingles with obvious surprise.

"Easy, guys," Jingles said. "He didn't say he helped me. He said he'd like to think so."

"I don't know," Harvey said. "If someone asked me if I discovered a cure for cancer, I don't think it would be fair for me to say, 'I'd like to think so.'"

"Yeah, I think Jingles is being a little too nice," Knickers said. "But at least he's been giving us our lessons for free!"

"What about the lima beans?" Bess asked her husband.

"Good question," Mulligan said. "Where in the world did that comment come from?"

Everyone else looked at Knickers too. They all had the same question.

"Aw, I knew you would ask me that," Knickers said, shaking his head. "It was what they call an impromptu speech. I was just tryin' to say that I'd do anythin' to be able to play like Jingles. Eating limas was the worst thing I could think of at the moment."

"Well, Jane Friend seemed to like what you said," Lucy declared. "She used it for her closing. I thought it was fun."

Stanley Sturrock sat in his recliner in front of the television, sipping brandy, and savoring his brief appearance on *Newswatch*. His friends would be incredibly jealous when they realized Jane Friend sat with him on his patio! She was so warm and friendly that he couldn't help but think there had been a spark between them. Yes, he was at least twenty years her senior, but that didn't always matter when it came to romance. The likelihood of a torrid affair with Jane seemed to increase more with each swallow of Courvoisier.

Less than five minutes after the show concluded, his phone rang and he debated whether to get out of his chair or not. After the fourth ring, he decided it might be a friend who saw the show or, better yet, Jane. He suddenly rushed to answer.

"Hello, this is Stanley."

"Yes. I'm the optometrist that was just on television."

"You can call my office on Monday and make an appointment."

"No, I never work on Sunday."

"How much? You mean how much do I want for a Sunday appointment?"

"You want to pay me five hundred dollars to see you tomorrow?"

"You realize, of course, that you still can't get contacts for at least another week."

"You don't care?"

"Twenty-nine Bloomington Road, right across from Goody's Restaurant, three o'clock. Just knock. I'll let you in."

Golfers! I'm glad I'm not one of them, Sturrock thought, as his phone rang again. After the fourth similar call, he let the answering machine do its job. The recorded message provided his office number. He heard the phone continue to ring nonstop until he dozed off hours later.

As Pat hoped, the festive mood of the morning carried right into the dance that night. Tables had been set for an anticipated turnout of 240. Only 162 tickets sold in advance, but there were always a fair number of walk-ups. Over four hundred beaming seniors packed the party room by eight-thirty!

Many brought signs they carried at the golf course and taped them to the wall. Others made a quick trip home to fetch their own signs or scratch out new ones to add to the décor.

Newswatch was the topic of almost all conversation. Not only Jingles, but the entire foursome, were viewed as dignitaries. A cluster of people encircled each of them the moment they walked through the door.

Given the size of crowd, Pat was proud to have added so many sweet delicacies to the long table of appetizers and desserts. Not a crumb would go to waste. Food was even more popular than alcohol at Leisureville parties.

Jingles led his wife to the dance floor for one waltz before being swept away by an array of other passionate dancers. Some were widows or divorcees and others let their husbands find their own amusement in the dessert line or at the beer and wine bar. Jingles knew he couldn't dance as well as he could putt, but the floor was full enough to hide him and he did his best Mulligan impersonation.

Pat sat with Lucy, wondering if she would get a chance to try other steps she had learned. Her eyes settled on Knickers, who was holding court across the room.

"You were right, Lucy," Pat said over the blare of the orchestra. "Knickers really stole the show with the lima beans business. That's all I'm hearing."

"Don't be silly," Lucy said, wondering where Harvey was. "Look at the signs on the wall! Your husband is the star of the show!"

"I don't know about that," Pat said. "There's something sneaky about that Knickers. What about what he did to our car?"

"Pat, that was just a joke! An elaborate joke, yes, but still a joke. Men like to have fun like that."

"He's not a man. He's a silly little boy," Pat said. "Lima beans! One of these days I'm going to tell him off."

"Well, I can't tell you how to think, but all the men around Leisureville think Knickers is the cat's pajamas. Harvey looks up to him like royalty. By the way, have you seen my husband?"

Harvey sat alone outside in a lounge chair beside the swimming pool. In all the excitement at the Plumlee house, he drank too much wine. Nonetheless, he held still another glass as he looked into the water, which was bright from lights beneath the surface.

Despite all the excitement of the past few days, he felt a deepening melancholy. He had been so happy for the last two years and felt it all slipping away. Things were never going to be the same. He took another swallow of the cabernet and chastised himself. His best friend was no longer good old Ray Plumlee. He was *the* Jingles Plumlee. What was going to happen to the Foursome now? The competitive balance was gone. Would Jingles even play with them much longer?

A raindrop fell from the sky and landed on his forehead. He looked at the pool, but saw no evidence of other drops hitting the water. Looking upward, he saw the glimmer of stars among only a few wispy clouds. Deciding that the single splash on his head was a message to stop his negative thinking, he collected himself and returned to the party.

Upon entering the ballroom, Harvey stopped in his tracks. Although the dance area was full of couples, only one of them was moving as the others just watched. At the center of the oak parkay floor, Jingles was doing some kind of dance with *Speed Bump* herself, the incomparable Ingrid Samuels! She had never attended a dance before, or any other organized community activity as far as he knew. Yet there she was, in a white minidress, in all her runway splendor, looking like that hostess of *So You Think You Can Dance*. She and Jingles were laughing and talking and oblivious to everyone else in the world!

The other couples seemed frozen like statues. They still clung to each other but their feet were glued to the floor. The men all stared at Ingrid and the women all looked at Pat, who was sitting next to Lucy. Pat wore a smile, but Harvey had a feeling that if someone touched her face it might crumble like plaster.

Harvey looked for the closest chair and collapsed into it. *To the rich or famous go all the spoils*, he thought. Jingles wasn't rich, but he sure was famous. He was suddenly thirsty for another glass of wine.

Pat watched her husband for what seemed like the longest three minutes of her life. It wasn't that Jingles had accepted an invitation to dance from the most beautiful woman she had ever seen that bothered her, what else was he supposed to do? The problem was that he seemed to be enjoying himself too much. The look on his face!

"All the other women are staring at me," Pat whispered to Lucy. "Are they expecting me to run out there and beat up that beautiful woman or my husband?"

Lucy laughed and whispered back. "Let's beat up the woman!" She formed her right hand into a claw and posed for Pat with a mock snarl on her face, which made them both laugh.

By the time the music ended, a line of men had formed behind Ingrid, all anxious for their turns to dance with her. Mulligan was at the front of it. However, she merely smiled at them all, waved, and headed straight for the exit.

Jingles made a beeline for his wife and escorted her to the parkay. "Well, all the mystery about Ingrid Samuels has now been solved," he announced. "I know her whole life story!"

"You heard her life story during one dance?"

"I'm a very good listener."

"When you really want to be," Pat said, with more than a hint of sarcasm.

Jingles tried to ignore the slight. Women were from Mars or Venus, he couldn't be expected to understand them all the time.

"She's an artist, a painter actually," he said. "That's why no one sees her around much. She has a studio in the house and paints portraits of flowers. Her canvases sell real well in galleries all over the place."

"I love flowers," Pat murmured, suddenly captivated by the image of the young widow, living by herself, standing hour after hour in front of an easel.

"And you know how everybody wonders about why she married a man so much older? Well, she was an art student back in college and he was a professor of art history. She said she loved him so much that she practically stalked him! He refused to even have lunch with her until after she graduated."

Ingrid hardly seemed like the stalker type to Pat, but she was drawn into the story. "Go on. Why does she choose to live here in a senior community?"

"She's just comfortable here and doesn't want to move. It's something about an aura, whatever that is."

"And why did she choose to come here tonight? I've never seen her at any of the events before."

Jingles leaned close to her ear and whispered, "She saw me on the news and wanted to visit with me, that's all." Why was Pat so curious? It all seemed perfectly logical to him.

"Well," Pat said, pulling her husband closer as they did the box step, "everything's fine as long as she doesn't start stalking you."

When the orchestra took a break before their final set of the night, Knickers summoned Mulligan, Harvey and Jingles to a conference by the pool. He lit a cigar and offered a handful from his breast pocket to the others.

"They're excellent," Knickers said. "I get them from a friend in the Dominican Republic."

Mulligan took one and the others declined. Jingles was sure Pat would smell it on him and file for divorce. Harvey could barely hold up his head.

"Here's what I wanted to talk to you guys about. Friday is Bess's and my fiftieth anniversary."

Jingles smiled, sure that Pat had the date recorded and a gift ready to go in the War Room. He wondered what she picked out.

Knickers continued. "I've decided to dust off the check book and do something really special. I'd like to take you all on vacation for a few weeks, you and your wives. Would you all be able to leave on Wednesday? It's a couple days before Halloween, Ichabod!"

Jingles reacted first. "That sounds fantastic! Right now is probably the perfect time for a getaway. Things have gotten hectic this week." *And there would be some interesting golf courses without a doubt!*

Harvey perked up. A week with just his friends sounded wonderful right now. No crowds. No being on the news. And no Ingrid dancing with Jingles.

Mulligan said, "You can count Mary and me in. Where are we headed?"

"Well, that's the fun part," Knickers said. "We'd all fly first class to the Island of Hispaniola. We can take our sticks and get in a few rounds on courses along the ocean."

"Haiti or Dominican Republic?" Harvey asked.

"Both. I have a great friend over in DR. His name is Juan Felipe."

He held up his cigar. "That's how I get these. Juan wants to give us a white stretch limo to use for the trip, with a driver and everything. His treat. He's been very successful in business over there."

"How do you know this Felipe?" Mulligan asked.

"He was one of the very first Dominicans to play ball over here. We were teammates in the minors and stayed friends through all the years. I've never gone to visit him and feel like it's time.

"I've grown more and more curious about Haiti too. Did you know that there have been over five hundred major league players from the Dominican and basically none from Haiti?"

Harvey interrupted. "Don't they play soccer in Haiti? More of a European influence?"

"Yes, that's true," Knickers said. "But the people from both countries have the same ethnic background and I assume the same great athletic potential. Here you have two separate countries on the same island, each with about nine million people, and only one has a passion for baseball. In the baseball country, the economy is pretty good, more kids go to school, and people live longer and happier lives. In the soccer country, everything is pretty tough. We all remember the news coverage after the earthquake a few years ago."

"How do you know all this?" Jingles asked. "I'm not even sure where Hispania is."

"Hispaniola," Knickers said. "Bess has been copyin' stuff off the computer for me to read."

"I never liked soccer," Mulligan said, blowing out a plume of smoke. "Just a bunch or running back and forth."

Knickers cut him off with a glance. "Anyway, the plan is to lie on the beach, play some golf, and tour around both countries a little. I just want to see everything firsthand and first class. We're going to the best hotels and restaurants. You all still have your passports, right?"

They all nodded. All four couples had been to Acapulco for the wedding of Harvey's granddaughter over a year ago.

Harvey stood up, all energized and eager to tell his wife the news. "I've never flown first class before!"

"As far as the money goes," Knickers said. "Just tell your wives that Bess and I have been saving up for this for a long time."

"Well," Jingles said. "That's the absolute truth!" Jingles stood to catch Harvey, who was already headed back to the ballroom.

"Hold on," Mulligan commanded. "Sit back down. You too, Harvey. I've got something else to discuss."

The men sat and gave Mulligan their attention. There had been some urgency in his voice, along with a hint of too much booze.

"Do you see all those signs on the wall in there?" he asked. "It's like Jingles is running for orfice . . . office . . . or something."

129

Jingles only now noticed that Mulligan was a good two and a half sheets to the wind. He wondered how his friend managed to drink so much when he seemingly spent the whole night on the dance floor.

"What *orfice* would he be running for?" Knickers asked, obviously teasing Mulligan. "Homeowner Association President?" Knickers knew all the attention on Jingles had to rankle Mulligan, who had always been the Lord of the Dances or whatever. Jingles' dance with Ingrid must have really gotten Mulligan's goat!

"We need to talk about what's been going on these last few days," Mulligan said, either ignoring or not hearing Knickers. "What's going on, Jingles? The three of us are just watching all this and are like, 'What the hell's going on?'"

The others just looked at Mulligan. Their chairs were suddenly uncomfortable.

"I'm a damned good golfer, especially for my age," he continued. "I've always felt like I could play with anybody. I go out on the course this week and suddenly I'm an old fool or something."

He looked at Knickers, then Harvey. "Speak up, you guys! I know you feel the same. You told me!"

"Mulligan, you shot a seventy-three today!" Harvey said. "You stepped up to the challenge!"

"I stepped up? I lost by a dozen shots! Nobody shoots a sixty. And who the hell got to dance with Speed Bump?"

Harvey didn't defend Jingles on the latter point. He figured all those mouth to mouth treats for her little collie should have rated him a dance too.

Jingles felt both anger and sympathy. Should he have to apologize for his good fortune? "Ingrid just wanted to congratulate me!"

Mulligan dropped his cigar and stomped on it. "Mary said you embarrassed your wife by dancing with Ingrid. I think so too."

Knickers burst out laughing. "Jingles embarrassed Pat? Don't you think Mary saw you standing there hoping for a dance with her yourself? You were more excited than the last time you had an eagle putt!"

Jingles nodded to Knickers. "And you must have danced with fifty women, Mulligan! Mary didn't seem to mind."

Instead of replying, Mulligan picked up his cigar refuse and tossed it in the trash can, leering at Knickers all the while. What was he supposed to say now? Maybe he should say what he was really thinking. He lowered his voice. "Okay. You've caught me being jealous. I confess. But I think we have to try and assess what's really happening here.

"Jingles, we know you and we know your golf game. What you've done the last few days is all off. You shot the crazy sixty-two on Wednesday and we knew it was a total fluke.

"Knickers turned up the heat on Friday by sticking you under the spotlight the best way he knew how. What did you do? Shoot an impossible sixty! Now, we are totally baffled. It's like one of those out of your body esss . . . periences.

"On Saturday, I throw even more wood on the fire. I put you in a situation that is sure to bring you back to earth, television and everything. You march right out and make every putt again.

"I guess what I'm saying is, 'who the hell . . . or what the hell . . . are you?'"

Jingles glanced at the other men and saw the same question on their faces. He wasn't surprised or insulted. This reaction was more logical than all their cheering had been. Had he shot one round of sixty-seven or something, it may have been okay. Repeated scores in the bottom sixties, however, were well beyond reason, just like the view through his odd lens.

Would his description of how the lens worked for him and Sid Wexler's explanation satisfy them or confuse them even more? Would they curse his good fortune or accept it like the story of the investment advice Knickers got from the bleachers?

This wasn't the time to find out, he decided. The men had been drinking and they were tired too.

Jingles chose his words more carefully than usual. "My contact lenses have made all the difference. You have to understand that I was playing blind before, at least compared to how I can see now."

"Yeah, yeah, yeah. Blah, blah, blah," Mulligan said. "We've heard all that and it just doesn't wash. You heard Harvey on the news! He was right. Nobody putts like that. Nobody!"

Jingles pointed to his right eye. "I've told you that everything looks different now."

Mulligan interrupted. "Yeah, the hole looks like a big, old bucket, you said. Guess what? You are shooting at the same hole, with the same ball, as the rest of us!" Ashes fell from another freshly lit cigar and landed on his shirt and tie.

"You have to accept that I can see better than most people," Jingles offered. "There you have it."

Harvey was now sitting taller in his chair. "I can accept it," he said. "My optometrist says my eyes are close to normal, but I couldn't see all those golf balls you were finding in the bushes. Your eyes must be better than normal!"

"I don't accept it at all," Mulligan said, tossing up his hands and dropping even more ashes. The tie started smoking all by itself. "The Golf God just decided that Jingles Plumlee should be able to see better than everybody else?"

Somehow Mulligan touched a nerve. Jingles tossed up his hands and raised his voice a little. "Maybe it was Mrs. Beckerman's five iron, like *you* said on TV. Or maybe I'm in the zone that Knickers talked about. It could be all of those things. I don't think I should have to apologize for it."

The other three stared in wonder. Jingles was angry? That seemed as improbable as a sixty.

"There's no reason for anybody to get upset," Knickers said. "We're friends here."

Mulligan pushed himself out of his chair and took a second to get his balance. "A week ago, we were a quartet, all playing the same music from the same page. Now we're *Gladys Knight and the Pits*. We all know who the lead singer is."

"I think you mean *Pips*," Harvey said, despite suspicion that the choice of *Pits* may have been intentional.

"Gladys Knight?" Jingles said. "Where in the world did that come from? What are we even talking about?"

Harvey felt stone sober. The tone of the conversation had awakened him like a dunk in the swimming pool. "We need to stop this right now. We *are* a quartet."

Looking directly at Jingles, Harvey added, "I apologize for all of us. You have never been anything but a great friend. We need to grow up, I guess. I think we all might be a little worried about the future of the Foursome now that you are playing like this. I think that's what Mulligan was getting at."

Mulligan nodded agreement, stumbled over to Jingles and held out his hand. Jingles grasped the offered hand with both of his and gave it an affectionate squeeze.

Mulligan said, "I'm sorry, Jingles. Harvey is right. You know that's booze doing my talking. This has all been so crazy. Sometimes we short guys feel like we have to kick everybody's ass to prove our worth."

"You'll never have to prove your worth, Mulligan," Jingles said. "No man ever stood by his wife like you did. You also do more for Leisureville than anybody. Hey, if you and Mary hadn't contacted Jane Friend, we wouldn't have even been on television tonight. This was *your* day!"

Mulligan tensed up again. *My day?* He had to force one of those grins that a losing candidate makes during a concession speech. "If you ever want more dance lessons, come and see me."

"If you ever need a new tie, come and see me," Jingles said, noting two fresh holes in Mulligan's red one.

Knickers snuffed out his cigar and carried the butt to a garbage can. "This vacation couldn't come at a better time and I'm glad you can all make it. I'm not playing any more golf 'til I get to the island."

"I second the motion," Mulligan said. "This meeting is adjourned."

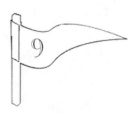

9

The Plumlees had a regular routine on Sunday mornings. They left the house at ten for breakfast at House of Pancakes and attended a church service at eleven. Unlike the restaurant, the church changed from week to week. After arriving in Leisureville, they decided to visit a variety of churches in the immediate vicinity before choosing one to join. They found twenty churches dotting the map within a few-mile radius. After several months, they started to enjoy the variety itself. Seven years later, Pat still chose among a dozen churches each week and told her husband where to drive.

As regulars at the eatery, they knew the wait staff and other patrons that shared their routine. Many of them watched *Newswatch* and were excited to question Jingles about everything from Jane Friend to golf to how his name changed since last Sunday, when they knew him as Ray.

Pat enjoyed the chance to tell the story of Lucy's nickname for her husband. Did they recall the Wild Bill Hickock sidekick Jingles? The patrons, mostly seniors like the Plumlees, remembered. The younger employees were clueless. Half the customers did their own Jingles impressions while the others listened and chuckled. The current Jingles ate his hotcakes and enjoyed the newfound attention.

On the drive home after church, Jingles turned to Pat. "I'm not sure we should keep that one on our list. The sermon got a little windy."

"Let me guess," Pat said. "You're disappointed that no one asked for your autograph at that church?"

That seemed a little harsh, he thought. *What was wrong with wanting to be around people sharing an interest in sports?*

She reached across his chest and touched his left breast pocket. "At least you got to use that Sharpie at breakfast. It's the first time you've carried a pen since high school."

"Yeah, well," Jingles said. "I still think the sermon went a little long."

They heard the phone ringing when they entered the house. Pat realized she now felt resignation instead of excitement. The phone had been noisy too often lately.

"It's for you, Jingles. He's from the Sun newspaper. He's sorry to call on Sunday and he did anyway."

"Hi, this is Jingles."

"Phil Smith, Phoenix Sun. I saw your story on WAZA last night, and we'd like to do a story about your golf."

"We get your paper on Sundays," Jingles said. "We like it."

"We had a photographer there yesterday morning when you played, but I was busy on another story. We got some great shots. This is going to be fun to write."

"What do you need from me?"

"I just need some time, maybe an hour or two. Are you busy tomorrow?"

"Actually, I'm not. My foursome isn't playing. You want to golf with me?"

"Sorry, I'm not a golfer, but I can't believe you aren't playing. If I were you, I'd be playing about twelve hours a day!"

"I could live with that," Jingles said. "And my wife would probably prefer it!"

"Could I come by your house at Leisureville in the morning? Around ten?"

"No problem. I'll leave word with Charlie at the front gate. He'll give you directions."

When Jingles disconnected, he sat at the kitchen table with Pat. "We're going to be in the paper! We can send copies of the story to the kids!"

Pat started to leaf through their Sunday Sun with renewed interest. "I wonder if anyone recorded last night's show. I didn't even think of that."

"You might call Mary Wettman," Jingles said. "If there's a copy in Leisureville, she'll find it."

The phone sounded again and Pat grabbed it. "What? A limousine? Let him in and give directions to the house. Thanks."

Pat headed to the bathroom to check her hair. "You aren't going to believe this, Jingles. There's a limo coming through the gate right now. A Mr. Fennel wants to see you."

"How do you like that," he said. "We'll be riding around in a limo ourselves come Thursday! Our vacation is going to be great."

"I don't know how Knickers and Bess can possibly afford it," Pat muttered.

They watched through the window as a black limousine pulled into the driveway and parked. A uniformed driver got out and opened a rear door. A gray-haired man in a dark three-piece pin-striped suit stepped out and walked deliberately to the front door. Pat opened it before he could knock.

He looked at Jingles and smiled. "I recognize you. That was an impressive show last night. My name is Derek Fennel." He took a business card from his coat pocket and handed it to Jingles.

Jingles handed the card to Pat without looking at it. "Please come in, Mr. Fennel. What brings you here?"

He said nothing at first. He walked into the house, looked around, and headed for the living room. Jingles and Pat looked at each other and raised their eyebrows.

Pat read the business card to her husband. "It says Derek Fennel, board of directors, PGA Champions Tour."

"Is this your sitting room?" Mr. Fennel asked, looking at the living room.

"It is," Pat said. "Would you like to talk in there?"

"That would be quite satisfactory. Do you have a cool drink? Preferably bottled water?"

Mr. Fennel sat in an armchair and Jingles took the couch. Pat scrambled to the refrigerator and returned with a plastic water bottle and a glass of ice. Jingles noticed that the glass was fancy crystal, not one of the plastic tumblers she normally used.

"I'll get right to the point," the gentleman said, pouring water into the glass. "I'm here representing both the Champions Tour and myself."

"Representing the Tour in what way?" Jingles asked.

"How do you think? We want to give you a chance to compete on Tour."

Jingles had to laugh. "I can't play on the Seniors Tour. I'm not qualified."

Mr. Fennel seemed perturbed by the laughter. "Please don't be sophomoric, Mr. Plumlee. The question isn't whether you can play on the Tour or not, it is whether you want to or not."

"Who wouldn't want to play?" Jingles said. "The problem is that I'm seventy-two years old. Didn't you know that?"

"I know far more than you might imagine. I had you checked out right after the program last night."

Had me checked out? "Well, even I know that nobody my age ever had any success on the Tour. Most of the guys are in their fifties."

"First of all, you are far too modest. Not a single one of those fifty-somethings can do what you did this past week."

The Sweet Swing

Jingles hadn't really thought about that. *Maybe it was true.* Maybe the bubble lens could open doors that didn't even exist a week ago. After all, he was on television last night!

"Secondly, your age is your biggest attraction to us. Personally, I'm eighty-one. I'd like nothing more than to believe that older people can be successful at this game. We think you'd be a major attraction."

"So you are saying what?" Jingles asked. "You'd let me play in a qualifying tournament or something?"

Mr. Fennel tapped the arms of his chair with obvious impatience. "Fortuitously, you golf far better than you listen, Mr. Plumlee. We want you in Orlando for the tournament a week from Thursday and Jacksonville the week after that. I'll guarantee you sponsor exemptions for the next four events."

Jingles stared at him. He didn't know what to say. He looked at Pat. "Can we afford to have me do that?"

Mr. Fennel interrupted, "No one expects you to bear the cost of this adventure. I'm a wealthy man, and I will cover your costs. I even have a wager with one of the other directors that you'll make top ten by your third event."

Now Mr. Fennel turned to Pat. "I think you'll rather enjoy accompanying your husband. There are lots of social events associated with every tournament. You can stay at fine hotels. It's a lifestyle many of the wives seem to enjoy."

Pat nodded like a bubblehead. "Of course he'll do it! We'll do it! It sounds wonderful."

"Fine," Mr. Fennel said, standing up and straightening his tie. "I'll have a courier deliver you a complete schedule, tour packet, and authorization tags straight away. In the meantime, plan on getting to Orlando several days in advance so you can get in some practice."

He took a folded piece of paper from his pocket and dropped it on the coffee table. "This will take care of your expenses for the next couple of months. Do you have any other questions?"

Jingles and Pat stood up from the couch, speechless.

"My cell number is on the card in case you recover your powers of speech and want to contact me. Now, if you'll show me out."

As the limo driver opened the door for Mr. Fennel, the old gentleman turned to them and said, "By the way, you can thank Jane Friend for getting hold of the PGA and advising that we watch the show. I just happened to be the one director living near Phoenix. I don't normally watch much television."

The Plumlees stood in the driveway, holding hands, and watched the limousine drive away. When it disappeared, Pat dashed back into the house to look at the check. Jingles sat down on the front steps.

Pat returned, sat beside him, and planted a kiss on his cheek. "It's a personal check for thirty thousand dollars, Jingles! It's payable to Ray Plumlee! We're going to Disneyworld! Let's leave soon so we can enjoy more time there."

She jumped back up and rushed into the house to call all the children. "Oh, my," she hollered back to him. "You are making life so much fun!"

Jingles pondered all that happened in a single week. He thought back to the moment he first looked at himself in the mirror with the odd right contact lens. He certainly didn't see a future like this!

A thought struck and he rushed into the house. Pat was already talking to their oldest daughter on the kitchen phone, staring all the while at the check in her left hand.

"I'm going to be playing on television," Jingles exclaimed. "Ask the kids if they get the golf channel!"

He could hardly wait to break the news to the rest of his foursome. How would they react? Would they be as excited as he hoped? Yes, of course. How could they not? Knickers, especially, knew what it was like to make it to the big time. He would be understanding when Pat and he had to cancel out on the anniversary trip. Heck, it would save him lots of money.

An hour later, Jingles was on the bed with a phone, mostly listening, while Pat continued to talk on the kitchen phone. She had the last of their four children on the line.

"Jingles, the limousine is back," she said over the phone. "They must be delivering all the stuff Mr. Fennel talked about. Can you go meet them?"

Jingles walked quickly to the front door and looked at the sleek black Cadillac with the dark tinted windows. Pat joined him a few seconds later.

When the driver didn't step out after a full minute, the Plumlees walked down the driveway and Jingles tapped on a window. A rear window opened, and a cloud of smoke escaped as if the car was on fire. Through the haze, the faces of Mulligan, Harvey, Knickers, and Derek Fennel appeared. Mr. Fennel's suit had disappeared in favor of a T-shirt.

Jingles grabbed the door to support his suddenly dead weight.

"Welcome to the Champions Tour," Mulligan said, raising a bottle of beer in a toast.

Harvey gushed, "Is this the best one ever or what?"

"How do you guys know Derek Fennel?" Pat asked, still with no understanding that she'd been *Knickered* right along with her husband.

"Meet Willie Freeland," Knickers said, patting *Derek Fennel* on the shoulder. "My old teammate and friend! And the driver is his buddy Fred."

Pat's entire body started to quake. The look on her face was so scary her husband had to turn away from it. She crushed the check she still held into a ball and threw it at Knickers. The paper wad glanced off his shoulder and caught Willie in the ear.

Knickers laughed at her fury. "That's what I call a brush back pitch, huh, Willie?"

Pat started to shriek in a voice Jingles didn't recognize. "Don't you ever come in our house again, Knickers Collins! That was just mean! It was sick. Don't any of you ever come in this house again! You are all just jealous of my husband!"

She turned and grabbed Jingles' arm and tried to lead him back to the house. He pulled his arm free, partly because he didn't share her anger, partly because his legs weren't steady yet. Pat hurried off by herself and slammed the door loudly enough to chase birds out of trees for a square block.

"I'm not jealous of her husband right now," Mulligan said, forcing a chuckle.

"How 'bout a beer?" Knickers asked, pulling a longneck from the ice chest between the two seats that faced one another, and twisting off the cap.

Willie and Harvey watched Jingles in silence. Pat had taken their breath away for the moment.

Jingles took a long swallow and sank to sit on the driveway in front of the open door. He looked at the stranger beside Knickers and shook his head. "That was the performance of a lifetime, Mr. Fennel," he said, replaying the entire visit in his mind. "Don't be *sophomoric*, Mr. Plumlee!" Jingles mimicked. At the same time, he knew he had been sophomoric enough to swallow the whole charade.

The others felt relief. All was well, at least with Jingles. Harvey offered the use of his guest room if Jingles needed it for a night or two.

"She'll be all right," Jingles said, hoping it was true. "Her biggest problem was the last hour. She's been on the phone telling all the kids about it. I'm telling you, she was already at Disneyworld!"

Willie addressed Knickers. "Artistically speaking, we might have just left a check for two cents behind. That would have shocked them enough."

"You may be right," Knickers said. "But this isn't an exact science. The *not knowin'* exactly how it will turn out is the excitin' part, don't you think?"

Knickers turned to Jingles. "I made one mistake in planning what Mr. Fennel would say to you. Harvey pointed it out a little bit ago. He thought you would catch it."

"No," Jingles said. "I believed every word."

Harvey said, "The Champions Tour event next weekend is in San Francisco, not Orlando. And that's the last tournament until January."

Jingles shook his head. "Never gave it a thought. If you waited another fifteen or twenty minutes, we'd have bought our tickets to Orlando.

"Anyone for golf?" Jingles asked, pushing himself to his feet. "I'm thinking of a quick eighteen on the executive course. I think Pat wants to be alone for a bit!"

"Would it help if I apologize to her?" Willie asked.

"There's probably a 5 percent chance it would help," Jingles said. "Would you risk your life for those odds? Sending flowers tomorrow would be a better idea."

Inside the house, Pat was calling Bess Collins. "Do you know what your husband just did to us!"

Bess took exception to Pat's tone. "Relax, my dear. Did it have anything to do with the limo I rented yesterday or the PGA card that I made and printed off the computer?" She laughed, presuming Pat would laugh with her.

"So *you* were in on this too! I thought we were friends!"

Bess said, "Where's your sense of humor? It was just a joke!"

"My sense of humor is *not* going anywhere with you on Wednesday, I can tell you that! You go on your fancy trip and have a great time! My husband and I will be staying home!" Pat shoved the off button on the phone and slammed it down.

Now the ugly task of calling her children back. How could she even explain such treachery from *supposed* friends? How many others had her children already called with the news? She had to hurry.

Back in the driveway, Knickers and the others turned down Jingles' golf proposal. They already drank too much beer and reminded him of the pledge of no more golf until they reached Hispaniola. The counter proposal was more beer at the Nineteenth Hole, where it would be free for a long, long time. Jingles passed on that to go to the driving range and work on his mid-range game.

Before leaving, he returned to the house to see how his wife was doing. He heard her sobbing and apologizing to their eldest daughter Sarah in the bedroom. He picked up the phone in the kitchen.

"Listen, girls," he said in his most soothing voice. "I'm really sorry about what happened. It's unfortunate that Pat got in the middle of what was a practical joke by my friends. I probably had it coming. I've gotten a big head lately.

"And, Pat, let me sit down and call the others as soon as we finish this call. None of this is your doing. You are totally innocent."

Jingles spent the next two hours on the phone, first with the other two daughters and then his son. He explained his unique friendships and mentioned some of the other practical jokes Knickers pulled, including the one with his car. They already knew the story about the salmon and had laughed about that for years. It was Jingles' son who air freighted the fresh fish to Phoenix. He quickly changed the topic of each conversation to the change in his golf game. All was fine with the kids.

Afterward he looked into the bedroom, where Pat was asleep on the bed, exhausted from the ride Knickers orchestrated. The phone rang near her head, and he grabbed it quickly so it wouldn't wake her. He carried it out of the bedroom and closed the door behind him.

Jane Friend was on the line.

"Speak of the angel," Jingles said. "You made all of Leisureville happy with your show last night." A thought flashed through his mind that maybe his partners weren't as happy as everyone else.

"You've made us happy too, Jingles. Our phones were ringing like you wouldn't believe after the show. People want to know more about you and I think you should oblige them!"

"Phil Johnson from the Phoenix Sun said the same thing earlier today," Jingles said. "He's coming by tomorrow to get information for a story."

"I know, Phil," she said. "He'll do a good job. Don't be surprised if the story is picked up nationwide."

"You're kidding, right?"

"Not at all. The Sun is part of a huge syndicate. They must have three hundred papers. Your story is an original. Nobody can recall anything like it."

"It's only golf, Jane." Jingles said, making an effort to be humble.

"And only thirty some million people play golf in this country, Jingles! There is also the fact that at least forty million people are over the age of sixty-five. You have a huge demographic." *And so did she when she covered this story.*

"What more can I do?"

"That's the fun part. You can play more golf for our cameras! The top sponsor for my show, Phoenix City Bank, wants to put together a promotional campaign that features you playing some exhibitions. We would film some of the action and have an ongoing feature on *Newswatch*."

"I'll start tomorrow!" *If it's not too late to start today!*

"Oliver Pruh is the bank president. He'd like to play golf with you at Desert Springs on Wednesday afternoon. He'll discuss the deal with you then."

"Wow! I've always wanted to play that course. The problem is that I'm going on vacation with some friends. We leave Wednesday. I'll be happy to play when I get back in a few weeks."

That wasn't what Jane wanted to hear. Not Oliver either. "Sometimes you have to strike while the iron's hot," she said. "Your story is a *right now* kind of thing. I didn't mention that if everything works out, the bank will pay you thirty thousand dollars."

There was that number again, Jingles thought. *$30,000.* But this was Jane Friend, not Derek Fennel. It was an amazing opportunity. However, if life taught him a single lesson, it was that friendship always came first.

He said, "Ask Mr. Pruh if three weeks from Wednesday would work for him, okay? This is a very special trip I'm going on. It's a friend's fiftieth anniversary. Tell him I promise to take him up on his offer afterwards."

Jane wasn't happy. She wanted to go on the air tomorrow night with a report that there would be more on Jingles Plumlee later in the week. Within days, the print media would be doing more advertising for her and she wanted to take full advantage. Beyond all that, Oliver was relying on her to seal the deal. He wanted to get something going before his big annual meeting in less than two weeks.

"Don't you think your friends would understand?" Jane asked. "You are a celebrity now. You have to take advantage of this chance."

"The world won't change in just a couple weeks," he answered. "Tell Mr. Pruh I can golf with him on Monday or Tuesday, before I leave. I'll explain it all to him. He'll understand."

Jane hadn't achieved success at such an early age without persistence. "Well, Jingles, I honestly don't think the deal will be there for you if you wait. That's a lot of money for a few rounds of golf."

"Tell me about it," he said. "My wife would go ballistic if she knew I might be turning down that much money!"

So, Jane smiled, perhaps there was a chink in Jingles' armor. She gave him Pruh's personal cell number as she'd been instructed to do.

"I hope everything works out," she said. "You're making me famous."

After the call, Jingles sat and looked at the phone. *I'm* making *her* famous? That was a little over the top, wasn't it?

He was still looking at the phone when it rang again. Knickers this time.

"I'm calling about our trip, Jingles. Your wife told Bess that you and she won't be coming. We've got to fix this fast!"

This was news to Jingles. He knew Pat was angry. In fact, he never saw her so angry. Still . . . "She'll feel differently tomorrow," Jingles said. "You don't realize what a great job you did on us. That was cold-blooded murder!"

"It was all in fun," Knickers said. "Harvey and Mulligan thought it would be a riot. I came up with the idea on Friday while you were busy shooting that impossible score."

Jingles laughed. "Maybe you should have concentrated on your golf instead."

Knickers was silent for too long and Jingles sensed he may have touched a nerve with his smack talk. As he learned last night, his partners were a little sensitive right now. Who could really blame them? At the same time, maybe

Knickers' trick actually did rub him the wrong way, at least a little. Why couldn't he compete with anybody now? He couldn't hit a ball as far as the younger pros, not even in the same zip code, but he could make up for it on the greens.

Jingles broke the uncomfortable silence. "I'm sorry I said that. I was trying to be funny and I'm not that good at it."

"No problem," Knickers said. "Just realize how important this trip is to Bess and me. It's huge to me that you come."

He was busting to tell Knickers all about Jane Friend's new proposal but caught himself. It was the wrong time to be bragging about his new opportunity. "Don't worry," he said. "Everything will work out."

Oliver Pruh sat in front of the computer in his home office, a surprisingly small nook in his sprawling manor behind the third green at Desert Springs Country Club. The space seemed even smaller given the size of the man, who was large enough to play tackle on a pro football team. He slept alone in one of the six bedrooms but rarely felt lonely. His work was his life. The most popular joke around the bank was: *What would Mr. Pruh call a sixty-hour workweek?* The answer: *a vacation.* His office at the main bank in downtown Phoenix was ten times larger, paneled in teak, and furnished in rich brown leather. However, he would be the first to say that the only furnishing of importance was a computer.

At age forty-eight, he had been head of the bank for six largely successful years. *Largely* successful, he was reminded, staring at the balance sheet for the failed Prescott Hills development on his screen. *Not totally successful.* Thinking of this Jingles character and how he might help advertise the bank was a welcome respite from thoughts of Prescott Hills.

The bank's major investment in the once promising golf course community was the only blemish on his otherwise perfect record. The project unexpectedly tanked a few years earlier when the owner/developer died of a heart attack and his surviving family walked away from the business. The bank now owned an idle golf course and a bunch of empty lots for its $16 million investment, which got larger by the day due to maintenance cost and real estate taxes. Until the housing market improved, there was no relief in sight.

Using that setback for motivation, Oliver had increased the number of accounts by an astounding 82 percent over the past three years alone. The bank's affiliation with Jane Friend's program played a significant role in that. However, there would be no rest for Oliver until other area banks had no customers at all.

Three years ago, he saw Jane on *Newswatch* during her first week on the job. He recognized star quality immediately. Within days, he increased the bank's advertising budget and acquired a major share of the show's commercial time. *Newswatch* and Phoenix City Bank were now solidly linked.

Maintenance of that link had been jeopardized a year ago, when Jane received a tantalizing offer from a station in San Francisco. Her romantic involvement with a star pitcher on the Giants further complicated the situation. Fortunately, Oliver solved the problem with two quick steps. He hired a private investigator to track the pitcher's social activity; the least he could do to protect a naïve girl like Jane. One week of surveillance on a road trip turned up multiple instances of infidelity and a report was conveyed to her anonymously. With one problem remedied, he worked a deal with WAZA to increase the bank's purchase of commercial time on other programming, as long as a major share of the increase went to a raise for the *Newswatch* anchor.

Oliver didn't normally watch the show, but Jane called in advance of last evening's broadcast and insisted that he check it out. He was glad that he had. The spectacle at Leisureville was remarkable. Those people adored this Jingles Plumlee and Oliver adored the business of senior citizens. They tended to park money in low-yield certificates of deposit or savings accounts. In turn, the bank put that money into loans for construction, home purchases, and business ventures that kept Arizona prospering right along with the bank. He had to put Jingles to good use.

The story itself was phenomenal. Yes, the Leisureville course was to golf what Taco Bell was to fine cuisine, but that didn't matter. Oliver used to play on courses like Leisureville before he had money. It was no picnic putting on marginally maintained greens, hitting from sparse fairways, or blasting out of kitty litter bunkers. Sixty? The old guy was a freak!

Jane called soon after the show. She demanded more Jingles coverage and told Oliver to make it happen. She laid out an entire promotional concept for the bank. Imagine if Jingles were to make scheduled appearances at some of the dozens of other retirement communities around the region. Well-orchestrated exhibitions matching Jingles against top local talent would create the same wild scene as that at Leisureville, wouldn't they? All of this could be brought to the public by none other than Phoenix City Bank and WAZA.

He knew it was a solid idea, possibly brilliant. Still, he vowed to sleep on it, and sleep didn't come easily. Organizing exhibitions would be time-consuming and costly. On the other hand, there might be lots of willing volunteers in the retirement communities. How would it affect his bottom line? Maybe, just maybe, it could generate a big influx of new customers.

He had called Jane back at noon today. He wanted *her* to broach the subject with Jingles, not because the concept was her idea, but because he doubted anyone could say no to her. He told her to float a $30,000 figure and lots of television coverage for a half-dozen appearances.

He also insisted that a meeting be arranged at Desert Springs. He wanted to assess the man personally before committing to the financial plunge. Now, at nearly 5:00 p.m., he awaited confirmation from her. His cell phone finally chirped and the calling number was Jane's.

"How did it go?" he asked.

"Good and bad," she said. "He's good to go but bad on scheduling. He wants to postpone things for a few weeks. He's going on vacation."

"Vacation? What kind of vacation?"

Jane smirked. Oliver didn't understand vacations, which he viewed as slacking. "It's a friend's anniversary or something."

"Did you mention the money?"

"Of course."

"Is he rich or what?"

"Yeah, right. Oliver, he lives in Leisureville!"

Oliver paused and thought. He needed Jingles Plumlee now! He wanted something special to excite his board of directors at the annual meeting a week from Thursday. A solid earnings report was not enough. A golf ball signed by Jingles would probably mean more to them.

Jane read his mind. "You might call his wife and see what she thinks. What woman could say no to you?"

You could, Oliver thought to himself. *I've asked you out a dozen times.*

"Mention the money to her," Jane said and gave him the Plumlees' number.

Pat was up from her nap and making dinner when she answered the phone. Jingles' note said he was at the driving range.

"This is Oliver Pruh," the caller said. "I'm with Phoenix City Bank, the prime sponsor of Newswatch."

"You must be looking for my husband," Pat answered.

"Well, before we try to steal some of your husband's time for the next few weeks, I thought it best if we touched base with you. After all, marriage is a partnership."

Pat was impressed to hear a man acknowledge that. "Go ahead and tell me about it. I'll listen while I work on our dinner."

Oliver painted a picture of Jingles playing exhibition matches at other retirement communities in the area, large turnouts of his fans, and more television coverage. He explained the necessity of getting started immediately while his story was fresh. He mentioned Wednesday as the date things needed to get underway.

"I can't imagine that he wouldn't love that," she said. "Did he say he would play?"

This was interesting, Oliver thought. *She said nothing about a vacation.*

"Maybe he wanted to check with you," Oliver said. "Just to make sure everything was okay."

"Really?" Pat asked dubiously. More than likely, her husband was still hoping to leave on the trip with his friends on Wednesday.

Oliver then said, "We plan to pay you thirty thousand dollars just to have Jingles play a little golf over the next month."

Her blood turned cold and she shouted. "You can tell Knickers Collins to just leave us alone!" She slammed the phone back into its holder. *That's the final straw*, Pat thought. *I never, ever, ever, want to see that man again!*

Dusk had settled over Leisureville by the time Jingles got home from the practice tees. He worked exclusively on iron shots in the 100-150 yard range, the part of his game that could use some dressing up.

Pat was waiting with loaded guns. "Do I have to get a restraining order against Knickers or something? Is that little boy of a man going to harass me forever? Why do you go along with his pranks as if they were funny or something?"

"Is this a bad time to talk about our trip?" Jingles joked, trying to lighten the mood. "I thought you would have gotten over Derek Fennel by now."

"Gotten over it?" she asked. "Knickers won't stop. He just had some Prude character call on the phone and try to make a fool of me again!"

Jingles walked to the stove, lifted the lid on the spaghetti sauce, and dipped a fingertip for a sample. "Are you sure the man on the phone wasn't Oliver Pruh from Phoenix City Bank?"

"He *said* he was, but I knew better when he said he wanted to pay us thirty thousand dollars," she said. "You'd think even a lummox like Knickers could come up with a different number the second time around."

"Knickers had nothing to do with it. Jane Friend called earlier while you were sleeping. The offer is serious. What did you say?"

Oh no, she thought. "I told him to stop bothering us and hung up."

I'll bet that impressed him, Jingles thought. "It's okay. I have his number. I'll call him and try to explain."

"What? You mean the bank really wants to pay you all that money?"

"Maybe or maybe not. They wanted me to start playing this week. I told them I'd play when we got back from the trip."

"You call him back right now and tell him you can play right away. And apologize for me."

Jingles shook his head. She was so predictable. This was going to be a problem. "We have to go on this trip, Pat. These guys are the best friends I ever had. And Bess is your good friend too."

"Oh, right. They've been planning this trip for the longest time. I think we found out about it *last night*. Or maybe it was this morning. Was it after midnight that Knickers proposed this trip?"

Jingles had a sinking feeling. Somebody was going to be very unhappy, probably everyone except his wife.

"You go ahead and go on that trip," Pat added. "I can use the time to pack my things and move out. Enjoy the spaghetti. I've lost my appetite."

She left the kitchen and headed to the War Room, smiling inside. She could revise her gift list now that an additional $30,000 just came along. She was already figuring how much would be left after taxes.

Jingles pondered his one remaining problem. Who should he call first, Knickers or Oliver Pruh? He settled on Pruh. The call to Knickers was going to be painful.

The bank president was gracious but curious about Pat's reaction to his call. Mostly he seemed delighted to have Jingles on board. He encouraged Jingles to play a practice round at Desert Springs on Tuesday, before their Wednesday date. After all, he would have to be at this best for the WAZA cameras that would film Jingles' round with him and the course pro.

With each digit of Knickers' phone number he pushed, Jingles felt his euphoria subside a little more. By the time the phone started to ring on the other end, all the air had rushed out of his balloon. He hated to disappoint anyone, but his generous friend was in a category of his own.

"I have amazing news," Jingles said. "Call it a coincidence if you want, maybe fate, but I just got a call from Jane Friend. Her sponsor, Phoenix City Bank, is going to pay me thirty thousand to go on my own Champions Tour. I'm going to play exhibitions at a half dozen of the other Leisurevilles around here."

Knickers waited for a punch line, but none came. He decided that Jingles was serious. "That's great! Congratulations are in order."

"They are going to film the rounds to put highlights on *Newswatch* again."

"When is that happening?" Knickers asked. "After we get back?"

"Well, that's a problem. I have to start this Wednesday. We can't accept your invitation."

There was an extended pause on Knickers' end before he said, "Don't worry, Jingles. They'll work around your schedule. You're the attraction."

"The money won't be there later," Jingles said, worrying that his words may not be necessarily true.

Again Knickers was slow to respond. "Okay, how about I give you thirty grand just to make the trip. Just don't tell anybody. Hey, it's our fiftieth."

Jingles knew Knickers was dead serious, and the offer both irritated and touched him. "Listen. I wish you and Bess the very best. You'll have four wonderful travel companions, and we'll have lots to tell each other when you get back. Tell Bess I'll be by with her anniversary gift before you leave."

Knickers started to say something but stopped, said bye, and hung up. He wasn't sure himself what was bothering him most. Jingles' desire to put his new talent on display was understandable but unsettling. He wasn't going to be able maintain his level of play, no one could. How would he handle that? Hot streaks ended just as suddenly as they started. He knew. He'd seen it all. Or at least he thought he'd seen it all until watching Jingles for the past few days.

The phone in the Plumlee house refused to stay silent. Jingles answered himself because he still stood next to it.

"Hey, this Jingles?" a man's voice asked.

"Yessir," Jingles answered. "Can I help you?"

"I think so. I own Super Putz, the family entertainment center just a couple miles from Leisureville. My name's Alex Levin."

Jingles knew the place. He drove by it every week on the way to Pancake House. Miniature golf course, go carts, and what looked like basketball courts and batting cages or something. The parking lot was always mostly empty, at least on Sunday mornings.

"I wanted to drop an offer on you, something you might really enjoy," he continued.

Jingles couldn't help being curious. "What do you have in mind?"

"Well, I've got a boy, he's eleven, almost twelve. I think he's the best putter I've ever seen, at least on our course here at Super Putz. I'm willing to give you two hundred bucks in cold hard cash if you can beat him. How's that sound?"

Jingles laughed. "It sounds like you have a lot of faith in your kid!"

"Actually," Alex responded, "I have a lot of faith in you. I figure if I get word out that you'll be playing a round on my course, it would be a nice promotion for the business. People aren't playing as much mini-golf as they used to. I'd consider it a favor even if you win my money."

Jingles hadn't played miniature golf in years, but the idea intrigued him. Would it be a genuine test for his new vision or just be ridiculously easy? He would find out. "When did you have in mind?" They settled on eight o'clock on Tuesday night.

Rows of tall Arizona pine trees stood like sentries on each side of the long driveway leading into Desert Springs Country Club. The huge white clubhouse with four prominent columns rising three stories sat at the end of it, perfectly framed by the pines.

"Now that is a picture," Jingles said, slowing down the Lincoln to prolong the view. "It looks a little like the White House."

"Yes," Pat said. "Definitely some Palladian influence."

"Pallady what?" Jingles asked. His wife still surprised him with her worldliness every now and then.

"Don't worry about it. I'm sure it has a bathroom. That's all you need to know." Pat listened to him whine about having to go for the last fifteen minutes, talking just like the *real* Jingles.

Pat agreed to make the trip with her husband, to chauffer his majesty around eighteen holes in a cart, by virtue of bribery. Oliver Pruh extended an invitation for them to dine at the restaurant after the practice round as his guests. He recommended the lobster!

As they parked in the lot, she took in the beautifully landscaped environment with a sigh. She appreciated Leisureville mostly because she had seen so little of this in her life. The whole placed seemed to glow in the success it represented.

Jingles led her to the pro shop, where Oliver instructed him to check in. The shop reminded her of the fanciest department stores in downtown Phoenix and a little of her house. The Berber carpet was the same deep blue color she chose for her master bedroom. Golf shoes were displayed on pedestals, not lined up on a rack. A half dozen mannequins displayed the latest fashionable golf wear, poised in putting or swinging positions with clubs. The place had the scent of big money, and the price tags documented it.

The gray-haired man at the desk wore a monogrammed golf shirt that matched the carpet. He grinned his recognition of Jingles Plumlee. "Welcome to Desert Springs! I'm Greg. I've been expecting you." He pushed a button on the wall, then walked out from behind the counter to shake hands with Jingles. He lifted Pat's hand and brushed it with his lips.

Pat was bemused. So many men were kissing her hand lately! Wasn't that practice normally meant for royalty or dignitaries? Actually, almost everyone was treating her with special respect, everyone except some supposedly best friends. Even Harvey and Irvin had stabbed her back by going along with Knickers and Bess and their cruel joke. While those two had called with apologies after she had words with their wives, the Collinses expressed no remorse at all.

A young man wearing the same attire as Greg stuck his head in the door and said, "Your cart is ready. It has some snacks in the wicker basket behind the passenger seat. If I may have your car keys, I'll grab your clubs." Jingles tossed him the keys and headed for a sign that said *Gentlemen*.

Greg told Pat, "There's also a cooler behind the driver's seat. It has a variety of drinks."

"You really didn't have to go out of your way for us," Pat said, although she was very grateful.

The man looked surprised. "It's not a problem, Mrs. Plumlee. All the carts go out that way."

"How much does it cost to play here?" Pat asked in a whisper, even with no one else around.

Greg smiled at her curiosity. "It's a private club, you know. You have to play with a member or at least be sponsored by one. It's one seventy-five after one in the afternoon. Two-fifty in the morning."

"What does it cost to be a member?"

"You know, I can't even tell you for certain. Suffice to say that my entire income for a year wouldn't pay the dues, let alone the initial membership fee."

"Oooh," Pat said. "The lives of the rich and famous."

"Rich, maybe," Greg said. "But none of them is as famous as your husband is right now!"

Jingles returned, carrying a large thermos. "Look what I picked up at the bar, Pat. I got you a whole jug of frozen margaritas! You can drink and drive."

Greg watched them roll off to the first hole, all smiles, giggles, and promises to bring the cart back in one piece. Yes, Mrs. Plumlee, the members here are rich. But none of them can buy the ability to play golf like the gentleman next to you.

Pat sat, sipped, and munched as she watched her man at work over the first few holes. Prior to the last week, she never actually watched him play, not once in the twenty years he'd been at it. He didn't play these holes like those at Leisureville on Friday and Saturday. Instead of teeing his ball between the markers, he had her drive him halfway to the green. At that point, he scattered a half-dozen balls on the ground and hit each toward the flag in the distance. Once at the green, he exchanged contacts on his right eye and proceeded to putt for a few minutes. He seemed to make most of them but showed no emotion in doing so.

Soon bored, she turned her attention to the course itself and the homes surrounding it. Was there a single weed living on the premises? She couldn't locate one. The cart path looked like a freshly paved highway. The paths she walked at Leisureville had cracks everywhere, with vegetation sprouting from them. The fairways here looked like the White House lawn. Obviously, Jingles' description of the clubhouse lingered in her mind.

And the homes! Each lot seemed like half an acre, space enough for six or eight homes in Leisureville. The same Arizona pines that greeted visitors out front, as well as other majestic leafy trees, provided shade for the homes. The entire area was an oasis. The home behind the third green appealed to her in particular. It stood at the center of what must have been two adjoining lots and had the same architectural flavor as the clubhouse. A walkway led from the golf course into the property, ending in a bridge that crossed over a swimming pool to the rear veranda. Pat could see her great-grandchildren at play in the pool, maybe slipping down a sliding board that she would have installed. Her daughters and son and their spouses could sit on the lovely terrace while she served fresh lemonade and Jingles cooked at the barbecue. How many bedrooms might there be? Enough for everyone. A woman could dream, couldn't she?

As they continued around the course, Pat pointed to each impressive house and listed the features she appreciated most. Her husband nodded, barely looking. He could pitch a tent and be happy as long as a golf course and playing partners were nearby. The course he would try to master for *Newswatch* tomorrow now had his full attention.

Pat viewed their marriage as an ideal merger of contrasting personalities, a pairing that made each of them better people. As a shy, studious girl, she loved Ray Plumlee by the time they were twelve-year-old classmates. She understood his friendliness toward her wasn't unique; he extended the same kindness to all the kids. But what girl wouldn't want to marry the nicest guy around?

Even in high school, when teenagers tended to divide into cliques, he remained the universal friend. Whether you tooted a clarinet in the band, grabbed rebounds for the basketball team, acted in the class plays, or studied continually in the library, he laughed at your jokes and applauded your efforts. Ray never seemed to look at your outfit, only your eyes. When you needed to sneeze, he was the first to offer a Kleenex. He was elected class president without even running for the office. A majority of the kids just wrote his name on their ballot.

While the happy-go-lucky boy strolled through life, she had plotted their merger. She stayed near his elbow in class to assist with test answers that stumped him. To be sure, he was frequently stumped. She offered help with math and English assignments because he struggled with those subjects even more than the rest. And she always had an extra brownie or cookie in her lunch bag.

In their junior year, she told him that going to the prom as his date would make her the happiest girl ever. Even though the prom was five months away, an eternity to a teen, Ray agreed to the date, as she knew he would. *No* wasn't in his vocabulary. She finished high school as his girlfriend while he, with her help, finished high school.

The birth of the Cleanery in the summer of their graduation secured their future together. Customers flocked to Ray for service and Pat made sure they got it. A marriage, a home, a family, and a retirement later, she had only one complaint with her husband: Sometimes he was just too darned nice!

Pat knew the luxury homes at Desert Springs were too expensive for them, but they might have done better than Leisureville. For a couple hundred thousand more, a much fancier development had been within reach. Had they sold the Cleanery, instead of turning it over to one of their daughters and her husband, they could have afforded it. For that matter, had they sold their home in Alaska, that would have done the trick too. The decision on the disposition of their business had tortured her. She always assumed they would sell the business to one of the interested buyers. It had been a major surprise when her daughter Amy went to Daddy and asked if she could take it over. It wasn't actually a request, of course, in that Ray knew only the one answer. Their third daughter, Rebecca, approached her father with a wish to purchase the house in Wasilla because she wanted to live where she grew up. Ray insisted she take it instead of buying it.

When Pat expressed concern for their own future, her husband had been sympathetic. He told her if she preferred to sell the business and house to their daughters, she was welcome to do so. He was sure they would be willing to pay for them. But for his part, he thought they could get by without inconveniencing the children. When she questioned the equity of giving a valuable business and home to two of the children while the others got nothing, Ray shrugged and said, "We're lucky. The others didn't ask! Tell them you'll balance the books in your will." Life was so simple for Ray.

Well, the Plumlees were getting by. They had saved enough money to purchase the home in Leisureville. Their retirement plan provided almost $80,000 in income last year. And there was the social security. Her marginal existence was his *Life of Riley*.

While Pat watched her husband practice his way through the back nine, she considered the recent excitement at Leisureville, the *Newswatch* program, the dancing, and the $30,000. In over fifty years of marriage, he had never disappointed her, not really. Now, for the first time, he was actually surprising her.

At the conclusion of the round, the Plumlees headed for the second floor restaurant with Jingles' favorite view: the course, of course. Caesar salad, mixed at the table. Smoked salmon chowder. Fresh lobster. While they looked at the dessert menu, the waiter brought a silver tray with a telephone on it.

"So, Jingles," the soft voice of Oliver Pruh said, "what did you think of my home course?"

"Well, Mr. Pruh, I'm not used to having so much grass under my ball. Hitting off your fairways is like hitting off a tee."

He laughed. "I'm glad you approve. Are you ready to show me and all of Arizona your stuff tomorrow?"

It was Jingles' turn to chuckle. "Don't even think about the cameras or it will take you off your game, Mr. Pruh. I can honestly say I don't even give a camera a thought. I found that out on Saturday. It's the beauty of golf. When you concentrate, it's like you're the only person there."

His own words made Jingles think. While the lens exaggerated the size of everything, it only allowed him to see what was directly in front of him. Like a racehorse wearing blinders, he had no peripheral distractions. Maybe that was a part of the magic of the lens too.

Oliver said, "The real reason I called was to insist that you try the cheesecake. One of you should order the chocolate one with all the strawberries on the side. The other should get the regular cheesecake with the blueberries. Then you can share. It's a life-changing experience."

"Thanks for the dinner and the tip. Let me put Pat on the line to say hello. I want to prove she can talk to you without hanging up!" After Pat conveyed her appreciation for the lovely dinner, the Plumlees ordered the desserts to take home.

On the way to the car, Jingles said to his wife, "I'm feeling cheesecake for breakfast, what do you think?" When Pat didn't say no immediately, he broke into a grin. Anything was possible these days!

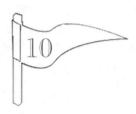

Upon returning to Leisureville, Jingles left to pick up his friends, who had agreed to accompany him to his scheduled match at Super Putz. The men were leaving for the Dominican Republic in the morning, and this was their farewell get-together.

From a couple blocks away, Jingles could tell something was up at the mini-golf complex. Multiple spotlights shot beams upward into the night, illuminating a banner that seemed to hang from the sky at least forty feet above the ground. As they drew closer, he could see the sign was suspended between a couple large helium balloons. Harvey read the message that was spelled out in dark blue letters on a yellow background: See Jingles putt! 8 pm Tonight!

"Well," Mulligan said. "Isn't *this* a slick promotion? Very clever." It wasn't all that different from some of the gimmicks he tried at his car lot in Chicago.

The parking lot was full and more cars were parked illegally along the road on both sides. Because it was only minutes before eight, Harvey volunteered to drop the others off and find a spot for the Lincoln . . . somewhere. Jingles nearly forgot to grab Pinger from the trunk.

The proprietor, Alex Levin, greeted them at the entrance. "I was getting nervous you wouldn't make it! What was I going to tell all these people?" He pointed at the course, where several hundred people surrounded his layout.

Jingles glanced at the course, which seemed modest at best, as many in the crowd yelled greetings or cheered his arrival. The spectators were a cross section of everybody, both old and young. When he waved to the group, they grew even noisier. The circus was in town!

"Here's my boy, Barry," Alex said, patting his son on top of the head. "He's going to give you a run for the money." The boy was short and skinny and wore shorts that may have fit someone twice his size beneath a Super Putz T-shirt. High-top Lebron James Nike shoes seemed oversized too. His outstanding feature was a mop of thick, curly, black hair.

"What color ball you want to use?" Alex asked.

Jingles reached in his pocket and produced a Titleist. "Is it okay if I use what I'm used to?"

"No problem," Alex answered. "The only rule is that you go first on every hole. As a celebrity, you should have honors."

Jingles asked for directions to a bathroom and left to install his right contact. He actually shivered in anticipation of performing, even at this odd venue, and even with a child for an opponent.

Mulligan nudged Knickers and whispered. "No wonder this place is hurting, the course is totally bland." He pointed to a sign that said: A No Frill Test of Skill. "Give me a couple carpenters for a few days, and I'd dress this place up. It needs ramps, windmills, tunnels . . . interesting stuff. No frills, no business. That's my conclusion."

Knickers nodded but was listening to something else. Not far off, he heard the sound of bats striking balls in the hitting cages. Even though it was the sound of aluminum bats, not wood, it played like sweet music.

Jingles returned, now wearing sunglasses, and took his place at the first tee. He placed his ball at the center of the mat and tried to study the putt. Because at least half of the overhead lights were burned out or broken, it was too dark to see with the shades. He took them off and stuck them above the visor of his cap.

The mini-fairway was made of concrete and covered with green outdoor carpet that had seen far better nights. It was frayed, worn, and covered with stains from countless spilled sodas and black holes from cigarette embers. Sideboards made from two-by-six-inch lumber contained a four-foot wide "fairway" that led to an eight foot square green. The distance to the cup was about twenty feet, and the only obstacles were two foot-long boards that stood halfway between the tee and the hole. There was six inches of clearance at the end of each board, along the sides of the fairway, and a foot-wide opening between them, right down the center.

In spite of the overt simplicity of the putt, Jingles' eye kept telling him *not so fast*! A path was worn into the carpet that led to the right of the cup. Even when he pushed his ball further to the right on the tee to allow a different angle through the center opening, there was no apparent solution. If he struck the ball hard enough to minimize the break, it could very well bounce right off the course. A two was the best score possible. He lagged the putt to within a few inches of the right lip and the onlookers groaned disappointment. When he tapped in for the deuce, Jingles seemed imperfectly human.

Five red and white clad cheerleaders stepped to the forefront after Jingles walked away from the hole. Looking about fourteen, they wore pleated skirts and sweatshirts emblazoned with an *M* and the snarling head of a big cat, probably a mountain lion. They each held pom-poms high over their heads and hopped and waved in synchrony.

"Barry, Barry, he's our man! Let's give Barry a great big hand!" They yelled the verse a second time, dropped their accessories, and started to clap together in perfect rhythm.

Jingles watched as the crowd started to clap along and realized he was clapping too! He was back in high school again, there was no escaping it. The cheerleaders were beyond precious.

Barry obviously thought so too. He wore a smile as big as his shorts and shoes. When the girls finished their routine, he dropped his blue ball at the far left edge of the tee and putted to the left side of the obstacles, not between them as Jingles had. His ball bounced off the sideboard and angled toward the hole, missing it by a few inches to the left before striking the backboard and ricocheting straight back into the cup. A double bank shot!

The cheerleaders sparkled again. "Putt it in, putt it in, right in!"

Jingles moved to the second tee, suddenly aware of the real reason he was designated to putt first on each hole. The kid had invaluable local knowledge!

"Nice work," Jingles said to his opponent. "That was impressive. You must play here lots."

Barry spoke to Jingles but stared at the girls with the pom-poms. "I play like ten rounds a day after school. You're totally meat."

Armed with a new perspective on how to take on the course, Jingles figured out a bank shot of his own for the second hole, a dogleg to the right. It too would require two caroms off the boards but seemed pretty straightforward through his right eye. He launched his ball off the left sideboard and then the back rail, where it thumped and stopped abruptly, well short of the hole. Again he settled for two.

Barry played his shot to the left side as well, but his aim was different. The blue ball angled closer to the far right corner than Jingles' Titleist had, bounced off two more rails, and dropped in for another ace. A triple banker!

"You're the man," Jingles acknowledged as the girls whooped it up some more.

The Sweet Swing

Barry nodded. "That's dry rot where you hit the board, that's what my dad calls it. You have to know where the soft spots are.

"Hey, you know what you remind me of?" the boy asked. "A cyclops. I mean, you got two eyes, but you only look through one."

Jingles was suddenly self-conscious. "It's how I aim, that's all." He decided to keep his head down as much as possible.

Over the next four holes, Jingles' lens proved its potency, and he aced three of them. Unfortunately, so did the kid.

Barry played as if he owned the place, which he sort of did. Still, Jingles had to admire such a great stroke coming from the young lad. It was one thing to know where to aim and another thing altogether to hold the line and proper speed. The kid had a gift. He should be featured on *Newswatch* too!

As he moved along the course, Jingles often noticed Harvey because he was s head taller than most of the crowd. But where were Knickers and Mulligan? He finally saw them joking around with the cheerleaders, seemingly oblivious to the match.

A surprise greeted Jingles on the seventh tee. The girls started chanting *his* name!

"Jingles, Jingles he's the man, let's give him a great big hand!" The whole place erupted in cheers from the spectators. He made a pretty straightforward hole-in-one.

"He's got style, he's got grace, Jingles made another ace!" the young ladies chanted and bounced until Barry's turn, then fell silent.

The boy frowned and looked wistfully at the backs of his former supporters, who had turned and walked off toward the next hole. He saw his father chasing them and shaking his arms in the air and then missed his putt badly.

Jingles rolled up a score of twenty-seven for the round and won by two shots. He put his sunglasses back on and shook eager hands and signed a few autographs before a somber Alex Levin passed him a wad of small bills.

Jingles sought out the cheerleading squad and gave them the money. "Go enjoy some pizza or something," he told them. "You were charming and beautiful!"

Finally, he accepted congratulations from his three friends.

"Giving the girls your prize money may have been a little overkill," Mulligan said. "Knickers promised each of them the newest iPhone if they would change their tune. The owner had hired them for nothing but a month of free mini-golf!" They all had to laugh. Cheerleaders for hire!

Harvey looked at Knickers and raised his eyebrows. "Those phones cost a fortune!"

"It's the least I can do for that company," Knickers said. "They've done well for me and Bess."

Mulligan pointed to the batting cages. "Hey, Knickers. Why don't you show us *your* stuff now. I'll bet you haven't swung a bat in ages."

"Somebody go grab some quarters then," the old ball player said. "We'll see what I've got left in the tank."

"Forget quarters," Harvey said. "You're showing your age. It's dollars now. I brought my grandsons here. A buck buys about ten pitches."

At the cages, Knickers picked out a helmet that fit and selected a piece of the artificial lumber. Aluminum bats with rubber grips! *What a sacrilege*, he thought.

"What speed do you want?" Harvey asked. "It goes from fifty to eighty miles an hour."

"Warm me up with sixty," he answered, and stepped up to the plate.

The pitching machine made some racket for a minute, a green light came on, and the first pitch came flying. Knickers took a big cut and missed.

Mulligan was hysterical. "Oh, man! So much for a dime a pitch! That was worth a hundred bucks right there!"

Knickers ignored him and moved into a bunting stance. He caught each of the next three pitches neatly with the bat, pushing one to the right, and the next two deliberately to the left.

When he started to take easy swings, he made better contact with each pitch. When the machine stopped, Harvey inserted another bill. Soon line drives started coming off the bat, one after another.

"Let's take it up a notch," Knickers ordered. "Seventy."

After a few foul tips, he started finding the sweet spot again. *Son of a gun, he still had game.*

"Crank it all the way up to top speed, Harvey," Mulligan suggested. "Let's put him to the test." Harvey served another dollar up and pressed for the top speed of 80 mph.

The ball became a blur to Knickers and left him swinging mostly at air. "That's why you don't see old men in the major leagues," Knickers pronounced. "Hitting a baseball at that level is the most challenging thing in all of sports."

Jingles was still wearing the lens with the bubble. Although he had never swung at high-speed pitching, he had spent plenty of time with a bat in his hands. In coaching Little League for decades, he hit countless grounders to his infielders and fly balls to the outfield. He also played slo-pitch softball for years and years. After watching the 80 mph pitches through his right eye, he was not intimidated, not in the least. He knew he could hit them.

The Sweet Swing

As Knickers slipped out of the cage, Jingles slid in. He removed his cap and sunglasses, set them on the ground, and found a helmet a little smaller than his friend used. He grabbed the same bat and took a few practice cuts before putting a dollar bill into the slot. The machine remained set for 80.

Assuming a bunting position like Knickers, Jingles waited for the pitch. The ball met the metal barrel and rocketed straight back at the machine, after knocking the bat right out of his stinging hands. Obviously the ball was moving a lot faster than it looked.

Harvey said, "Turn the speed down. You're going to get hurt."

Jingles stepped back and just watched as the next pitch buzzed past.

"When you bunt, you move the bat back as the ball arrives, like you're catchin' it with a glove," Knickers offered. "I give you credit for standin' in there."

Jingles bunted the next eight pitches with increasing success. He fed the machine another bill and took an open batting stance at the plate.

"Watch this," Knickers whispered to Mulligan. "He'll never touch it."

Feeling like he had a sense of the timing, Jingles started his swing early and adjusted to the ball. Crack! He popped the pitch straight up into the netting and felt a surge of adrenalin. He could do this! By his final few swings, he was hitting every pitch solidly.

When he turned to face his friends behind the screen, only Mulligan and Harvey stood there. Both appeared to be dumbfounded. "Where's Knickers?" he asked.

"Long gone," Mulligan said. "I think he felt like you were showing him up."

"I have no idea how you did that," Harvey said. "Seriously, that ball was coming in like a rocket or something. I can't believe you could hit it. It's like you're superhuman or something."

On the way home, Jingles tried to fill the uncomfortable silence in the car with his own chatting. Knickers sat in the passenger seat looking out the side window. The other two, in the back, were wondering what to make of it all. Jingles talked about how much he would miss them for a couple weeks and how everything would be getting back to normal by the time they returned.

When they reached the security gate, Harvey spoke, "I think Jingles is blessed with abnormally great eyesight. It's always been there but he needed prescription contacts to bring it out.

"Think about the great Ted Williams, the best hitter of his era and maybe of all time. He was no freakish athlete or anything, but he had freak 20/10 vision. It was a proven fact. In a nutshell, that meant he could see the same detail I can, but from twice as far away! A baseball had to look as big as a softball to him.

"That makes me wonder if abnormally good eyesight is a major factor for all the great athletes. You can go on the Internet and see how tall Ben Hogan stood and even how much he weighed. But how good was his vision? Nobody talks about that . . . even though it could have been the biggest part of his success. How do we know? It's all pretty fascinating, don't you think?"

Harvey waited for a response, but nobody was talking. "Well, here we are at Sleepy Hollow! Enjoy all your golf, Jingles. I'm pretty sure we'll be thinking about you all the time."

As he got out of the Lincoln, Harvey added, "If I were you, I'd go get your eyes checked tomorrow. I'll bet anything you have extraordinary vision that will explain everything. Maybe you're the Ted Williams of golf!"

After delivering Mulligan to his door, Jingles parked in Knickers' driveway and snagged the anniversary gift from the trunk. It was some kind of newfangled coffee making system that had been awaiting this day on the floor of Pat's office. Jingles followed Knickers to the front door.

Once inside, Jingles noticed something different about the interior. After reflecting for a moment, he realized that a collection of baseball photos on a wall had been replaced with a huge painting of yellow tulips. He handed the gift to Knickers and brushed by him to get a closer look at the art.

"This is a new look for you and Bess," Jingles said. "Those baseball pictures were here ever since I met you."

Knickers nodded and seemed to force a smile. "Classy, don't you think?"

Jingles was relieved that his friend finally spoke to him. While admiring the painting, he saw the name *Samuels* printed in the lower right corner. "Where in the world did you get an Ingrid Samuels painting? She told me she painted flowers."

Knickers chuckled. "Actually, I bought three so I could give one to Harvey and one to Mulligan for Christmas. Ingrid herself was your present!"

Jingles spun, stared at his friend, and felt a lump rise in his throat. "Are you saying that Ingrid didn't just happen to show up at the dance?"

Knickers called out to his wife. "Bess! Jingles is here! He knows about Speed Bump!"

Bess trotted out of the kitchen with a grin that matched her husband's. "Don't tell the others yet, Jingles. Let them stay jealous a while longer!"

"Did you see the faces on those two when you danced with her?" Knickers asked. "I thought they were going to start crying!"

Bess slapped Jingles on the shoulder. "You should have seen your own face! You were gawking at her like a teenager while you danced."

Knickers put the gift on the kitchen table and headed to the fridge to grab some beers. "All of Leisureville will be talkin' about that night for a long time."

Jingles accepted the drink and could only shake his head. Knickers was on a roll these days; nothing turned out to be what it seemed. He thought of the bubble lens in his pocket, and again wondered if Knickers might have something to do with that too.

He looked to Bess. "I'm really sorry that Pat is so upset with you guys. You have to understand, she's more serious than a lot of people. She doesn't laugh all that much. I have to laugh for both of us sometimes. She'll get over it. She always does."

"I love Pat," Bess responded. "Just because my husband and I are cut from a different kind of cloth doesn't mean we think any less of her. She's a great person."

Knickers reopened the front door. "Let's take a walk, you and me. I'd like to have a little heart-to-heart."

The men left the house with beers in hand and started up quiet Fairway Lane. Knickers was fortunate enough to live just half a block from the golf course and led Jingles in that direction. The first car to drive by slowed down and stopped when the occupants recognized Jingles. They congratulated him and wished him well.

As the car moved on, Knickers sipped from his bottle and asked, "Exactly what are they congratulatin' you for? I mean, really?"

The question seemed odd and caught Jingles off guard. "Well, the course record, I guess. For my golf."

"Well, I was impressed with that too . . . until tonight. Now, instead, I'm just wonderin' about it. I saw a couple of things that bothered me. First, I noticed that you putted with just one eye, your right eye, open. It was the first time I saw you play without them sunglasses. That just didn't sit right. And then, when you started hittin' those fastballs the same way, well then I knew something was really off. It's hard enough to hit a baseball with two good eyes . . . damn near impossible for someone our age."

Jingles understood the doubts. "The ball looked so big to me that hitting it was no real problem. I just had to time the pitches, which wasn't that hard because they were all the same speed."

Knickers held up his hand with the bottle in it. "Stop. Just stop. Why do you keep your left eye closed? Just answer me that."

"Because it only works that way. My right one that is."

Knickers shook his head. "Again, stop! I'm lookin' at you right now and both your eyes are open. They seem to work!"

"But I'm not wearing my other right lens right now. I'm wearing two regular contacts."

Knickers drew a deep breath. He guessed there had to be more to the story, but no idea what that might be. "So the lens you hit baseballs and golf balls with is *not a regular contact*? What the hell is it?" The men had arrived at the clubhouse and Knickers turned down the dark eighteenth fairway.

Jingles realized that he *wanted* to tell Knickers about the lens. He had wanted to from the start. Beginning with his trip to the optometrist, he told his friend everything, recalling every detail, every sensation. When they finally reached the seventeenth green, the men sat on Tom Klein's bench in the blackness. Knickers had asked no questions or even offered a single observation throughout the entire story, so Jingles asked for his thoughts.

Knickers rubbed his chin the way he always did while thinking. "Well, I'm not nearly as impressed with your golf as I was yesterday. I doubt anyone else would be either if they knew it was some kind of a trick."

Jingles felt his face redden. "Really? Is that what you really think?" He cursed himself for having shared his secret so readily. He should have stayed quiet like maybe Ben Hogan did.

"So what about Ted Williams?" Jingles asked. "He hit over four hundred one season. He's in the Hall of Fame. Are we supposed to think less of what he did because he could see better than everybody else?

Knickers vigorously shook his head. "That was different. His eyesight was God-given."

Jingles looked up at the stars in frustration. "Then why can't you see my bubble lens as God-given too? Heck, I've always believed the Lord works in mysterious ways!"

Knickers still looked unconvinced, so Jingles fired his last volley. "To tell the truth, we have no idea what kind of vision or contact lenses pro golfers have. If I got a defective lens that works this way, others could have the same thing."

"Well," Knickers said, as he stood for the walk home, "I just don't know. I give you credit for tellin' us you felt like you could see better than anybody. You did say that.

"But as your friend, I'd advise you to take a step back and think more about this. Come with us on the trip tomorrow and we'll all talk about it."

As much as Jingles didn't want to believe it, maybe Knickers was jealous like Pat said. "I'm committed to playing golf for Phoenix City Bank," he answered. "I really hope you have a wonderful time."

"Should I assume you want me to keep your secret from the guys?" Knickers said.

Jingles surprised himself with the quickness of his response. "You can tell Mulligan and Harvey the whole story on your trip. I know they'll be fine with it." *At least he hoped so.*

The Sweet Swing

As Jingles pulled up to the Desert Springs clubhouse Wednesday morning, he conjured up an image of what Oliver Pruh might look like. The soft voice on the phone suggested a smallish man, perhaps with a balding head and bifocals perched on his nose. Wasn't that how a bank president was supposed to look?

However, the Oliver who walked to his car to meet him stood about six-four and was built for pro wrestling. Jingles realized it was he himself that looked more like his idea of a banker, now minus the glasses and always minus the brains.

His hand disappeared in Oliver's grasp. "Phoenix City must be a big bank," Jingles said, looking up into the banker's eyes. "At least judging from the size of its employees." The comment was so goofy it made Oliver smile.

"I'm guessing you were a football player," Jingles continued.

"A lot of people tried to put me in shoulder pads," Oliver said. "I just didn't take to them too well. Trust me, I run like a banker."

"But I'll bet you can put a golf ball in orbit!" Jingles returned.

"I'm kind of special like that," Oliver said. "I'm the only guy I know that can hit a ball three hundred yards sideways."

"If you stand sideways on the tee, everything should work out then!"

Jingles knew the bank president reminded him of someone. Then it hit him. *Little House on the Prairie*. The Michael Landon show. Oliver was that huge former football player who played the friend with the easy-going, soft-spoken manner. Merlin Olsen. Merlin Olsen without the beard! What was the name of his character on the show? He'd have to ask Lucy.

Oliver introduced Bo Smolinski, a rangy man in his forties that was nearly the same height. Bo was the Desert Springs pro and would be playing with them.

Bo appraised Jingles warily, like a Homeland Security guard eyeing a passenger in a baggy overcoat. "I read about you in this morning's *Sun*," he said. "You are quite the sensation. Rags to riches in a week."

Jingles wondered if Mr. Pruh had mentioned the $30,000 to the pro. He hoped not. He then looked down at his new shirt and slacks that Pat purchased at Sears for the occasion. "Oh," he said, "my wife picked out a new outfit for television."

Bo decided that Jingles was joking around and extended a fist for the old guy to bump. Jingles happily returned the gesture and felt good about his playing partners.

A single cameraman from WAZA sat lazily in a cart, ready for the day's unusual assignment. Until Saturday, he had never filmed on a golf course. This was like a day off for a drive in the country, he thought, as he lit a smoke. From thin air, a man appeared and handed him a container for the proper disposal of cigarette butts. With *Desert Springs* scripted on the side, it would make a great souvenir.

When the threesome stepped to the first tee, a couple dozen club members gathered around to watch, as well as most of the clubhouse staff. Herman Winston, owner of Eagle Optics, was among the group of members.

Herman had taken the day off to watch his new hero in action. Without even realizing it, this Jingles was turning his business into a gold mine. On Monday morning he got a call from an optometrist named Sturrock, the doctor that performed Jingles' exam. Sturrock reported an amazing surge of requests for eye exams and contact lenses as a result of a *Newswatch* feature on the old golfer over the weekend. By the end of the day, a bunch of other optometrists inquired about moving their business to Eagle Optics, evidently after making inquiries with Sturrock. The flow of new business continued throughout Tuesday and showed no sign of slowing, especially not after the story in the sports section this morning, where Eagle Optics was specifically mentioned. This Jingles Plumlee was a godsend. The value of his company was growing by the minute.

As Jingles addressed his ball, music started to play from Herman's cell phone. The other members looked angrily at Winston and Jingles stepped back from his ball. Herman shrugged an apology and distanced himself from the tee. "What is it, Martha?" he asked in a whisper, after looking at the calling number. "I told you no calls."

"I apologize if I'm wrong, Mr. Winston, but I thought you'd want to know this. I just took a call from Karl Zimmer. He says he will be exercising his option. Fifteen million will be deposited to our account on December first." Herman dropped his phone. Miracles would never cease!

Jingles put his drive in the middle of the fairway, at least sixty yards behind those of the other two men. His Titleist settled in a deep divot, probably the only one in an otherwise immaculate fairway. *That was the nature of the game*, he thought. *You just never know.*

Playing from the poor lie, his 160-yard approach fell short of the green by a good twenty yards. He chipped to within ten feet and took his medicine, a par four.

Smolinski took honors with a birdie from fifteen feet and shot Jingles a self-satisfied smirk. The Ray Plumlee of old spent a lifetime ignoring such looks. They had always bounced off him like BB's off a rock. Harmless. But now he was Jingles. He was feeling new oats.

"You know, Bo," he said. "I'm used to playing for a little something to keep things interesting. How about a buck a hole and you've already got one in the bank?"

The Sweet Swing

Smolinski grinned. What was the old fart thinking? There was a big difference between playing with old hackers in Leisureville and playing on a real course like Desert Springs. This was *his* domain.

"Name your poison," Bo said, glancing at Oliver to make sure there was no objection from one of his member bosses.

Oliver nodded his okay and studied Jingles. He hoped he wouldn't have to cancel the promotional deal. Frankly, he saw nothing special about Plumlee's play on the first hole. For a fleeting instant, he even considered making a similar bet with his guest. Oliver was used to gambling with other members, just a little something to make it interesting. However, his conservative banker instincts quickly prevailed. There was something about the confidence in Jingles' limping strut.

At the conclusion of the round, Smolinski walked over to Jingles with slumped shoulders. He withdrew his wallet, pulled out a five and a one, and handed over the cash.

"What size do you wear?" he asked Jingles. "I'm going to give you a Desert Springs polo shirt and jacket. You own this course and your clothing ought to say so. Your sixty-four beat my own best score ever by two shots."

Oliver had been patting himself on the back all afternoon. Jingles was incredible! From tee to green, his game showed impressive consistency; hitting thirteen of eighteen greens in regulation was ample proof. But with the putter named Pinger in his hands, his game became a magic act. He made the ball disappear into the cup from nearly everywhere! A double-breaking snake from thirty feet? No problem. Twenty-foot downhill testers? Passed with flying colors. Eight-foot knee-knockers? Child's play.

He had inquired about Jingles' habit of removing his right contact lens so frequently and his constant use of eye drops. His new bank advertising representative explained that his right eye was sensitive and he avoided irritation that way.

Jane Friend greeted the golfers after the round. She looked at Oliver and he lifted his arms as if signaling a touchdown.

After giving Jingles a warm hug, she asked, "So how did it go out there today?"

"Well, I made a couple new friends, that's always a good day!"

"And he's going to make a few dollars," Oliver added. "We're going to set up for Sunland on Sunday." Sunland was a four-thousand home development not far from Leisureville. The retirement community was similar, but larger.

"I loved the article in the *Sun*," Jane said. "Your star is rising, Jingles!"

Jingles had read the article over breakfast. The writer was very kind in his story, which Pat attributed to the Belgian waffles she served on his visit.

Jingles figured the large photo of him standing over a putt might be framed and on their wall by the time he got home.

"I have almost no time before I have to leave for the station," Jane said, motioning to her cameraman to set up for interviews. "We'll have to get moving."

She talked to Jingles about his round and sudden stardom and heard the pro's observations about the talented visitor. Oliver announced the bank's new affiliation with Jingles and discussed the golf exhibitions that would begin on Sunday.

After Jane rushed off, Oliver invited Jingles and his wife to his home for dinner the next night. He promised to grill steaks on the terrace and serve up a *Newswatch* viewing for dessert. There would also be a contract to review and a check for half the payment in advance. He gave Jingles directions to his home and hustled off to work on plans for the Sunday exhibition. So much to do. So little time.

The Plumlees were preparing to leave for a practice round at Sunland on Thursday morning when they received a call from Charlie at the front gate. "A Larry Weinstein is here to see you. Should I let him in?"

Pat thought of the huge billboard not more than a mile away. Larry Weinstein Cadillac. "Go ahead," she said. "Thank you."

"Here's another surprise," she said to her husband. "Larry Weinstein wants to visit. He's on his way through the gate right now."

"That name is familiar. Where do I know it from?"

"Well," she said. "For starters, his picture is on a giant sign between here and the gas station. You've probably seen it a thousand times."

She looked at her husband. It wasn't registering. "How about all the late-night television commercials? Larry Weinstein Cadillac?"

The lights came on for Jingles. "Oohhh. The Cadillac guy! He's famous!"

"And here he is," Pat said, pointing out the window. "Live and in person."

The Plumlees walked outside to meet their guest, who was talking as soon as he opened the door of a shining blue Cadillac convertible. "Jingles Plumlee! There you are! What a pleasure it is to meet you!"

Jingles and Pat shook hands with a middle-aged man dressed in a cowboy hat and bolo tie. Larger than life, just like his billboard.

"Can we go inside? I have a great opportunity for you, the deal of a lifetime!" The Plumlees followed the cowboy into their house.

"How would you like to drive any car on my lot for an entire year for free? No charge at all! Even the one outside if you like!"

Jingles looked back over his shoulder at the car in the driveway. He never drove a convertible in his life. The thought gave him goose bumps.

Pat looked at Larry Weinstein through narrowed eyes. She didn't know what to think of a man in long pointed boots that wasn't riding a horse.

"Let me put you in a fifteen-second commercial for Larry Weinstein Cadillac, and I'll put you in the sweetest drive you ever experienced! It's that simple. That's all there is to it. It won't take an hour. We'll film right here on one of the greens at Leisureville. Picture this: You'll make a long putt . . . that's a snap for you, Jingles, am I right? Then you'll turn to the camera and say, 'Golf is a breeze when you drive to the course in a Larry Weinstein Cadillac! That's it! Done! And you *will* be driving to the course in a Weinstein Cadillac after that."

Jingles looked at the salesman in amazement. He never heard anyone say so much without taking a breath. It was a special talent.

Larry had Pat's full attention. After the car trick Knickers orchestrated, she no longer loved her Lincoln. "Can I get you a cup of coffee?" she asked.

"Can I get you a Cadillac?" he asked in return. "I'll have a camera guy here tomorrow. Your husband will be on the tube by next week! A half dozen times a night between ten and twelve. Heck, I'll put his face on my billboards too. How would you like that? The best of cars for the best of golfers! I've never made an offer like this before!"

When Larry finally paused to breathe, Jingles said, "I am going to be playing lots of golf the next few weeks. We could use a second car. I've always thought Pat would look great behind the wheel of a car like that one." He pointed to Larry's ride.

Larry looked at Pat. "You can come to the lot with me right now, Mrs. Plumlee. I have hundreds for you to choose from. Let's seal the deal!"

Jingles looked at his wife, nodding approval of the idea.

She said, "We are on our way to the Sunland golf course right now. My husband needs to practice. Why don't I come by in the morning?"

"Of course," he said. "No problem. One of my dealerships is less than five miles from here. You've seen the lot on Flagstone Road, right?"

She had. "What time would be convenient?"

"Ten o'clock would work. Can I set a time to film? How about four in the afternoon?"

Jingles nodded. "I guess we could use the first green at that time. Not many golfers start that late."

Larry clapped his hands. "It's a deal then. I'll have the contract ready for you to sign in the morning!"

"One question," Jingles said. "I don't have to wear a cowboy hat, do I?"

On Thursday evening, an hour before *Newswatch*, Pat stood on the veranda of Oliver Pruh's home at Desert Springs. She looked upon the same swimming pool, the same bridge spanning it, the same vast lawn that she admired beyond the third green two days earlier. It was a small world!

Jingles looked at Merlin Olsen, busy seasoning steaks on the grill, and thought this was no *Little House on the Prairie*. It was Little Mansion on the Fairway.

"It's a big house for just one person," Pat said to Oliver. It was a big house for a family of ten, she figured.

"I never set foot in 70 percent of it," he said. "It's all about keeping up appearances for my job. I could live in a cottage."

And I *do* live in a cottage, at least compared to this, Pat said to herself.

Jingles broached a subject he wished he could avoid. "I'm afraid my report on practice at Sunland is not so good."

Oliver turned from the grill and stared at Jingles. "What do you mean?"

"They aerated and sanded the greens within the last week or two. Ever tried to putt on a parking lot? I can make pars, but I don't think you want to pay for pars."

Oliver understood and felt embarrassed. He assumed the course condition would be comparable to Leisureville; he didn't even check it out. The homeowners association people with whom he made arrangements never mentioned a potential problem with the greens.

"What can I do to help? Do you want the course shut down for the next couple days? They could hit the greens with lots of water and roll them a few times."

Jingles shook his head. "Hundreds and hundreds of people will be playing that course over the next couple days, I wouldn't take that away from them."

That's ridiculous, Oliver thought. Sunland would close the course for sure if he threatened to cancel the event. It was the right business decision. He started to tell Jingles that very thing but stopped for some reason. Instead he said, "Would it help if they watered the greens more often than usual between now and Sunday?"

"I think lots of water would help the most. Maybe they could really saturate them the next two nights. To be honest, you spoiled me the last couple days with your course."

And you spoiled me, Oliver thought. Jingles' ability to perform well on Sunday had been the least of his worries. He pulled out his cell phone and called Sunland on the spot.

When the steaks were cooked to a perfect medium, they dined alfresco on the veranda. For an entire hour, the Plumlees talked about their family life in detail without a word about golf. All their children still lived in Alaska, the

The Sweet Swing

greatest state of all. They talked of fishing adventures, whales leaping in the bay near their old home, even moose grazing in their yard. The time flew by.

Oliver decided they were different than any people he knew; different in a good way. There wasn't a pretentious bone in their bodies. They spoke from the heart without a moment's hesitation. The more he was around Jingles, the more pleased he was to see him starring in such a unique fairy tale.

They watched *Newswatch* in Oliver's library, and no one spoke during the final five minutes of the show. The Jingles segment began with an aerial view of the Desert Springs layout as Jane did a voice over. "This is the scenic Desert Springs Country Club. Peaceful and tranquil. It is twenty miles away from Jingles Plumlee's home course in Leisureville and a world away from the frenzy you saw on *Newswatch* last Saturday night." The scene reverted to footage from the earlier show with a thousand people crowded around a green, dogs yapping, and the many signs on display.

And then they were back at the sedate country club. "Jingles visited Desert Springs yesterday to test his game on one of the area's top layouts, with less than thirty quiet observers."

The camera showed Jingles leaving a ten-foot putt an inch short. "Did the seventy-two-year-old have problems on this golfing day? Yesirree. On this putt, he looked like you or me!" *The twelfth hole*, Jingles thought and winced. *I never made a putt that I didn't hit hard enough.*

The next "highlight" showed Jingles blasting from a sand trap. "Did he find his way into trouble? For sure!"

"But did he play a solid round of golf? You could say that he did." The entire television screen became a giant scorecard. "Add 'em all up and the score is sixty-four, just two strokes shy of a course record!"

The next thirty seconds showed Jingles making putts from all angles and distances. "You are watching every putt that Jingles took on Wednesday, all twenty-three of them. Eighteen makes and all of five misses! You can watch them all again online by going to Newswatch.com and clicking on Jingles."

In Oliver's den, Jingles winced at a few of the misses. In truth, he had felt a little off his game, a little distracted. Had Knickers told the others the story of his lens yet? What did they think?

Jane appeared beside the club pro. "This is Bo Smolinski, the teaching professional here at Desert Springs, who witnessed all sixty-four shots yesterday. Bo, you read about Jingles Plumlee. You heard about him. Now you've played with him. What did you think?"

Bo showed some polish and smiled right into the camera. "You hear the expression all the time: 'Putting is half of the game.' If you ever doubted that, watch Jingles play. He's a surgeon on the greens. His putter is his scalpel, and he sliced up this course like very few have ever managed to do. We've had many young professionals and top amateurs play Desert Springs, and he could play right with them. If he ever needs a caddy for the Champions Tour, he can just call me."

Jane addressed Jingles next. "So you heard Bo, do you think the Champions Tour is in your future, Jingles?"

Jingles, trying to ignore the camera like he did when he played, laughed. "Unless my birth certificate is wrong . . . and my mirror says it's not . . . that's not going to happen. I'm just happy to be playing so well and making new friends."

Jane asked, "Are you aware that there has been a stampede to optometrists this week? Everyone wants contact lenses because of your story!"

"No, I didn't know. But I'm sure glad. Since I got contacts, I feel like a new person. I'd like everyone to see as well as I do."

Listening to himself, Jingles cringed. The words hurt coming out of his mouth yesterday and now they hurt his ears. *No one was likely to see as well as he did*, but what was he supposed to say? His vision was the result of a manufacturing error? Everyone seemed so happy with his play. Why should he complicate things? He just wanted to golf. Could he help people by motivating them to get their eyes checked? *He'd like to think so.*

"Well, you can schedule me for an eye appointment right now," Jane said. "My game can use all the help it can get."

For the balance of the show, Jane interviewed Oliver about the upcoming tour of senior communities and focused on Sunland. She concluded by referring viewers to the show's website for the latest on Jingles.

After the Plumlees discussed the show with Oliver, he went to his desk and returned with Jingles' contract and a check for $15,000. Jingles signed the legal document without reading a word, despite Oliver's protests. He handed the check to his wife, who zipped it safely in her purse.

As Oliver walked the Plumlees to the door, Jingles said, "Thanks for dinner and the contract. It was a great day. And tomorrow Pat starts driving a Larry Weinstein Cadillac!"

Oliver jerked to attention. "What about Larry Weinstein?"

Pat beat Jingles to the story and provided every detail of the car dealer's proposal. Oliver nodded his head slowly without saying a word.

Only when she finished, Oliver said, "I know Larry. We handle his banking. Would you mind if I talked to him on your behalf? I think you could get a better deal."

"I don't understand," Pat said. "We're getting a new Cadillac for a whole year."

Jingles trusted Oliver fully. "Of course you can talk to him."

"Just don't talk him out of it," Pat said and winked.

The Sweet Swing

With his guests gone, Oliver took thoughts of Larry Weinstein to his desk and sat down. He took a pen and paper from a drawer and started to write a few figures. How many additional Cadillacs could Jingles actually sell for Larry's five dealerships? One hundred? Two hundred? Five hundred? Possibly a lot more. People loved the Jingles story. The article in the *Sun* was one of the biggest local sports stories ever run. *Jingles*. The name itself was built for marketing. When he polled his board of directors by phone to get approval for the marketing concept, they were not only positive but positively excited. If Jingles maintained his game in the weeks ahead, how many other advertising opportunities might fall in his lap? Golf clubs. Golf apparel. How about the American Optometric Association? Like Jane said on the show, people were lining up for eye exams. At his age, Jingles had about the most unique appeal out there. What retired American didn't want to be just like him? What golfer didn't envy him?

Now that Oliver helped provide Jingles with the opportunity to showcase his talent, he felt a responsibility to help him make the most of it. Besides, Phoenix City Bank was in on the ground floor. Any additional publicity for Jingles added value to that relationship. He checked his phone book for a home listing for Weinstein and found it. Larry himself answered on the second ring.

"Hello, Larry. Oliver from the bank here. Sorry to bother you at home."

"Well, well. If it isn't the man I just watched on television a while ago. How are you, big buckaroo?"

"I'm doing well. I just called to touch base on the deal you want to do with Jingles."

Larry's antennae went up and he was quiet for a second. "He told you about that, did he? Well, I like the guy's story and thought I'd stick my neck out and give him some local support."

"I think you're on top of a great idea, Larry. A commercial and billboards for the use of a Caddy for a year, is that it?"

"That's pretty much it. The wife seemed real pleased."

"What do you figure a year's use of a car will cost you, maybe twelve thousand in depreciation? Fifteen thousand tops?" *Even less if you pawn off a demonstration car*, Oliver thought.

Larry was quiet, so Oliver continued, "You'd make that back on the sale of just a couple cars, wouldn't you?"

"You know how this business goes, Oliver. You can never be sure. I'm willing to take a chance is all."

"Well," Oliver said. "I know you're aware that the bank is going to have Jingles in the news constantly over the next month, and hopefully much longer. I'd feel better if you gave the Plumlees the title to one of your cars tomorrow. Maybe a new convertible like you drive. You know, instead of a loaner for a year."

"Hold on there, Oliver! You're talking about a sixty-thousand dollar car! That dog won't hunt."

"Well, I don't mean to rain on your Escalade, Larry," Oliver said. "But I think that dog will hunt just fine for Horst over at Copper State Mercedes Benz. You see, we all want to be just like Jingles. If we can't play golf like him, we can at least sport the same wheels."

"I thought bankers were supposed to make their customers money. I feel like this is a stick-up!"

"It's not a stick-up, Larry. It's a heads-up. Jingles' name is going to be gold. It is right now. You are a genius to be grabbing him early."

Larry laughed. "Well, I guess the Plumlees owe you one. They'll get their new car tomorrow. You got them a deal."

Oliver said, "Not quite. A couple more things. I'd like to see a real production company film the commercials for you, not the homemade stuff you've been running late at night. I'll find the right company and have them call you tomorrow. They'll do two or three different spots so you aren't running the same thing over and over. I'd want to see the finished commercials for final approval, of course. After all, we have a big investment in Jingles as well."

"Well, Oliver, I feel like you've bent me over and spanked me. Tell you what, I want a Weinstein Cadillac sign on Jingles' golf cart for these exhibition matches."

What an excellent idea, Oliver thought. *Leave it to Larry.* "You understand that we already planned on having our bank's sign on top of the cart, as the sponsor of the events," the banker answered off the cuff. "I think we could put a small sign on the back of the cart, right behind the golf bags."

"Do I have to get that in writing?" Larry asked. "And how about a half dozen tickets to each of these matches? I've heard that Sunland is going to be about impossible to get into. I just checked on it."

"No problem," Oliver said. "You'll be Jingles' personal guests."

"Are we done then?" Larry asked.

"That's pretty much it," Oliver said. "You'll write up the contract so it's good through the end of December. That's about sixty days. You'll have an option to extend it for another sixty days after that for $30,000. After all, he's going to owe taxes on the damn car!"

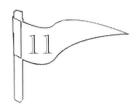

11

On Friday afternoon, Herman Winston sat in his office at Eagle Optics with an ear to the phone. "Okay, okay," Herman barked at his attorney. "But I want to know more about this Sherman MacPherson company. If they are so hot for Zimmer's lens, why can't they close the deal now?"

Herman looked at the calendar on his desk and counted the days until the December first option expiration. "It's thirty-two more days until then, why can't they close the deal now? I want my money!"

He tapped out a tune with his fingers on the left arm of his chair and rolled his eyes while his attorney talked. Lawyers never got to the point in a hurry. Not at $250 an hour. Herman tried to figure out how much $15,000,000 would earn in interest each day. That's what he would be losing every day for the next month! Then again, that was the very point. Sherman MacPherson wasn't going to part with the cash until the last minute for the very same reason.

"Well, stay on top of it," Herman ordered. "I don't want them spitting the hook at the last minute." Martha buzzed him from her reception desk outside his door. The next appointment had arrived.

"Gotta go!" Herman said and put down the phone.

Mark Roarke, Herman's marketing director, walked in, nodded, and handed him a single sheet of paper. His boss liked information in summary form. Sitting down in the chair in front of Herman's desk, he noted how clean the office was and how empty. There were no papers on the desk, no file cabinets, not even an in basket. It looked like a hotel room when you first checked in. It was a far cry from his office, where the desk was piled high and the chairs caught the overflow. Running a department that employed only him, a single assistant, and a secretary was no picnic. Herman made him release his second assistant the previous month as part of the budget trimming process.

Roarke said, "That's the basic number that our consultant came up with for the value of Eagle Optics in today's market, based on the last year's revenue."

Herman's eyes darted right to the bottom line: $17 million. Hell, he was getting almost that from Zimmer!

"Of course," his director said. "That number is low given the turn of events."

"Go on," Herman said. "I'm listening."

"You're aware that this whole Jingles thing has rocked our world. Our orders are up 320 percent this week."

Herman grinned. The stars had fallen into perfect alignment. "Tell Martha to put Jingles Plumlee on our Christmas card list, okay?"

Roarke shrugged. "We've had to turn away 74 percent of that new business because we can't deliver in reasonable time parameters. And that's despite offering overtime to all our operators."

The grin disappeared from Herman's face.

"According to our manufacturing department, you have only a couple options," Roarke continued. "You can either hire enough technicians to kick out lenses in three shifts, twenty-four seven, or you can subcontract with some other manufacturers that will handle our excess and ship under our brand name. The problem with hiring more technicians is that it could easily take a month or two for recruitment, screening, hiring and training. Personnel would need some new positions to do all that. That would require time too. In the meantime, we would be losing out on this unique opportunity to expand our customer base. Doctors will stop sending us orders when they know we can't fill them in a timely manner. A lot of them know that right now. By the time we geared up to meet today's volume of orders, the volume could be gone. Therefore, option one is problematical."

Herman said, "Not problematical. Out of the question. I told you I'm looking to get out of this business, not deeper into it. I'd like to walk away right now!"

"Which brings us to option two," Roarke said. "We could subcontract out our excess. We could probably do that quickly. The problem there is that our margin on the increased volume would be small and we would lack quality control."

Herman slapped the arm of his chair. "Proceed with that immediately. It'll increase our income and keep our customer base growing while we exercise our third option."

Roarke asked, "What third option?"

Herman shook his head, wondering why he had to do all the thinking. "Sell the company right now! We are riding a wave. Everyone knows we put the eyes on Plumlee. Get the word out to the majors about our volume of orders. Tell them Eagle Optics is on the auction block. Give them all the information they need and invite them to tour our facility."

Roarke considered Herman's suggestion. "You could probably get some serious interest if you had Jingles under an exclusive promotional contract."

Herman's tossed the director his snake eyes. "Why should I have to do that? You just said business is rolling in like crazy. I didn't have to spend a nickel."

"I think what we've had is just a knee jerk reaction and some favorable word of mouth. What's going to stop one of the majors from signing Jingles to promote *their* lenses? I'll bet most of them are talking about that very thing right now."

Herman slapped both of his armrests this time. "You're forgetting that he's wearing *our* lenses. We don't have to pay him in order to publicize that fact."

"Sure," Roarke said. "He's wearing them today. But he could be wearing another company's lenses on Monday and doing their TV commercials too."

"Sounds like risky business to me," Herman said. "Hitching up your wagon to a seventy-two-year-old horse seems a little risky, especially one that walks around like it threw a shoe. Personally, I think he's a flash in the pan. Golf is a much more difficult game than Jingles is making it look right now."

The director shook his head. Herman's notorious frugality could cost him plenty. "Perhaps you'd be interested to know that I got an e-mail from AOA today. They are contacting all the members to gauge interest in signing Jingles to a nationwide promotional contract."

Herman made a sour face. He had little regard for the American Optometric Association. They had been sucking dues out of him for as long as he could remember.

"The point is, if you really want to piggyback on Jingles, you have to act now," the director continued. "We could turn him into an invaluable asset of Eagle Optics alone. Our brand could go through the roof. One of the majors might buy you out for twice the price you are looking at now."

"Okay," Herman said, looking at his watch. He had a tee time in an hour for nine holes before dark. "Here are your marching orders. Call our attorney and have him draft a contract for Plumlee. I want it simple and irresistible, something he would sign at a glance. I want him to give us exclusive marketing rights for say, the next ten years. He'll wear our optics alone."

Roarke took notes. "And how much do you want to pay him?"

Herman took a deep breath. "Do you feel absolutely certain that I can sell this company for at least twenty-five million if we get his signature on a contract?"

"I think you could sell the company for much more than that."

"Then give him a hundred thousand. All payable on signing."

Roarke nodded his agreement. "And what is his scope of responsibilities under this contract?"

"I'll leave that for you to figure out. Have him wear a dang hat with our name on it. I don't care as long as Jingles is committed to us and no one else."

Roarke grinned and stood to leave.

"Hold on there," Herman said. "I want you to send out that message to all the majors that we're up for bid. Do it today and make sure they understand we have an exclusive contract with Plumlee."

"But we don't..."

Herman glared at Roarke. "They don't know that. They'll leave him alone as long as they *think* we do. And by Monday we will. Meet me here on Monday morning at nine and give me a report."

The marketing director hustled out the door. So much for his weekend plans.

Jingles sat at his kitchen table on Sunday morning, perusing a story in the sports section of the *Sun*. The headline read: *Jingles Takes on Sunland Today*. Now it was just Jingles. One name. A name that still seemed foreign. For days now, he felt like he was reading about someone else.

The day's schedule called for meeting with Oliver at a restaurant near Sunland at 12:30. Tee time was an hour after that. In the meantime, Pat and he would attend service at a church near the restaurant.

The greens at Sunland had improved over the past couple days, allowing him to feel more optimistic about his prospects. They were slow and soft. He could target the flags with his approaches. The fairways were rock hard and provided added distance to his tee shots.

Jingles walked to the bedroom to see if his wife was ready. Due to the challenge of finding attire suitable for both church and the golf course, Pat was still undecided. He had no problem; he could just remove a sport jacket, change shoes, and walk to the tee.

With a few minutes to kill, he decided to do some putting on his living room green. He went to the bathroom to get his putting lens. Standing over the sink, he was lifting the right lens toward his eye when Pat walked through the door and bumped him. The lens dropped from his fingertip into the sink below, where it slid toward the open drain. He reached for the moving lens with his left hand while trying to close the drain with his right. In feeling for the drain knob, he accidentally turned on the cold water! Like a cup swallowing one of his putts, the hole in the sink swallowed his lens. He stared down in disbelief. It all happened in a second.

He finally turned off the water, and another horrible thought struck him. Without the flood to sweep it away, he could have retrieved the lens from the elbow trap in the plumbing beneath the sink! He had sealed the fate of the lens by flushing it away himself!

Jingles looked from the drain to the ceiling in disbelief. *So this is what you had in mind for me! This has all been some kind of test? You want to see what I am going to do now?*

He turned to Pat, who sensed a problem. "Don't panic," Jingles said breathlessly, more to himself than his wife. "I just lost my right contact down the drain!"

He stumbled from the bathroom, clutching his chest, hoping that might keep his heart from bursting. The bedroom seemed to spin around him. What should he do now? He thought of Oliver and how he hated to disappoint him like this. Pat still had his check. They could return it. How about the new convertible in the garage that made Pat giggle like a little girl when she drove it? They could return the keys to Larry Weinstein. And how about the sheer wonder of playing great golf? He would miss that most.

Then he saw the faces of Knickers, Mulligan and Harvey. They were smiling at his misfortune, those devils. They had their old Ray back, or thought they did. What they didn't know is that he had no desire to ever step on a golf course again.

His mind then jumped to Sunland. Thousands of people would be there within a couple hours, no getting around that. *He couldn't run or hide.* He'd have to play this last round of his life and do the best he could. He put his other right contact on his eye, dropping it twice in the process.

He rushed past Pat, who had been watching him without saying a word, and headed to the garage. "I can't go to church. I have to practice putting without the lens. Pick me up at the practice green when it's time to meet Oliver!"

He rushed out the door without looking back. He couldn't stand the thought of seeing Pat's face right now. She would probably be crying. Or would she? She probably didn't even understand the true value of the lens. He certainly hadn't explained it to her in any detail.

In the garage, he opened the trunk of the Cadillac, which had pushed the Lincoln outside to the driveway. After grabbing his putter and some balls from his bag, he drove Birdie Chaser toward the practice green.

During the six-block drive, a handful of walkers greeted him with exaggerated smiles and waves. Even Speed Bump stopped and waited for him to pull over for a visit. Jingles, however, saw none of them. He was trying to gauge the extent of his forthcoming humiliation.

The bubble lens had been worth ten, twelve, maybe even fourteen strokes a round, he figured. That was how many putts he would have missed without it. On the other hand, maybe he was discounting the overall benefit of the regular lenses. It was a fact that now he hit the ball as crisply and as straight as ever. It was the absolute truth, he assured himself. The lenses would at least make his putting game better than it had been before Mrs. Beckerman clubbed him; he hadn't even tried them on the greens since looking through the bubble for the first time.

What kind of score could he put on the board at *Sunland*? Par wasn't an unreasonable target. Even seventy was within reach if he could concentrate and stop feeling sorry for himself.

Then the cloud of reality settled over him. There were probably hundreds of golfers his age in the Phoenix area alone that could shoot par on a course like Sunland. Maybe even his competitors today! He could see tomorrow's headlines: Jingles Returns to Earth, Jingles Bungles, Jingles Proves He's Human. He had to summon the strength to deal with it all.

Testing his regular lenses on the otherwise empty practice green proved utterly fruitless. Impending doom had seized his entire body. He couldn't think, couldn't stop shaking. Dropping Pinger, he collapsed beside the green and tried to calm himself.

Accidents happened. Wasn't the creation of the lens itself an accident? His receiving it was yet another. This final accident was the last chapter of what had been an improbable story from the very first.

One of his first thoughts after watching the lens go down the drain, returned to him. *He couldn't run or hide.* Why not? Perhaps the right thing to do was to call in sick like many of his own employees had done all too often over the years. In this case, there would be no deception at all. He *was* sick! He never felt so sick.

As he continued to ponder, the right answer came forward. *Honesty was the best policy.* He would tell Oliver the entire story of the lens and let him decide what should be done. After all, the exhibition was the bank's investment and it was the reputation of Phoenix City Bank that was really at stake. However, knowing the right thing to do didn't the make prospect of actually doing it any more pleasant. A day that had begun so beautifully was now the ugliest day ever.

A car horn sounded. He looked up and saw Pat in the convertible. She got out of the car, walked part way to the green, and called to him. "C'mon," she said. "We're going to church. You need church more than practice right now."

The clock on the wall at Hog Heaven, a diner just minutes from Sunland, displayed a time of ten minutes past noon. Oliver sat alone in a booth, reading about Jingles and the forthcoming exhibition in the paper.

Although nervous about the event, given the size of the anticipated crowd, he felt that he planned reasonably well. Eighteen branch managers "volunteered" their time for the afternoon with minimal protest. They, in turn, would supervise a similar number of resident helpers.

Initially, Sunland's spokespeople agreed that attendance would be limited to community residents. Outsiders could enter only with passes exclusively controlled by Oliver himself. Yesterday, however, he reluctantly approved a Sunland request to sell one thousand additional passes to the general public, the proceeds of which would support the community's library. They assured him that parking would not be a problem; it was under control.

The number of requests for media passes took him by surprise. All the local television stations would be represented as well as many newspapers from around the state. Major publications *Golf Digest* and *Golf World* had writers coming. Best of all, ESPN assigned a small crew to cover the event. Phoenix City Bank was in store for a major shot of publicity, not just the grassroots promotion he originally anticipated.

One thing was absolutely certain; his decision to promote the bank with Jingles could already be viewed as profitable. The bank opened over three hundred new accounts on Friday alone! On an average day, the bank picked up seventy-four new accounts and closed a slightly smaller number. His board of directors would be impressed at their meeting on Thursday.

Oliver looked outside and saw a new silver Caddy pull into the parking lot. His star had arrived! However, Jingles didn't look like his normally cheerful self when he walked up to the booth. Were those tears in his eyes? Had he been crying?

"I have to tell you, Oliver," Jingles said brokenly. "We can never thank you enough for what you've done for us. When Larry Weinstein told us that car was ours to keep, we couldn't believe it. Pat loves it!"

And I love her, Jingles thought. When he got in the car back at Leisureville, she had said, "You need church more than practice . . . so you can give thanks for your wonderful wife. I got a pipe wrench from the garage, opened the trap under the sink, and got your precious contact lens back. It was stuck in a wad of my hair. I always dye my hair at that sink."

Jingles had kept an arm wrapped around her shoulders throughout the church service and now kept a hand clasped over her knee while they sat at the table. While they each enjoyed a stack of pancakes, Oliver talked about the headline in the morning paper. Interestingly, he made the same observation Jingles had. "You know you are a star when you are referred to by just a single name. Soccer had *Pele*. Basketball had *Magic*. Baseball had *Babe*. Now golf has *Jingles*, another one name wonder!"

Pat grabbed her purse from beside her on the seat. "I almost forgot, Oliver. We got this letter in the mail and had two interesting calls I want to talk to you about." She handed him the letter.

"Wow," Oliver exclaimed. "*Ping* golf clubs! They are interested in having you endorse their clubs, Jingles!"

Pat said, "I wondered if you could talk to them for us, Oliver."

Jingles looked at Oliver and shrugged apologetically. He didn't want to put him to any more trouble.

Oliver said, "I'd be happy to do that. I play Pings myself. Did you notice that, Jingles?"

Jingles fibbed, "Of course, I did." And fibbed again, "And you hit them really well!"

"What else do you have?" Oliver asked Pat.

"Well, it's just two names and phone numbers that I wrote down," she said, handing another paper to the banker. "They both want to meet with us right away to talk about more endorsement contracts. One is the Eagle Optics company that made my husband's contacts. The other is the American Optometry Association or something like that. They wanted the same."

This was very interesting, Oliver thought, as he looked at the notes. "Herman Winston, the owner of Eagle Optics, is a member at Desert Springs. I think I saw him at the course on Wednesday. I e-mailed AOA two passes to the golf today."

Oliver tucked the papers into his right rear pocket. "I'll call them tomorrow and let you know what's cooking. Speaking of which, we all better get cooking. It's almost one o'clock!"

Taking the lead in his car, Oliver pulled out for the five minute drive to the course, where two parking places were reserved beside the clubhouse. A half mile from the entrance to Sunland, they were stopped by a line of traffic and the banker had a bad feeling.

Still a quarter mile from the gate with just ten minutes remaining before tee time, Oliver had to make a decision. He stepped out of his car and walked back to talk to Jingles. "We're going to pull off the road right here and walk in. That way we might be just a little bit late. I'll carry your clubs."

With Jingles' bag on his shoulder, Oliver started walking along the side of the road with the Plumlees. As they passed each car, the occupants recognized Jingles and started to wave and honk their horns.

A cloud of dust on the berm ahead grew larger and a golf cart took shape. Jane Friend had decided a rescue mission might be in order. She smiled as Pat and Jingles climbed in beside her and Oliver jumped on the back. "I had a feeling you might be stuck out here. You aren't going to believe what you are about to see."

A minute later, they whirred past the barrier at the entrance, where a red-faced gatekeeper confronted a group of angry people. Jane turned to look back at Oliver. "Poor planning makes for great television. A crazy reality show is what we have here. Are you the man I should be thanking?"

Oliver pretended not to hear and Jane said, "Well, I guess it's clear that you are!"

Every single driveway was plugged with three or four cars. Lines of cars were parked on both sides of the streets, leaving just a single lane in the center.

Jingles had decided that the Sunland development had to be quite a bit older than Leisureville. The homes were smaller here, all painted white, and roofed with gray shingles. Most had canvas canopies shading the windows. It looked fine to him but Pat never would have considered it.

Jane continued to poke fun at Oliver. "Some are saying we have at least five thousand people milling around the course. I'm thinking more like six. You told me there would be about four, so you were close."

Oliver wasn't in the mood for conversation. Clearly there had been a major breakdown in the lines of communication and the buck stopped with him. Keeping the bank's costs to a minimum had seemed prudent. How was he to know that Jingles would attract so much interest? He vowed to hire a PR firm to take care of the exhibitions going forward, if he survived this one.

Many in the crowd recognized Jane and Jingles as they drove toward the first tee and word quickly spread down the fairway to the green. A gallery this size might be small for a pro tour event, but at those tournaments people were scattered over an entire course. Here they were packed around a single 370-yard hole for the most part.

The scheduled competitors were waiting by the tee. Howard Spencer, sixty-five, was a former butcher from New Jersey and the current Sunland Club Champion. Sam Shumway, fifty-three, had been the club pro for close to twenty years.

Jane elbowed Oliver and pointed to another more familiar man by the tee. Slim Jim Gerken, Arizona's senior U.S. Senator, stood waving at the huge gathering. To Oliver's dismay, he held a driver as if he planned on using it.

Oliver walked over and shook hands with the twenty-four-year DC veteran who should have had the *Slim* dropped from his moniker long ago. "You are looking well, Senator. Did you come to watch Jingles play?"

"Hell, no," Gerken said. "I'm here to help you promote your bank, Oliver. I understood there was just a threesome, so I dumped everything else on my schedule." The senator waved at the throng of seniors, the age group that voted more regularly than any other.

Oliver didn't care much for the senator personally. He didn't like his politics at all. But most significantly, he didn't want a novice golfer making a mess of the exhibition. However, Gerken was very influential in the Senate and had close friends on the bank's board of directors.

"Enjoy your round, Senator," Oliver said, "and try not to hurt anybody!" He laughed as if he was kidding.

After Oliver gave the volunteer scorekeeper a minute to add Gerken's name to the scoreboard, he took the microphone for the small audio system set up behind the tee. "Welcome residents of Sunland and your many, many, many, many . . . many, many guests!"

The portion of the crowd that heard Oliver roared appreciation of his humor. He looked at Jane, standing only a few yards away, and lifted his eyebrows a few times. She laughed and shook her head.

"Phoenix City Bank, the premiere caretaker of retirement savings throughout the State of Arizona, is delighted to bring you this day of golf.

"First on the tee is a special guest, the Honorable U.S. Senator Jim Gerken!" Oliver was handed a note card with a long introduction by one of the senator's staff but tucked it in his pocket instead of reading it. Just letting the politician play was enough butt-kissing for one day.

Jane leaned close to Oliver and whispered, "I don't know how *honorable* it was to crash our party."

He whispered back. "Just don't give him any air time."

Oliver watched the senator address his ball and expected the worst; he had played with him at Desert Springs on a few occasions. Senator Gerken didn't surprise him. He sliced his drive badly and the ball flew at spectators to the right of the fairway. The ball hit an elderly man's metal walker and bounced right back into the fairway. Everyone seemed to laugh or applaud or both, with the exception of Oliver. The last thing he wanted was an injured spectator and not just for humanitarian reasons. He hadn't even considered the liability issue. Poor planning. Then again, he hadn't planned on Senator Gerken.

The Sweet Swing

Oliver next introduced Howard Spencer and Sam Shumway. Both hit nifty drives well down a fairway with the consistency of concrete. The club pro's drive rolled to within fifty yards of the green! Perhaps Jingles would have some competition.

For Jingles' introduction, Oliver handed the microphone to Jane. She was a celebrity in the eyes of everyone; it was good public relations. As soon as the crowd heard her voice, it erupted with applause. Oliver smiled, knowing that he planned at least one thing right.

"Has anyone here heard of Jingles?" she said into the microphone.

She then yelled it. "Has anyone here heard of Jingles?"

The crowd started to yell in response and some held up signs like they had seen on television. Jane hollered the question still louder. The people started to chant Jingles' name and fell into unison. Oliver looked and listened in awe. It was a pep rally! The only thing missing was the band. Jane shrieked the question for a fourth time and handed the microphone back to Oliver. That was it, her entire introduction.

Oliver had studied the crowd as it watched and reacted to Jane. They were children looking at a puppy; she was the cutest, sweetest thing ever in their eyes. He saw the adorable puppy as well, but knew the breeding was very different than the spectators realized. She had the intelligence of a German shepherd, the energy of a retriever, and the tenacity of a Rottweiler all rolled into one. If she wore a puppy collar, the tag would say: Return to Phoenix City Bank.

Jingles stood on the tee, casually taking practice swings while waiting for the spectators to quiet down. With his special right lens safely in a case in his pocket, he kept thinking of his wife, Pat the plumber. He looked around for her, but she was lost among the countless faces.

The chant continued. The message in the roar of *Jingles* was suddenly clear. It wasn't him, the individual, they lauded. It was the very idea that life didn't have to lose vitality when age robbed one of beauty, strength, or even alertness. Jingles was living the dream. Their dream. Older could indeed be better. He was their living proof. The people were cheering for themselves.

Reflecting again on the bubble lens, he vowed not to disappoint his wife, Jane, Oliver, Larry Weinstein or anyone else on this unforgettable day. He had risen from the dead and would take advantage of his second chance. The hard fairways provided opportunities he never enjoyed before. He made half a dozen eagles on par fives during three practice rounds . . . *six* eagles, when in his previous life there had been none! The greens had improved. He could put up a low number, he just knew it.

Jingles teed his ball down to take full advantage of the extra roll a low shot provided. His mind turned the people into shrubbery, the noise into music. His body swung the club as it always did and his drive flew down the middle of the highway of a fairway. With countless yards of roll, the Titleist stopped barely over a hundred yards shy of the green.

Oliver ushered him to a cart sporting a large Phoenix City Bank sign on the roof and red, white, and, blue streamers on the back that waved when the cart moved. Each of the four golfers had his own chauffeured cart and Oliver was his driver. The blue Larry Weinstein Cadillac sign on the rear of his colorful little limo surprised Jingles and pleased him too.

While waiting for Senator Gerken to play his second shot, and then his third, Jingles wondered how his friends were doing in the Dominican Republic. Were they playing golf right now? Probably not. They would have finished their play in the morning. What time was it there anyway? Probably a four-hour time difference. Were the men talking about him and the bubble lens?

Finally, it was Jingles' turn to hit his approach. With the greens waterlogged, he aimed his nine iron right at the flag itself. His ball dropped within ten feet of the pin and hopped no more than a foot. Minutes after that, in front of the 10 percent of the crowd that could actually see the green, he limped up to his ball and made his first birdie of the day.

On what would prove to be a day of broken records, the first to fall was the length of time to play nine holes. Had it ever taken a foursome three full hours to play a front nine? Anywhere? The golfers waited an eternity on each tee as the crowd arranged itself around the fairway ahead. Senator Gerken's play contributed to the problem too. His cart followed a connect-the-dots pattern that had far too many dots.

The event caught a major break on the tenth tee when the senator informed the group he was leaving. The play was running longer than anticipated and he had a dinner engagement. Gerken got his first ovation of the day when he waved good-bye and drove off. Oliver was so pleased he decided to vote for him in the next election.

When the banker looked at the large scorecard, he even thought of running for the senate himself. If the election was today, and he had Jingles' endorsement, he would win in a landslide. The scorecard read:

Shumway	-2
Spencer	-1
Jingles	-9
Gerken	+17

Jingles, alone in understanding his ability, was nonetheless amazed. Had anyone ever played nine holes in nine under? He thought of Harvey. Harvey

The Sweet Swing

would know for sure. In any case, Jingles knew he had been both as good and as lucky as he would ever get. The two par fives were the key. Jingles reached both in two: one with a five wood, the other with a three iron. Two eagles! The first came courtesy of the five wood approach itself, which left just an eighteen-footer. The other came off a forty-foot putt from the fringe. That was the longest putt he faced! Two eagles. Five birds. Two pars. One miraculous front nine.

Oliver was thinking ahead to the frenzy that might follow the round. *Thinking ahead.* He had not done that adequately to this point. The crowd needed to be controlled. A full-scale press conference would be in order; where could that take place? He needed to get back to the clubhouse a couple hours in advance.

Larry Weinstein, of all people, came to the rescue. He tapped Oliver on the shoulder and said, "If you'll let me drive Jingles for the back nine, I'll write him a check for the thirty thousand option right now."

Oliver looked at the cowboy hat above the pleading grin. "It's a deal, cowpoke. Just obey the speed limit!"

Oliver advised Jingles of the driver change and the reward for it. Jingles, in turn, looked over at the cart and gave a thumbs-up to Larry, who was already behind the wheel.

Life with Larry was different on the back nine. He proved to be the proverbial new sheriff in town. Where Oliver sat in the cart and waited for Jingles at each green, Larry raced the other carts to the green so he could arrive first and tend the pin. He made a huge show of walking to center stage and waving to the encircling gallery. After a couple holes of this, Sam Shumway noticed Larry's boot heels were carving up the greens and asked him to stay off them.

Jingles assumed Larry's behavior must be a car dealer kind of thing. Mulligan acted much the same in the limelight. However, he didn't care what Larry did. Pat was losing sleep with concern about the option and how they would pay the taxes on the new car. He could hardly wait to see her face when he handed her the check. He would call it a finder's fee!

Over the final holes, Jingles wasn't quite as good or nearly as fortunate. Still, six birdies and three pars were nothing to sneeze at. He knew that fifty-seven would likely be the best round of his life. Not bad for a great-grandpa!

After his final putt, Jane rushed to his side to protect him from the onrushing horde. She was one person for whom the crowd would willingly and readily part. She led Jingles back to his cart for the short drive to Sunland's fenced-in tennis courts, which were set up for the press gathering.

Larry Weinstein, who most of the crowd already recognized but now appreciated, shook hands and passed out business cards. He wrote $1,500 on the back of each card, along with his initials. The holder of the card would get that much off the price of their Weinstein Cadillac; $100 for each stroke Jingles played under par.

Jane drove slowly through the foot traffic, steering with her left hand and patting Jingles on top of the head with the other. It reminded him of the way he patted his Labrador retriever after it fetched a mallard or goose. If Jingles had a tail, it would have been wagging. He was thrilled to have pleased Jane. Her first *Newswatch* show had triggered the whole thing. That was only eight days ago! How could his life change so much in one week?

"I'm going to your home in Alaska," she said. "I'm leaving right after Monday night's show. Do you think Pat would like to come with me?"

Jane had decided a special half-hour program on Jingles was in order. She would focus on his background before coming to Arizona, the story behind the man so to speak. The idea was only an hour old, but she always worked quickly. She had bounced the idea off Oliver, who agreed to have the bank sponsor the entire program if no other advertisers were willing to participate, which seemed unlikely. One call to her station manager and it was a done deal. A replacement would anchor *Newswatch* for the three days she would be gone.

"Can I go too?" Jingles asked.

"Dream on," she said with a grin. "Phoenix City Bank has plans for you. You have to get ready for Raven's Nest next Saturday."

"I'm guessing my wife would love to go with you. We haven't been home in over a year."

Jane hoped Jingles was right. Having Pat with her would open the doors to all the interviews she needed. Her producer was already trying to locate a film crew out of Anchorage.

"There she is!" Jingles said, pointing to his wife, who stood next to Oliver on a tennis court. "We'll ask her right now."

Jane counted over twenty media people lined up to enter through the gate. In addition to a reporter from ESPN, there were writers from USA Today, the Associated Press, and the national golf publications. The rest were from media around the state. She knew the Jingles story would be very competitive going forward. Hopefully, she would be the first to chase it to its roots in Alaska.

Pat was delighted at the prospect of the trip but reluctant to leave her husband alone. Oliver clinched the deal by inviting Jingles to be his houseguest while she was gone. He would have a golf course right outside the back door!

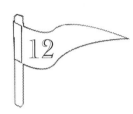

Mark Roarke was waiting outside the boss's office on Monday morning. Almost 9:30 and still no Herman. Finished with the feature story on Jingles' day at Sunland, he read the Ernie Wilson column titled "Jingles Turns Back the Clock."

Yesterday was turn back the clock day, the start of Daylight Savings Time. It's the one day of the year we can all sleep an extra hour without consequence.

Obviously, no one told Ray "Jingles" Plumlee, age 72, to turn back the clock by just an hour. He turned his back 40 years!

Jingles minus 40 would be 32. That's when golfers are in their prime.

It's an age at which a few, as in maybe one in a zillion, could walk onto a regulation golf course and shoot a ridiculous 15 under par 57.

Funny thing about Jingles, though, in addition to his name, is that he did that very thing at Sunland yesterday. He did it front of 6,000 incredulous spectators, including me. His game is beyond that of golfers in their prime. His game is beyond belief.

Like the others that watched, I wanted to see an optometrist afterwards. Unlike the others, who want to play golf like Jingles, I wanted to make sure I saw what I thought I did.

Jingles plays a different game than mortals. He puts the ball on the green when he should but makes putts when he shouldn't. Thirty feet away with a two-foot break? No problem. Forty feet up a hill and then back down? Why not? Through the windmill, up the ramp and through the clown's nose? Probably just as easy. For Jingles.

These are the scores for his last five rounds: 62; 60; 61; 64 and 57. That's not the sports story of the year. It's not the story of the decade. It's the story of forever.

Why, you ask?

Who is your choice as the best golfer of all time? Snead? Hogan? Palmer? Nicklaus?

Let me just ask this: How was his game at the age of 72?

Ray "Jingles" Plumlee. The story of forever.

The Eagle Optics owner finally arrived and Roarke stood to greet him. "Good morning, sir. I have some very good news for you."

Herman motioned him into the office and nodded a greeting to Martha, his secretary, who handed him coffee with two sugars.

"Did you see SportsCenter this morning, Mr. Winston?" Roarke asked.

Herman shook his head no and sat at his desk.

"Well, I suggest you turn on your television," he said, pointing to the wall-mounted flat screen. "The story changed your life."

"Spare me the drama," Herman said. "What do you have to tell me."

"Like you asked, I put together a package with our annual report, inventory of equipment and appraisal and sent it out to the ten companies that met my profile as potential buyers of your company. I also included information on last week's order volume and our long-term agreement with Jingles Plumlee. I e-mailed it out on Friday evening."

Herman nodded. "So you got Plumlee all signed up?"

"Well, not yet. I talked to his wife on Saturday, but she said I had to deal with Oliver Pruh from Phoenix City Bank, that he was handling his business for him."

"So how did that go?"

"It hasn't. He hasn't contacted me yet."

"Okay, so what's your good news?"

Roarke held out the sports page from the *Sun*. "As you can read here, Jingles put on a real show at Sunland yesterday. Over six thousand people watched him shoot a fifty-seven. ESPN has a big feature on it! Jingles talks about his lenses from Eagle Optics right on the air! Says they changed his life."

Herman nodded again. "Charitable of him. Go to his house and give him that check for a hundred thousand right now. I want his name on the dotted line."

The Sweet Swing

"Hold on," Roarke said. "I haven't even reached the good part. I got two calls on my cell before seven this morning. Companies on the east coast. They both want Eagle Optics. Like right now! I guess they are sports fans."

"They talk money?"

"Let me just say this. They are willing to factor in foreseen growth. One mentioned twenty-five million. The other wanted the chance to prepare a bid. They both asked me to e-mail a copy of our contract with Jingles."

Herman rubbed his hands together. "Don't go through Pruh. I'd rather we avoid that. Go find Plumlee and show him a check with his name on it."

Home was no sanctuary for the Plumlees on Monday morning. The phone had been unplugged since the previous night, but well-wishers started beating a path to their door at breakfast time. The solution had been to station Jingles on a lawn chair throne in the driveway. Pat served coffee in foam cups while he talked to his admirers and fed biscuits to their dogs.

Did you see the SportsCenter broadcast on ESPN this morning?

"No, haven't had the chance."

What did it feel like to shoot a fifty-seven?

"Actually, I felt like I was watching someone else play. It couldn't be me."

Are you going to play on the Champions Tour?

"As soon as cows fly. Seventy-two-year-old cows."

How does our Leisureville course compare to other places?

"It's fantastic. Mulligan Wettman does a fabulous job staying on top of it."

Will you autograph this?

"Sure, but remember, I'm just your neighbor."

Would you consider becoming the club pro at Leisureville?

"Maybe after I retire," he joked.

Two hours into the impromptu reception, Pat poured the last cup from her twelfth pot of coffee when a Cadillac as new as her own pulled up in front of the house. The driver introduced himself as Mark Roarke of Eagle Optics, the company that made Jingles' contacts. He wondered if he could have a word alone inside the house.

Jingles excused himself from his guests and went inside with Pat and Mr. Roarke, who was all suited and briefcased up. Jingles was delighted to see a face from Eagle Optics, someone he could thank in person for his lenses. *Someone he could thank for screwing up in such a great way!*

"I have to tell you," Jingles said. "Your company has changed my life." *That much was absolutely true.*

Roarke opened his case and took out the contract. "You don't know how much! We're here to take care of you even more, Jingles. We want you to sign an endorsement contract with our company. We'll make all your contacts for you for the rest of your life!"

Pat interrupted. "Didn't Mr. Pruh from the bank call you? We gave him your number."

Mr. Roarke cleared his throat. "No. He hasn't called and this is a matter of some urgency to us."

"How did you get through the gate?" she asked. "We didn't get a call."

"I had to see you right away, so I followed another car through when the bar lifted."

Pat nodded. Of course he couldn't call. She had the phone disconnected.

Roarke looked at Jingles. "The urgency here is that we would like you to advertise our contacts so that others will be aware of them and can benefit like you have. We'll pay you well to do that for us."

Jingles laughed at the suggestion. There wasn't much chance that anyone else would benefit like he had. Pure, simple luck. "You don't have to pay me to do that. I've already told everyone where my contacts came from. It's a known fact."

Pat shook her head angrily behind Roarke, and Jingles rolled his eyes.

"I know your intentions are good, Jingles," Roarke said. "But other companies are going to approach you about advertising their contact lenses and we want to insure that we, as the producers of those lenses, receive the appropriate credit. It sounds like you agree with that, right?"

Jingles said, "I need to talk to my wife in private for a moment. Would you mind?" He led Pat to their bedroom.

"What is it?" she asked impatiently.

"I can't take their money. The contact lens that's responsible for my golf was a mistake."

"A mistake?" she said, her eyes doubling in size. "That lens you keep under your pillow is a mistake? You seem to value it more than life itself!"

"Sid Wexler said so. I showed it to him the day I got it. He said it was flawed in manufacturing or something. There's a bubble in it. For some reason it works for me."

"Why haven't you told me that? That's a silly secret to keep."

"He told me not to wear it because it was defective. I thought you would say the same thing. What am I talking about? *You already tried to take it from me.*"

Pat said, "Think a minute. If Eagle Optics made your lens, who is most likely to be able to make you more just like it? If you show it to them, maybe they can duplicate it. You wouldn't have to worry about losing or breaking the one you have!"

The Sweet Swing

Her words made sense to him, and Jingles kissed her. She was such a bright woman! He led her back to the kitchen and said, "Mr. Roarke, if I brought my lens to your company, do you think you could duplicate it exactly?"

Roarke thought it was a weird question. Obviously, all lenses cut to the same prescription would be the same. Didn't everyone know that? "Of course we can duplicate them. I guarantee it. We have all the best equipment and staff."

Pat glanced at her husband with a "So there!" look, then turned her attention to their visitor. "How much are you offering?"

Roarke took a check from his inside coat pocket and showed it to Pat.

"Jingles," she cried out. "It's a hundred thousand dollars!"

Her husband barely heard. Eagle Optics could duplicate his lens! All his worry had been for nothing. He really hadn't understood the technology at all!

Pat's mind flashed to Knickers for a moment, and she looked out the window to see if anyone else was in the car. Wait, Knickers was out of the country. And her husband was a *real* celebrity now.

Roarke spread four pages on the kitchen table. "The contract is right here. I'll be happy to go over it with you. You can sign and take that check to the bank!" His hands were shaking. His whole body was shaking. Please, let this happen!

"Well," Pat said, her eyes playing ping pong between the check and the contract, "we still have to refer you to Oliver Pruh at Phoenix City Bank with that." She nodded at the contract.

Roarke laughed nervously. "Oh, you don't have to worry about the contract. I can summarize it for you in five minutes. Jingles doesn't actually have to do anything."

"Do you know where the main branch of the bank is?" Pat asked. "I'll call him now and try to set up an appointment."

Mr. Roarke could see the resolve in her eyes, the set of her jaw. There was no benefit in pushing things any further. Not *too* much further anyway.

"It's important that we see Mr. Pruh now," he said. "Frankly, I'm not authorized to extend this offer past today. Popularity can be a fleeting thing. We know we can bank on Jingles' fame right now, but who knows what tomorrow might bring?"

Pat reconnected the phone and dialed a number stuck on the wall on one of her yellow Post Its. Oliver answered his personal cell phone.

"Hi, Oliver, it's Mrs. Jingles," she said, winking at her husband. "There's a Mr. Roarke at our house from Eagle Optics. I think his name was one of those we gave you yesterday. He has a contract here he wants us to sign . . . ."

Mr. Roarke and Jingles watched Pat nod and listen and nod some more. Finally, she handed the phone to Roarke.

"One o'clock should be fine," Roarke said. "Herman Winston and his attorney will probably be with me, just to let you know. See you then."

Oliver pocketed the phone, looked at the time, and called his secretary on the intercom. "No more calls this morning," he said. "And cancel my eleven-thirty and the luncheon reservation. I have some people from Eagle Optics coming at one. Keep my schedule clear for the half hour after that. And thank you."

It was just 10:45, but Oliver felt guilty for having ignored the Plumlee's personal business for even this long. The guilt intensified when he considered his own good fortune. He had an early call from a member of his board of directors who was so delighted with the Jingles publicity that he was proposing a $300,000 bonus for Oliver at the annual meeting. Oliver already received a salary of $1,650,000 plus his Desert Springs membership, but the bonus was nothing to sneeze at. He had Jingles to thank for it.

After an early start to the day, Oliver already had a public relations company lined up for the coming exhibitions, starting Saturday. The total tab would be around $20,000 per event, but things would go more smoothly, especially for him. The money was now a non-issue.

He had set his alarm for dawn so he could catch an early edition of *SportsCenter*. Their video was fantastic. Six thousand spectators looked like five times that number. Jingles was charming and humble, looking great in his PCB cap. A couple of the top PGA pros weighed in on Jingles and said his putting was confounding. A few golfers might have a single round with twenty-two putts, maybe once or twice in a lifetime, but nobody could do it consistently like Jingles. Maybe the most telling tribute was the demeanor of the broadcasters; they seemed to love presenting the story!

One thing was clear. Jingles needed a top agent right now. For that matter, he needed one last week. He would be blitzed with calls for interviews and appearances that he may or may not want to accept but couldn't afford not to. With the publicity would come financial opportunities far beyond his deals with Weinstein Cadillac and his bank. Lots of them. Clubs. Clothing. Golf shoes. Balls. And of course AOA and Eagle Optics. A good agency would not only negotiate deals but find more of them. It would also help the Plumlees deal with all the pressures of fame they were just beginning to feel. It was time make some calls.

It was 1:00 p.m. before he knew it. His secretary announced the arrival of the Eagle Optics people. The banker met Herman Winston and two other gentlemen at the door. "Always a pleasure, Herman. Good to see you." Oliver shook his hand.

There was no smile on Herman's face. "This is Stanley Wilhelm, my attorney," he said, nodding to his right. "And my marketing man, Mark Roarke." Oliver offered them seats.

Herman sat and said, "So when did Phoenix City Bank start consulting on business like this? We simply want to sign Plumlee to a promotional deal."

Oliver flashed a disarming smile. "Jingles is a friend, Herman. He just asked for my help. It's all a little new to him."

"My company is a major client of Phoenix City Bank, as are my wife and I," Herman said. "I hope you view us as friends as well.

"As you know, we helped Plumlee by making his contacts and now we're even going to pay him for the privilege. We think he can help us sell a few more. We're offering him a hundred thousand to sign on with us." Herman looked at Roarke, who passed the prepared contract across the desk to Oliver.

"Give me just two minutes," Oliver said. Two minutes was more than enough time to get the drift. Eagle Optics wanted limited rights to his name and likeness for advertising for the next ten years. During that time, his sole obligations were to wear their lenses exclusively and promote the prosthetic eyewear of no competitor. Oh yes. And wear a hat with their logo when he played golf. He basically had to do nothing at all. Payment for the entire contract duration would come at signing.

"Your contract looks good. I just don't have any sense for the value it should have. In fairness to everyone concerned, I'm going to pass this matter on to Jingles' new agent. I may have found one to recommend. Have you heard of the Quinn Group? They represent all kinds of sports figures."

Herman shook his head. "That won't do, Oliver. I want to sign Plumlee today. Not tomorrow. Not the next day. You know full well that his present popularity can disappear as quickly as it came."

"So why are you trying to lock him in for the next ten years?"

"That's the tradeoff for us. We're prepared to pay him in full right now. We want the time in case his popularity endures."

Oliver nodded understanding. "I'm sorry, there's just no way for me to know if the money is right."

"The money is right!" Herman practically yelled. "The Plumlees were ecstatic when Roarke gave them the figure! They just wanted you to look over the contract. If you are going to interfere with this, I'll have to consider finding a new home for our accounts."

Oliver didn't like the threat. At the same time, he knew he shouldn't even be having this conversation during his workday for the bank. "Okay, Herman. You counsel me. I'm sitting here wondering what the big companies in your business might pay Jingles to wear their lenses. What might they offer? Five or ten times that amount? If he takes this deal right now, he'll never know."

Herman took a sideways glance at Roarke. Oliver said exactly what Herman feared most. Verbatim. If this negotiation went to an agent, Eagle Optics would be left in the dust. There would be no big pay day for him.

Herman glared back at the banker through slits beneath his brows. "And how much is Phoenix City Bank paying Jingles? Are you paying him as much as Wells Fargo would?"

That was different, Oliver thought. The bank had gotten into the game early. *Early. Five days ago.* "I can't divulge the terms of our contract with Mr. Plumlee."

"Here's the deal, Pruh," Herman said, almost spitting the name. "You gave this figure yourself. Tell Plumlee he can have that half million dollars if he signs the contract right now. After that, there will be no offer, no more deal."

The larger offer caught Oliver off guard. On the one hand, a brand new $400,000 came into play from thin air. That was exciting. On the other hand, the game must be bigger than he thought. A half million was an enormous number for a relatively small business like Eagle Optics. Oliver was well aware of the amount of activity in their accounts.

Herman's attorney spoke for the first time. "Mr. Pruh, you will call Plumlee and convey Mr. Winston's offer right now. It's your fiduciary responsibility to do so. If you don't, you can explain to the Plumlees about how you lost them so much money. You won't have to explain the loss of dozens of large accounts that I will orchestrate to your board of directors. I'll do that."

Oliver considered the lawyer's message. Things were getting ugly. The bottom line was that the Plumlees had been prepared to take a fraction of what was now on the table. They would be elated with the windfall. On top of that, Eagle Optics was a local business that employed local people. Most importantly, if something happened to Jingles or he lost his touch, the money would be his regardless.

He pushed a switch and asked his secretary to get the Plumlees on the line. Less than a minute later, he was talking to Pat. "Is your husband available?"

"No. He's over at the course filming some commercials for Larry Weinstein. You can talk to me. Are you calling about the Eagle Optics offer?"

Oliver knew Pat was the lead Plumlee on financial matters. "Yes. I'm here with company representatives at my office. I have no objection to the contents of the contract. It would basically keep Jingles wearing their lenses for the next ten years. He doesn't have to do anything other than wear their hat."

"What does the hat look like?" she asked.

Where in the world did *that* come from, Oliver wondered. "I'm sure they'll come up with a hat you approve of."

"But what about your bank hat that he wears now? How many hats can he wear?"

Oliver had to chuckle at that one. "He wouldn't have to wear our hat anymore."

"What if something happened to him in the next ten years? We aren't getting younger, regardless of what Jingles may think."

"It wouldn't matter. The only way to violate the contract is if he wore or promoted different lenses. You get to keep all the money."

Pat sighed. "Well, it sounds like we are going to make a hundred thousand dollars! I can't wait to tell Jingles."

It was the moment for which Oliver was waiting. "Actually, the figure has been adjusted. It's now five hundred thousand."

She was silent for so long Oliver got nervous. Finally, she said, "I don't know what to say."

"How long will Jingles be? I need the two of you here at the bank as soon as possible."

Winston interrupted, "Tell them that Roarke will be at their house with the contract immediately. I'll need to go downstairs and move some money around."

Oliver passed that message to Pat, then said, "I ask only one favor. Would you consider opening an account with Phoenix City Bank?"

Late on Wednesday night, Jane Friend sat alone in her room at Wasilla's Last Frontier Motel, pecking away on her laptop. Her two days in Alaska had been a whirlwind of interviews and fantastic footage. She had enough prize material to fill a two-hour show. The challenge would come in condensing it to the twenty-two and a half minutes of air time.

How should the show begin? Should she go with the photograph of Jingles at age ten, standing proudly beside his father while holding up his first trophy, a Canada goose? Jingles' first birdie! Or should she start with a look at the snow-covered golf course on which Jingles hit his first tee shot at the age of fifty-one? Her film crew came upon a cow moose and calf browsing on willows along a fairway! Or why not go with a vista of the rural Plumlee home with the dramatic white mountain range in the background? The sky had been an incredible clear blue.

At a Tuesday night reception at the Plumlee house, Jane met all four of the children, their spouses, eleven grandchildren, and even a couple of the great-grandkids. Wishing to be part of the festivity, Jingles called from Arizona and visited for an hour as the family passed the phone.

Their love for their father and grandfather showed in twinkling eyes as each talked and listened. To a person, their reaction to his sudden stardom was joyful disbelief, something akin to the way families of lottery winners must feel.

A community reception and potluck took place at the elementary school gym earlier tonight and the town turned out in force. In addition to a wealth of interview opportunities, Jane's group was treated to Alaska culinary delights. They sampled smoked and pickled salmon, salmon caviar, trout, halibut cheeks, and moose stew, perhaps the destiny of the two they filmed at the golf course.

Jane gathered perspectives on Jingles Plumlee, the man the community knew simply as Ray, while the cameras caught all the discussion.

A former golf partner, considerably younger than Jingles, shared some background on his friend's golf. *Ray was about a five or six handicap at the time he retired and moved to Arizona. Once he got to playing all the time, he improved some. I remember playing with him when he visited four or five years ago and he shot a seventy-three. Due to his age, or so I thought, his game started slipping a couple years ago. I know he was real unhappy about it. Last time he was here, a little over a year ago, he shot seventy-eight I think. I wouldn't have taken his money if I knew he was half blind! This is all like a miracle as far as I'm concerned, but it couldn't happen to a nicer guy. Ask everybody here and they'll tell you the same.*

Another golf buddy had received a call from Jingles just a week earlier. *Ray told me about getting contact lenses that let him see like he couldn't believe. He said the game that had been testing his patience for twenty years suddenly got easy for him. He promised to come up next summer and show off.*

A school teacher of Jingles, now ninety and going strong, recalled vivid memories of her student. *Ray was always a good boy. I remember when he just started to drive and had a rusty old blue pickup with a blade on the front. Every time we had a snowstorm, which is often around here, he'd be out plowing everybody's driveway because he thought it was fun. As a student he wasn't the sharpest tack on the bulletin board, but I always passed him. Who wouldn't pass a boy that plowed your driveway for free?*

Another friend appreciated his sense of humor. *Ray had a joke for every occasion. Well, he knew a few jokes and used them all the time. The one I heard a hundred times was about his custodial business. Every time someone asked him about it, he'd say it was the easiest job in the world for him because he was the only person he knew that could clean up a room just by leaving it.*

And there were many who applauded his generosity. *When any group of kids needed a donation or sponsorship, Ray was there for them. If the cheerleaders wanted new uniforms, he was first to put money in the hat. Every soccer, basketball, hockey or baseball league had a team sponsored by the Cleanery. When it came to Little League, he'd always coach the team too. He coached kids for thirty years and not a one of them will ever forget him. Just ask around. There are probably twenty of his former players walking around in here.*

One of those former Little Leaguers talked about his old coach. *Coach Plumlee had a special way of teaching us patience at the plate. He could never throw a strike when he pitched batting practice! In all fairness, though, he taught us to play the game the right way. There was never any fooling around. He taught us that the best way to have fun was to play well. The best way to play well was to take practice seriously. He called it "serious fun" and it was.*

"Jingles," Jane said out loud. It made you smile to say it or hear it. Pat told her the story of the unusual nickname's origin, which was as recent as Jingles' success. Now that was irony. He catches the name because he's complaining about his declining golf game. The very next day his game turns completely around and then some. Maybe that should be the lead to the show!

Jane sensed this story could vault her career. WAZA already marketed lots of Jingles footage to other stations and continued to do so. Newswatch.com had over three million hits in the last week. The number would really take off after the special. She wanted to craft it perfectly.

Before shutting down the computer, she did a final e-mail check. The only new message came from Oliver: *Hope your trip is exciting and fulfilling. I couldn't be more envious. I can only imagine how excited the family and hometown friends must be. Look forward to hearing all about it on your show.*

Interesting. The Oliver she thought she knew would have asked only about her take on the potential of the story, the business side of things. The emergence of Jingles was having an effect on the staid banker, bringing out a side of him she hadn't seen. His growing affability was rather charming. The bottle of peppermint schnapps that awaited her in the room when she arrived had surprised her too. The attached note said: *Something to keep your toes warm, Oliver.* The thought itself warmed her heart.

She mused about life for a minute, considering the domino effect of a single event. A woman accidentally tosses a golf club, noteworthy only because it sends a man on a trip to an optometrist that he may never have made. Corrected vision reveals a talent no one could have imagined. A whole community is energized. *Newswatch* airs a human interest story. Millions parade to have their own eyes examined. Her own career receives a jolt and she's in Alaska, of all places. A rock of a banker discovers he indeed has a heart. Larry Weinstein moves Cadillacs like hot dogs at a ballpark. Jingles banks rewards. The dominos just continued to fall.

Tapping *Reply*, she wrote: *Alaska is breathtaking. We will have to come here on vacation someday. Warm regards, Jane.*

We, she thought. That ought to knock him for a loop. Maybe even more than the thought of a *vacation*.

She turned off the computer and prepared for a nap before a wakeup call scheduled for 3:30 a.m. After an early drive to Anchorage with Pat, they would fly on to Seattle together. From there, she would return to Phoenix while Pat flew to Los Angeles to meet her husband and his newly hired marketing agent.

Wearing the new flannel nightgown Pat had given her, replete with a cow moose on the front and emblazoned with the name of the state, she crawled into bed and switched off the light. She closed her eyes and envisioned another way to start the show. The Alaska State flag was seven gold stars in the formation of the Big Dipper, all on a field of deep blue. She would start with the image of the waving flag and zero in on the Big Dipper, which would fade into the actual constellation in a star-filled sky. The screen would track to the location of the North Star, to which the Dipper pointed, and zero in on that. The North Star would fade into the smiling image of Jingles. Her technician could do all that in a half hour on the computer. Why not? Jingles *was* the North Star. He was also a star north of seventy years old.

And there was the North Pole. The name *Jingles* reminded people of Christmas. Why not start with a map of Alaska and zoom in on the town of North Pole? She could run with: *Christmas came early for Jingles Plumlee when Santa delivered his new contact lenses.* Too corny? There was so much to think about. So many choices.

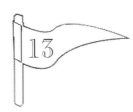

13

Jingles looked out the window of the jet from the comfort of a roomy seat in first class. He didn't know how he'd feel about riding in the front of a plane; he had only passed through that section in the past. It wasn't all that bad. The plane was circling LAX and he could see nothing but a network of buildings that extended to the horizon. It was a world away from Wasilla. Even the Phoenix area seemed desolate in comparison.

Not wishing to be alone in the vast city, he wondered if Pat arrived a half hour ago as scheduled. Handling success on the golf course was easy; life off the course made him uncomfortable without close friends around.

Oliver had entertained the PCB board of directors at his home last night and served up Jingles as the main course. Even as he spoke with one or two guests at a time, he could feel the curious stares of all of them throughout the evening. Worst of all, they expected him to talk all the time. His preferred role in conversation had always been as listener. That's how you learned things. Your own talk was mostly a recap of what you already knew.

When he asked others about their jobs and families, they brushed the questions away and pushed to know about his putting style, his endorsement opportunities and his upcoming exhibition at Raven's Nest. When the subject turned to Alaska, they didn't just smile at his old hunting and fishing stories, they roared their approval. When he talked about his career operating the Cleanery, his old joke about being able to clean up a room just by leaving it was celebrated as the funniest thing they ever heard! *The Ray in him knew better.* He had seen countless reactions to the joke in the past and none were so enthusiastic. It was his putting that had improved, not his sense of humor.

In the midst of it all, he had wondered what his friends might be doing in the Dominican Republic. Did they miss Pat and him? He certainly missed them. He would like nothing more than to sit down to a game of pinochle. Well, almost nothing. He would have most preferred to be in Wasilla, seeing all his old friends and family.

Oliver had fired up the big screen at just after 10:00 p.m., when Larry Weinstein's first commercial featuring his new spokesman was scheduled to air. Within minutes, Jingles stood over a teed ball with his driver on Leisureville's first tee, looking too good with all the makeup.

"There's only one right way to drive on a golf course," he said, taking a smooth, graceful swing at the ball. "And that's right down the middle." Another camera showed the ball landing in the center of the fairway. The scene immediately changed to Jingles driving the new Cadillac convertible into the parking lot. "And only one right way to drive *to* the golf course. That's in a Larry Weinstein Cadillac." A map of the Phoenix area appeared and showed the locations of Larry's dealerships.

"That was world-class," one of Oliver's guests said.

"As good as anything you see on the major networks," said another.

"Even better," said still another.

Everyone applauded when Jingles dropped a forty-foot putt on the next commercial spot fifteen minutes later. The ad began with him leaning over his ball with Pinger in his hands. Just before his stroke, he said, "There's only one right way to get the ball to the cup." He struck the putt and the camera tracked it up a swale and down the other side with a sweeping break. It plopped loudly into the hole. The commercial ended with the same scene of him driving up to the course, this time pointing out that there was only one right way to get there. Again, his new acquaintances praised the ad lavishly.

He joked that the putting commercial took a while to produce because they had to wait for him to actually make the putt. It was true. The fourth try was the charm.

Jingles felt relief when the visitors finally left. Sensing that, Oliver patted his shoulder and told him, "That's show business. Thanks for your patience and good humor. You're my hero."

A couple practice rounds at Raven's Nest had gone well. Oliver had the foresight to foil the media that staked out the course by disguising Jingles as just another tourist. Dressed in a floppy hat and shorts that showcased skinny snow-white legs, no one recognized him. Having lived all his life in Alaska, where the open air was either too cool or too laden with mosquitoes,

The Sweet Swing

Jingles never wore shorts out of habit. As an adult, he never owned a pair until Tuesday morning.

After the plane reached the gate, Jingles gathered his sport coat and small suitcase from the overhead rack. The coat was the one Pat told him to bring, along with the plain white dress shirt, dark blue tie, tan slacks and dark brown loafers. He bid farewell to his hostess Jennifer, who he learned was studying to be a nurse, lived in Phoenix, and had a cat named Phoenix as well. No one on the plane seemed to recognize him. He decided that may have been because he always wore a hat on the golf course.

Outside of security, Jingles saw the tall, heavily built man in the black suit for whom he was looking. He held a sign that said *Mr. Brown*.

"I'm Mr. Brown," Jingles said when he walked up to him.

The man smiled and extended his hand, which Jingles shook. Judging by the man's surprise, Jingles figured out he wanted the suitcase, not the handshake. The man smiled even more at Jingles' confusion and said, "Your wife is outside in the car. Did you have a good trip?"

"It was fine," Jingles answered. "But I'm glad you were here to meet me. This place is a little scary. What's your name?"

"I'm Simon, and I've lived here for twenty years. LA still scares me at times."

Simon led him to a silver limousine parked right outside the exit. He opened a rear door and revealed Pat and a tiny but beautiful young blonde lady, both sporting welcoming grins. Jingles slid into the seat and hugged his wife as if she'd been gone for years instead of days.

Pat said, "This is Gillian Constantine. She was in the Olympics about twelve years ago. She works for the Quinn Group."

He reached out and took the young lady's small hand, gripping it gently, as if it were porcelain. "You must be a gymnast," Jingles said, "judging by your size."

Gillian squeezed his hand with the strength of a lumberjack and smiled at his wince. "That's right," she said. "How was your trip?"

Jingles was trying to remember her from the Olympics, which he always watched from beginning to end with Pat. Her dimples stirred his memory. "The trip was fine," he said. "How did you do in the Olympic competition?"

Gillian made an exaggerated frown. "I was the girl who fell off the balance beam on the first day. I fractured my ankle and it was over for me."

"Oh no," Jingles said, now remembering the whole tragedy. "You were one of the favorites to win, weren't you?" He recalled her picture on the cover of various magazines and the accompanying story that touched so many hearts at the time.

"So goes," she said, dismissing the subject. "I've been working for Mitchell Quinn for the last six years. I've been assigned to you and Pat. I don't mind telling you, everyone at the office is jealous of me. They think you are the greatest thing ever."

Jingles laughed and looked at Pat. "That's a coincidence. Everyone we know would envy us if they knew we met you."

"We are quite the contrasting pair," his agent said. "My athletic career was over at seventeen. Yours is starting at seventy-two!"

Although Gillian tried to learn all she could about her new client, the Plumlees pushed her to answer all their questions about gymnastic training and the Olympics. The role reversal seemed odd to her, particularly since Jingles was the top sports story of the day.

The limousine headed directly to the Quinn Group office downtown, where they would meet Quinn himself. Gillian informed them that Simon would take their bags to the hotel directly across the street from the office.

A half hour later, the limousine stopped in front of a fourteen story building, all shining steel and dark glass. The former gymnast led them through the lobby to the elevator and upward, where the Quinn Group occupied much of the ninth floor.

Once there, Gillian walked to the closest door and spoke into an intercom. "Jingles is in the house." A buzzer sounded and the door unlocked.

Inside, they were greeted by a group of over thirty people, all holding glasses of champagne and wearing t-shirts printed with Jingles' smiling caricature. As if choreographed, they all turned around at the same time. On the back, some of the shirts said: Age Is No Handicap. Others said: Who's Your Granddaddy? One said: The Old Putter Works Just Fine, Thank you. Jingles laughed at the latter; it was an expression Mulligan often used after making a long putt.

The man in the Old Putter shirt emerged from the others and introduced himself as Mitchell Quinn. He was about Jingles' height, very tan, and sported the unnaturally perfect teeth of a movie star. He looked to be no older than forty.

Quinn ushered the Plumlees around the room to meet each member of the welcoming congregation, who were all his employees. He pointed out the gallery of framed photos on the wall—all present or former clients. Jingles recognized most of the names and faces. There were stars of baseball, football, hoops, and hockey. Skiers, bicycle racers, skateboarders, boxers, swimmers, race car drivers, and even a few golfers. The last photo Quinn pointed out was most familiar of all. How did they get a photo of him?

Gillian, who had disappeared for a moment, reentered the room wearing one of the T-shirts in an extra small size. Quinn nodded to her, and she

The Sweet Swing

announced to everyone that the Plumlees had to leave for their meeting. She led the Plumlees into an adjoining conference room.

The table in the meeting room had at least twenty chairs, all empty, and Gillian led them to two near the head of the table. A large projection screen on the wall, at least six feet across, showed an Internet web page featuring footage of Jingles making putt after putt on greens he recognized from Leisureville, Desert Springs, and Sunland. It was a highlight reel.

Mr. Quinn walked into the room and closed the door behind him. He sat at the head of the table, where a large laptop computer was open.

"That's the official Jingles website," he said. "We got it up and running late yesterday afternoon. It's jinglesgolf.com. Can you believe that jingles.com and jinglesplumlee.com had already been registered by other people? It's a fast moving story!"

Jingles and Pat looked from the screen to Quinn to Gillian and then to each other. Pat said, "Our kids are going to love this."

"Everyone is going to love it," Quinn said. "Anyway, let me get started. I have a lot to cover and I'd like to do it in an hour. The reason that your friend Pruh recommended us, I think, is because we already knew so much about you when he called on Monday. We'd been following your story from the get-go, which was what, barely two weeks ago? You are going to be surprised by all I have to tell you. I'm going to ask that you hold your questions until I'm finished.

"We are happy to have you because we've never had a client like you. Nobody has. The round you played last Sunday at Sunland, under a media microscope, made you fifteen or twenty million dollars at a minimum. If we play our cards right, which is what we try to do here, it could be much more."

Jingles heard Pat take a deep breath and felt her grasp his knee. He looked at Gillian and smiled in a way she took as apologetic, or possibly embarrassed.

"The web page you are looking at has highlights right now and links to every media story about you that has been printed right through today. The most important part of this is right here." He brought an arrow on the screen to the top right, where it said *contact information*.

"This is where every company in the world that wants to do business with you can connect with us. No more phone calls and no more mail for you to worry about. You can get an unlisted land line for your home if you want, but Gillian has cell phones to give you so we can reach each other at all times. Please keep them charged.

"The biggest news first. Nike wants you. We can screw around forever with endorsements for clubs from one company, balls or shoes from another, clothing from someone else, but Nike is *the name* these days. Nike makes and markets all those things all over the world. In your case, they will not be outbid. You bring them a demographic they've never had before.

"When we negotiate with Nike and everyone else, we're going to be looking at deals like the one you just signed with that little optical company in Arizona."

Pat said, "Oliver did a great job for us with Eagle Optics."

Quinn dismissed her remark with a wave of his hand and a look of annoyance. "No, he didn't. But I'll get back to that. The only thing I'm referring to is the fact that the money came up front. When you are seventy-two years old, about to be seventy-three on February fourth, you have to think of *the right now*. You have to be realistic. We have to get your money now."

Pat thought about their contract with the Quinn Group. Oliver e-mailed it to her in Alaska. She printed it at her daughter's house and read it on the plane. The agent got 20 percent of all contract proceeds in the first year and 10 percent thereafter. Is that why he was talking about getting the money immediately? She would have to think more about that.

Quinn continued, "Whether it's Nike, a car company, a bank, or a pharmaceutical company, we'll be looking to get the bulk of any contract paid immediately.

"Now back to what happened to you with Eagle Optics. The day they made Jingles' contact lenses was their best day ever. Well, the second best. The best was when you signed your endorsement contract with them. The owner of the company has it up for sale, up for auction really, and he's going to make twenty or thirty million extra because of Jingles. A larger company will pay that money just to cash in on the publicity and sales generated by the whole Jingles story. Let's face it, every golfer is suddenly thinking the only thing holding him back is poor vision. Call any optometrist in LA right now. They'll tell you their business is off the charts in the last week. The bottom line is that a large optical company would have been happy to give *you* a bunch of that money instead of Eagle Optics. They would *rather* have given it to you. Conservatively speaking, I'd say you cost yourselves six or seven million by signing that deal with Eagle Optics." *And cost me 20 percent of that*, Quinn thought.

He added, "You have to ask yourselves the question: Why didn't Pruh tell you to wait until you met with me? You signed with me later the very same day!"

Jingles and Pat looked at each other. It wasn't an unfair question to ask. Maybe Oliver would explain at some point. At the same time, they had been ecstatic to get what they did.

The Sweet Swing

Jingles said, "Live and learn. We know Oliver did his best and I'm the one who signed the contract, not him. And remember, we are only here doing business with you because of Oliver."

Chalk one up for Jingles on that observation, Quinn thought. "Next we have Cadillac. The little deal you made for yourself with Weinstein in Phoenix grabbed their attention. Would you believe that guy already sold thirty cars to people that watched you play last Sunday? Today he could use an extra dozen salesmen. They are absolutely buried with customers after your commercials aired last night. We can go to the other car companies, and we will, but Cadillac is intrigued. And after all, you are driving a Cadillac."

Jingles said, "Oliver got us the deal with Weinstein. He arranged for a really good company to make the commercials too."

Quinn listened to another interruption stoically. Okay, he learned his lesson. No more belittling Oliver Pruh, at least not in front of the Plumlees.

"The American Optometric Association has thirty-six thousand members. They want to sign you right now for obvious reasons. They are talking a half million and I'm thinking three point six. That's a paltry hundred bucks per member.

"Bank of America slash Visa is on the verge. As soon as we get your public appearances rolling, I think we'll get a really large offer there. More on the appearances in a minute.

"Hilton Worldwide sees you as a potential asset for its advertising. It has thirty-two hundred hotels in seventy-seven countries. Lots with golf facilities associated with them. Again, I think Hilton wants to see how the people embrace your public appearances. Wynn Resorts is in the running if Hilton doesn't step up.

"ThinErgy, the new weight-loss supplement company that you've no doubt been hearing about, is ready to toss you two million right now. I'm talking today!."

Jingles couldn't stay quiet on that one. "Weight loss? I've weighed 165 pounds for the last fifty years!"

"No, sugar," Pat added. "I'm his ThinErgy. I watch what he eats."

"Listen up," Quinn said. "Here's a quick Marketing 101 class. Jingles eats a half-gallon of ice cream before bed every night. Boom! In one month, he's 190 pounds, and they take a photo. One more month of dieting and work with a personal trainer and he's 165 and like a brick. They take his picture again, and he's the centerfold for AARP magazine. Before and after. People assume the *before* photo is before he became a great golfer. They buy ThinErgy. It's just the way the consumer thinks."

"Isn't that a dangerous thing to do?" Pat asked. "I mean gaining all that weight?"

Quinn laughed. "Robert De Niro, who is smaller than Jingles, gained sixty pounds for the movie Raging Bull. He didn't earn anywhere near two million for that movie, did you know that? You don't have to make up your mind right away. That opportunity will be there.

"As a senior citizen, you are an ideal pitchman for all kinds of medicinal stuff for arthritis, Alzheimer's, and on and on. I have someone working exclusively on that angle.

"And then we have international. Golf is so big everywhere these days and your story hasn't even hit in Europe, China, Japan. Personally, I'm expecting some impact there. Big impact."

Quinn went on to explain the process of screening and selecting the right package of endorsement offers, the importance of controlling the mix and amount of television, radio, and print media, and even how their personal lives would be affected along the way. It sounded like a recording, but was fascinating nonetheless.

"As far as your golf goes, I think this news will make you happy," he said, finally smiling. "The Champions Tour starts up again in the middle of January. I not only have sponsor exemptions lined up for the first two tournaments, I have a two hundred thousand dollar appearance fee lined up for the first one."

It was Jingles' turn to squeeze Pat's knee under the table. Wait until he told Knickers about this!

"Now back to the public appearances. For the rest of this month, I want to put you on the road. Letterman, Leno, Oprah, Good Morning America, the works. This is beyond a sports story. It's a story everybody cares about. They'd all put you on tomorrow if they could get you. Because of that and other considerations, you are going to have to drop the rest of your tour for Phoenix City Bank. I'll work that out with Pruh."

Jingles raised his hand and Quinn nodded. "I have to honor my commitment to the bank. If it wasn't for Oliver, I wouldn't have been on *SportsCenter*. I owe him for everything."

Quinn looked at Pat and said, "There is no advantage to having your husband play any more of those exhibitions at this point and possibly a big downside. What if his play falls off before we get the endorsement contracts we want in place? Your financial security comes first."

Jingles said, "I need to play on Saturday at Raven's Nest. Pat bought eighteen plane tickets for most of my family to fly down from Alaska for the weekend. I'm not worried about how I'll do. I practiced there this week. If I shoot worse than sixty-four, someone should shoot me! Wouldn't another good round just help you make good deals?"

"It's all about risk," Quinn said. "Everything is perfect right now. You have a great presence for television and Gillian will help you perfect it. The more people see you and learn about you, the more they will like you. The safe play is to just talk about what you've already done to everyone who will listen. You shot a fifty-seven, dammit! It doesn't get better than that. You can go on the Champions Tour in January with your fortune already in the bank and nothing to lose."

Jingles considered what the agent said and it made absolute sense. He was a smart guy. Still, it didn't matter. "I will play Saturday and we'll see how it goes. I know the bank has already spent time and money getting ready for this event. We'll talk about the rest of the exhibitions after that."

Quinn knew it was time to back off. "All right then. I'll get you back there on Saturday in time for the exhibition."

Pat nudged Jingles with her elbow. "We have to be back home by tomorrow afternoon. The family is arriving."

Quinn said, "I'll meet you halfway on that one, Pat. Gillian will make reservations for you and her to fly back to Phoenix early in the morning. She'll need to help you go through all your mail and phone messages. If I understood Mr. Pruh correctly, Jingles hasn't done any of that this week.

"As for Jingles, the two of us are flying to Carmel to play a round at Pebble Beach with some Nike people. We can't miss that."

Jingles' eyes bulged. "Pebble Beach? No, we can't miss that."

"And then tomorrow night," Quinn said. "We have front row seats for the Lakers game with people from the Optometric Association. I promise to get him back in time to play on Saturday.

"Okay, then, that's it for me," he added, looking at his watch. "Gillian has a couple hundred other things to go over with you. I'll have a car pick you up at the hotel tomorrow morning at seven, Jingles."

Jingles remembered his clubs were in the trunk of the Cadillac. "I don't have my clubs!"

"Not to worry," Quinn said. "I think Nike has their own plans for that."

He quickly left the room, removing his Jingles shirt as he walked. The same thought occurred to both Jingles and Pat: Whose shirt would he be wearing next?

Soft gray clouds shrouded Raven's Nest golf course on Saturday but there was little threat of rain. The only genuine threat to the most celebrated day in the history of the senior community was the absence of Phoenix City Bank's featured performer, Jingles Plumlee. The scheduled start was fifteen minutes away and there was no sign of him.

The substantial media presence had been abuzz for the past hour over a last minute change to the cast of golfers for the exhibition. Tommy Jenks, a twenty-three-year-old sensation on the PGA Tour, eighteenth on the year's money list and the fourth place finisher in the British Open, was going to play. Raven's Nest had the right to choose the competition, and Jenks's grandfather, a local resident, convinced his grandson to join him in representing the home crowd. It was Jingles and the two Jenks.

Or was it? Many in the media suspected that Jingles got cold feet at the prospect of facing off against one of the world's top players. Tommy Jenks, one of the longest hitters in the game, would likely turn the senior community layout into a pitch and putt.

Oliver, Pat, and Gillian looked into the sky to the north, watching for the helicopter that was supposed to be delivering Jingles to the course. Gillian had been on her cell phone much of the morning, learning of the cancellation of a scheduled flight due to mechanical problems, the acquisition of private jet transportation, and finally the chopper.

Standing much taller than the others, Oliver was the first to spot the low-flying dot and pointed. As it drew closer and took shape, the crowd around the first hole heard the sound of the engine and rotor. Soon the chopper circled overhead, exciting the crowd with the rush of wind. It landed on the fairway, just thirty yards in front of the tee.

Once the engine shut down and the blade spun lazily, a door opened and Jingles popped out, turned and waved to the pilot and hurried in a limping trot toward the tee. The fans cheered the grand entrance as the pilot restarted the engine and headed back to the Phoenix airport.

Jingles hurried directly to his friends and greeted them. Pat handed him a white cap with Eagle Optics in blue-and-gold block letters above the bill. His golf spikes were sitting on the seat of the cart, and he quickly laced them up.

Oliver punched Jingles lightly on the arm. "Glad you could make it."

Jingles nodded. "Me too. Can you even believe I played Pebble Beach yesterday? I dreamed of playing seventeen, with the island green, for the last twenty years. I'm finally standing there on the tee, taking it all in, and then put two in the water and make a triple bogey! A total choke over a sentimental moment. I still shot seventy without my own clubs. I played Nikes, and they weren't too bad."

"So," Oliver said, "you can make putts at Pebble Beach too."

"I made a few, even with a borrowed putter."

Oliver pointed to the scoreboard atop another cart. "Ever heard of Tommy Jenks?"

The Sweet Swing

Jingles had taken his driver from his bag and was starting the same exercises he normally performed in his garage. "The pro golfer? Sure. He was leading the British Open after the first two days."

"Do you want to meet him? He's going to be your competition today."

Jingles finally looked to where Oliver was pointing. "Wow. How did you ever pull that off?"

Oliver laughed and shook his head. "It pulled itself off. I didn't know until an hour ago."

Pat grabbed Jingles arm and led him off to see his children and a large delegation of spouses and grandchildren. They had trouble reaching the family, who were being greeted by dozens of Jingles' fans. He stood and watched for a moment, taking a mental picture he would always cherish. They all looked so proud, so caught up in the moment.

His son Mathew dashed over and kissed his cheek, before standing at arm's length, staring his father in the eyes. "Just one question, Dad," he said. "Who the heck are you? Really. I'm positive this can't be happening."

As Pat explained last night on the phone, the entire family was staying at Oliver's home for the weekend. He insisted. They filled not just every bed, but every couch and a bunch of inflatable mattresses as well.

Jingles barely had time to say hi before heading for the first tee, where Tommy Jenks's grandpa, William, was being introduced. He was the same age as Jingles, but seemed more muscular and fit. He could still fly a ball well over 230 yards and his drive rolled out to close to 250.

Tommy Jenks was a lanky kid with long blond hair that flowed from the back of his cap to the tops of his shoulders. Jingles saw the Nike swoosh on his shirt and cap and wondered how soon he'd be wearing the same. He figured the young pro would lay waste to the course, which had no rough and few hazards. In most cases, if you missed a fairway you would just roll into an adjoining one. There was no danger in swinging for the fences and Tommy Jenks would be letting the big dog out.

The pro's drive came off his club like a missile and seemed to hiss just a few feet above the ground for a hundred yards before starting to rise. As the ball disappeared into the sky, Jingles wondered if it might even reach the green, which was 360 yards away. Having never seen a tour pro play in person, the drive took his breath away.

A deep male voice, one of Oliver's hires, had introduced the first two golfers to the huge gathering. Now he heard the voice of Jane Friend. Jingles hadn't seen her and still couldn't locate the source of her familiar holler, *Has anybody here ever heard of Jingles?*

As the clapping and cheering commenced, Jingles walked around the tee, slapping extended hands and exchanging as many hellos as he could, just the way he had been instructed to do by Gillian. People *like* talent, she said. But they *love* a talented person that shows them some love.

Tommy Jenks was poking his grandfather, looking around, and laughing at the spectacle.

Jane popped out of the crowd, repeating her question into a handheld microphone, and walked beside Jingles around the tee. Up the fairway, some of the oldsters started hopping up and down.

Gillian was holding out her cell phone, sharing the noise with whoever was on the other end of the line.

Jingles thought of his family witnessing all this and tears started leaking from his eyes. He tried to blink the tears to a stop but couldn't do it. He had to walk off the tee to his cart and sit down.

The sound of Jane's voice was replaced by the blare of music from at least a dozen speakers spread from the tee halfway down the fairway. It was Leisureville again! *Jingle Bell Rock*. Jane grabbed Tommy Jenks' hand and pulled him to the center of the tee and started to dance. He did his best to follow along. Soon the whole place turned into one big dance; Christmas had arrived over a month early!

Jingles looked up and saw Oliver dancing with Gillian in front of his cart. They were as caught up in the whole scene as everyone else. His unexpected breakdown was over. Now he felt just amusement in watching a lumbering giant cavort with a limber munchkin. He was reminded of the work of his favorite Alaskan artist, Victoria Owens, who drew or scrimshawed images of animals dancing together. Oliver was a grizzly bear and Gillian was a seagull.

He picked up his driver, walked to the tee, and set up his Titleist. Yesterday at Pebble Beach it had been a Nike and he noticed no appreciable difference. He was glad that he wouldn't be making any sacrifice in the name of earning endorsement dollars. The moment the music stopped, he put metal to surlyn and knocked his drive down the middle, about fifteen yards shy of the elder Jenks' ball. The crowd whistled approval of a shot that was a full 120 yards behind that of the younger Jenks.

As they headed down the first fairway, Jingles said to Oliver, "How do I go about thanking you for setting up my whole family at your house this weekend? Let's see, with Pat, that's nineteen houseguests."

"You forgot Gillian, that made twenty!" he said with a grin. "Finally, I found a good use for that house! I think they had fun being together like that. We all went out to dinner and then went back to the house and kicked back. There were people sleeping everywhere."

"I understand you even gave up your bedroom?"

The Sweet Swing

"I did. I left around ten and slept at the bank. You've seen that big leather couch in my office there."

"And you and Pat have made plans for tonight too?"

"We have. I've got caterers putting a nice dinner together. Afterwards we'll watch Jane's special on yours truly. It aired last night and I have it recorded."

Oliver stopped the cart, and Jingles pulled his seven iron from the bag. After a moment's hesitation, he pulled the eight instead. His approach landed short of the green by a couple yards and went no further.

"They must have just watered the course down, at least around the greens," Jingles said, hopping back in the cart. "A few days ago that ball bounced right up there."

After young Jenks chipped to within a foot of the flag, Jingles was faced with a forty-five-footer from well off the putting surface. His long putt veered off-line before reaching the short grass, and he had to settle for par. Jenks took the lead right off the bat.

At the second tee, Jingles asked, "How did you get the driver's seat back from Larry?"

Oliver laughed. "He's so busy selling cars that he couldn't leave the lot! Your commercials are a big hit."

"That's what Mr. Quinn said. He mentioned that we might get a national car deal with Cadillac."

"That's great. Did Quinn think the contract with Weinstein was okay?"

"He seemed happy with everything. He's really excited about Nike."

"And was he okay with the Eagle Optics contract?" Oliver asked, watching Jingles' reaction closely. A friend of Oliver's told him that Herman Winston had been bragging about his deal with Jingles at the bar in the clubhouse at Desert Springs. He said that he was going to make a fortune on the sale of his company because of it. Oliver had been harboring a sick feeling in his stomach ever since.

Jingles noticed the concern in his friend's voice and thought before he spoke. "You see all those Plumlees standing over there?" He pointed to where his family was standing in a group about fifty yards away. "They wouldn't be standing there right now if it wasn't for that contract. You did very well."

After Tommy Jenks blew through the five-hundred-yard second hole with a driver, nine iron and eight-foot putt for an eagle, his lead over Jingles, who made birdie, increased to two strokes.

On returning to the cart, Jingles said, "I'm going to shoot you a sixty-three or better today, I can feel it. But I think Jenks will shoot a fifty-three!"

211

Jingles lost no more ground over the next seven holes, despite missing a couple greens and one long birdie putt. The pro was a monster from tee to green, but just a talented mortal with his putter, especially on greens he never played previously. With the scoreboard showing one Jenks at -7 and the other at +3, Jingles was a solid -5.

On the par-five eleventh, Jingles got the kind of break he needed. His chip from twenty yards off the green rattled off the pin and dropped for an eagle. When Jenks two-putted for birdie, his lead was a single stroke. The gallery, which had been in Jingles' corner from the start, was revitalized.

For the next six holes, the two put up identical scores of four birdies and two pars. Jenks was hitting most of his approaches stiff and making putts of under ten feet. Jingles was dropping mostly twenty-footers and canned one putt from almost double that distance.

On the final hole, Jingles hit his best long approach of the day. A seven iron from 140 yards hit the front of the green and rolled to within a foot of the flag. Without thinking, he raised the club in the air and posed like the Statue of Liberty; this birdie would result from a great golf shot, not a lens-aided putt. For some reason, that suddenly seemed to matter. Unfazed, Jenks lobbed a short wedge to within six feet.

For just the second time of the day, Jingles didn't need to wear his special right lens onto the green. The young Jenks took the flag from the cup and invited Jingles to tap in, which he did. He waved his white hat as he left the green, leaving the pair of Jenks to finish the round.

William left his long birdie try short and finished off his seventy-nine.

That left the young pro alone to knock in his short putt and collect the winner's purse, which consisted of nothing more than the glory of beating a couple guys fifty years his senior. He went through all the motions, then hit his ball firmly. It caught the lip and spun out. The exhibition ended in a tie.

Tommy Jenks and Jingles stood near the center of the green and shook hands as cameras clicked away. That very scene would be featured on sports pages all around the country on Sunday morning.

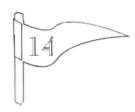

14

Walking into his Eagle Optics building on Monday morning, Herman Winston was counting down the days to his retirement. In exactly twenty-one days he would receive his fifteen million from Karl Zimmer. Soon thereafter, he would sell his company to the highest bidder. That was the plan for the glorious future.

Herman was actually glad to see Mark Roarke waiting outside his office. All his marketing director did these days was bring more good news. His projection of the sale price for the company kept growing every day.

"Morning, Martha. Morning, Mark," Herman said with uncustomary courtesy. "Did you see our boy Jingles all over the news today? He's wearing our name on his head like a halo!"

"You won't believe the e-mails I have today," Roarke said, following his boss into his office. "We have two new players in the game today. Are you ready for this irony? One of them is the German company, Fokus. That's where Zimmer came from. They are suddenly wanting a footprint in the United States!"

Herman laughed aloud. "Yes, that would be ironic."

"It makes perfect sense," Roarke continued. "The Euro is at a dollar forty. We're rather cheap for them. It's the first company outside the U.S. that I've heard from."

"Well, just tell them the same as everyone else. Noon on December twelfth is auction time. Jingles goes to the highest closed bid and brings the rest of the damn company with him."

Martha Porter tapped on the door and opened it. "Manufacturing is here to see you," she said, referring to the head of that department. "He says it's important."

The director of manufacturing, Joe Cole, walked directly to Herman's desk and put a contact lens on it. "We have a problem. This lens was returned to us in the mail over the weekend. It came from an elderly woman in Flagstaff."

Herman glanced at the lens and then to his problem bearer. "And what is that?"

"The problem is the lens. It's one of Karl Zimmer's! How in the hell did a lady in Flagstaff get one of those lenses?"

"You are sure about that?"

"Definitely."

Herman wrapped his hands around his face. This wasn't the way he wanted to start this day or any other.

"Well," Herman said. "If she returned the lens to us, she obviously got it from us. Was she harmed in any way? Are we in trouble?"

"No, no," Cole said. "We just got a note saying it was no good and she wants a replacement. She thought it might have been damaged in shipping or something. When one of my people looked at it, he realized what it was."

"Dammit," Herman said. "You're the one who has the buttons Zimmer made! I thought they were under lock and key!"

"You're right," the director said sheepishly. "I was so shocked over this that I didn't even think to check. We have exactly fifty-four of them. I'll go make sure that everything's in order and I'll be right back." He rushed out of the office and down the hall.

Herman and Roarke sat quietly, staring at the walls. Both understood the full ramifications. If one of the unlicensed lenses ended up harming someone, everything could be lost. The option would never be exercised. The value of the company would plummet. Liability? Herman didn't even want to think about that.

The marketing director returned in just a couple minutes, breathing hard and holding a piece of paper. "We have fifty-two of them!. Karl Zimmer signed out two of them on September first at eight-fifteen in the morning. The note says they were for the director's meeting that day."

Roarke thought back to the meeting, when he sat right beside Zimmer. He remembered the two buttons! Zimmer had been playing around with them. "I saw Zimmer holding them. I'm positive. He dropped them on the table and picked them up again."

"And they were never returned to us," Cole said. "My secretary put the note in the bag and forgot about it."

Herman was sweating despite the air conditioning. "You have two things to do right this minute. Find Zimmer and ask him what he did with those buttons!"

"Are those two things or just one? You said two things."

"And fire your secretary!"

At her desk outside Mr. Winston's office, Martha Porter started to cry. She heard every word of the loud conversation on the other side of the door. She knew exactly how two of Karl Zimmer's buttons had been cut into contacts. They had been right there on the floor after the meeting. She picked them up herself and took them to manufacturing. They looked just like all the others! Why hadn't she asked about them or thrown them away? Her mistake would cost her. She would get fired like Sally down the hall.

Like the honest employee she was, Martha marched right into the office and told her story. The men allowed her to leave the room before the yelling started.

Herman's face was scarlet. "Exactly what kind of a place am I running here? This is a joke! It's like kindergarten or something! I hate this place!"

"At least we know where we stand," Cole said. "At the most, two of these lenses got out there and we already got one back. I'll stop all production right now while we examine every button down there. If it's still here, we'll find it."

Herman's heart suddenly fluttered and he looked at Roarke, who was already staring intently at him, nodding his head. Herman said, "I don't think that will be necessary."

Both Roarke and Herman said the name at the same time. "Jingles Plumlee!"

Roarke jumped from his chair. "Sweet Jesus! Jingles asked me if we could duplicate his contact lenses! I had no idea what he was really talking about. He's scheduled to be right here at our building today at three o'clock. He's hoping we can duplicate his lens for him!"

Cole said, "You mean to tell me that Jingles' golf is all tied to Zimmer's lens? Mr. Winston, how could you let Zimmer go? The man's obviously a genius!"

Roarke winced at Cole's ill-timed words and braced for an explosion from the boss. Luckily, Herman didn't hear a word. He appeared to be lost in thought.

Through closed eyes, Herman was watching Jingles play at Desert Springs, constantly applying eye drops, yes, to only his right eye! He thought of the many times Jingles talked on television over the last two weeks, always alluding to his excellent vision, to how he thought he could see better than anybody. Most of all, he knew Jingles made more putts than humanly possible. Eaglevision! Everything now made perfect sense.

What was the value of Zimmer's lens now? Certainly not fifteen million. Possibly more like billions. Did Zimmer *know* that Jingles was using his lens? Was that why he found an investor so readily? There was suddenly a lot to consider.

"Okay," Herman finally said. "This is how things are going to go right now. If any of you say one word about this to anybody, and I mean anybody, I will fire all of you.

"Martha, come in here. I know you can hear me and you are part of this. If you all stay silent about this until my company is sold, I will give you each a bonus of a full year's salary.

"Cole, I want you to go back to your department and cut another of those Zimmer lenses right now. For the right eye only. The prescription's on file back there."

Cole said, "He might want more than one spare."

"It's not for him, idiot. It's for *me*. *My* prescription is on file."

Roarke tried not to laugh. "Plumlee is going to want more lenses. That's why he's coming."

"Well, he's certainly not going to get any of *these* lenses," Herman said, pointing at the one on his desk. "If we *knowingly* put an unlicensed lens on his eye we could face all kinds of problems."

"But we already know he has an unlicensed lens on his eye!" Roarke said.

"You know that?" Herman barked. "You've examined him? I didn't even know you were trained in optometry. What we know is that two of our secured experimental lenses disappeared from storage. One of them is right here. We can't know where the other one is."

Roarke decided it would be better to stay quiet.

Cole stepped up to the plate. "So how are we going to handle Jingles?"

"I'm going to have to think about that," he said. "Now off with you two!"

Herman watched the men leave before opening a desk drawer and taking out a copy of Zimmer's report. He remembered seeing a host of problems, but only now admitted to himself that he should have had the material reviewed by experts. He had no background in optical engineering, just knowledge he picked up along the way. He was merely an astute businessman that had a profitable enterprise drop in his lap when his stepfather, the founder, passed away. He would read the report more carefully this time.

Seventy miles from Eagle Optics, Jingles sat behind the wheel of the convertible, motoring north toward Prescott with the top down. With the temperature in the sixties, Pat and Oliver wore light jackets, just as he did. Conversation was difficult due to wind and noise, so each enjoyed the view, lost in individual thoughts.

They were making the drive at Oliver's request. For an undisclosed reason, he wanted to show the Plumlees the Prescott Hills Country Club complex. Jingles knew it might be a long time before he had another opportunity to make such a trip, so he readily accepted. After a visit to Eagle Optics this afternoon, he would be heading back to Los Angeles for a few days before traveling to New York and Chicago.

Just as they reached the outskirts of Prescott, Oliver instructed Jingles to take a left toward the hills to the west. A scattering of trees and lower-lying vegetation soon gave way to majestic ponderosa pines, oaks and junipers. Just an hour north of Phoenix, they had entered a different climate. The annual temperature ranged from the seventies in summer to fifties in the winter. The area even got a dusting of snow some ten days a year.

Oliver, riding in the backseat, leaned forward so that his head was between the two Plumlees. He explained that Prescott Hills, a country club and luxury housing project, had been the dream of Ivar Barthelson, a major developer in the region for over forty years. He purchased the rolling, forested property in the early 1980s with the idea that the project would be his crowning achievement and he would live out his own retirement there.

Phoenix City Bank participated in the project with the security of knowing that the developer himself was more than matching the bank's investment and offered the substantial acreage as collateral as well. Because Barthelson did nearly all the work with his own construction company, he had a reputation for keeping costs to a minimum. The bank had worked with him on a number of smaller projects over the years and everything had gone well.

Unfortunately for Barthelson, the luxury retirement home market plunged disastrously at just the wrong time. At the stage of the development when buyers should have been making their deposits and choosing floor plans, the sales office was deserted. In the midst of dealing with all the financial problems, Barthelson tragically died and his company died with him. Prescott Hills fell into the lap of Phoenix City Bank when Barthelson's estate could not pay property taxes and outstanding obligations.

A ten-foot wooden fence appeared along the right side of the road and continued for a quarter mile before Jingles turned into the entrance. Plywood covered the windows of the security station. A chain link fence blocked the road.

Oliver left the car and opened the padlock with one of his keys. He swung the gate open and returned to the car. A road sign indicated they were on Oakmont, a blacktop surface that looked brand new. Oliver explained that the road ran in a huge oval around the entire property with a half dozen streets dissecting it. There were 300 half acre building lots, each of which already had a driveway, cleared space for construction of a home, a septic tank, electricity, and Prescott city water access already in place. The city, anxious to see the huge development become a reality, had extended its water line to the property in cooperation with Barthelson. The lots all featured mature trees and were cleared well back from the road. The homes would all be relatively secluded and well shaded.

As they neared the back of the development, the land opened up into a golf course. Unlike the courses Jingles was accustomed to seeing and playing, this was carved from the wilderness with minimal alteration to the terrain. Each tee was elevated on a grassy mound with split log stairs leading up to it. Most fairways didn't begin until at least a hundred yards out from the tee. The price for missing one would be a trip into the bushes or trees. It was no place for novice players.

Like the tees, most of the greens appeared to be elevated. It seemed the course had been constructed by clear-cutting only where necessary and bringing in vast amounts of fill. The grass looked and smelled as if it had been cut recently, but the course was not manicured.

They rounded a bend and a clubhouse appeared on a hill at the right side of the road, the only building they had seen. Per Oliver's directions, Jingles pulled up to the front door and parked. The entire structure was made of Ponderosa pine logs from the property. A local sawmill still had two acres piled with cured logs and lumber that Barthelson intended to use on homes in Prescott Hills. Given the small number of homes and prospective members, the building wasn't especially large, but had a rustic elegance to it. The true beauty was at the rear, where a dozen large picture windows showcased a view that was part natural, part landscaped, and all wonderful. A stream meandering through the golf course, Gold Creek, had been dammed with large boulders, creating a large pond and a six-foot waterfall. Beyond that were the first tee and eighteenth green, divided by a tall stand of pines, and wooded hills beyond. A huge deck behind the building featured four free-standing fireplaces to brighten and warm evenings for restaurant and bar patrons. Jingles could easily envision sitting on the deck with the Foursome, enjoying that late morning beer.

The garage adjoining the pro shop held a couple dozen golf carts, lined up like soldiers, ready for action. There were also riding lawn mowers and other maintenance equipment. Oliver explained that the bank had a caretaker to keep the fairways, tees and greens cut to a manageable level. A full crew would be hired when it was time to put the course in playing condition.

Oliver suggested they take a couple carts for a quick drive around the course, so Jingles and Pat followed him along the gravel cart path. He stopped briefly at each tee so they could take in the postcard worthy view of each hole. Obviously, the course had been designed with loving attention.

When they reached the fourteenth hole, Jingles left his cart and climbed four stairs to the tee. He looked out at a green entirely surrounded by a pond. It was Pebble Beach! In the trees to the left of the green, he could see the only existing home in the development.

When they reached the bridge that crossed the water to the green, Oliver left his cart and motioned for the Plumlees to follow. They walked up a stone path toward the rear of a spectacular two-story log home.

Oliver said, "This was to be Ivar Barthelson's retirement home. He built it as a model to show prospective buyers. He also used it for an office and a place to feed his work crews every day. What a boss, huh? His employees always had a hot meal at noon and a cold beer after work, mostly here on this shady terrace."

Jingles sat on a bench beside an outdoor fireplace like those behind the clubhouse. It was easy to imagine growing old in such a place, sitting by a crackling fire and looking down at the island green. Actually, the surroundings felt like Wasilla on a fine September day. He turned to ask Pat if she felt the same, but she had disappeared into the house with Oliver.

The house was bright and open, all large windows, oak floors and beamed ceilings. An eight-foot wide split log staircase led up to the second floor, which had four comfortable bedrooms, two with balconies to enjoy the setting behind the house. Nearly the entire main floor was open, with the kitchen and dining area on the right, the living room with a vast stone fireplace in the center, and a den with a pool table and wet bar on the left. Twelve-foot ceilings and equally tall windows had the effect of pulling the outdoors into the house.

"Ivar named this house *Ponderosa* after the Cartwright house on *Bonanza*. What do you think of all this?"

Pat wrapped her arms around herself. "There's a peace about it, a tranquility, that I really, really like. I feel like I'm back home in Alaska."

Interesting, Jingles thought, his sentiments exactly. "I don't think there is any doubt how we feel about it. I'm going to feel good for a long time just remembering it."

Oliver said, "Let's talk then."

The idea hit the banker on the back nine of Raven's Nest on Saturday, as he watched another large crowd respond to Jingles. How could he make up for the horrible mistake with the Eagle Optics contract? Whether the Plumlees begrudged him or not, Oliver was convinced his decision cost his friends millions. He didn't want to live with that guilt if he could avoid it.

Prescott Hills was a prospective answer. The bank was into the project for $16 million plus. Another three million would make the development market ready. One builder claimed he could construct homes similar to Ivar's model, not logs but stick-built with log accents, for $480,000 each. With a sales price of $700,000 each, the project could yield a significant profit.

The question was: *How do you get buyers interested?* The answer was *Jingles*.

Oliver continued. "I want to sell you this house."

Jingles looked at his wife and back to Oliver. "We've been wondering about why you brought us here for the last two hours. We love the house. We like everything about this whole place. The only problem is that we love having neighbors. We like having friends close by."

Pat nodded her agreement. "Thanks to you, we can actually think about living in a place like this. If it wasn't so lonely here, I'd be begging to buy it."

Oliver shook his head in amazement. Perhaps because things had happened so quickly for the Plumlees, they still didn't understand the power of fame. "Here's the way it would work. Phoenix City Bank sells you this house for a reasonable amount, say one dollar." He had to stop and smile as they looked at each other.

"With Jingles as the resident club pro, I think we could immediately draw the publicity we need to generate sales. I talked with the owner of the largest real estate company in Prescott yesterday and she says this place would take off immediately if Jingles was the face of it. She's seen this house already."

Pat tugged at her husband's arm. "Think of all the people in Alaska, Jingles! This is exactly the kind of place they want to retire; a place that feels like home but without the cold and snow. This could be Alaska in Arizona!"

Jingles looked at Oliver. "What Pat is saying is true. Alaskans like to be around other Alaskans. There's sort of a bond between us."

A fantastic idea, Oliver thought. He could recommend that to the real estate company. They could begin their marketing in Alaska!

Oliver said, "My proposal goes like this. You become the first owner here and the pre-build sales start in another month or as soon as I get the golf course back in great shape and the rest of the street lighting in place. The payoff for you is this house and 10 percent of the profit when the project is complete. That could be several million. As for the bank, we'll get back our investment and hopefully a tidy profit as well."

Jingles took out his wallet and removed a one dollar bill. "Do you accept cash?"

The wheels in Pat's head were spinning. "Wait, Oliver. Doesn't Mr. Quinn have to get involved in this? We signed a contract."

"Your contract relates to endorsements. This is a personal investment for you. Before you part with your dollar, though, there are a couple other things I want you to know."

The banker led them to the back door, where he grabbed a fishing rod that leaned on the wall beside it. The Plumlees followed him down to the pond, where he turned over a rock, found a worm, and strung it on a hook.

He handed the rod to Pat. "Just flip it underneath the bridge. Right around there," he said, pointing to the spot.

The worm barely touched the water before being snapped up by a foot-long rainbow trout. The fish darted across the surface and tugged at the line as Pat held on, elation on her face.

Oliver said, "The pond is part of Gold Creek. Ivar created three ponds like this by damming up the stream. You saw one of them at the clubhouse and there's another coming up. They all have trout that he stocked and some other fish too.

"There's one other building on the property that you'll see on the way out. It's a barn with stables for twenty horses. There are thousands of acres of state park land all around us for people to enjoy on horseback. It's another feature that Ivar wanted to offer."

"And another good reason to name his house Ponderosa," Pat said, still watching her fish splash around.

Jingles folded his dollar bill, placed it in his right palm, and shook Oliver's hand. Feeling the bill within their shake, the banker grinned and said, "I guess this means we have a deal."

At exactly 3:00 p.m. Martha Porter watched the Plumlees walk through the glass doors at the entrance to Eagle Optics. They held hands as they strolled up the hall, laughing and chuckling and looking like a pair of teenaged lovebirds. She popped out of the chair behind her desk and hurried to greet the famous golfer.

After exchanging pleasantries, Martha invited them to sit and have some of the iced tea she had just brewed. Once they sat with their drinks, Martha began an apology. "I've been calling your number for hours and got only the answering machine. Mr. Winston won't be able to meet with you today or for the next few weeks. He had to leave town due to a death in the family."

"We haven't been home," Jingles said. "I'm so sorry to hear about Mr. . . . Winston? But I think we're here to see a Mr. Roarke about getting my lens duplicated."

Martha opened a drawer and produced a couple plastic lens cases. "Mr. Winston is the owner of the company and has authorized no one else to speak with you, Mr. Plumlee. However, he did have two additional pairs of contacts prepared for you." She pushed the cases across the desk toward Jingles.

Jingles looked at Pat, wondering if she was as curious as he. How could they duplicate his bubble lens if they didn't even have it?

His wife suggested that he try out the new ones. Having become proficient at exchanging lenses after all his practice, Jingles had one of the new right lenses on his eye in seconds. He looked at Pat, shook his head, and tried out the other right lens. After no success again, he even tried the left lenses. All were clear and perfectly normal. No bubbles.

Jingles turned to Martha. "This isn't at all what I expected, Mrs. Porter. I think Mr. Winston would want to have Mr. Roarke talk to me."

"He'll see you himself as soon as he returns, Mr. Plumlee. That's all I can tell you . . . and that he wishes you continuing good fortune on the golf course. We all do."

Jingles turned to Pat and shrugged. She took the two new sets of lenses, put them in her purse, and thanked Martha for the iced tea. Taking her husband's hand, she led him out the way they entered.

Standing behind the flimsy door of this office, only ten feet from his secretary's desk, Herman Winston had listened closely. His company was in a precarious position and matters had to be handled perfectly.

Jingles' possession and use of the unlicensed lens had to remain confidential for two reasons. From a legal perspective, the FDA would skewer his company if there was evidence that Eagle Optics knowingly, or even just irresponsibly, put an uncertified product into circulation. However, as long as Jingles didn't bring the lens to the company's direct attention, which he had not to this point, and Eagle Optics did not inspect the lens, the company maintained what his attorney called *plausible deniability*. The second reason to maintain secrecy was financial as well; he was intent on finding a way to stop Zimmer from exercising his option. Public knowledge of the real key to Jingles' success would make it impossible to stop Karl and his financial backers. The functionality of the lens would be proven beyond a doubt.

Amidst all the doubts and questions swirling in Herman's mind, at least one certainty consoled him; Jingles would continue to keep his secret. The old guy obviously wasn't too bright . . . he apparently thought his lens could be duplicated like a sheet of paper going through a copier . . . but he was smart enough not to talk about it. Human nature was so predictable! Who would worship Jingles and pay him lots of money if they knew the true source of his ability?

Earlier in the day, Herman had become the fourth person to wear the telescopic lens, joining the ranks of Karl Zimmer, Jingles, and the woman in Flagstaff. If not for knowledge of Jingles, he would have rejected the lens as readily as the woman had. The view was just so radically different . . . like looking through a ship porthole from perhaps a foot away. You had to accept that the bulkhead blocked your peripheral view before you could focus on, and appreciate, the magnification of what was right in front of you. Based on his self-examination, using the eye chart in Karl's former office, Herman documented Zimmer's claim of 20/5 vision. It was truly remarkable.

Life would be much simpler now if he had recognized the significance of Zimmer's work and invested in it. At the same time, he now remembered exactly why he hadn't. The entire premise of Zimmer's research at the start was that he could produce binocular vision. A month before submitting his final report, the German told him that two-eyed vision was off the table . . . the lens could only function on a single eye. One-eyed vision? It seemed preposterous. Use of only a single eye seemed more like sight restriction than enhancement. He had closed his mind to *eaglevision* right then and there.

Fortunately, Zimmer's financing people had delayed payment for the option until the deadline of December first. There was still a window of opportunity to somehow change their thinking. That fat lady had not sung yet.

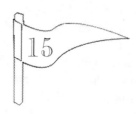

In a hotel room high above the hustle of downtown Los Angeles streets, Jingles was trying to sneak in a nap before dinner. However, it wasn't easy to relax while in the process of becoming rich beyond his wife's wildest dreams.

A Tuesday afternoon meeting with Nike representatives had gone well. Beyond well. The Battle at the Nest, as the headline on the *Los Angeles Times* Sunday sports page described the match between Jingles and Jenks, pushed Nike to immediate action. The contract Jingles signed an hour ago totaled eight million dollars. The money would be paid in four equal installments over the next year. The company held a lifetime worth of annual options that could be renewed at its discretion, which was of little consequence to Pat. The eight million was just fine and that was guaranteed.

Tomorrow's meetings included Hilton Worldwide, Visa and AOA. The American Optometric Association had thus far been unwilling to part with more than a million, far less than the number Mr. Quinn had in mind. For his part, Jingles was glad for that. He wanted no affiliation with AOA, or even Eagle Optics for that matter. By not fully disclosing the details of his bubble lens, he was basically *pulling a Knickers* on innocent people that just wanted to see better. While that had never been his intention, his careful choice of words and lack of candor had snowballed. No, there would be no contract with AOA. When the owner of Eagle Optics returned, he would show him the lens and offer to return their half million dollars. There were lots of other endorsements from clients willing to reward Pat and him for his golf, not his eyesight. He would stick with them only.

The Sweet Swing

His thoughts turned to Knickers, Mulligan, and Harvey. They were due back from their vacation today, or was it yesterday? Pulling the cell phone from his pocket, he punched in Harvey's number. Lucy answered.

Jingles said, "Como estas?" It was one of a few Spanish phrases he learned in Mexico.

Lucy paused. "It's Jingles, isn't it?"

"Well, it's not Andy Devine! How was your trip?"

"A lot of shopping in the markets, a lot of driving, a lot of eating and drinking, and a lot of watching you on SportsCenter. They have the same shows over there in both Spanish and English."

"We're in Los Angeles of all places. Pat is out shopping."

"What's Harvey supposed to do with those three sets of golf clubs in the garage?"

"Oh, those. They were delivered last week. Pat picked them up at the post office. I told her to put them at your house for a welcome home present. They were sent by different companies for me to consider, but I'm hooked up with Nike. Harvey can try them out and see if he likes them. He can let Knickers and Mulligan try them too. Can I talk to him?"

"Jingles, is that really you?" Harvey asked. "I'm on the other line."

"Yep, it's me. I wish I could have met you at the airport. Now the best I can do is invite you to our house for Thanksgiving supper! That's the next time we'll be home."

"We can't believe what's happened, Jingles. We're gone for a while and the whole world changes. You're the most talked about man in the country! I swear it."

"It just happened, Harvey. My golf keeps getting better."

"Wow, that's unbelievable. This whole thing is unbelievable. I guess you won't be golfing with us anymore, huh Jingles? We told people that we were your regular golf partners and they laughed at us!"

"Well, how was your trip? I can't wait to hear all about it!"

"It was good. I read that you were in talks with Nike for an endorsement contract. Have you met Tiger Woods?"

"No, but I played at Pebble Beach and met all the Los Angeles Lakers. Did Knickers get to see his friend over there?"

"We all did. He's a great guy. Did you really play Tommy Jenks to a tie?"

"On the Raven's Nest scorecard, yeah. On a real golf course he would kill me. You can't imagine how far he can hit a ball. You have to see it up close to really appreciate it. How is your game? Did you play lots of golf?"

"C'mon, Jingles. I've got no game. They said on the news that you are going to play on the tour in January. Knickers says he's a fortune teller! He says it all started when he played that trick on you."

"It'll be interesting to see what I can do. Did you get to Haiti?"

"We did. It's kind of a mess over there. Where do you play next?"

Jingles stopped to think. He was talking to one of his very best friends and it was like talking to someone he just met! Why couldn't they have a normal conversation? Was *normal* officially gone from his life?

"Harvey, let's talk about your trip first. Take me through each day."

"C'mon, Jingles. We were on vacation. You're the one who's been on a trip. When a golfer makes a long putt on the Golf Channel, the announcers say they *Jingled* one in! You can't watch that channel for five minutes without hearing your name mentioned. The most famous pros in the world are talking about *you*."

Jingles felt an awkward tug at his gut. Harvey was his friend, not his fan. "Don't take that seriously, Harvey. You *know* me. I'm just lucky to have the ability to see better than anyone else."

"I know. Knickers told us all about your right lens. I remember you telling me that you rotated lenses because of irritation. Now I understand that better."

Again, Jingles felt his stomach tighten. He had been telling Harvey only half the truth, maybe less than half, and now Harvey knew that too. He took a deep breath and popped the question that been nagging him for weeks. "What did you guys think about my whole crazy story?"

Harvey cleared his throat. "I'd rather you ask them personally. The general drift is that they feel like it's your contact lens shooting your scores, not you. It's all about that *big as a bucket* you were always talking about. I ask them when they ever saw a contact lens swing a golf club, but it doesn't change their thinking."

Jingles pondered Harvey's disclosure. "Well, those guys are probably right for the most part. You all know how I played before I got the lens. I don't recall Nike knocking on my door back then.

"Anyway, welcome home. Please use Birdie Chaser while I'm gone. I'll call again soon and I'm sure Pat will be in touch with Lucy. Oh, and don't forget to open the compartments on those three new golf bags in your garage. They're full of Oreos."

Calls to Knickers and Mulligan confirmed their ambivalence. Were his friends changing or was he? The strength of relationships forged over years had to prevail, didn't it? Knickers didn't seem to want to talk about his trip. He sounded like he didn't believe his old friend was genuinely interested. He never mentioned the upcoming journey to the Champions Tour so Jingles didn't say anything about it either. Mulligan's primary interest seemed to be whether he and Pat would be leaving Leisureville now *that their ship had come in*. Jingles didn't have the heart to mention Prescott Hills. Mulligan was cordial yet distant and said he would look forward to Thanksgiving. The topic of when they might reunite as a foursome was never addressed.

Jingles considered Prescott Hills. A new development like that would need a leader like Mulligan to organize and head a new homeowner association. It would need a personality like Knickers around the clubhouse to keep things lively and entertaining. And Harvey. Who could do without a friend like Harvey around? Always loyal and supportive.

The door opened and Pat entered, dropping plastic bags on the floor in a heap. He had insisted that she do some shopping after the Nike signing. Shopping of a different kind. Shopping for herself for once!

"Did you find something you liked?"

"I didn't find much I didn't like," she said. "But I only bought half of it."

"I was just thinking about Prescott Hills. Don't you think you'd miss all your friends in Leisureville? Like what about Lucy? You girls are peas in a pod."

"Of course I'd miss them," Pat said, sitting down on the bed and looking her husband in the eyes. "Just like I missed so many friends when we left Alaska and moved to Arizona. That was the hardest of all. Well, leaving the children was harder still."

"Do you think Harvey and Mulligan and Knickers might bring their wives and move to Prescott Hills too?"

Pat looked at her husband and shook her head. "They seem happy right where they are. Besides, they can come up and visit as often as they like. We'll have three guest bedrooms and we're only an hour and a half away."

She waited for a response and got none. "I'm going to shower and get ready for dinner. Gillian is picking us up in an hour. Some people from Cadillac have flown into town and they are entertaining us tonight! I'll set your clothes out."

Jingles reclined on the bed and looked at the ceiling, suddenly wondering when he would be golfing again. Life was so simple on a golf course and he had been staring at ceilings entirely too much lately.

Herman Winston scheduled his first and hopefully only meeting on Wednesday for 9:00 a.m. He shot eighty-eight at Desert Springs on Tuesday and was anxious to get back to the course. The lens was everything Zimmer said it would be, including painful to wear after a short time. The key was to do what Jingles figured out on his own, wear the lens for putting only.

Roarke and Wilhelm arrived right on time. As soon as Martha handed them their coffee, Herman was ready to begin. This was no time for small talk.

"Okay, Wilhelm. As I explained to you yesterday, I want out of that option contract with Zimmer. If he thinks he can buy a billion dollar property for fifteen million, he has another thing coming. What did you come up with?"

"I came up with nothing," the attorney said. "If he puts fifteen million in your account by the end of the workday on the first of December, he owns the exclusive rights to the lens. You didn't ask me to write a contract you could break. You asked for a contract that would guarantee you *a ton of money*, those were your words, if he could come up with it."

"Well, Wilhelm, you didn't surprise me. I was pretty confident you'd come up with a goose egg, so I've done some thinking."

Roarke and Wilhelm looked at each other curiously. What now?

"We have a lady in Flagstaff who got one of Zimmer's unlicensed lenses because he gave it to her."

Roarke interrupted. "Zimmer didn't give her the lens, we did."

Wilhelm said, "It's my understanding that the lady simply returned the lens and that there was no complaint on her part."

Herman held up his hands and glared across his desk at the men. "Zimmer failed to return two buttons to inventory. We have proof of that. Therefore, he is ultimately responsible for what happened to the woman in Flagstaff."

"Nothing happened to the woman in Flagstaff!" Roarke said.

"What if something *did* happen to her," Herman said with a grin. "What if she tried to wear the lens and it caused trauma to her eye?? What if she sued us over it?"

The attorney said, "She claimed no such thing. Why are you even creating such conjecture?"

"Conjecture this," Herman said. "If this lady sues us for damage caused by Zimmer's lens, are his money people going to part with fifteen million on December one? Are they going to feel so confident about getting FDA approval?"

Herman saw that his attorney was finally listening. He nodded his satisfaction and pointed to the report on his desk, *The Status and Future of Eaglevision*. "Wilhelm, you'll find everything you need right in this report. Zimmer reviews all the potential problems that could occur if the lens is used improperly. In the case of this woman, bring them to life. Even Zimmer himself won't be able to refute them."

"Have you lost your mind?" Wilhelm asked. "You want us to sue ourselves?"

"We wouldn't," Herman answered. "You draft the lawsuit and then get some bonehead ambulance chaser in Flagstaff to file it right before

Thanksgiving, a few days before the option expires. All he has to do is get it signed and filed, and then go on vacation for a week. We'll give him twenty thousand cash for his trouble."

"And the woman?" Roarke asked.

"I had her looked at," Herman said. "Seventy-eight and widowed. She's half-crippled by arthritis and lives on social security mostly."

"Let's say a lawyer comes to her door with some great news. He's settling disputes with Eagle Optics about some bad contact lenses they mailed out and her name is on his list. If she signs a complaint, he can promise her ten thousand dollars within a week or two. I ask you, what is she going to do?"

Wilhelm knew that most people would accept such an offer readily. "And you want to do all this just to scare off Sherman MacPherson?" the attorney asked. "They'd smell a rat in a second."

"What rat?" Herman said. "We are obligated to advise them of the lawsuit because it relates to the Zimmer lens, whether we view it as frivolous or not. We simply convey the irrefutable facts. The suit alleging eye damage from the lens was filed and we hope to settle it quickly. We send them a copy of it. We acknowledge that the lens in question was the Zimmer lens, and we hold *him* accountable for its distribution. We also say that we hope this doesn't compromise the closing on the option."

The attorney said, "Sherman MacPherson would ask for an extension to the option contract until the litigation runs its course. That's what I'd advise them as their attorney."

"I thought of that," Herman said. "If they do, we'll demand that the money be held in escrow pending the result of litigation."

"That would be reasonable," the attorney responded. "They might be perfectly willing to do that."

Herman lifted his hand to stop him. "Yes, they *might* do that. However, they *might not*. Would they want that kind of money tied up for long? Would their investors approve of that?

"And what are they going to think about relying on Zimmer? After all, he put an unlicensed lens on the eye of an unsuspecting woman. Their investment is based on faith in him. Let's destroy that faith and see where it takes us. There's too much money riding on this for me *not* to take this chance. I know what these lenses can do. Believe me, the world wants them."

Wilhelm shook his head. "It's illegal, unethical and wrong in every way. Take your fifteen large and be happy. I can't do that."

Herman rolled his eyes at the brief sermon. "It's called business, that's all. Would a fifty thousand dollar bonus ease your mind any? This can all be done in a single day of your time. I know you're capable of doing it without a chance of it being traced back to you or us."

Roarke said, "Wouldn't a lawsuit against us spoil your efforts to sell the company before the end of the year? Things are looking so positive right now."

A response came quickly from Herman, who apparently had every angle figured out. "The lawsuit will be settled the day after the option expiration. The woman will acknowledge, in taking my money, that there was no wrongdoing on our part."

He looked to his attorney. "You can draft up the settlement agreement in advance. Just give it to the bonehead at the same time you give him the other paperwork. He'll like that."

Herman turned back to Roarke. "If Zimmer exercises his option, heaven forbid, I lose the big payday and console myself with the scraps. Then we sell my company as scheduled and get another forty million."

Wilhelm asked, "And if Zimmer doesn't exercise?"

Herman beamed. "Then we have a whole different outlook. We delay the sale of the company, examine Jingles' lens and issue a press release. It says we have discovered that Jingles Plumlee has been wearing an unlicensed lens to which we have patents pending. We apologize to him for Zimmer's mistake and express relief that the lens caused him no harm. That ought to shake the world! How much will someone pay me then?"

Wilhelm didn't share Herman's optimism. "Shearson McPherson will see through what you did and sue you. And there's the FDA issues."

"One bridge at a time," Herman said. "We cross one bridge at a time."

Early on Friday afternoon, Jingles and Gillian Constantine sat in the otherwise empty conference room at the Quinn Group. They were watching tape of last night's Jay Leno program. She wanted Jingles to be as comfortable as possible with the surroundings, the timing, the whole feel of the program. You could never be too well prepared.

She turned off the tape and asked him to practice his grand entrance. He walked around the table, which represented his steps to the center of the stage, and stopped at the front of the room. Extending his arms as if he held a seven iron, he took an easy swing and held the follow through, all the while smiling at Gillian. He would be doing the same thing in a few hours on the actual show, and she would be in the front row.

"Remember, you hold that pose for about five seconds and then start nodding to the audience with a nice smile. It's going to remind people of Johnny Carson. He used to pretend to swing a golf club all the time. People are going to love it!"

"I saw Johnny Carson do it," Jingles said. "Do you have any video of that? I could probably copy the way he did it."

The Sweet Swing

"Why didn't I think of that?" She lifted her cell phone, dialed a number and asked someone to find some old footage on the Internet.

"Okay," she said. "We'll see what they can find. Now, let's go over the questions again. These are the basic things he's going to ask." She pushed a key on her laptop and the questions popped up on the big screen.

"Where did you ever get a name like Jingles?" she read. "That's the very first question."

Jingles smiled and said, "Some people think that's a funny story. My friend Lucy Green gave me that name because I reminded her of the Jingles character on the old Wild Bill Hickock Show. Then I turn to the audience and ask if anybody out there is old enough to remember Wild Bill. And then Jay is going to say, 'I'm old enough. Jingles was played by Andy Devine, right?' and I tell him he has a great memory and then about how the Jingles character was always whining about something or the other. My neighbor thought the name suited me because I was starting to whine about getting old and losing my golfing ability. And then Jay says, 'Well, I've heard of ask and you shall receive, but *whine* and you shall receive? That's a first. I think I'll start whining that I need a raise!'"

"That's right," Gillian said. "It's a great story."

The door opened slightly, just enough to accommodate Mitchell Quinn's head. "Big news, Jingles. You'll be playing golf on network television on Sunday the thirtieth. The Senior Skins Game. You're in!"

Quinn turned to Gillian. "It's a 10:00 a.m. start time on the Big Island. Pull all the info on it and prep Jingles for tonight's Leno show. He's going to want to talk about it." His head disappeared and the door closed.

Jingles looked at his new friend in shock. "Just like that? How can that be?"

Gillian flashed her dimples while keying up information on her computer. "I knew there was talk about it. I just didn't know if it would happen so I didn't say anything to you. It's all about Nike. They pull lots of strings."

"But I thought the field was already set."

"Here it is," she said. "Mitchell copied me on the e-mail. Appleman is out. Pulled a muscle doing yard work it says. A press release is probably going out as we speak."

"What incredibly bad luck for him," Jingles said, surprised that someone of Appleman's stature would be doing his own chores in the yard.

"Sure, it was bad luck, bad luck for him that the people want to see you! Don't worry about him. He'll probably get paid more not to play than he would have earned in prize money for his favorite charity anyway."

"When will Pat and I be heading over there?"

"Well, you're booked through the day before Thanksgiving, and you want to fly back to Phoenix for the holiday. I suppose we can fly to Hawaii sometime late on that Friday afternoon. You'll have time to practice on Saturday."

Jingles took his own cell phone from his pocket and called Pat, who answered on the first ring. "Are you ready for this? We're going to Hawaii to play in the Skins Game right after Thanksgiving! Could you call Lucy and have her tell everybody to watch the Jay Leno show tonight?"

After listening for a minute, he said, "Ooohh, that's right. It's not on until really late there. Tell her to at least tape the show so they can watch tomorrow."

Gillian had waited patiently, checking the rest of her e-mail. "Everything okay?"

"I guess. I was just hoping that my friends could watch tonight, but it's not on the air until kind of late. That's why I never watch it. I don't know many grownups that stay up that late."

She pushed another button on her computer and an e-mail appeared on the big screen. "At least they can watch *On Demand* in the morning, right?

"Look there! More good news. Your deal with Hilton is done. You'll be filming not far from here on Monday. They want to get a spot ready to run in the days before the Skins Game, while you're in the headlines. And then in December you'll be flying to some of the most exotic locations in the world . . . and that means so will I!"

Jingles knew Pat would want to know the contract amount but figured Gillian could tell her. The whole situation seemed unfathomable to him.

His coach had more instructions. "It's time for you to go back across the street and get ready. The limo will pick us up at one forty-five in front of the hotel even though the taping isn't until five. We have to allow extra time for the drive. Twelve miles can take twelve years around here!

"Bring your white Nike polo shirt and black slacks with you. Can't wear them in the car. We'll be eating Chinese on the way."

At Leisureville's Sleepy Hollow, Harvey had been drinking coffee since after supper. On nights before golf, he normally hit the hay at ten. Tonight Lucy and he would be up later to watch Jingles.

GAF, *Golf After Jingles*, had begun on Wednesday morning for Harvey. His new playing partner, Walter Crabtree, had been recruited to fill out the foursome. Walter was just sixty-six and a former educator as well. He was the 2013 Leisureville championship runner up and played around scratch.

Knickers, Mulligan, and he all had new contact lenses in their mailboxes when they returned from their trip. He didn't notice any improvement in his

The Sweet Swing

game and was considering going back to his glasses. For whatever reason, Knickers and Mulligan refused to even try the new eyewear.

As the time for Leno approached, Harvey suddenly wondered if the two of them were even watching. *How could such close friends not be watching?* Based on their behavior for the last couple weeks, however, Harvey suspected they might be fast asleep under their covers.

Jingles' play had become a sore subject for the trio even prior to the revelation about the defective lens. The first record-smashing round at Leisureville was an unlikely wonder. The second came as a total shock. The third, with all the accompanying coverage, served to scramble their brains.

Once armed with knowledge of Jingles' secret, however, their discussions became passionate, even heated, arguments. When a member of *their* foursome made his way from *Newswatch* to *SportsCenter* the very next week, an all-out war of words ensued. Ultimately, they had to agree to stop talking about Jingles altogether in order to salvage their vacation.

Mulligan's position on Jingles had jumped around from day to day, but he seemed to have settled on the idea that Jingles was in bed with the devil. Knickers alleged that Jingles was somehow cheating the game and himself with his trick vision and forecast a very bad ending to it all. For his part, Harvey believed it was a fairy tale, a bedtime story. He would wake up in the morning, *Ray* would pick him up in front of his house for another round of golf, and the story, the dream, would be over.

The one part of *Ray* still present for each morning round was Birdie Chaser. Although the foursome's new member owned a cart and offered to drive, Harvey preferred driving the loaner himself. He had purchased a jumbo box of Milk Bones, placed a bag of them under the seat, and stopped to treat each passing dog. The jingle bells on the red ribbon still hung from the rearview mirror.

Sitting next to Lucy on the couch, Harvey watched a Leno monologue that seemed too long, until he came to a Jingles joke. "And then there's this golfer Jingles that we're all reading about." He had to pause while the audience, aware that Jingles was a featured guest, applauded.

"He's almost seventy-three years old. At the time most guys that age are losing the use of their putters, he's just finding his!" There were lots of cheers and a shot of the band leader, covering his mouth in feigned shock.

Lucy asked, "Can they say that on television?"

"I guess that's what we miss by going to bed so early," Harvey said and started laughing.

When Jingles was introduced, the band started to play what had become his theme, *Jingle Bell Rock*, and he walked out from behind the curtain, stopped, and faked a golf swing.

Lucy stood right up. "That's the most beautiful thing! He did it just like Johnny Carson. He even looks like Johnny! Jingles is wonderful!"

Harvey was overwhelmed by what he saw and driven right over the edge by his wife's ecstatic response. His eyes got damp. That was his friend standing there. His best friend!

The audience wouldn't stop clapping and the band wouldn't stop playing. Tired of just nodding, Jingles started to fake a few putts. Finally, Leno walked over and saved him.

"He doesn't even look nervous," Lucy said. "How can he not be nervous? Pat must be so proud."

When they sat down, Leno asked Jingles about his name. Jingles told the story of how she, *Lucy Green*, had given him the nickname. Lucy was beside herself. She started crying like Harvey.

After a commercial, Leno asked Jingles about life in Leisureville.

Jingles said, "I've spent my retirement years playing with the best group of guys you could ever imagine. That's what golf is all about, right?" My partner is Harvey Green, a retired high school principal from Indiana. We play with Knickers Collins and Mulligan Wettman."

Leno slapped his hands on his desk and looked at the audience. "You've got be kidding me! *Knickers* and *Mulligan*?"

"That's right. Knickers, who is Mickey on his Topps baseball card, used to play for the St. Louis Cardinals. He got the name because he wears knickers to play golf. As far as Mulligan goes, golfers will know where that name comes from."

Leno said, "I know all about mulligans. I wouldn't play golf without them!"

"Mulligan's real name is Irvin. He does a great job as the head of the homeowner association."

"I understand you are from Alaska. They have golf there?"

"Oh yes," Jingles said. "That's where I started playing."

"Tell me something," Leno said, lowering his voice a little and leaning toward his guest, "I've always wanted to know this. What kind of distance do you get when your balls are frozen?"

"I'm not going to touch that one," Jingles said and started laughing.

"Well, frozen balls won't be a problem where you are playing next. I see you are going to be in the Senior Skins Game in Hawaii on the last day of this month."

Jingles nodded and waved to the cheering audience. "That's my understanding. I'm looking forward to it."

"But hold on a second, I heard you got into the Skins Game because of a leg injury to George Appleman. You didn't do a *Tonya Harding* on him, did you?"

Jingles smiled and winked. "Who me?" He then took another pretend golf swing as he sat there, as if he might be swatting someone's knee. The writers were on target; the audience thought it was hysterical.

It wasn't until the conclusion of the show that lights went out in most Leisureville homes. The Wettman and Collins houses were no exception.

Early Wednesday evening, the day before the American holiday of Thanksgiving, Karl Zimmer stood waiting for his elevator ride up to the offices of Sherman Macpherson. He had been summoned to report to the office straight away.

When an elevator door opened, a stream of smiling, laughing people poured into the lobby. It was nearly 6:00 p.m., and most were on their way off to enjoy a late November vacation.

The Sherman MacPherson office was open but seemingly deserted when Karl arrived. With no receptionist on duty, he walked down to Mark Sherman's office and knocked on the door.

"It's open," said the familiar voice of Sherman.

Before Karl could even sit down, Sherman said, "I have some very bad news for you, Karl. It's certainly been bad news for us. Our deal to purchase your lenses is gone."

Karl grabbed the back of a chair. The situation was shockingly familiar. He felt the same way when Herman Winston told him he was eliminating his Research and Development Department at Eagle Optics. He tried to calm himself. There had to be some mistake, some kind of misunderstanding.

Sherman waited for Karl to speak. When the inventor said nothing, he continued, "A courier delivered us some news right after lunch this afternoon. A lawsuit has been filed against Eagle Optics over injuries caused to a customer. I assume you know something about this."

"I've heard nothing of it," Karl said. "What does it have to do with the business of buying my technology?"

"I thought perhaps you would know something since it was one of your lenses that caused the injury."

Karl felt the relief of knowing that such a thing was impossible. "That's not true. I have the only lenses that have been made. I've told you that."

Sherman held up a batch of papers. "Let me summarize this for you. A lens definitively identified as one of yours was delivered to one Madeline Hanover of Flagstaff, Arizona, about two weeks ago. In wearing the contact, she was injured in the way described in this lawsuit. Her injuries are right in line with the potential problems you documented in this report." He slapped his hand down on a copy of Zimmer's report.

"I can assure you that I had nothing to do with this woman getting one of my contacts. The fifty-four disks that I created are in the possession of the Manufacturing Department. You can call Mr. Cole there right now and he'll confirm that."

Sherman spoke through clenched teeth. "I have been on the phone with Eagle Optics people all afternoon, mostly their attorney, and there is no need for more questions."

"How can you say that? There are nothing but questions!"

"Let me ask you one," Sherman said. "They have fifty-two of your disks in their possession and a note, signed by you, that you took two of them out of inventory on September first. They were never returned. The question is: Where are they, Karl?"

Karl sat down in the chair to think. Yes, he remembered signing out two buttons for the directors' meeting. He didn't remember returning them. Where were they? They were probably in the pocket of his lab coat. The coat was hanging in his old office.

"I'm confident the buttons are in the pocket of my lab coat. I'm sure of it. It was an honest mistake. That would not explain how one could be cut into a lens and delivered to a customer."

"Your old company was more forthcoming about this than you are. You left your buttons in the conference room, on the floor to be specific. A clerical employee picked them up and mistakenly took them to their manufacturing plant."

It seemed plausible to Karl that he might have dropped them; he had been upset. "Why would an employee do that?"

"How about because they didn't know any better, and you should have. You have put Eagle Optics at risk because of it."

Karl decided he couldn't argue that point. He made a mistake. "Something about this still isn't right. These lenses are extremely different to wear. If you put one on, it would actually shock you at first. I do not believe that a woman would put it on and continue to wear it long enough to harm herself."

Sherman stood and lifted his suit coat from the back of his chair. "Karl, I've learned a lesson today that I've also learned a few times in the past. If something seems too good to be true, it often is. I love the potential of your lenses and until today, I really liked you. We've invested a lot of money and God knows how many hours pursuing this, but we're pulling the plug. I suggest you check out of your hotel room right away because we're done paying for it. The rental car too. It's over."

Karl's mind was whirling. "Have you considered that maybe they changed their mind and don't want me to exercise the option? The timing of this is a little strange, don't you think?"

Sherman walked to the door and held it open for Karl. "Strange? You think the timing is strange? Have you considered what could have happened to us if this suit had been filed *next* week, *after* we exercised the option? Stop thinking of just yourself! Our only consolation is that it could have been much, much worse for us."

"Give me a chance to go back there and straighten all this out. I'll get it cleared up by Monday. At least give me that chance."

"There's nothing for you to fix. What are you going to do, talk the lady into dropping her lawsuit? We don't feel good about this investment any longer and you may well have serious problems of your own. Eagle Optics isn't very happy. Your bumbling has cost them fifteen million."

"Please!"

"Our decision here is final. We have a whole list of safer investment opportunities waiting for us. We are crossing you off our list and moving on to the next project. The money is already committed elsewhere. I'm going to head off on vacation like everyone else and try to forget about all this. Have a good life, Mr. Zimmer. And a happy Thanksgiving."

Jingles carried the turkey to the head of the table and started to carve the bird in front of the guests. It was a Plumlee tradition.

"Don't cut yourself, Jingles," Lucy said. "You're going to need all those fingers in Hawaii on Sunday!"

Mulligan glared at Jingles' hands. "You've probably got them insured, right, Jingles?"

Pat tapped lightly on her wine glass with a spoon. "I want to propose a toast." Everyone looked from the turkey at one end of the table to Pat at the other and lifted their glasses.

"Here's to good friends forever!" They all sipped their wine.

The Sweet Swing

Jingles put down his glass and continued to cut into the sixteen-pounder. "Tell me about Walter Crabtree. All I know about him is that he beat me three and one in the club championships a couple years ago and then beat Knickers too."

"He probably wouldn't want to play you now," Harvey suggested. "He's a nice guy and a really good golfer. He's been playing around even par every day so far."

"His wife is nice too," Lucy said. "Her name is Virginia."

Jingles continued to cut and place meat on a platter. "Our special request before dinner is to have each one of you tell us your favorite part of your trip to the island. Let's start with the anniversary girl, Bess."

Bess pointed to her chest, raised her eyes and mouthed a silent *me?* She was the least talkative of the group and Jingles wanted to get her going.

"That's an easy answer for me. My favorite part was when the guys went off golfing or to a baseball game and left the girls alone. I'm not going into details of the mischief we got into, but let's just say the men over there are fond of tourist women, even old ones like us!" Lucy and Mary laughed and winked at Pat. They would all talk about that later.

Mary said, "For me, it was the ocean. It didn't matter if I was floating on it, walking along the shore, or lounging beside it, I loved it."

"I liked the ocean too," Lucy agreed. "But if I had to pick my favorite thing, I'd say it was dinner every night. There was just something neat about going to unique places, trying new dishes, and getting dressed up. Our husbands all looked so handsome over there."

Mulligan decided to speak next. "Is this a trick question? You know I liked the golf best of all. Who doesn't love hitting an approach shot to a green you've never seen before. It's what I assume heaven is like: a different course every day."

Harvey looked contemplative, obviously taking the question seriously. "My favorite thing was watching Knickers, watching him light up around his old friend Juan Felipe. Watching him watch baseball! I got a view of Knickers I never had before. I always thought he loved golf more than anything, but no more. He has baseball running through his veins and I think it's a great thing."

"I agree with you on that," Mulligan said. "I felt it too."

Knickers was the only one left to respond. Pat looked at him cautiously, not knowing what to expect. She had gotten over all his practical jokes; life was proceeding too beautifully to dwell on those any longer. Still, he was an enigma to her.

"I'm gonna depart from my normal bullshit ways," he said. "I'm gonna be honest for this once. There were a lot of things I really liked about the trip and some things I didn't like. I didn't like that Ray and Pat weren't with us. I'm not sure who this Jingles is, but I know Ray personally. He's a helluva guy."

Harvey quickly glanced at Jingles, who had stopped cutting the bird in mid slice. Jingles looked up at him, not Knickers. The look told him that Jingles now understood what Harvey tried to tell him. Knickers wasn't happy with the new Jingles.

Pat was visibly upset by Knickers comment, but managed to stay silent. She wished she had kept her pledge to never let him in the house again!

Everyone was quiet, so Knickers continued. "I didn't like that they aren't playin' hardly no baseball in Haiti. I don't know if baseball is *the* answer to their problems there, but it darn well could be *an* answer. It keeps kids busy, and it gets people excited. And there's always the dream. In the Dominican Republic, kids dream about bein' big leaguers, and they see role models all around them, people like Juan Felipe and hundreds of others. Haiti doesn't have those kinds of heroes that kids look up to.

"I liked seein' my old friend Juan, and it made me happy that we could feel such a bond after so many years. I liked watchin' baseball bein' played by people that love the game. I liked seein' my friends havin' such a great time. I liked the night that Harvey sucked it up and smoked a cigar with Mulligan and me.

"But what did I love? Two things come to mind. I loved celebrating fifty years with a woman that means everything to me. I know lots of people think I'm a cool guy and all, especially me, but all my coolness comes from her.

"The other thing I loved was a weird scene at the most unlikely place. Near the end of our trip, we were staying at this big hotel in Haiti, and I went downstairs to find a cup of coffee real early in the morning. There was nobody in the restaurant yet, but a bunch of the employees were gathered in the bar watchin' Deportes on a big screen TV. The announcers spoke Spanish and all the people too. All those employees, old and young, women and men, were laughin' and pointin' and talkin' all at the same time. I understand a fair amount of Spanish after coachin' so many foreign players over the years, but the announcers kept sayin' one word in English. The word was *Jingles*.

"And were they talkin' about golf? No. The television was showin' an interview of some men in Wasilla, Alaska, who were talkin' about their Little League coach from twenty years ago. They were standin' on a snow covered baseball field reminiscin' about the values of hard work and . . . . *fair play* . . . they learned from a man now suddenly famous for putting golf balls. The Haitians thought it was funny that people played baseball in Alaska, where they had only a handful of baseball weather days a year!

The Sweet Swing

"And I started laughing too. I was thinking about Haiti, where they have almost nothing' but baseball weather and hardly anyone plays. I was wonderin' how someone like Jingles or even me could possibly change that."

"Wow," Bess said. "You never even told me that."

Everyone was silent for a minute, either touched by Knickers' eloquence or confused by the message. The other ladies exchanged glances that said, *What was that all about?*

Lucy tried tapping on her glass with a butter knife. "My turn to toast! Here's to Knickers and Bess, our gracious and wonderful hosts for a vacation we will always remember!"

Everyone sipped.

"And here's to Pat and Jingles for this lovely Thanksgiving meal!" Mary said, raising her glass again.

"Which you better start eating before it gets cold," Pat added.

While the guests filled their plates, Jingles opened another bottle of wine from his well-stocked liquor cabinet. The group was in a toasting mood. One glass was his limit because the next activity of the day was a long drive to Prescott Hills to show the development to the other men.

Over dinner, Lucy said, "Why don't we all share our favorite moment from the Leno Show? I know we all loved it, so let's share!"

"I think we all know your favorite part, Lucy," Bess said. "You heard your name on national television!"

Mulligan looked bursting to talk. "My favorite part was when Leno said that old guys like Knickers and Harvey were losing their putters! Mary will tell you that's not a problem for me!"

"That's not what she tells me," Bess said. Everyone laughed, even Mulligan.

"I recorded the show and watched it a few more times," Harvey offered. "I liked the whole thing, obviously, but I liked what you said about playing with your friends, Jingles. You said that was what golf was all about. I hope we get to play together again soon."

Jingles got up to gather dishes from the table. "Speaking of that, I want to take you guys for a long ride in Pat's new car after dinner. I want to show you a golf course that we can all play together in the not-so-distant future."

Pat addressed the ladies. "I want to hear all about the mischief that Bess referred to. I can hardly wait for the men to leave."

Jingles had all the keys for Prescott Hills. Oliver gave them to him when he met them at the airport. He hoped his friends would share his excitement about the place.

The drive passed quickly as Jingles probed for every detail of the trip to the Caribbean. He learned all kinds of things. Mulligan made a hole-in-one on the first day of the trip. Harvey helped Knickers translate for everyone after listening to instructional tapes on basic Spanish for only a few days. They traveled everywhere in the chauffeured limousine and ate lobsters and fresh fish almost every night. While the earthquake had struck Haiti several years ago, the destruction remained highly visible.

The men didn't seem overly curious about their destination until they actually pulled up to the chain link gate and Jingles got out to unlock it.

"I can't believe we're still in Arizona," Mulligan said. "Look at the size of these trees."

"It's a lot cooler here than it was back in Leisureville," Jingles said, once back in the car. "That's why I gave you all sweaters."

Jingles drove to the clubhouse and told them about the history of Prescott Hills as he remembered it from Oliver. When they arrived at the clubhouse, Jingles took a small ice chest from the trunk and carried it to the deck beside the pond. He opened each of the men a Sam Adams and let them take in the view.

"We can even take a ride around the course in the carts," Jingles said, leading them to the garage. They took two carts and headed off down the path, with Jingles driving Harvey in one and Knickers taking Mulligan in the other.

When they finally got to Ponderosa, Jingles drove off the cart path and right up onto the rear terrace. "I want you guys to take a look at this house and tell me what you think!"

Jingles gave them the walking tour and pointed out all the features that had so impressed Pat and him. He explained that there were no restrictions on the size of pets here, that there was even a barn for horses.

Remembering the trout, Jingles took the spinning rod from beside the door and led the men to the pond around the island green. The second stone he overturned revealed a worm and he baited the hook.

"Are you a fisherman, Knickers?" he asked, handing him the rod.

"Not for about twenty years," he replied.

Jingles hoped that the trout Pat caught hadn't been a fluke. "Well, try tossing this little worm over there under the bridge!"

Knickers tossed out the bait and nothing happened. *Sometimes things don't work out the way you hope*, Jingles thought. Suddenly the rod doubled over and a fish took off with Knickers line. A trout twice the weight of Pat's jumped out of the water and splashed back down.

Knickers chased it around the edge of the pond as the other men watched. "Do you have a net?" Knickers yelled. "Somebody get me a net!"

The others walked out on the bridge and leaned on the railing, offering no help. Jingles looked from Knickers to the green, then back at Ponderosa.

The Sweet Swing

This felt perfect. Finally the trout tired and Knickers lifted it from the water. It was a Kodak moment, but no one had a camera. He posed for a moment and then released the fish.

"You put on a good floor show, Jingles," Mulligan said and lit a cigar.

Harvey turned to Jingles too. "You've been very mysterious. What brought us out here?"

"Why did you haul us out here to Yosemite National Park?" Mulligan added from behind a cloud of smoke.

"That's Pat's and my new house right there," Jingles said. "Pretty much a gift from the friendly people at Phoenix City Bank."

Mulligan immediately asked, "So you're dumping Leisureville?"

Jingles half-expected the comment. "We probably won't move for a year or two until most of the construction is done around here. Until then, we'll be staying where we are."

"What construction?" Harvey asked. "I don't see anything going on. Fill us in."

"There are three hundred lots, and they are all going to have homes similar to this one."

"You mean the lots are all sold?" Harvey asked.

"None are sold yet," Jingles answered. "Just ours."

Knickers rubbed his hands on his pants to get rid of the slime. "So how are they going to sell them? The market isn't so good for houses that cost what? Seven or eight hundred thousand?"

"The golf course is great," Mulligan said. "I think the place has nice potential. But like Knickers says, the market isn't so good."

"The bank thinks I can help sell the development," Jingles said. "Oliver, he's the head of the bank, wants me to serve as club pro. Pat and I think lots of Alaskans would like it."

Knickers started looking for another worm. "So the plan is that people will buy into this place so they can be neighbors of the great Jingles?"

"I don't understand!" Harvey objected, glaring at Knickers. "Why are you ripping Jingles? You're all mixed up. A couple hours ago you said you loved how the people in Haiti responded to his story!"

"No, you're mixed up, Ichabod." Knickers scolded. "I think you missed my point. I saw grown men standin' on a field in Alaska talkin' about what a difference Jingles made in their lives by bein' their coach. He didn't even play golf back then. If an experience like that can be so memorable for kids in a snow-covered state with less than a million people, what could it mean in a country of nine million that have almost nothing but baseball blue sky? I'm a fan of what he did as a coach, not for what he's doin' on the greens right now."

243

Jingles tried to shake off Knickers' remark. "I want you guys to move here too. Pat and I talked about it. We'll buy three more houses in here that you can use for as long as you want. That's what I brought you here to tell you."

Knickers handed the rod to Harvey. "Here, you can try catchin' one of Jingles' fish."

He then turned and looked at the new owner of Ponderosa. "Now I know how you must have felt when I tried to bribe you to come on our vacation. We're your friends, Ray. We're not Jingles fans. When this is all over, we'll still be your friends. And at least *I* will still be living in Leisureville, where I've been happy for the last eight years."

Mulligan tossed Knickers a cigar. "I hate it when he says what I'm thinking before I can. I guess we've been partners for a long time."

Harvey's face turned red, and his Adam's apple pointed directly at Knickers. "You know what?" he said, his voice an octave higher than normal. "I am a Jingles fan! Why the bitterness? We all wish that lens had come to our mailbox, don't we?"

Jingles turned and walked to the woodpile beside the house and returned with an armload of logs and kindling. The other men watched him in silence. He arranged the wood in the fireplace and asked for a lighter. He flicked up a flame and held it to the smallest piece of kindling. A cozy little blaze erupted within a minute.

He motioned for everyone to sit around the fire and wished he had more beer. "Just go ahead and talk freely, like I'm not even here. I really care what you all think."

Mulligan wiped sweat from his forehead, despite the cool temperature. "I have to say that you've handled it a little like a politician. Believe me, I know how that works. You talk in generalities but avoid the specifics. Why is it that you don't come right out and tell the world that you got a freak lens that makes everything appear so large that the game becomes simple. I think it's because you want to keep up the illusion that you're a great golfer. Tell me if I'm wrong."

Harvey was still flushed, but his voice returned to normal. "What illusion? He is a great golfer! It's like the perfect storm; his golf game was already phenomenal, except for the putting. This lens comes along and Jingles becomes the perfect golfer. You could give each of us that lens, but it wouldn't produce the scores that Jingles gets, not even close.

"And you think he should tell the world about it, Mulligan? Is that how you would advise him as his agent? You said you wished he hired you!"

Knickers raised his hand to stop Harvey. "The *problem* with the lens is that I don't think it's fair. If a baseball player puts cork in his bat, he can hit the ball further. That's why it's against the rules. You read all the time about how some baseball players use steroids. It's wrong because it isn't fair to those who don't."

"Not fair?" Harvey objected, heating up again. "He didn't go out and cork a bat or use steroids! He put in the lenses that a doctor ordered for him! You're a stickler for the rules, Knickers. Is there a rule about eyewear in golf? I never heard of it!"

Mulligan chimed in again. "Knickers didn't say he was breaking the rules. He said it wasn't fair . . . more like Jingles was breaking the code of fairness."

"The code of fairness?" Harvey said. "What's that? When did they put that in print?"

Jingles stared into the flames, as if by sharing Knickers' physical view he would better comprehend the mental one. Was Knickers right? Without a doubt, the lens gave him an advantage. Was it unfair? That seemed like a more complex question. He continued to think without saying anything.

Mulligan continued. "Nobody's saying you are cheating or anything like that, although the effect is kind of the same."

"I guess I'm not a deep thinker like you guys," Jingles said quietly. "One day I'm struggling to maintain my game and the next day this contact lens comes along. It seemed like a gift. I want to believe it was just meant to be." He looked at each of his friends and they were all staring at the fire.

"Please," Jingles continued. "Tell me what you would do in my place. I have lots of people, lots of friends, that are relying on me now."

Mulligan said, "I wouldn't worry so much about all your *new* friends. If they weren't part of your life before you were shooting fifty-nines, they probably don't matter. Nobody's paying you out of the goodness of his heart. I don't think you understand that. Look at that big log house over there. Why did somebody give you that? Because you're a nice guy? No. They did it because they are angling to make money for themselves.

"I'll tell you the difference between you and them. I don't even have to tell you, you just showed us. You wanted to give us houses like yours *only* because you are a nice guy. You have nothing to gain but our company, so thanks for the offer."

"It's the same with Eagle Optics or Larry Weinstein or Nike," Knickers said. "They give you a little because they can make a lot. It's just business. You don't owe them anything if you don't take their handouts."

Jingles looked at Harvey, who seemed quiet all the sudden. "If you were me, Harvey, tell me what you would do. Would you wear the lens and make the money and let people make a fuss over you?"

Harvey slowly shook his head. "I can't say for sure. This all happened so fast, but I'll tell you something. I have never met anyone that I think more highly of than you. I can't imagine you ever doing the wrong thing, which does lead me to a question. How do you endorse contact lenses for a company when your own is just a fluke? How do you or the company justify that?"

Jingles stared at Harvey for a moment, then lowered his head. "I really can't justify that. Somehow I got the impression they could make more lenses just like the one I have, but now I know that was stupid. They have no idea that I have a defective lens. I'm planning on giving their money back. If I'm going to benefit financially, it's going to be because of my golf, not my eyes."

"What the hell's wrong with you, Jingles!" Mulligan shouted. "Your golf and your eyes . . . make that eye . . . are one in the same! You can't separate the two."

"You want to know what I'd do in your shoes? I'm going to be honest, and it hurts. I would have done exactly the same as you even though it's dead wrong. Heck, I pushed you right in this direction. I saw something amazing happening and called out the media dogs! You never even had a chance to think about what was going on before your feet were buried in it. You didn't go out of your way to screw anybody. You just got dealt a straight flush and you're making it pay. Thing is, deceit just isn't in your nature. This is deceitful."

Harvey said, "I'm listening, but I'm not getting it. Who is getting screwed over? Jingles has just played in some exhibitions. No one else has been a loser, really. People are just entertained. Even the Skins Game is only an exhibition for charity."

"Okay," Knickers said. "Here's another way to look at it. If others could see the cup through Jingles' eye, if they knew how much easier it was for him to putt than Tommy Jenks, do you think they would be so excited? I don't think so. I mean how many people want to watch me in a slam dunk contest if the basket is only seven-feet high for me and ten for everyone else?

"Am I far off, Jingles? Do you feel like you are dunking at a seven-foot basket?"

Jingles considered the comparison. Actually, Knickers wasn't far off. Putting was almost that easy.

"But look how far Tommy Jenks could hit the ball," Harvey offered. "Jingles' putting just leveled the playing field."

Knickers chuckled. "If you think seventy-three-year-olds should be on a level playing field with twenty-three-year-olds, that's your business. I don't think you really believe that.

"Jingles, it was a very entertaining experience for a few days. I'll give you that. I wouldn't mind playing a few rounds with a lens like that too. But I figure you should only mess with people for so long. You can't let them go on believing it's possible to get seventy miles to the gallon forever.

"And let me go back to what Mulligan said a while ago. If it's all good and fine, why don't you just tell the world how it really is, like you told me? Would Nike want your name on a contract? Would the bank have given you this house?"

Harvey felt badly for Jingles. The tone of the others was overly harsh. "Why can't we just accept the lens as a gift from above? Let's just be supportive like friends should be."

Knickers snorted. "If God gives a damn about how anybody plays golf or baseball or any other game, I want a refund for every dollar I ever tossed in the collection plate at church! We just came back from a country where people are struggling to eat. God has bigger things to think about.

"And I held back one other thing that I disliked about our trip because I didn't want to say it in front of the girls. I disliked *me* for driving around in a limo where all those people were starving. That's not who I want to be. That's not the way I've lived my life and it will never happen again."

Mulligan clapped his hands for Knickers. "One last thing, Harvey. There are lots of ways to show support for a friend. One of the most important is to let them know when they're wrong."

Jingles stood up. It was time to be heading back to Leisureville. "I'm going to think about everything you all had to say. I'm also inviting you to Hawaii for the Skins Game, if you'd like another island vacation."

There were no immediate responses to the offer. The drive home was long and quiet.

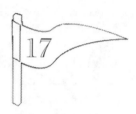

Martha Porter owned a one-bedroom condo just ten minutes from her job at Eagle Optics. Thanksgiving was usually a quiet holiday for a woman of fifty-five who never married and had no relatives living nearby. This one had been no different. She sewed a couple new outfits for her collection of Barbie dolls, watched some television, and baked a Cornish game hen for her evening meal. She called it her Barbie turkey.

She had been Herman Winston's secretary for eleven reasonably satisfying years. While her job lacked excitement or challenge for the most part, she never had to work late or on weekends. Her salary was sufficient to cover her modest housing expenses, keep her 2005 Toyota running, and put food on the table for her and on the floor for Cosmo, her cat.

The bonus of a full year's salary that Herman promised would amount to $34,000 before taxes. According to the agreement she signed, she would receive the bonus as soon as the sale of the company was finalized. The money would go a long way toward securing her future, especially since she may not have a job after the sale. That's why she had surprised herself when she jotted down Karl Zimmer's phone number in New York before she left work yesterday.

She wondered how the Zimmers were spending the holiday. It couldn't possibly be a happy one for them. Her prayers that Karl would successfully exercise his option had gone unheeded. All the benefits of his amazing invention, the contact lenses that made Jingles Plumlee such a sensation, would go to Herman Winston instead. Herman Winston: *The man who had been turned into the devil by greed.* She had heard everything.

"Well, Cosmo," she said, looking at the cat that today sported a gelled stand-up hairdo like the Seinfeld character Kramer, "we're not going to let money turn my head, are we?"

She picked up her phone and punched in a number. Karl Zimmer was no longer registered at the hotel. Had he left a forwarding number? Yes. They had his cell phone number.

Karl answered his cell. She recognized his accent immediately.

"This is Martha Porter from Eagle Optics, Karl."

"Yes, Martha."

"Where are you?" she asked out of curiosity.

"I'm in a taxi here in Phoenix. Just coming home from New York."

"Well, I know that things aren't going well for you. We got word that you would not be picking up the option on your lenses on Monday. I want to see if I can help," she explained what had transpired in Herman's office over the last two weeks in detail.

When she could think of nothing more, she said, "I hope this information will allow you to complete the purchase of your option on Monday."

Karl wondered how he could reach Sherman. The offices were closed until Tuesday; there had been a sign on the door to that effect. What if he couldn't reach him? What if Sherman wouldn't listen when he did? He would have to find an attorney tomorrow. An attorney could tell him what he should do.

"Martha, I can never thank you enough for what you've done. If this works out the way I hope, you will always have a job with me. And a much bigger bonus than the one Winston offered."

Martha loved the idea of working for the kind German. "I think you should call Jingles Plumlee as soon as possible. He deserves to know too. Jingles left me his card with some phone numbers." She gave him the numbers for Jingles and her own number as well.

Before hanging up, she asked, "If you could avoid telling anyone at Eagle Optics where you got this information, I'd be thankful. I just want you to get what's properly yours."

Jingles, Karl thought. He heard people talking about the golfer while he was in New York. So this Jingles was wearing the other lens! It would be interesting to speak with the only other man to experience *eaglevision.*

Karl called the first number Martha provided and got no reply. The second number produced an answer after several rings. "This is Quinn," the voice said. Mitchell Quinn was the only person working on the holiday.

"I'd like to speak with Jingles Plumlee, please. This is the man who made his contact lens."

"You are with Eagle Optics?" Quinn asked, almost spitting the last two words. Jingles' cheap contract with that company still rankled him.

"No. I'm the man that made the telescopic lens that this Jingles is wearing. Eagle Optics is trying to steal it from me."

"Holy shit," Quinn whispered. "What telescopic lens? What are you talking about?"

Quinn sensed the hesitation on the other end. "I represent all matters for Jingles. Please tell me all about it."

Karl told him the whole story from the back of the cab. About halfway through it, Quinn was already checking on evening flights from Phoenix to Los Angeles.

When the story was complete, Quinn said, "Here's what you need to do, Karl. There's a seven-thirty flight from Phoenix to LA on United. I will take care of everything for you. I promise. Can I book you a seat?"

"I suppose so," Karl said. "We're almost to my apartment. I can drop off my wife and have the driver take me right back to the airport."

"Can you e-mail a copy of the report you were talking about before you leave?"

"Yes, I will do it from my computer in the house before I leave. Just let me write down your e-mail address."

Gillian was waiting for the Plumlees at the airport in LA on Friday morning. They walked up to her in the company of two other passengers.

Jingles stepped forward to give her a hug and whispered in her ear. "I'm anxious to hear what Mr. Quinn said about my lens, but we need to talk about that in private."

She turned her head and whispered back, "Nothing yet."

Pat introduced Lucy and Harvey Green. "They are two of our very best friends from Leisureville." They exchanged handshakes, and the Greens made a fuss about meeting the Olympian, as she figured they would.

Pat continued. "They'll be traveling with us to Hawaii later. I got tickets for them on our same flight. Do you think you could see if there are a couple more rooms open at our hotel over there? Oliver will be coming too. He's going to caddy for my husband!" *Did Gillian seem to brighten up when she mentioned Oliver?* It made her curious.

Gillian said, "I'm worried that the hotel may be full. The event is going to be very well attended by fans and media alike."

"You can always stay in our room," Pat said to Lucy. "They usually have two beds."

The Sweet Swing

"And Oliver is a big boy," Jingles added. "He's resourceful enough to fend for himself."

Gillian said she would find something, not to worry. "And listen, the flight to Hawaii doesn't leave for six hours, and Mr. Quinn has apparently cleared your schedule for the day. I thought there was a contract or two to sign, but I guess they can wait. Why don't you just enjoy yourself touring around town. You want to see Universal Studios? Take the Hollywood tour?"

"Universal Studios!" Lucy said. "That's for me." They all agreed.

"Will Oliver be going over on our flight?" Gillian asked.

Why the apparent interest in Oliver, Jingles wondered. Glancing at Pat, he noticed her raised eyebrows as well. Jingles answered, "No. It's the midnight special for him. He has to work all day." A frown spread across Gillian's pretty face.

Pat whispered to her husband, "I think there might be something going on between Oliver and Gillian!"

Jingles whispered back, "He's old enough to be her father."

"He is and he isn't," Pat answered.

"What do you mean by that?"

"He *is* old enough, but he *isn't* her father."

The limo sat outside the baggage claim area, right there at the curb. Harvey couldn't stop grinning. Jingles had been awed by the flashy transportation too, but not so much this time around. Knickers words about never riding in a limousine again were still at the front of his mind.

As they arranged themselves in the car, Jingles suggested that Pat sit with the Greens toward the front. He had business to discuss with Gillian. Late last night, well, after returning from Prescott Hills, he had taken a long walk by himself that led to Tom Klein's bench. From there he called Gillian to explain everything about the uniqueness of his lens. Hopefully, the agency could guide him in the right direction.

Once comfortable beside his advisor, Jingles asked, "You've heard nothing from Mr. Quinn? I thought it would be a rather huge deal to him."

"I thought so too," Gillian answered in a conspiratorial whisper. "I called him last night and got nothing but his voice box. I left word that there was big news about one of your contact lenses that could be a real game-changer. Today he's been in a closed door meeting and will accept no interruptions. I've heard nothing."

Game-changer, Jingles thought. *In so many ways!* He'd simply have to wait.

He shifted gears. "I can play on Sunday for the charity of my choice, right?" She nodded. "So how hard is it to set up a nonprofit corporation. How long does it take?"

"You can basically do it online in very little time as long as you have all the information. We have people at the office that can do that kind of thing lickety-split."

"That's what I want to do then," he declared, nodding his head. "I'd like to get it set up before the press conference tomorrow afternoon in Hawaii." He took out the notes that Harvey wrote during the plane ride and handed them to her.

"I can work on it for the next few hours," she said. "The driver can drop me at the office before you head off on your tour."

Jingles tipped his head toward Harvey, who was staring intently out the windows with his wife. "I'd like you to take Harvey to the office with you. He understands a lot of things better than I do and knows just what I want. I know there will be blanks to fill in and he's the man for the job. And show him the pictures on the wall. He'll get a big kick out of that."

Gillian's phone sounded. "It's Mr. Quinn!" She listened, then put her hand over the phone. "Do you have that contact lens with you?"

"Right here," Jingles said and touched his front left pants pocket.

"Mr. Quinn wants to have someone look at it for you. I'll return it when we meet for the flight to Hawaii."

Jingles handed her the case. He pointed to the R compartment and surprised himself with how easily he let it go.

"I have it," Gillian said into the phone. "I'll be there in about twenty minutes."

After she returned the phone to her purse, Jingles said, "And just one more favor. When you get to the office, see if you can help Harvey find a phone number in the Dominican Republic for Juan Felipe, the former major leaguer."

By Saturday morning, Karl Zimmer was weary of hotels. He had been in New York for months and now two nights in Los Angeles. He hoped to be settling into a regular lifestyle again soon. Perhaps today Mr. Quinn could finally give him good news. The contact lens that brought fame to Jingles Plumlee was definitely one of his. He held it in his hand and examined it yesterday morning. Mr. Quinn said it was the final piece to the puzzle, the last thing he needed to know.

As Karl headed out of the hotel for the walk to the Quinn Group office, a beautiful Los Angeles fraulein was crossing the street a half block away, all long legs and five-inch heels. Beneath the designer sunglasses he purchased yesterday, Karl opened his right eye to take in more detail. He knew his wife would give him an elbow if she was beside him, but hey, she wasn't. He continued to appreciate the legs until the girl disappeared around a corner.

The Sweet Swing

His lenses had more uses than just tavern games and golf! Karl laughed at his own silliness.

When he reached Quinn's office, the receptionist buzzed him in and led him to the room where he spent most of the previous day and nearly the entire night before that. There had been so many questions, so much review of his report, and more conversation with Martha Porter.

Quinn was sitting in front of his computer when Karl entered his suite. He immediately rose from his chair and crossed the room to the couch, where he patted the cushion beside him, inviting Karl to join him.

"Well, Karl, it's finally time for a decision on how we can help you most. I've talked to my attorney and he tells me you have a solid case against Eagle Optics. Obviously, Herman Winston has a lot to lose and will spend big money defending himself, so you'll need a deep pocket too." Karl nodded appreciation for words he wanted to hear.

"So here is an alternative I can provide," Quinn continued. "I will purchase your option rights from you for ten million dollars. I'm willing to put that much at risk because I believe in what you've done." Karl wondered what risk there could be, given the accomplishments of this Jingles Plumlee.

"You can then go ahead and sue Eagle Optics. Who knows, you might end up owning the whole company!"

Karl shook his head vigorously. "But I wouldn't have the rights to my lens! You would own them!"

"That's true," Quinn said. "But you don't own them now either. The clock is ticking. Ten million is a lot of money to fund your fight against Eagle Optics."

Karl glared at the man as he stood and walked to his desk and gathered some papers. Did this Quinn think he was a fool? His lens was far more valuable than any damages a court might award.

Opening his right eye, Karl looked past Quinn to his computer screen. From sixteen feet away, he could see every word. He read the first paragraph, stopped, and looked back to the top to start reading again. It wasn't an e-mail. It was a formal letter that had been attached to an e-mail. The letterhead was ChinaLink, the massive conglomerate with hands in nearly all aspects of Chinese life.

Quinn returned with a contract, spread it out on the coffee table, and started to review it. Karl leaned back on the couch, put his hands behind his head, and pretended to listen. He continued to read the letter through his right eye. *Our scientific team has reviewed your report on the Jingles Lens in sufficient detail. We are willing to meet your full price of $300,000,000 U.S. plus $3.00 U.S. royalty per lens with one necessary provision. We require an exclusive thirty-day option period in which to examine and evaluate the actual product. In* *consideration of that exclusivity, we will forward a nonrefundable payment of $30,000,000 U.S. upon receipt of both a signed copy of the attached agreement and thirty of the lens prototypes from the listed inventory.*

"Scheisse!" Karl said aloud. No wonder Mr. Quinn doesn't mind putting $10 million *at risk*. China was the logical place to go. Getting approval for production and distribution would be a snap over there, especially for ChinaLink. Why didn't he think of that? Quinn was smart and fast, in addition to being something less than honest. First it was the owner of Eagle Optics and now this Quinn stranger; everyone was out to take advantage of him.

Obviously, he realized, Jingles was the reason for ChinaLink's lightning-quick action. It takes real imagination to read a report and figure out what it all can mean. It was Jingles the magic golfer that put instant substance into that report. They wanted *the Jingles Lens*. He wanted to meet this Jingles.

Karl abruptly stood and Quinn stopped talking. "I need you to make some changes to that contract. You don't have to pay me anything up front, just pay Eagle Optics the fifteen million for my option. We'll share the proceeds from the sale of my technology fifty-fifty." That was the split with Sherman MacPherson and the first numbers that came to mind.

The veins bulged on Quinn's neck. The stretched skin looked white against the darkly tanned background. "How in the world would I ever recover my investment that way? I'm trying to help you!"

Karl pointed to the computer. "Why don't you read your e-mail? You'd see there's nothing to worry about."

Quinn looked from the computer screen to where Karl was standing. How could he possibly know what was on the screen?

Karl enjoyed Quinn's confusion for a moment, then reached up and touched the right lens of his sunglasses. "Never underestimate the power of the lens. Have a copy of a new agreement sent over to the hotel immediately. I'll review it and get back to you when I have the chance."

Karl started for the door and turned. "You know, on second thought, we'll split the three hundred million down the middle, but I'll take all the royalties. Jot that down."

Quinn started to stutter. "H . . . how do I know that they'll even exercise? I can't know for sure."

"Well, the thirty million option fee is guaranteed," Karl answered. "That will get you your money back right there. Half of the thirty is fifteen. No risk at all."

"I'll need to see that agreement at my hotel ASAP, as you Americans like to say. I have plans for the weekend." According to the newspaper, Jingles

The Sweet Swing

was playing golf in Hawaii tomorrow. Karl was hearing the call of the islands. "Remember, Mr. Quinn, the clock is ticking!"

On his balcony at the Hapuna Beach Prince Hotel, Jingles looked down at the parking lot four stories below. Pat suggested that his stardom should have merited an ocean view, but that was the last thing on his mind. When Gillian had returned his contact case and bubble lens at the LA airport, the attached note from Mr. Quinn conveyed nothing more than good luck wishes . . . not a single word about the lens! When Gillian told him that her subsequent calls to Quinn from Hawaii went unanswered, Jingles decided to take charge for a change.

With the noon press conference only twenty minutes off, Pat, the Greens, Oliver and Gillian were gathered in his room. He awaited only Jane Friend. Although she was part of the media, she was also like part of the family now.

After a tap on the door, Jane entered. She looked radiant and sported an orchid in her hair. "What's up?" she asked. "Doesn't everybody have to get downstairs?"

Jingles asked everyone to join him on the balcony, and they crowded around him. "Do you see the Lexus at the end of the lot? The red one?" He pointed and everyone nodded. "Can any of you read the license plate number?"

"Are we supposed to guess?" Lucy asked. "I mean obviously no one can see the numbers from here."

"Four, seven, nine, letter C, four," Jingles said. "Does anyone want to go down there and check?" When no one answered, he turned around to check their reactions. There was more confusion than amazement on their faces.

"Okay, let's go inside then," he continued. "Oliver, will you take a dollar from your wallet and stand over there against the door?" Oliver did as asked.

"Now," Jingles continued. "Does anyone here believe they have excellent vision?"

Jane answered first. "I'm sure I do. I just got a new prescription because of you."

Jingles instructed Oliver to hold up the bill and Jane to walk toward him until she was close enough to read the serial number. From a range of about six feet, she started to read. "I see an F and a one." She tilted her head slightly forward. "Seven, seven . . ."

From his position at the foot of the bed, about eighteen feet away, Jingles finished the serial number. "Four, seven, five, nine, zero, and letter G. Is that right, Jane?" He had removed his sunglasses and ogled the chart with one eye while the other was closed tightly.

255

As everyone studied him, Jingles began his story. "It's a blessing to have good vision, but when you can see this much better than everyone else, I've decided it's a curse." He told the story of the lens and his golf as quickly as could. He credited his friend Knickers Collins with helping him *see the light*.

When Gillian said they couldn't delay going to the press conference another second, Jingles concluded by telling the group that he would never wear the lens again, at least not for golf or any other competitive game. It was all about the code of fairness. Perhaps next week, when they returned to Phoenix, Jane could do a special show about his vision and decision.

The ballroom of the beautiful hotel on the emerald Kohala Coast of Hawaii's Big Island was crowded. All of the six hundred chairs in front of the small stage were occupied, some by the media and the rest by resort guests. Still more people stood at the sides and rear of the room. The only empty seats were the five behind the table and podium on the stage.

In a hallway outside, Gillian gave Jingles last minute coaching on his forthcoming adventure. "I'll be right there in front of you, not twenty feet away. Just talk to me and the people around me."

"I'm not worried," Jingles said. "I've had lots of practice by now. I know I've thrown a lot at you the last couple of days, but you have risen to every occasion. Thanks for everything."

A side door to the ballroom opened and the host for the press conference said it was showtime. The four golfers followed him into the room and to the speakers' table, where they sat in their assigned seats. Because Jingles was the hot ticket on the island, he was scheduled to make his opening remarks last.

The other competitors in the Senior Skins Game were Sam Sitton, fifty-five, who had been the Champions Tour leading money winner for two of his five years on the circuit, Earl "Scruffy" Welton, fifty-three, a bearded giant of a man who had won two of the Tour's major championships on the year, and George Blackwood, fifty, who just recently qualified to play with the older golfers and won the other two Senior majors. Each smiled through a flattering introduction and took the podium for a couple minutes. Their remarks followed the pattern Gillian had predicted. They expressed their gratitude for the invitation, complimented the resort, expounded on the beauty of the course, and discussed the charities they chose to represent.

Only Scruffy Welton broke the pattern. Rather than basically repeat the first two speakers, he mentioned the fabulous parties of the last few nights and demonstrated the hula he learned at a luau on Friday. In a game dominated by mostly serious-minded competitors, Scruffy had always been a crowd favorite.

Sitton was playing for breast cancer research and Blackwood championed the Kids Need to Read Foundation. Welton, whose early years on the PGA Tour were derailed by alcohol abuse, was playing for his own foundation, Welton for Youth Wellness. According to him, the foundation contributed $9 million to his hometown Houston City Schools for extra counseling positions over the last decade.

As Scruffy concluded his brief speech, Jingles looked out at his small contingent among the crowd. To the right, about ten rows back, sat Harvey, Lucy, Pat, and Oliver. He knew that all of his family was sure to be watching on television, along with most of Leisureville and Wasilla.

The emcee made a few comments about Appleman and conveyed hopes for a rapid recovery. He mentioned that the injured golfer had already been extended an invitation to compete in next year's event, news that was warmly applauded by the gathering.

"By popular demand," he then said, "we have broken tradition and invited a nontour golfer to participate in the Skins Game for the very first time. Ray Plumlee, a man known throughout our country as *Jingles*, has captured our imaginations and hearts almost overnight. I don't have to tell you his story. It's been chronicled by every sportswriter over the last several weeks, and celebrated by every optometrist." He paused while everyone in the room laughed and started to clap. "I got contact lenses for the very first time last week! Did any of you do the same?" Hands went up throughout the ballroom. "Ladies and gentlemen, I give you Jingles!"

Jingles stood and took his place in front of the microphones. The audience was all standing as they clapped, whistled, cheered, and called out his name. The other golfers at the table looked at each other and laughed, then each turned and gave Jingles a thumbs-up. Jingles nodded and smiled and waited, looking at Gillian all the while. When she finally nodded, he lifted his arms and everyone took their seats. How did she know they would do that?

"I'm not here today because I'm a great golfer. These three men are great golfers and so is Mr. Appleman. They have proven it over long professional careers that I have enjoyed watching right along with everyone else that loves the game. But again, I'm *not* a great golfer. I have been lucky enough to suddenly play some great golf, luckier than any of you can possibly imagine right now.

"My greatest luck of all is in being able to launch a new charitable foundation. When you get to be my age, you will start thinking more and more about how you can make a difference in the world. I commend these younger men up here for having already done so much. I think they would all tell you that when everything is said and done, it won't be the trophies on their shelves or the balance in their bank accounts that defines their lives, it will be their sense of how they helped others."

For a second time, the audience stood and applauded. This time Jingles felt it in his knees and put his hands on the podium to keep his balance.

"My friends and I have talked a lot recently about what we might do to make a difference. There are so many worthwhile causes and missions out there in the world. Each person has his own ideas about what counts most. In my case, I believe in what team sports can mean in the life of a child. It's not just about the games themselves, it's about a special feeling of working hard to achieve team and personal goals. It's about exercise, feeling the goodness of sweat, and dealing with both success and failure. It's all of those things.

"Some of my friends just returned from a trip to the island of Hispaniola. They saw two entirely different countries there in the Dominican Republic and Haiti, which we all know was plagued by problems long before the earthquake struck and put that country on the front page. Despite being neighboring nations of matching population, the contrasts are more glaring than the similarities."

Jingles stopped briefly to pick up his notes. "In Haiti, the literacy rate is just 53 percent, compared to 87 percent in the Dominican Republic. Life expectancy is just sixty-one in Haiti, compared to seventy-four in the Dominican Republic. In Haiti, per capita income is six times smaller." He looked at Harvey, who had collected the data, and nodded.

"The national pastime in the Dominican Republic is baseball. The season never ends. Over five hundred past and present major leaguers continue to be part of the culture there, inspiring others to succeed at whatever they choose to do. Haiti has no such recognizable heroes. Haiti has no baseball to speak of. My friends and I believe it should. We don't think baseball is the answer to solving the many problems in Haiti, but we think it can be one of them. Most importantly, it's something that we understand and feel capable of providing.

"I will be playing for the new Baseball Is an Answer Foundation and plan to volunteer my time and effort to its cause. I see it like *Field of Dreams*, one of my favorite movies. I believe if we fund construction of hundreds of ball fields throughout Haiti, employing local people to build them, and start youth baseball programs from the ground up, the children in that nation will flock to them. In doing so, we will also be building a bridge between the two countries of Hispaniola. Among the first to cross that bridge will be many of the Dominican baseball heroes, ready to inspire, promote and teach.

"The foundation will be headed by Mickey Collins and Juan Felipe, former major leaguers. Mr. Felipe is a resident of the Dominican Republic and has assured us that dozens of former and present baseball professionals from his country are eager to step up to the plate and make this plan happen.

"While golf will be my mission tomorrow, it will be the final day of that mission. I will not be attempting to play on the Champions Tour. I will not be competing in any other organized golf events. My full attention going forward will be to help make Baseball Is an Answer a success. Thank you very much."

Three thousand miles to the east, in Leisureville, Mulligan and Knickers sat in front of a television with their wives. They watched and listened in wonderment.

"Surprise, surprise," Bess said, and punched her husband on the arm. "I guess he pulled one on you!"

Knickers hopped up from the couch. "I'm on my way to Hawaii, anyone coming with me!"

"I'll find reservations," Bess said. "Just give me a second."

"We'll take my car to the airport," Mulligan offered. "Mary and I will go pack a bag and pick you up in fifteen minutes."

"How far is Hawaii?" Knickers asked.

"What's the difference?" Mulligan said over his shoulder as he went out the door.

In the Hapuna Beach ballroom, the questions came like machine-gun fire.

How can you just walk away from golf?

"I'll be lucky to be able to walk around this course tomorrow. We won't be using carts. I haven't walked a golf course in over ten years."

Seriously, how can you quit now?

"I enjoy golf. I *loved* coaching Little League. I did it for thirty years."

Do you have a physical problem standing in the way? Something to do with your limp?

"I only tend to limp because my left knee is stiff sometimes. It's nothing."

What about your endorsement contracts? What about the deals with Nike, Cadillac, Hilton and the others we've been reading about?

"That's a very good question. Fortunately, we haven't spent any of their money yet!" He pointed to his spouse in the audience. "There's my wife Pat, sitting right there. "Pat, we still *do* have the money, right?" Everyone laughed while she squirmed at the unexpected attention.

What about your millions of fans? Aren't you worried about disappointing them?

That question hit him like hammer, even though Gillian told him to expect it. He lowered his head to collect himself. What would everyone think when he made a full disclosure about his lens in a few days, as he was planning. He already decided to sit down with an optometrist first, for a full evaluation and explanation.

He remembered his planned answer. "There's no shortage of sports heroes in our great country. I think everyone will appreciate my decision in time. I'm most concerned now with finding fans in Haiti. Baseball fans!"

How can people donate to your foundation? It sounds like a fine idea.

Jingles looked at Gillian, who was smiling. Always smiling. "We'll have a web site up and running soon. We'll let you know within the next few days. From what I understand, it will be updated regularly with lots of photos."

Have you practiced on the course yet?

"I only arrived late yesterday. My practice round is scheduled for this afternoon."

How do you expect to handle such a challenging layout and the windy conditions?

"Actually, because it's the Skins Game and not medal play, I at least have a chance. A lucky shot here or there can make all the difference. I just hope not to embarrass myself too much." That was the absolute truth. To his way of thinking, forcing himself to expose his unaided game to a national audience was a form of punishment for his recent sins.

The host walked over and whispered to him. Jingles nodded and said, "That's it from me for now. I'll take questions, if anybody has them, after the golf tomorrow."

Questions were now directed to the remaining three golfers, but the subject remained the same. Most of the press asked for their thoughts about Jingles' game and his surprise announcement.

Pat had watched the proceedings with mixed emotions . . . anger, embarrassment, frustration, and some pride too. Her husband was dashingly handsome and unassumingly charming behind the microphones. Lucy even whispered *George Baily* in her ear a couple times!

Jingles' ability to handle his earliest interviews had surprised her. However, the man she saw on subsequent television appearances and today flabbergasted her. Where had that talent been hiding for over fifty years? And although her unexpected public introduction was embarrassing, the glow of it remained.

Still, through all the fluff, anger prevailed. Had her husband just given away everything? Would they have to return all the money? He *had* made the remark about how they hadn't spent it yet. Was she about to step back in time to where she was a month ago? How humiliating would t*hat* be?

Of all people, Knickers Collins was responsible! Everything had been fine until they went home for Thanksgiving. *Why did her husband have such a*

The Sweet Swing

so-called friend? One thing was certain, Knickers was now officially out of her life, and her husband's too. She could demand it!

Or could she? She resented the fact that he announced his intentions in front of the Greens, Oliver and the others without discussing them with her first. Surely she could have changed his mind, that was a foregone conclusion. *Was that the very reason he chose not to talk to her in advance?*

Oliver had watched Jingles' presentation without really hearing. His thoughts were on how Jingles' decision might affect the Plumlees' lives. The Eagle Optics contract was secure. They could keep that money because the contract only stipulated that he wear their hat and their lenses, not play golf. Larry Weinstein would have no objection. He already took a pile of chips to the cashier and the Skins Game appearance would result in added windfall in the short term. As for the contracts negotiated by the Quinn Group, he really couldn't be sure, but that might be a mess. His heart went out to Gillian in that regard.

He chose not to worry about Prescott Hills. *Que sera, sera.* Whatever will be, will be. His hunch was that the project would do just fine, especially if all the lots could be sold in the next few months. The Jingles story certainly wasn't over.

Neither was its impact on Oliver himself. Jingles first brought him business success and then excitement and joy. Now he had even helped the banker capture the affection of a wonderful lady, opening the possibility of starting a family.

After listening to Jingles' summary of why he would no longer wear the lens, Oliver considered what he might do under similar extraordinary circumstances. The insight of this fellow Knickers was indeed compelling. If Jingles had shared as much information about his sight with him, would he have come to the same conclusion as the old baseball player?

Definitely not. His world view was altogether different than that of either Jingles or his friend. He would have had the lens scientifically evaluated under an agreement with a major optics company. Some of the greatest discoveries in history originated from accidents like manufacturing errors, more than most people realized. If scientists could learn enough from the lens to reproduce it commercially, there could be a very happy ending to Jingles' story. He would talk to Jingles about that very thing.

Jane Friend wandered around the back of the ballroom, eavesdropping on conversations. While she was now in touch with the reality of the situation, perceptions were an important part of any news story as well. Jingles' revelation in his hotel room added new depth, a fresh twist. He was wise to choose her to help him present his story. She was compassionate. She understood. She would help others understand. And her ratings would fly off the chart!

Harvey looked on with glassy eyes, awed by what was taking place, and amazed by his presence in the inner circle. Lucy and he had considered both Arizona and New Mexico as retirement destinations. Even after settling on Arizona, they looked at four or five different developments in the Phoenix area. Why did they select Leisureville? Was it because dogs were so welcome and Lucy thought she *might* like to have a pet one day? That may have been it. For whatever reason, they certainly made the right choice.

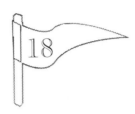

Two hours before tee time for the 2014 Senior Skins Game, Jingles sat in a corner of a restaurant on the ground floor of the Hapuna Beach Prince Hotel. The other competitors were busy on the practice tees, honing their swings, or on the green, fine-tuning their putting strokes, but Jingles wasn't used to a regimen that would only wear him out. He had to rest up for the 6,700 yard walk around the course. Besides, there was little inspiration in knowing even his best play would embarrass him; the lens would remain tucked in Pat's purse.

Knickers had been right. While the lens was a godsend, he misinterpreted the reason for the strange gift. It was intended as a test of his personal character. It had taken the wisdom of a true friend to help him recognize that. He hoped that the Baseball Is an Answer Foundation would help Knickers in return.

Jingles' party had pulled two tables together to allow room for seven chairs. Jingles sat at one end of the table, with Pat to his left and Harvey at his right elbow. Oliver, Gillian, and Lucy filled other seats and only Jane Friend's chair was empty. Two uniformed officers stood a few yards off to discourage interruptions from fans or media people.

Gillian seemed distracted, even distraught. As she had explained to her client, all communication with her boss was inexplicably absent. She knew that Jingles' announcement had to trigger immediate calls to Mitchell Quinn from both current and prospective clients, but she hadn't heard a word from him, not a single response to her messages. According to fellow employees with whom she checked, Quinn had left the office at noon on Saturday and had not returned. The whole thing was a mystery.

Jingles felt both admiration and deep sympathy for Gillian. One of his worries about his decision had been how it might impact her and her relationship with her employer. While she kept her smile until the end of the press conference, her spirits seemed to plummet ever since. Concern for her was going to further disable him on the golf course. A young lady like Gillian deserved only the best.

Jane arrived at the table and greeted everyone before taking her seat. The buzz on the grounds all centered on the old fellow from Alaska and Arizona. Did he bring the incomparable putting stroke to Hawaii? Could he compete with these established pros, as he had with Tommy Jenks, on a course that was the furthest cry from Raven's Nest? Network executives were on Cloud Nine, looking for record viewership for an event of this kind. She watched Jingles closely, trying to imagine what he might be thinking.

Suddenly Jingles stood, spread his arms, and called out to the security men, "Please let them join us. Those are my good, good friends."

Pat looked up and saw Mary and Bess walking toward them with their husbands trailing behind. Oliver and Jane pulled a third table into line to create space for the new arrivals.

Mulligan was decked out in a bright yellow suit and white patent leather loafers. "I told Knickers there was no way you'd be on the practice tee but he insisted that we look."

Knickers, in a plain gray suit, gave Jingles a hug that lifted him off his feet. "I knew you wouldn't be there. I just wanted to see how real golfers hit the ball. Scruffy's a hero of mine!"

"That figures," Jingles said and chuckled.

"And now you are my hero too, Jingles! You've seen the light and turned mine on too. Baseball *is* an answer! I talked with Juan on the phone from Los Angeles last night . . . didn't realize it was after midnight for him. He said the people there are totally stoked and ready to help."

Knickers turned to everyone and said, "I don't care who knows it now. I have over twenty million bucks that's been burnin' a hole in my pocket. It's all goin' to the new foundation! Harvey, you're gonna be the chief financial officer. Mulligan, you are CEO. You'll both earn salaries too! Well, very little ones."

"Hey, how about me?" Jingles asked.

Knickers laughed and winked. "Your future is in politics. You told me everythin' I wanted to hear!"

Pat, Mary, and Lucy stared at Bess. Twenty million! How could anyone keep a secret like that?

One of the security men got Jingles' attention. He limped over to see what the officer wanted.

"There's another person here who insists you'd like to talk to him." The guard pointed to a dark-haired man standing beside the other security guard. "He says he wants to tell you all about your contact lens."

Jingles motioned to the man to join him at another table as the others watched with curiosity. Mulligan said he recognized the stranger as another passenger on their flight to Hawaii, that he sat only a couple rows away.

Gillian went to the table and asked if Jingles wanted her to join them. He said he would be just a minute, not to worry.

Karl Zimmer introduced himself and said, "I assume you are aware that you have been wearing my telescopic lens on your right eye for the past month?"

"The lens I got from Eagle Optics?"

"Yes. The one that I examined on Friday in Mr. Quinn's office."

Jingles could only stare.

Karl continued, "The lens that allows you to see into a much larger, more vivid world?"

Jingles grabbed a scruff of hair above his left ear. "You mean that the lens is not some kind of accident? It's supposed to work that way?"

"It is. I call it *eaglevision*. I developed it while under contract to Eagle Optics and they have been trying to steal it from me."

"Hold on," Jingles said. "I'm not a very private person, not anymore. I want you to tell everyone about this. Please come join us."

He ushered Karl to the other tables and asked him to take a seat at the center, with his back to the room to prevent any eavesdropping.

"This is Karl..."

"Zimmer," the man said.

"I think he has a very interesting story to tell us."

For the next thirty minutes, only Karl spoke. His audience sat in numb silence as he told his entire story. He began with his boyhood in Germany and carried it all the way to Quinn's office and his trip to Hawaii.

Pat took the special lens case from her purse and handed it to Karl. "Here's your lens. My husband already decided never to wear it again. That's why he said he was finished with all his exhibitions."

Mulligan said, "You were so right, Knickers. You had a premonition. You thought there had to be some explanation more reasonable than an accident. Who could ever guess it would come with a story like this?"

Oliver shook his head; so much for doing something commercial with the lens. He'd been thinking of nothing else for the last twenty-four hours.

Gillian's fair cheeks were bright pink. "I can't imagine how Mr. Quinn could know all this and not tell Jingles! He had every right to know. We had a responsibility to tell him. Mr. Quinn told me the lens was fine when he gave it back to me. He said nothing about any of this!"

Oliver said, "I think it's rather obvious. He had bigger fish to fry. He didn't want any complications."

"So what are you going to do?" Gillian asked Karl. "Are you going to make this deal with Quinn Group?"

"I don't want to. That's why I came here. I signed the agreement with Quinn, but I left it at the desk at the hotel. I knew I could call and have him pick it up if I had no alternative. The deadline is tomorrow."

"Did you bring a copy of the agreement by any chance?" Gillian asked. "I just want to check something."

Karl lifted his briefcase from the floor and opened it on the table. He withdrew a copy and handed it to the lovely fraulein.

She opened her mouth wide. "This isn't an agreement with Quinn Group! It's a personal agreement between you and Mitchell Quinn."

Mulligan had moved to the front edge of his seat. "Karl, you mentioned that the only reason these people want to pop hundreds of millions at the drop of a hat is because of Jingles, am I right?"

"That is exactly why. He's the living proof. In time, everyone will learn about the capabilities of *eaglevision*, but seeing what he has done gets people moving more quickly."

"Well, what's in it for Jingles?" Mulligan asked. "He's the guinea pig that made it all happen!"

"Again," Karl said. "I don't want to do business with Mr. Quinn if I don't have to. He tried to deceive me, don't you agree? What do you call it when someone offers to pay ten million in exchange for hundreds and hundreds of millions?"

Mulligan smirked. "I'd call it a very good deal for him!"

"Can I ask Karl a question, Jingles?" Harvey asked.

"Of course," Jingles answered. "You don't have to ask me."

"Karl, would you be interested in having a nonprofit corporation be your partner on this deal?"

Karl smiled and nodded his head. "You mean the baseball answer thing that Jingles talked about yesterday? It's in all the newspapers this morning."

Harvey glanced at Knickers to see if he was paying attention. Knickers took the cue. "I have the fifteen million to buy out your option. My problem is that it's all in stock and I can't come up with the money by tomorrow."

Oliver leaned forward. "If you can show me documentation of the stock holding, I can float the fifteen million from Phoenix City Bank for the time necessary to clear a stock sale."

Knickers looked toward his wife. "Bess, get out that laptop of yours. She can show you the money right now!"

Oliver grinned at all the enthusiasm. "The Eagle Optics account is with our bank. I can just make the deposit and notify Winston. It sounds like the scoundrel will be very surprised. And I know a great lawyer who would be happy to handle a lawsuit against him, Karl. And he won't require a dime up front."

Harvey scratched his nose and looked at Oliver. "It might take a while to clear a stock sale. First Knickers has to transfer the shares to the foundation. It's for tax reasons."

"That's correct," Oliver said. "The longer it takes, the more interest we make on our secured loan. It sounds to me like the foundation will be able to afford the interest.

"Can we assume, Mr. Zimmer, that you are offering a 50 percent split of the proceeds to the Baseball Is an Answer Foundation?"

"Yes, that is right," Karl answered. "I like your American game of baseball."

Mulligan had borrowed Harvey's pen and was writing on a napkin. "In all fairness, I have to point out that would be a worse deal than you negotiated with Quinn. Didn't you say that all these royalties would go to you?"

"Once we have secured the rights to eaglevision," Karl said, "we aren't under any pressure to take the ChinaLink offer. I think Mr. Quinn was just grabbing at the first and easiest opportunity to cash out. Once every other company knows what only ChinaLink knows now, the price for the technology could multiply." Then Zimmer surprised everyone with a big grin. "I'm willing to bet your money on it!"

"For what it's worth," Oliver said. "I know a number of consultants that would stand on their hands for a chance to help you negotiate the best sale of Karl's invention. Would you like me to help you find one?"

"No ChinaLink, if we can avoid it," Knickers said. "I'd rather sell to an American company!" Everyone smiled at Knickers' patriotism.

"How many Little League diamonds would a hundred million build?" Mulligan wondered.

Oliver pushed himself out of his chair. "I'm going to have to leave for Phoenix right now if I'm going to take care of this. Karl, you and Knickers will have to come with me. Jingles, much as I hate to say it, you are going to need a new caddy."

"Gees," Jingles said. "I forgot about the golf. I have to tee off in half an hour!"

Knickers nudged his wife. "Bess can go with you. Either one of us can sign and she has better handwriting. I have to carry Jingles' damn clubs."

Jingles chuckled at the prospect. "Right, like you could carry my bag for the next four hours."

"There's three of us," Harvey said. "We can rotate the bag on every hole. Will they let you have three different caddies?"

Gillian finally smiled again. "They'll let Jingles do anything he wants."

Pat looked sympathetically at the Olympian, who seemed to be an innocent victim of all the shenanigans. "What are you going to do, Gillian? You don't strike me as someone who would want to work for Mr. Quinn after all this."

Jingles knew his wife was right. "Gillian, you leave word with Mr. Quinn that his company is fired. I'm hiring just you instead!"

Mulligan's jaw dropped, and he looked squarely at Jingles. "Stop and think for a second! When news comes out that you've been wearing this new high-tech lens, your stock will drop like a rock, won't it? There won't be any fans and there won't be any endorsements. You'll just be seen as a guy that fell into some good luck . . . and that's a best case scenario. Some will think the whole thing was some kind of charade. Hell, you're going to need an air traffic controller more than an agent. Shit's going to come flying at you from everywhere!"

Jane Friend had been sitting in a trance. How could the best story of her life keep getting better by the day, by the minute! "There will always be a few who throw shh . . . stones at others," she said. "I think I can portray Jingles as the most innocent of victims. He's going to come out of this with his head up."

Lucy reached over and held Gillian's hand. "You can start by finding Jingles a book deal." Everyone turned to Lucy. "This is the most amazing story I've ever heard. There isn't anybody, golfer or not, that isn't going to be fascinated by all the intrigue, all the consequences, everything."

"Damn right!" Knickers said. "I've already got a name for it. How about *The Sweet Swing of Jingles Plumlee!*"

"I'd go for *Eagle Eye*," Harvey said. "Karl says that his lens provides the vision of an eagle."

"*The Lens*," Mary Wettman offered. "Call it just that."

Oliver looked down at Gillian. "The book is a great idea, and I have another offer for you, Gillian. Jingles and I have a beautiful residential development with three hundred homes to sell. You can have a contract

The Sweet Swing

with Phoenix City Bank to market them. You'd be perfect. Have you ever considered living in Phoenix?"

Gillian looked pleased by all the concern. "Right now we have a Skins Game to play. Let's see if Jingles can win a few dollars for his new foundation!"

The crowd around the first tee at Hapuna covered an acre, stretching all the way to the practice green, where Jingles had been last to appear and last to finish. The spectators anticipating a clinic on expert putting were disappointed. He made a few here and there, but demonstrated less precision than Sitton, Blackwood, and Welton.

Preparing for the walk to the tee, Jingles' three friends completed a series of coin flips to determine who carried the bag first. Harvey won the first hole and would be followed by Mulligan, then Knickers. All three wore bright yellow tags on strings around their necks, signifying their official capacities at the event.

"It's going to be a long day," Jingles said to Harvey as they walked a rope-lined pathway, both slapping palms and bumping fists of enthusiastic fans. "The wind here seems to work against me on every hole, at least the ones where it hurts the most. They tell me it picks up every afternoon."

"Stop whining, Jingles," Harvey said, his eyes focused on all the smiling faces around them. "You're living the dream today."

Jingles gritted his teeth. Living the dream? In a matter of days, the world would know he was basically a fraud. He would have to call his children right after the round to give them a heads-up.

"How about you play and I carry the clubs?" Jingles offered.

Harvey, apparently unconcerned with his friend's dilemma, just laughed. "You must have me confused with Mulligan. He'd take you up on that offer!"

Harvey drew a deep breath when they were clear of the fans and looked upon the first fairway. "Will you look at this course! I didn't even know green came in this shade!"

Everything looked gray to Jingles. He looked up at Harvey and asked, "What do you think people will say when they know the real story?"

"I have no idea," Harvey said. "But does it really matter? I'm proud of you. Knickers and Mulligan are proud of you. We're going to build lots of little baseball players in Haiti and help build up a whole country at the same time."

The announcer described the format for the day's play. The first nine holes had a value of $50,000 each. In order to win a hole in Skins competition, one golfer had to make a lower score than all the others. If no single golfer got the lowest score, the prize money for that hole was added to the next. Basically, it was a progressive jackpot. The back nine got even more exciting when the value for each hole jumped to $100,000. The total prize money for the charity event was $1,350,000.

Each of the professionals received a fine introduction and warm greeting before his tee shot. Mere mention of their career victories and major tournament championships sent a shiver up Jingles' spine that served to clear his a head a little. Sitton and Blackwood each drove 290 yards into what was still only a light wind. Sitton found the fairway and Blackwood caught the rough to the right. Scruffy Welton, looking more like a lumberjack than a golfer, crushed his drive thirty yards past the others.

"My gosh," Harvey whispered. "How can you even play with these guys?"

"Thanks," Jingles responded. "That's the way a caddy is supposed to build a golfer's confidence. Let me build yours. Tommy Jenks hit the ball much further!"

Jingles' introduction was more succinct. "And now, representing Leisureville, Arizona, Golf Course, Ray 'Jingles' Plumlee."

Jingles teed his Nike ball and took a couple warm-up swings with his Nike driver. The first hole was a 366-yard par four. It required a drive of 190 yards on the fly to reach the fairway, which began on the other side of a gully full of bushes. In his practice round yesterday, the wind had been howling at 30 mph into his face and he couldn't even reach the fairway. He tried to forget everything but his simple swing and the ball.

The gallery watched his straight tee shot clear the hazard with five yards to spare and bound out to about 210 yards. Jingles exhaled and let Harvey snatch the club and return it to the bag. It was going to be just another round of golf; he would keep telling himself that all day.

"I had to pray a little on that one," Harvey said. "That was close."

"Keep praying," Jingles said. "It's about a hundred and sixty yards from there. Usually that's a five for me, but I better go with the four or even a three into the wind."

The others had to wait for him to play the short drive before proceeding up the fairway. Jingles kept their wait short. After one practice swing, he hit a high shot from a good lie . . . too high, and landed on the front fringe. With the pin toward the back of the green, he would have a putt of at least sixty feet.

Harvey and Jingles watched the others, anxious to see which would make a birdie and take down the initial prize money. Blackwood played from a poor lie in the rough and fared no better than Jingles. His ball stopped within a foot of the older man's ball. Sitton stuck a gorgeous wedge within six feet of the flag and the crowd around the green went crazy. Welton had a chip of only fifty yards and almost nailed the cup

The Sweet Swing

on the fly. His ball took one hop forward and then spun backward, not stopping until it rolled to eight feet in front of the hole. A great effort and a little misfortune.

Jingles waited for Blackwood, whose ball was slightly further from the flag. He used a nine iron to chip within two feet. The shot was soft, controlled, and confident. A thing of beauty.

For Jingles, a putter was the only way to go from the fringe. After taking a quick gander for himself, he asked Harvey for his thoughts.

"Aim a foot or two right and hit it hard enough," Harvey answered.

A foot or two, that narrowed it down, Jingles thought and laughed. He gave the ball a smack and missed long and to the right. His five-footer wouldn't matter. Sitton or Welton would make birdie, probably both.

Scruffy was next, and his putt appeared to be pretty straight. When his ball stopped short of the front lip, everyone groaned, including Harvey and Jingles.

Sitton turned the groans into cheers with a solid birdie. He tipped his cap and celebrated a $50,000 contribution to breast cancer research.

The next five holes proved uneventful, at least in terms of prize money. Everyone made par on the second hole, a result Jingles celebrated like victory. Three and four were halved by Sitton and Blackwood and then Welton and Blackwood. The pros were taking target practice at the pins. The fifth hole was a short par three and Jingles missed a 25-footer that actually caught a piece of the hole before spinning away. Two of the other three golfers converted birdies from inside fifteen feet. Six was halved in pars without anyone giving the cup a scare with his birdie putt.

The seventh hole was a 178-yard par three. The large green looked like an oasis in the dunes as it was mostly surrounded by a sand trap. The wind had picked up appreciably, and Jingles watched as each of the others left seven or eight irons well short of the flag near the back of the large undulating green.

"I'm not proud," Jingles said to Harvey, who held the bag for his third turn of the day. "I'm hitting the three wood. Even that might be short if I hit it too high."

Harvey said, "Might as well. You hit it as straight as your irons."

Jingles teed the ball low and lined it into the teeth of the breeze. The shot landed safely on the right front of the green, hopped once, and rolled quickly forward. Catching the right to left slope, his ball veered right toward the flag.

The spectators behind the tee started to holler. "In the hole! In the hole!" Jingles' ball barely missed the cup on the right and stopped only a foot past it. He was actually going to make a birdie at Hapuna!

The three pros congratulated Jingles for the near ace. He told them all to sink their own birdies and assumed that at least one of them would. If not, *Baseball Is an Answer* would have its first official contribution of a whopping $300,000!

"It's going to be a proud walk to this green," Harvey said. "The beauty of golf is that you never know! That was some shot. I figured the par threes would be your best chance against these guys."

Jingles laughed, totally caught up in the moment. "Even a blind squirrel finds an acorn once in a while!"

The large gathering around the green held its collective breath as first Welton missed, then Blackmon. Everything boiled down to Sitton's twenty-two-footer that would break sharply to the left. With big money at stake, he took extra time to survey his line and the suspense grew. He knew his putt was off-line immediately and lowered his shoulders in disgust.

Jingles was glad to have only ten inches to negotiate for his birdie. Even with his head spinning, he tapped his ball into the cup. Harvey rushed over and lifted him off his feet, oblivious to all the people and cameras. "That was the greatest thing I've ever seen. I could live to be a hundred and never feel like this again."

Knickers and Mulligan met them just off the green. They both squeezed him with the same enthusiasm as Harvey.

"You just hit a homerun to win the World Series!" Knickers yelled.

"For the St. Louis Cardinals?" Jingles asked.

"Who else?"

A security guard worked his way through the crowd with three women in tow. Pat greeted her husband like a returning war hero.

Mary Wettman said, "Pat told me she could make love to you right there on the green, Jingles! I'll take seconds."

Jingles raised his eyebrows. "Did you say it'll take seconds?"

"No," she laughed. "I said I'd take seconds! Oh, you know what I mean."

Mulligan moaned. "I've lost my wife. I'll have to take up with Speed Bump."

"How about you, Lucy?" Harvey joked. "Are you in the Jingles love-line too?"

"I'm kind of partial to the caddy," she said. "Since I hear Scruffy is already married."

Knickers slapped Jingles on the shoulder. "You just built at least a dozen Little League fields! Heck, maybe twenty or thirty. How does that feel, coach?"

"We can put a sign on each of those fields," Mulligan added. "'Built by Jingles Plumlee's tee shot on Hapuna's seventh hole!'"

The Sweet Swing

Jingles was jubilant. He never expected to win any hole, let alone one with such a huge prize. There was nothing left to worry about for the next few hours. He had accorded himself well against all odds. All the family and friends had reason to cheer a feat accomplished without *eaglevision*.

With no winners on eight or nine, the stakes were piling up again. A victory on the tenth hole would net the winner $200,000. Each subsequent flag represented another waving $100,000 bill.

"Is there such a thing as a hundred-thousand-dollar bill?" he asked Harvey who had the bag again on the tenth fairway. Harvey was the only person Jingles knew who might know such an answer. Other than Oliver, maybe.

"There was," Harvey said, without hesitation. "I even know which president had his picture on it."

"If you're waiting for me to guess, forget it," Jingles said.

"Well, it was Woodrow Wilson. The bill went out of circulation before the middle of the twentieth century."

"Question number two," Jingles said. "Can I get there with a three iron from here or will it take a wood?"

"I'd go with the *Wood*row Wilson," Harvey laughed. "A wood to win some Woodrows."

Jingles hit the wood and his ball ran over the green and into the bunker behind it. "Hmmm," Jingles said. "I was thinking three iron. Good thing I get a new caddy on the next hole."

The Skins Game became an excruciating grind as the round wore on, at least for the three professionals. Jingles didn't threaten to win a hole and didn't mind; he'd happily ride the laurels of Number Seven forever. The crowd groaned with each missed birdie attempt and cheered the many successful efforts. Unfortunately, each time one of the pros made a birdie, another matched it. On the fifteenth green, with $700,000 riding on his birdie putt, Scruffy missed a five-footer and proceeded to hit himself on the head a few times with his putter.

On the sixteenth tee, Jingles lucked into a real opportunity to fatten the foundation's new bank account. It was the final par three and just 165 yards. The last two holes were difficult par fours, especially the eighteenth, which played to an elevated green. Chances of success on those holes were minimal at best. On this hole, however, two of the pros fired right at the pin and missed the green on the left. The resulting chip shots would be difficult. Blackwood saw what happened to the others and played to the open right side of the putting surface, leaving himself with a thirty-five-footer.

Jingles aimed for a spot midway between Blackwood's ball and the flag and took a smooth swing with his four iron. The shot tracked perfectly, hit the green and took a favorable kick to the left. His ball parked pin high and only twelve feet from the flag.

"My heart can't take this," said Harvey, who was proving to be Jingles' lucky charm. "I'm not even going to rattle you by saying how much you could win!"

"It would be eight hundred thousand for the hole and over a million on the day," Jingles said. "Go get my contact lens out of Pat's purse, and I'll make that putt ten times out of ten."

"Do you mean it?" Harvey asked. "I thought she gave it to that Zimmer."

"I was just kidding around. She did give it to Karl. I'm going to make this putt anyway. I can see a lot better now than when I was wearing my old glasses. You hear me? I'm going to do it!"

The gallery smelled roses for their favorite and hollered support as he approached the green with a limp more pronounced with each passing hole. He tipped an Eagle Optics cap that he would rather burn than wear. However, Oliver's parting words had been wear the hat, keep Winston's money, and give it to your charity if you don't feel comfortable keeping it.

Welton and Sitton chipped up from off the green, leaving putts of just a few feet for par.

Blackwood's long birdie putt looked good right off his putter and better as it approached the cup. With only a few feet left, Jingles thought it actually had a chance. It caught the lip, spun around, and dropped in the side door! Blackwood raised his arms, looked at Jingles, and mouthed the words, "*good luck!*"

Just like that, Jingles' twelve-footer now looked hopelessly long. Putting for an $800,000 prize for the foundation would have been kind of fun. *Having to make it* to keep all that money in play for the group was not enjoyable at all. It was pressure. The pressure of good competition.

He decided the putt should break only a couple inches to the right. That was it. Hardly more than the width of a ball. He'd tried to pick out a single blade of grass as a target, but noticed only a small clod of dirt about two inches to the left of the hole. Ignoring the cup itself, he looked only at the dirt and made it his target. Silence surrounded him as if he was the only person on the Big Island. Even the birds seemed to understand the significance of the moment. The silence was broken only by the click of his putter striking the ball.

He refused to look up, concentrating on his follow-through. Knickers was so right. He had been cheating the game with Karl's lens on his eye. With it, a putt like this was automatic. That wasn't how the game was meant to be played.

Sam Sitton was first to shake his hand and Scruffy was close behind. Even George Blackwood gave him a fist bump. The game was still alive

The Sweet Swing

and the crowd loved it. Winning $300,000 in a match with these young gentlemen was a miracle, but making that clutch putt was ecstasy. He actually pumped his fist! Amazing.

The seventeenth was an aesthetic disaster for all the players. No one hit the par four green in two and it became a chipping contest. Jingles missed a par putt from fifteen feet, and the next two players halved the hole with successful putts.

Mulligan was on the bag and asked, "What if no one wins the million on eighteen? Do you just keep playing?"

"That's a good question. I assume we will. Or maybe *they* will. I'm about tuckered out."

Knickers assumed the caddy position for the final regulation hole. "Howdy, stranger," he said with a goofy grin. "Long time, no see."

Jingles cocked his head and said, "You meant to say that, didn't you? You know, *no see*."

"You have me confused with Mulligan the Punster, but hey, that's kind of funny now that you mention it. Tell me the honest truth, how much difference could your lens have made today? You're the only one to win serious money as it is."

Jingles had been thinking of that very thing all day. "Well, look at it this way. I've made two putts all afternoon. One from a foot and another from twelve. That's it."

Knickers shrugged. "You really haven't been all that close to the pins."

Jingles smiled. "You noticed! It doesn't matter. I would have made a bunch of them. You can take that to the bank. I believed I could make everything with that lens and I was right most of the time, but it was more than that. I played better because I was so confident. My whole game was better."

Knickers patted him on the back as he had been doing throughout the round. "You've handled this whole thing as well as any man could. Take my word for it. Now give me some sugar on this last hole."

A gust of wind sent Jingles' hat tumbling into gallery. "No sugar here. It's four-forty straight into the wind. I couldn't get there with two drives! On top of that, the green is on top of a ten-foot mound."

Knickers leaned close as if he had advice no one should hear. "Your swing is always so controlled. You've got firepower in reserve. Try reaching back for a little extra and swing like Mulligan. And tee your ball low so you hit a wind-cheater."

Jingles followed the instructions well. His drive never climbed higher than twenty feet and caught a good roll down the left center of the fairway.

"Just that easy, you're halfway there!" Knickers said. "Another seventy yards and you'd be right there with the rest of them."

Jingles tried to think of something other than his next shot. "What's going to happen to golf when the new lenses hit the market for everybody?"

"That's an excellent question. Maybe they'll change the rules so they won't be allowed. If not, they'll have to make the holes smaller I guess."

"How about baseball? You saw how much it helped me. A batter could pick up the spin immediately and a fastball would appear to slow down . . . slow down a lot."

Knickers glared at Jingles. "Baseball will never allow those lenses! The game has tradition, integrity. Forget it."

They reached Jingles' ball and looked out over two hundred yards to an embankment rising up to the green. With the putting surface well above them, only the white flag at the top of the stick was visible, just a dot on top of the hill.

"I'll hit the three wood to the base of the hill," Jingles said. "Maybe I can pull off a miracle with the wedge."

Knickers handed him the driver.

Jingles handed it back. "That's my big dog. I need the three."

Knickers pushed the big dog right back. "You'll hit this just like your drive off the tee. The exact same shot. Just visualize it. You'll land just in front of the hill, take a hard bounce into it, and maybe kick right over the top and get yourself a birdie putt. Just one sweet swing."

"Let's pretend you're a catcher again," Jingles said. "I'm the pitcher on the mound. I'm going to have to shake off that call. If I stick my ball on the side of that bank, I'll have no chance of hitting a great chip."

"No pitcher ever shook me off! They knew I'd kick their ass. You stand over that ball with your driver . . . it's a decent lie . . . and you pretend it's my face looking up at you. Imagine how you felt when I just told you about pouring gas in your car. I saw it in your eyes. You wanted to crush my fool skull!"

Jingles needed to hear no more. Even though he never hit a driver without a tee in his life, he'd hit it just to make Knickers shut up. Pretending it was a three wood, Jingles extended his backswing for a little extra punch and let it fly. The contact was clean, and the ball rocketed in the direction of the white dot on the hill. The ball landed a few feet shy of the bank, skipped into it, and bounced right over the top!

"There you go," Knickers said. "It pays to listen."

And they both listened. The huge crowd at the green began to scream even louder. And louder still. A mighty roar then carried all the way to Knickers and Jingles, knocking both men to their knees.

Hundreds from the gallery started running across the fairway toward them. Scruffy Welton, who stood closest to the green, took the white towel from his bag and waved it over his head. Sitton and Blackwood and both their caddies looked back at Jingles and Knickers, then fell to their knees too.

Moments earlier, millions of knees had touched millions of floors in millions of homes across America. They had all just witnessed old Jingles Plumlee's sweetest swing of all.

Epilogue

The Nineteenth Hole

Nearly a year later, on the Friday after Thanksgiving, four senior golfers walked into the Nineteenth Hole and sat at their customary table with a view of Leisureville's eighteenth green. Knickers Collins held four fingers in the air and Nick delivered four Sam Adams drafts.

"It's been nice being home for a few days," Mulligan said. "But, man, the place has been going to crap without me."

Harvey nodded. "Yes, the golfers are already driving carts on the fairways again. It's like you're a distant memory, Mulligan."

"What time is the wedding on Sunday?" Knickers asked. "I hope we have time for a full round in the morning. I've been wanting to play that Hapuna Beach course ever since Jingles taught it a lesson last year."

"Oliver said the wedding is flexible," Jingles said. "They'll wait for the best man and the rest of the Foursome to finish their golf game. It will be kind of fun to keep a banker waiting."

Mulligan smacked his lips after a gulp of cold brew, "I don't know about you guys, but after just a few days here, I'm anxious to play near the ocean again. I'm so spoiled I . . ." Music from his cell phone interrupted him. "Yes, Martha, what can I do for you?"

Martha Porter, formerly of Eagle Optics, worked in their office in Haiti. Despite receiving a gift of $10 million from Karl Zimmer, she wanted to work for the foundation and now resided on the island full-time. Her office was part of an earthquake-damaged motel in Port-Au-Prince still undergoing renovation as the headquarters for the Baseball Is an Answer Foundation. Even though the Foursome left only days ago, Martha missed them already.

Empowered by a $640 million share of the money for Karl Zimmer's invention, they had been touring Haiti, monitoring construction of ball fields large and small, negotiating the acquisition of additional sites, supporting coaching seminars, distributing huge amounts of baseball equipment, and playing some golf too. Over a hundred major leaguers from the Dominican Republic had joined the cause and were doing much of the heavy lifting. The number of Haitian youth enrolled in official Little League already topped a hundred thousand.

While Mulligan chatted with Martha, Knickers asked Jingles, "How did you enjoy your ride out to Prescott Hills last night? How are things goin'?"

"I'd say there are at least a hundred homes under construction right now. Ninety percent of the homes should be up within the next three years."

Harvey nudged Jingles with his elbow. "It's kind of fun to think that we sat out there a year ago and wondered how they would ever sell those lots."

"Well," Jingles replied, "once Knickers bought one, everybody had to have one!"

Mulligan concluded his conversation and poked his partner. "Knickers, when do you start building your summer cottage up there?"

"They'll get started in a few months. And it's not a vacation home! I'm movin' there for good when Jingles does."

Jingles added, "Pat and I have decided not to officially move for at least another year or two. We want things to quiet down a little. Let's play a few rounds up there when we get back from Hawaii, shall we?"

"I don't mean to bring up business while we're on vacation," Harvey said. "But I just learned that the Jingles lenses are headed to market in China any day. We'll be looking at some nice added income for the foundation. A two-dollar royalty doesn't seem like much, but who knows how many of those lenses they'll sell?"

"I still can't believe you guys outvoted me and gave the thing to ChinaLink," Knickers grumbled.

Mulligan smiled at his buddy's misery. "What can we say? We're international goodwill ambassadors."

"What's Karl Zimmer doing these days?" Harvey asked. He hadn't seen the German since the fateful day of the Skins Game. News that Zimmer had settled with Herman Winston for just the return of the option payment had surprised him . . . until he learned that Sherman MacPherson sued the owner of Eagle Optics for everything else he had.

"He's living the high life in New York City," Jingles answered. "A patron of the arts or something."

Three elderly women walked into the tavern, one of them Gladys Beckerman, and made their way to the men's table. All were after signatures on their copies of Jingles' book.

On Gladys' copy, Jingles wrote a note inside the cover. *To Gladys, the young lady who single-handedly made this book possible and will always be my shining star. Love, Jingles.*

"Is the book still selling after the big rush a few months ago?" Mulligan asked. "We haven't talked about my royalties yet. I think you owe me a beer for every time my name was mentioned."

Knickers laughed. "And how many times were you mentioned, Mulligan? I'm sure you counted."

Harvey signaled for another round. "I don't know that number, but they did a heck of a job on that book. I've read it four times."

Jingles leaned back in his chair, his hands clasped behind his head. "Gillian is my little heroine. She took a difficult situation and turned everything to gold. I tell her it's the gold she wasn't able to compete for in the Olympics and she always laughs."

"Almost shutting out the competition at the Senior Skins Game, without the Jingles lens, didn't hurt your cause any," Mulligan pointed out. "You gave her a little something to work with."

"I still think she feels badly about being a bridesmaid at Oliver's wedding, instead of the bride," Jingles mumbled.

"Yeah, imagine the luck of that big oaf Oliver," Mulligan said. "How did he ever rate having two beautiful young girls after him?"

"Well, he loved Jane for a long time before he ever met Gillian," Jingles said. "She just came around in the nick of time."

Mulligan suddenly sat at attention. "Speaking of good-looking women, check out the lady that just came in the door!"

A stunning young brunette in a chic business suit walked into the Nineteenth Hole, sporting both cleavage and a briefcase. Most of the tables were full of men, and every head turned. She looked around, spotted Jingles, and made a beeline for him.

Jingles grinned and winked at his friends. It was good to be a celebrity!

"I'm so lucky to find you," she said. "I know it's holiday time and all, but I have to talk to you. It's a business proposition. Could I have just a few minutes?" She pointed to the only empty table.

Jingles normally referred such requests to Gillian. However, this beauty was cause for exception. He knew the other men would be jealous, so he followed her to the table, looking back once and winking again.

"I'm Samantha Furlgood from Kennecott Pharmaceuticals," she said. "We're interested in having you as the pitchman for our brand new product."

Jingles shook his head in amazement; this would make the third new endorsement offer in the last month. "Can I order you something to drink?"

"Maybe later," she answered with a coy smile. "Our new drug is called Uplift, it's like Viagra times ten. We expect it to sell in the hundreds of millions in the very first year. You are going to find our offer hard to resist."

Jingles put a finger to his lips. "You may be talking a little too loudly," he whispered, suddenly wishing he *had* referred the lady to Gillian. It wasn't a product he felt comfortable discussing with a woman.

"Are you kidding?" she said, still too vocal. "You are going to want to shout when you try this product! You can maintain an erection for a whole week!" Jingles cringed, sensing everyone in the place probably heard her.

She moved her chair closer to his, until their legs touched beneath the table. Though nearer, she didn't turn down the volume. "We thought we could play off your whole putter thing. There could be millions in this for you."

Gosh, Jingles thought. *Did she think he was hard of hearing? Some people just assumed that older people couldn't hear well.*

"We'll put you in every living room in America, telling the whole world they can play just like you!"

On a scale of one too ten, Jingles' embarrassment level hit ten. This didn't seem like something she should be talking about in a bar full of men, even elderly ones. And so vocally! Women weren't so aggressive back in the day.

Every man in the tavern was watching and straining to listen. The bartender was wiping down the adjacent table . . . for the third time.

Samantha Furlgood turned and looked at the gawking patrons. "Every one of you is interested in improving your sexual performance, am I right?"

Some of the men nodded, others dropped their jaws in surprise or shock. All of them stared. Harold Perkins raised his hand like a schoolboy and shouted, "I am!"

She took something from her briefcase and displayed it on the palm of her hand. "Of course, we don't expect you to endorse our product without trying it yourself. Look how the pills are shaped! Just like a . . ." Jingles extended a hand to cover her mouth, to keep her from yelling it out. He could see what they were shaped like.

Most of the other patrons rushed toward Jingles' table to see what the lady held, like guppies attacking a flake of food.

Jingles suddenly wondered what his friends must be thinking of all this. He turned his head and saw Mulligan and Harvey slapping their table, bent over in laughter. Knickers leaned back in his chair, arms folded across his chest, grinning at the whole scene . . . a portrait of an old child at play.